CROWN OF SOULS

Books by Ronie Kendig

The Warrior's Seal (A Tox Files Novella)
Conspiracy of Silence
Crown of Souls

THE **TOX** FILES
—2—

CROWN OF SOULS

RONIE KENDIG

BETHANYHOUSE
a division of Baker Publishing Group
Minneapolis, Minnesota

© 2017 by Ronie Kendig

Published by Bethany House Publishers
11400 Hampshire Avenue South
Bloomington, Minnesota 55438
www.bethanyhouse.com

Bethany House Publishers is a division of
Baker Publishing Group, Grand Rapids, Michigan

Printed in the United States of America

Library of Congress Cataloging-in-Publication Data
Names: Kendig, Ronie, author.
Title: Crown of souls / Ronie Kendig.
Description: Minneapolis, Minnesota : Bethany House, a division of Baker
    Publishing Group, [2017] | Series: The Tox files ; book 2
Identifiers: LCCN 2017012337| ISBN 9780764231117 (hardcover) | ISBN
    9780764217661 (softcover)
Subjects: | GSAFD: Christian fiction. | Adventure fiction.
Classification: LCC PS3611.E5344 C76 2017 | DDC 813/.6—dc23
LC record available at https://lccn.loc.gov/2017012337

Interlude titles taken from John Hay's "Hymn of the Knights Templars," recorded in Thomas R. Lounsbury, ed. (1838-1915) *Yale Book of American Verse* (1912). Hymn #197

Scripture quotations are from the King James Version of the Bible and the *Holy Bible*, New Living Translation, copyright © 1996, 2004, 2015 by Tyndale House Foundation. Used by permission of Tyndale House Publishers, Inc., Carol Stream, Illinois 60188. All rights reserved.

Cover design by Kirk DouPonce, DogEared Design

Author is represented by the Steve Laube Agency.

17 18 19 20 21 22 23   7 6 5 4 3 2 1

To Victoria (Robertson) Kendig, my amazing mother-in-law. As a journalism professor, you poured your soul into teaching your students how to be better, stronger writers, and you turned a flagging program into an award-winning one! You have always inspired me. I remember when Brian and I were dating, I saw your first book manuscript and was so in awe of you. And I thought, "Maybe I could do that, too."

Together, may we pass on our love and passion for the written word to the next generation, and the one after that, too. Infect them all!

I love you, Mom.

But the worst enemy you can meet will always be yourself . . .
You must be ready to burn yourself in your own flame;
how could you rise anew if you have not first become ashes?

—Friedrich Nietzsche, *Thus Spake Zarathustra*

1

It took one ten thousandth of a second—exactly 0.000169 seconds—for the bullet to rip through his shoulder. The sniper shot shoved him backward onto the sun-warmed beach. In the chaos and shock, his mind powered down to microscopic analysis. Though it only took seconds, the pieces came in numbingly slowly.

What . . . ? What had happened? Cole "Tox" Russell struggled against the quagmire of sights, smells, and sounds to figure out how he'd landed faceup on the beach, staring up at a picture-perfect blue sky and puffy clouds. Confused, he blinked, his breath trapped in his throat.

His first clue was the warmth spreading around his shoulder blade and down his back. Sliding across his right pectoral and abs.

"Cole!" Blond hair spilled over a knotted brow and wide eyes.

Get up, idiot! He pushed up from the sand.

A volcano erupted in his shoulder. Fire. Needling, explosive fire. He howled and arched backward. Gripping his shoulder, he found it slick. Dark, shiny. Blood. Heaviness weighted his limbs. Shock. Blood loss. He sagged against the beach, disoriented.

"Cole? Cole!" Haven reached for him.

Haven. Right. They'd been walking the beach, talking about . . . about what? He struggled to remember. To think.

About what?

Mom—they'd been talking about his mom, whom Haven had just visited for a party.

"She's good—misses you still," Haven had said.

He nodded, thinking, aching to see his mom again.

"Here." She angled in with her phone to show him a photo. "I convinced her to take a selfie."

His heart clenched at his mom's beautiful smile, instantly recalling her laughter. Her advice. Her wisdom.

Haven's bright green eyes studied the photo, then him. "You have her smile."

His throat was raw.

Haven's words had filled him with reassurance about his mother's welfare but had also drowned him in a squall of grief, because he'd never see his mom again. It was own fault. His decision five years ago had declared him *persona non grata* with the U.S. government and severed his familial ties.

"Cole? Cole, talk to me!" Haven's voice pitched. "There's so much blood!"

He dragged his gaze to her, feeling strange. A little . . . hungover.

Panicked, frantic eyes darted over him. *"Ram, help!"* Her primal scream scraped its way out of her throat.

In a plume of dust and sand, a tornado of curses and olive skin whirled into view as Ram Khalon slid up to his three-o'clock position. "You'vebeenshotdon'tmove." His words tumbled over one another as he slammed both palms against Tox's shoulder.

Fiery shards exploded at the touch, pinning Tox to the ground. *"Augh!"*

Shot? He couldn't have been shot. He was in Virginia. Home. Safe. "I'm fine." He hated this—hated the look in Haven's eyes. The worry in Ram's voice.

"Maangi!" Salty wind pulled Ram's shaggy hair free of its pony-tail and tossed it into his blazing eyes. "Keep still, you hardheaded son of a—"

Whoosh! Maangi wedged in beside Ram to take over. "How bad?"

"Entry and exit—"

"Get my kit!" Maangi mashed one hand to the wound, another to Tox's carotid artery. "Okay, Sarge—"

"Car keys," Ram demanded.

"Right pocket." Maangi was assessing, looking, squinting. "Sarge, I'm going to check the bleeding."

Gritting his teeth, Tox squeezed his eyes against the pain. Against the situation. Who had shot him? It'd only been a few seconds ago that Haven had been sharing about her visit to his parents' estate in Maryland for his mom's sixtieth birthday.

"I hear you're really good at air guitar," Haven said with a mischievous laugh.

"No no no." Roughing a hand over his face, Tox growled. "Please tell me she doesn't still have that video."

Haven laughed even more. "You were pretty cute at four."

He hung his head. "I should've destroyed that a long time ago. I was buck naked."

"Were you? I only remember your grunt-song," Haven said around another laugh.

He snorted, knowing full well his nudity could not have been missed.

"So, no repeat performance?"

"—ox? Hey! Tox, talk to me, man."

Only at the frantic words did he register the darkness clouding his vision. He blinked, and piercing light shot through his corneas. Hollowed hearing unplugged slowly and pulled him back to the chaos. Maangi was working on him with Ram. Had he already gotten the kit?

If Chiji Okorie hadn't flown home to Nigeria for his brother's funeral, he'd quote a Scripture. About God protecting Him. Crazy how much Tox wanted to hear those words right now. This wasn't a mortal wound, but it was significant. He could tell by the way Maangi moved, the ferocity in his eyes. Tension hovering so thick, it'd take a bomb to eradicate it.

Maangi angled into Tox's view, cutting off the vibrant blue sky. "How you feeling?"

Tox grunted. "Like dog meat." Entry and exit wounds, Ram had said. A sniper, then, since he hadn't seen anyone with a gun nearby. "We safe?" They should get to cover.

Maangi said nothing. The others towered over Tox, expressions etched with rage and shock. He could relate. "Cover," he reiterated. At least, he thought he did. His body was going into shock, thoughts and limbs rubbery. Movements jerky, uncoordinated.

"No more shots," Victor "Thor" Thorsen called.

"Only one shot? Was the sarge targeted?"

"Here? Why?"

"Who cares. Let's find this guy," said Barclay "Cell" Purcell. Angry. Hateful. "Show him what dead feels like."

Tox fought to distract himself from the pain. He'd been shot before, but not on home turf. Not where he should've been safe. They'd been on the beach for the Fourth of July. Early in the day, before fireworks started. Before dark. A volleyball game—the team and some family members. Shouts as they played. Barking dogs. Cries of children. Little faces.

"The kids." Tox bit through the fire to sit up.

"Down!" Maangi barked, pushing hard against him.

Nausea swirled with the pain, flopping Tox onto the beach. He was going to lose it. Vomit. Pass out.

Lost a lot of blood.

Swallowing hard, he relaxed a little. Were they still in danger? "Sitrep," he wheezed, then wet his dry lips. His words sounded like sandpaper against stone. There'd been four kids. A baby. A pregnant wife. Three girlfriends. "The kids," he moaned again. "Get them"— was someone using a cattle prod in his shoulder?—"safety."

"Easy," Ram said. "They're good." His hands moved toward the kit, then back to Tox's shoulder. "Foster's getting them out of here. They're leaving. "

Foster. Someone's friend. Or was it brother?

"Always in charge." Ram snorted. "Thor, Cell, and Keogh have taken VVolt to check the buildings and find the shooter. Neutralize him before he can hurt anyone else."

"Good," Tox whispered. A touch weighted his palm. Reflexively, he tightened his fingers, knowing only one person would try to hold his hand. He peeled his attention from the blue sky, past Ram's furious expression and Maangi's hair dark with sweat as he aimed white gauze at Tox's shoulder, to—"Haven."

She was beautiful. More than he could've dreamed. Too good for him. In danger because of him.

"Go," he said. "Get to—"

"I'm not leaving." Her eyebrows rose, fire in her green eyes.

"Don't argue," Tox grunted.

"Just did," she said with a smirk.

"I mean it. Go."

"Shut up and roll onto your side," Maangi ordered, then to Ram, "Help, so we don't destabilize him."

As pawing hands shifted Tox onto his side, he gritted his teeth. Sticky warmth slipped over his dorsal muscle. Blood from the exit wound. But not gushing. Good.

"Sand's doing its job," Maangi said, "packing the wound, slowing blood loss. They'll have to clean it out."

Sirens howled in the distance. More eyes on scene, making the sniper's escape more difficult. Tox shifted his attention to the buildings in the distance. Roughly eight or nine hundred yards out. Three shadows shimmied up to the wall. By the tactical approach used to infil, they were his guys, the military working dog, and sometime Wraith asset, Drew Keogh. But Tox couldn't see—

"Hey!" Maangi snapped, his brow sweaty. "Keep still, or I'll make sure you feel this."

He didn't like his team going in without backup. Without him. If the shooter was still there . . . He tensed. But he didn't have enough in him to fight a combat medic, let alone a sniper. Tox slumped back.

Warmth compressed his hand again. Haven's face was streaked with dirt and blood.

Blood? "You hurt?"

Lips thinned as she fought tears, Haven shook her head. And then it hit him—the blood on her face was his. Before the shot, he'd been staring across the beach at Ram, who lifted a hand as if to call him back. Then came the puff of red around Tox's shoulder. *His* blood. Haven had been walking with him, arms linked. . . .

Three inches off, and she would've taken the bullet.

Guilt tore at Tox for exposing her to this. That she had to see him laid out. "Go."

"Here," Ram shouted.

Emergency lights splashed across the buildings and vehicles in the lot. Seconds later, two EMTs carrying a stretcher and medical bags crested the small rise from the parking lot and jogged down the beach toward them.

Maangi called out to them, "My name is Tane Maangi. I'm a combat medic. Single gunshot wound to the right shoulder. Entry and exit wounds. No major arteries hit, as far as I can tell."

Ram stepped away, but his bare feet remained in Tox's peripheral vision. Watching over him. When Maangi shifted aside for the EMTs, a chill swept Tox's spine. Wanting to reassure Haven, he squeezed then released her hand. As the EMTs loaded him onto a stretcher, a foam wedge propping his torso up off the exit wound, he let himself analyze the incident one more time.

A lazy Fourth of July before fireworks.

The team—playing volleyball.

The families—gathered around the grills and picnic benches.

Tox—with Haven. Fifty yards off. The time between the crack of the rifle and the instant he found himself on the ground . . .

As they secured him in the ambulance, he stared down the length of his legs, a terrible fear digging into his gut. "Haven, come with me."

She gave him a smile, apparently reading into this insistence, and climbed in, staying out of the way of the EMTs.

Asking her to come wasn't about sentimentality. This was about insurance. Guarantees. Making sure Haven didn't eat a bullet, too.

It was stupid, but she couldn't shake from her mind the glittering grains of sand in Cole's hair. Glints of gold in his dark brown hair. Framing his head and face.

As Haven washed her hands, red swirled in dizzying circles down the drain. Spiraling. Vanishing. Like life. The stress and grief of the afternoon's events tumbled out in a choked sob. She held the back of her hand to her mouth, stifling it. Gripping the edge of the sink, she swallowed hard. Closed her eyes.

But doing that only gave her mind the freedom to shove Cole's ashen face, splattered with his own blood, back to the forefront. The measured breaths she took didn't ease the band of pressure tightening around her temples.

He's stable, she reminded herself. *The doctor said he's stable.*

But her mind refused to surrender the image of him flat on his back at her feet. Holding hands one second, ripped apart the next. He had lain there, staring up the sky. Red pooling across his shoulder.

Going from near bliss to shattered world in a heartbeat. Thinking he was . . . dead. He hadn't moved, not for several excruciating seconds. After all she'd gone through to have him in her life, to be dating him, to be the bridge between him and his parents—who still didn't know he was alive—and then to think he was dying . . .

Voices outside the bathroom door shoved steel down her spine. *Pull it together.* Haven scrubbed with the antibacterial soap, digging the dark spots from beneath her nails, then dried her hands. She stuffed the paper towel in the trash and returned to the small hospital room.

A shape peeled off the wall. The man stood straight, shoulders back, chin up. Thor. "They said this was his room." He glanced at the empty space where a bed should be.

Strange, the instant comfort she felt at finding one of Cole's guys waiting. She offered a smile. "He's in surgery but stable." She swallowed and hugged herself.

"Surprised he already has a room." Thor went to the window.

Haven watched as he glanced out. "Pays to have the president as your brother. Galen pulled strings, sent security—"

THWAP!

Haven jerked when he ripped the cord on the blinds, snapping the room into near darkness.

"Least he's good for something," Thor muttered as he returned to the door, spread his legs shoulder-width apart, and folded his arms. Standing guard. Since Cole wasn't here, who was he guarding?

Me. The thought struck her. Alarmed her. Yet comforted her. "And the others?" Was it too much to hope that they'd caught whoever had done this?

"Ram's making calls. The team just left the site."

Site. Not the beach. Because now it was a crime scene. Someone had tried to kill Cole. Throat suddenly raw, Haven swallowed.

The door punched open. In a blink, Thor somehow had a weapon cradled in both hands, aimed at the opening. Shadows gave way to light, and Ram entered. Stepping to the left, Thor holstered his weapon.

Ram held a souvenir T-shirt out to Haven. She frowned, but when he nodded to her blouse, she glanced down and felt a simultaneous rush of dread and nausea as she saw her white sweater splotched with Cole's blood.

He moved to the bathroom, flicked on the light, and set the shirt on the counter. "We'll stand watch so you can change and clean up."

Clean up? She'd already—

Ram flicked a finger along his jaw.

In the bathroom, Haven noticed tiny red dots along her jawline and cheekbone. Grieved, she washed her face, changed into the shirt, then considered her sweater. Even if she could figure out how to get Cole's blood out of the fabric, she couldn't fathom wearing it again. She dropped it in the waste bin before returning to the room.

Ram was at the windowed door, peering through a slit in the blinds, the only barrier between them and the busy hall. He turned with a nod. "They're bringing him down now."

When he reached for the handle, Haven's pulse quickened. She strained to see around Ram. Two nurses guided a bed down the hall, trailed by matching police officers, then into the room. The bed creaked past her, affording a clear view of Cole—pale, unconscious, the bedding drawn up to his chin. As the nurses anchored the bed and secured his IV line, Haven drifted closer. They plugged in the heart-rate monitor, then folded his bedding down a bit, exposing his bandaged shoulder and a sling that anchored his arm to his abdomen. He lay with his left side slightly elevated to alleviate pressure on the wound in his back.

"Dr. Calvert will be in shortly, but the patient should start waking soon," the brunette nurse said before leaving and pulling the door closed behind her. The uniformed officers remained outside.

"You want to get some rest?"

Haven glanced at Ram, who gripped the foot of the bed. "No, thanks." She wasn't leaving Cole, not until he opened his eyes and told them he was okay. Insane, but she needed that reassurance. His reassurance. His voice.

Ram nodded, his gaze swinging back to Cole. "Not the first time he's eaten lead. He'll be good."

These were the punches the guys rolled with every day. Despite Ram's words, she saw something in his eyes. Protection. Annoyance. "Anything from the others?" she asked.

"Giving reports to the FBI and NCIS, then heading here."

15

NCIS seemed odd, but considering what Cole and his team did, maybe it wasn't, with the proximity to the naval base and where he'd been shot. Galen had wanted to send Secret Service, but that would defeat the whole keeping-Cole's-identity-a-secret thing.

Cole's leg shifted as he moaned.

"Here we go," Ram said with a wry smile. "Hey, Tox, you with us?"

Cole turned his head but didn't open his eyes, which raced back and forth beneath his lids.

"Haven's here," Ram said. "Toughen up, old man. Don't let her see you cry like a baby." When Haven frowned, he shook his head, reassuring her that this tough talk was normal.

He gave Cole's leg a light slap. "C'mon. Quit slacking. Fight it."

Cole blinked his eyes open. Groaned. His brow rippled, clearly searching for clarity, for understanding. His lids drooped closed.

"Little groggy from the anesthesia," Ram explained. "You're at the hospital."

Cole stretched his neck with another moan, but then slowly his blue eyes broke free. "D—" The word died on his lips. He grimaced and cleared his throat. "Did you get him?"

Ram looked down.

Cole huffed, and his eyes drifted shut. Anger, irritation, and defeat clustered in the shadows of the room, mocking them.

Adjusting and again clearing his throat, Cole said, "Tell me."

At those two simple words, Thor and Ram slipped closer, as if restricting the information they were about to hand Cole. Fluidity existed between Tox and his team that translated into its own language and made Haven feel a bit left out. But she kept her mouth shut, paid attention, and learned.

"Maangi took Cell up on the roof, said he could tell where the shooter set up, but that's it. No casing. Nothing left behind."

"Ah, good," droned the baritone voice that belonged to the doctor. "You're awake." Dr. Calvert sauntered into the room, placed a notepad on the cabinet beside the bed, then bent over Cole. He checked Cole's pupils, then his vitals. "Well, your wounds were clean, through and through. No damage to peripheral organs or tissue. We debrided the wounds, then stitched you up."

"What medications?" Cole asked, his gaze still clearing of the anesthesia.

Dr. Calvert nodded. "We had strict orders that none beyond the anesthesia and IV antibiotics were to be used." He looked around as if to confirm this, but when nobody responded, he went on. "They'll prepare a script for antibiotics, but for a tough guy like you, I'd think this is a walk in the park."

Cole grunted, tugging at the sling.

"That's to keep your arm immobilized. The less it moves, the better your chances of not further injuring the wound or tearing the stitches."

At the annoyance skidding through Cole's expression, Haven stifled a laugh.

His gaze met hers briefly before bouncing back to the doctor. "When can I leave?"

Now Haven did laugh.

"Your vitals are almost where I'd like them to be, but your BP is a bit low, so I've ordered observation." Dr. Calvert started for the door. "I'll check back in the morning."

"*Morning?*" Cole barked, scowling.

A smile twitched the corners of Ram's lips.

"There's no reason to keep me here," Cole called after the exiting doctor, his voice hoarse and groggy despite his efforts. "What if he comes back to finish the job?" He shifted and tensed, pain digging deep crevices into his brow.

"See?" Haven shook her head. "You're in pain."

"Had worse."

"Maybe, but this time you're going to follow his instructions." She reached over the rail and touched his hand. "Besides, morning is only four hours away."

Going still, Cole frowned at her, then looked at the wall clock. With a grunt, he settled back against the bed, lost in his frustration. But then he homed in on something in the hall.

Light pushed into the room as Cell and Maangi entered, followed by Sergeant Drew Keogh, an Air Force Security Forces handler, and his patrol explosives detector dog, VVolt N629. The Belgian Malinois trotted over to Cole's bed, sniffed it down, then came to

Haven, hauling in the scents from her clothes before he slumped to the cool floor.

Cole's gaze brightened. "What'd you find?" Always in charge, always on edge, always on mission.

"Whole lotta nothin'," Cell groused as he dropped into a chair at the foot of the bed and leaned back, hands behind his head.

Maangi came to Haven's side and rested his forearms on the rails. "Whoever did this is good. If I hadn't known what to look for, we would've missed his setup. No casing. No marks, just a slight disturbance of the dust."

"So it was a sniper."

"He could've hit anyone. There were a lot of us on the beach," Keogh said.

Cole and Ram exchanged glances that telegraphed their doubt of that statement. Then they looked away from each other, as if unwilling to face it.

No, unwilling to discuss it. The realization startled Haven, unseated what little confidence she had at the moment. What could be so bad that they wouldn't talk about it? Or . . . "Me," she said, watching for a reaction. "He could've been targeting me."

"You?" Cell snorted.

But she'd seen the small shift in Cole's expression that confirmed her theory.

Cell shook his head. "I doubt you have enemies who'd snipe you on the Fourth of July."

"I've helped put away some pretty sick individuals," Haven said.

"See?" Cell lifted his hands as if she'd just made his point. "They're sick, and yet you call them *individuals*."

"They're still people."

"The ones we encounter, we don't put away." He placed his hand on his chest. "We put them *down*. Like dogs, like the pieces of—"

"Hey." Cole glared at Cell. "Mouth."

"Whatever," Cell muttered.

The bed's safety bar lowered. Apparently while she'd been having a verbal duel with Cell, another silent dialogue had happened between Ram and Cole, because the former stalked to the bathroom and set sweats and a shirt on the edge of the sink. Surprise held Haven fast as Ram then exited the room, requesting the location of the doctor from someone in the hall as the door glided shut.

"What's—" Haven turned and froze.

Having removed the IV line from his hand and tossed it aside, Cole swung his legs over the edge of the bed.

Cell came out of his chair, opening the door for Keogh, VVolt, and Thor, who took up positions outside. Cell then blocked the door.

Haven struggled to keep up. Nobody had given orders. Nobody had said a word. Yet they moved and operated. Doing something that felt an awful lot like breaking Cole out of jail.

"What are you doing?" she demanded, her voice pitched.

"Leaving." Feet planted on the floor, Cole stood, pulling the bed-sheet with him and hooking it around his waist to cover backdrafts.

"What? No!" She lunged to his side. "The doctor said you should stay."

Sheet bunched in his left fist, Cole grimaced. He touched his right hand to his shoulder as he took his first step.

Haven braced him, acutely aware of his warm, bare skin beneath her touch. But the flash in his eyes said he didn't want help, so she stepped back. "Cole, you should—"

"*Trust* me," he ground out, then trudged into the bathroom and barricaded himself inside.

What just happened here? What had she missed? Haven turned around, staring at the empty room. Apparently his team trusted him—anticipated him. They'd clearly taken his silent orders. And she had hers—*trust me*—yet . . .

Almost as quickly as Cole vanished into the bathroom, he reappeared in the sweats. Sans sling and shirt, baring his toned, muscular chest. Lord help her, she didn't need that distraction, too. His plaintive, frustrated expression drew her to his side. Cole was used to giving orders, helping others. He wasn't used to asking for help. But that was what he was doing now. Again, *without* words.

"You shouldn't be doing this," she said, taking the shirt.

"That's why you're helping me."

"That's not what I'm talking about, and you know it, Cole Russell."

With care, she slipped the shirt over his head, then stretched the arm out so he could ease into it. "Just because you and your men speak a silent language doesn't mean I do." She adjusted the shirt so it wasn't askew.

He hesitated, and she braved a look into his blue eyes, which held both worry and protection. "It's not safe here. You're not safe here. We need to leave, because we can't control who comes and goes."

She sighed. "I'm here with you. There's no safer place."

"Wrong."

She blinked.

"Haven, they targeted *me*. That means anywhere near me is not safe."

3

She wanted an explanation, but that required time. It also meant someone else could hear. Tox couldn't risk that. But he hated the look she was giving him. One of hurt and longing. He didn't know what to do with it, since he'd spent the last dozen years soldiering and barking orders. Almost half his life. The only half still alive.

He turned to Cell, who stood in the doorway, and gave a curt nod. Cell unfolded his arms and left, heading to his nine. In the hall, Thor fell in behind him.

Using his injured arm, Tox took Haven's hand. "C'mon." He caught the door before it closed and tugged it open a fraction, waiting. Listening.

"What—"

"Shh." He felt annoyance flick through his face before he could stop it. He should give her some reassurance, that his irritation—

Voices came from the far end of the corridor.

Tox slid out and eased her behind him. She started left, tugging his shoulder and making him wince. "No," he said, guiding her right. Giving her a nudge at the small of her back. "Go. Hustle."

Maangi took up his six, and they hurried down the hall, then

21

banked left, where they found the stairs. He steered Haven into the stairwell. Gritting his teeth did little to stifle the jarring of each step. It felt like someone swinging a bat at his shoulder. They stepped into the parking garage and spotted a waiting black SUV. Ram sat at the wheel.

Haven hesitated, but again he urged her on. Aimed her into the back seat. Maangi took the front passenger side. Doors had barely shut when Ram pulled away.

Buckled in, Haven looked at him, eyes filled with concern and fear.

Tox needed a distraction and shifted his focus. "Cell? Keogh?"

"Created some good confusion," Ram said, the vehicle gliding up the ramp and out of the garage.

They burst into a black night awash in city lights and headed north back toward DC, to a location only Ram knew about. A safe house. Silence chased them through the streets and onto the highway.

Strange, needing a safe house in their own backyard. Getting popped on his home turf ticked off Tox. He'd find this person and even the score.

It took an hour, but they finally veered into what had once been an industrial part of the city just outside the Beltway. Red-brick warehouses had been divided into condos. One in particular waited in anonymity, its garage door yawning wide as their SUV's tires hit the lip of the drive. Before the streetlights had even snapped out of sight, the heavy door slid shut. Ram watched the rearview mirror, not moving until they sank into total darkness. A fraction of a second later, light bloomed in the cement garage.

"Clear," Ram said.

Climbing the wrought-iron steps up to the condo, Tox wondered whose name was on the lease. Ram's? Someone else connected to the Mossad? But Ram wouldn't take them somewhere exposed. At the top of the landing hung a barn-style door, which Ram accessed with a code and thumbprint. Cold darkness embraced them as they entered and took in their setting. Two-story, open concept, with a mixture of wood floors and stained cement. Modern furniture gathered around a massive fire pit in crisp, clean lines. The far brick wall ran from floor to ceiling, and a second level hung over an expensive gourmet kitchen. Bedrooms, he guessed.

"Nice place," Maangi said as light stroked the lacquered floor of the living area.

"Clear to talk?" Tox asked, watching Haven wander to the leather sofa and perch on the edge.

Ram nodded.

But that he hadn't said there were no devices made Tox hesitate. "Who owns this?" The Israeli-American's ties to the Mossad seemed as far-reaching as underground cables in New York.

"It's safe," Ram said. "No devices."

Again he hadn't answered the question, and Tox wasn't sure he believed the assertion that the place was device-free.

Ram must've noticed his hesitancy, because he stalked into the kitchen, flipped a switch, throwing light across the loft, and opened the fridge. "The hit on you wasn't random."

Tox nodded, his mind buzzing too much to stay still. Bracing his injured arm, he walked the loft, eyeing framed prints and crevices where devices were often concealed. Most common were lights and electrical outlets. But everything seemed right, original.

"You were the target." Ram produced two bottles of water and handed one to Tox.

With a nod, Tox accepted it.

"So that dovetails options." Ram guzzled his water, his narrowed gaze on some fixed point in time.

"I'm sorry," Haven said, lifting a hand as she came to the island, "why are we convinced Cole was the target?" She slipped onto one of the barstools.

Tox didn't want to answer that because he hadn't processed everything yet. But he wouldn't just shut her out. "I wasn't near the team. I was with you."

"So doesn't that leave open the distinct possibility that I, too, could've been the target?"

"No."

"Why? Why do you say no?"

Though he wasn't used to explaining himself, he appreciated that she wanted to understand. But was it because she sought to learn, or because she was worried about him? He felt Ram's eyes on him and gave the explanation. "The shooter was skilled enough to conceal his presence and escape unnoticed, so the possibility that he hit the wrong target is unlikely." When her lips parted, Tox knew he needed to head off her argument. "You and I walked a straight line down the beach. If we had weaved or crossed paths, the hit could've been a mistake."

She paled. "But we didn't."

Tox nodded. "He aimed at me."

"And then there's the fact that it was a perfectly placed shot." Ram's gaze held too much meaning.

Meaning Tox couldn't sort. "Yeah, that's where I lose the trail."

"A message?"

"Probably. But what?"

"Mess—what? Wait." Haven touched her fingertips to her forehead and huffed. "Could you two bring this down to *Attempted Murder for Dummies*—emphasis on *dummies*—please?"

Tox felt a smile crowd out his processing. "Sorry. Ram and I—"

"I get that this is all second nature to you, that it's a puzzle to solve," she said, her words edged in frustration. "But I was there. I saw you get shot. I had your blood on my hands. I thought you were dying."

When her voice cracked, Tox clenched his jaw and set down his water, appreciating when Ram silently slid out of the kitchen to give them privacy.

Haven clawed her fingers through her hair, elbows propped on the counter. "Sorry," she whispered, face shielded by her arms. "I'm not very good at this."

"At what?"

"This." She wagged her hands around. "Everything. You and your men move, you operate, you talk without talking. None of you ever seem fazed."

"It might look that way—"

"Yes," she snapped, her green eyes sparking with irritation, "it does."

"Haven, this is what we do. When we get ambushed, we do every-thing to get to safe ground, then sort it out. It's normal. We have to step back and analyze. Go through it all, so we know what to do next."

"Yes, but I don't. And I don't want to—" She bit off her sentence and lowered her gaze. Sat back on the stool. Said nothing.

Send him on a mission. Have him neutralize targets. Extract VIPs. Lead a team. Deal with terrorists. He could handle all that. Excel at it. But put him in a room with this woman, with Haven, the one person who'd believed in him when nobody else had, and he was . . . inept. Lost. Ineffective. And she still hadn't spoken. "What?"

"Nothing," she muttered as she pushed off of the stool and went to the fridge.

He might not be good at relationships, but he was smart enough to know she'd just set a landmine at his feet with that response. Now to figure out how to step around it.

Or step to her. Tox moved to her side. "What do you want to know? What don't you want to do or be?"

She swallowed, as if ready to refuse to answer, but then she deflated. "I don't fit in with them, Cole."

He frowned, angling sideways toward her to avoid jarring his shoul-der. "With who?"

"Your men."

He barked a laugh. "Good."

She scowled, the hurt plain on her face.

"They're hairy and they smell."

She snorted. "That's not what I meant—"

He slipped his hand around the back of her neck, her thick blond hair warm against his fingers. "They're soldiers. And I wouldn't want you to know that life, to have to operate the way we do. Ever."

"But I feel . . . lost when you're talking, operating."

She wanted to be a part of it. Which didn't make sense.

"It's dangerous."

"Yes, but it involves you," she said, eyes rife with meaning.

Might as well rip his heart out. "Look," he said, digging into his resolve, into his desire to be better for her, "because this isn't yet classified, I can tell you what I saw, what I worked out, but I can't always. And I won't. There are things I will do, things I know, that you will never hear about."

She nodded. Her job with the FBI as a deception expert demanded privacy, too.

He traced the edge of her jaw, and in response, her eyelashes fluttered. He liked that. Liked that *he* caused it. "You're so beautiful."

"Don't," she said with a growl. "Don't think that works."

Guilty as charged. "But it does work." He'd noticed the clues—her leaning into his touch. The soft intake of breath. When he stepped in closer, testing his theory, she breathed a little more raggedly. He drew his thumb along her lower lip.

"Cole." She tried to sound stern, but he heard the hitch in her tone. Saw color flush her cheeks.

He tugged her closer, bracing his shoulder and anticipating the twinge of pain that came, and angled toward her mouth.

"This so isn't fair," she muttered, resting her hands on his biceps.

He caught her mouth with a teasing kiss. Felt her draw in a breath. And wondered for the thousandth time since they'd been reintroduced how he'd gotten so lucky.

Tox kissed her, sliding his hand to the small of her back and pulling her in tighter. Her arms snaked up his shoulders, and though he tensed as she skimmed past his wound, he didn't let it bleed into the moment.

He eased back, bouncing a look between her hooded eyes and those full lips, then went in for the kill again. She was eager, yet conservative. Soft and sweet.

And he was getting too far out of his depth.

Tox eased off, sliding a row of kisses along her jaw and beneath the lobe of her ear.

Haven leaned into him. "You're not getting off that easy, Russell."

Busted. "It takes time, Haven. To know me, to know the team, to know how to operate. We've had a dozen years to work it out." He stroked her cheek with his thumb. "You'll pick it up. Probably faster than they did. Besides"—he tilted in for another kiss—"we've got time."

* * * *

— DAY 2 —
ARLINGTON, VIRGINIA

In a leather chair, Ram Khalon crossed his legs, propping his ankle on his knee. Sipping coffee did nothing to jar him from this nightmare. He was livid. Someone had come after one of the team on their own territory. Not cool. He wanted answers.

No, he wanted someone dead. Namely the person who'd lain behind the scope of that rifle and put a round through Tox.

Seated around the large dining room table, the members of Wraith waited for the live feed of the conference call to come through. The first to sign in was Major General Antonio Rodriguez, whose grim expression mirrored their determination. His presence was vital, since Wraith operated under his purview.

"Where are you?" he asked, leaning in toward the camera, his assessing gaze taking in their setting.

"Safe," Tox said tersely.

"Call's untraceable," Rodriguez noted, his question implicit.

"Necessary." Ram shifted. "Considering the circumstances."

Another window popped up on the screen, shrinking the general's by half. The intense face of the CIA's Deputy Director for Operations, Dru Iliescu, filled the new box. A second later, the images shifted and a third window appeared, planting Levi Wallace, FBI assistant special agent in charge, below the others.

"Seems we're all here now," Rodriguez said. "Tell us what you know."

After skating a brief look at Ram, Tox focused on the members who comprised Wraith's oversight. "Pretty straightforward. We were on the beach, celebrating the Fourth. Guys were playing volleyball. Families and friends were there. I was off to the side with Haven Cortes when I was shot."

"Any eyes on the shooter?" Rodriguez asked.

"We sprinted to the most likely spot for the nest," Cell said, picking up the story. "Three-story building. Got up there, but he was gone like the wind."

"VVolt caught no scent either," Keogh offered, the Malinois's ears swiveling at the mention of his name.

27

"Nothing was disturbed, save a spot of dust," Maangi put in. "If I wasn't a sniper and didn't know what to look for, I would've missed it. He made the shot from 1,100 yards. Without killing or maiming the sarge."

"That's lucky," Rodriguez said.

Tox grunted. "Nailed me in the shoulder—no permanent or devastating damage. Didn't tag Haven or anyone else." He shook his head. "That's not luck."

"A miracle," Rodriguez offered, though everyone knew it wasn't.

Sitting sideways at his desk, Dru Iliescu tapped a pen on its surface. "What're you thinking?"

Ram expected and received another long look from Tox. They'd both had the same nagging feeling. When Tox dropped his gaze to the table, Ram took the cue. "It's a message." He let out a long breath. "To Tox."

"From who?" barked Rodriguez. "And what message?"

Shaking his head, Ram saw Tox doing the same. "Unknown on both accounts."

"I agree," Iliescu said, adjusting in his chair. "The shooter was skilled enough to infil, take the shot, and not kill Russell. Just as flawless of an exfil—and we all know, once you take that shot, everything's compromised." He nodded, apparently buying where their thoughts were going. "This guy made a shot from a significant distance. But we don't know the quality of the shooter—we're only talking a couple of inches from the heart to the shoulder. Easy miss in less-than-ideal conditions." He rubbed his chin. "So our agency refrains from making a definitive call about motive. There's enough room for doubt that he just wasn't a good shooter."

"But he still targeted the sarge," Thor countered.

"Again, I agree." Iliescu's chair squawked as he faced the camera full-on. "Rodriguez or Wallace, you have anything on a possible tango responsible?"

"Negative," Rodriguez said.

"Same," Wallace muttered. "We have a team going over surveillance videos, monitoring flights and electronic as well as audio traffic. Nothing has come up within the U.S."

Iliescu was scribbling notes. "We'll go over international profiles of assets and known hostiles capable of shots like this, then start narrowing the field." He tossed down his pen and stared at the camera. "I'll update the director on what's happening. You in a safe place?"

Tox gave a single nod.

"Okay, keep us posted." Iliescu ended his feed.

Wallace lingered for a moment, and Ram figured he was wondering if Haven was there. At one time, Wallace had had a thing for her. Actually, Ram was pretty sure the ASAC *still* had a thing for the deception expert.

"Tox," Wallace said, "be careful. Wouldn't want you or anyone else to get hurt."

Tox's jaw muscle twitched as he received the veiled warning about Haven's safety.

"Hey," Cell injected, "we got this, dude."

"Take care," Wallace said with a hint of resignation, probably annoyed nobody would say Haven was safe. But it wasn't his place to worry about Tox's girl. He hung up.

That left Rodriguez. "Did the doc say how long you'd be out?"

"I'm fine," Tox said.

Rodriguez laughed. "I doubt it. That bullet tore a hole through your body, Russell." He scrubbed his scalp in frustration. "Look, stay there, wherever that is. We don't have anything for you right now anyway. And until we know who is responsible for this, best you stay low."

"I'm not letting an invisible shooter terrorize me or control my movements."

"Aren't you? You're in a safe house." The general's point made Ram tuck his chin to conceal his smile. "And Khalon, don't think I haven't figured out that this hideout belongs to you."

They all thought they knew so much about him. Let them flounder in their guesses.

"A'right," Rodriguez said with a huff. "I'll be in touch. Oh—have you notified the president, or do I need to?"

"He's aware," Tox confirmed.

"Good. Stay in touch."

When the screen went black, Ram sat back and folded his arms.

It'd been a necessary but fruitless call. But the agencies were working, both domestically and internationally, to profile and rout whoever had attacked Tox. Find the shooter and deliver him some justice.

Tox rubbed his forehead, then climbed out of his chair, wincing. Bracing his shoulder made his movements stiff as he went to the fridge and pulled out the OJ.

"So how long do we stay holed up here?" Cell asked.

"You don't." Tox set his glass down hard on the granite countertop as his gaze flicked to each member of Wraith. "Go home. Take care of your families."

A nervous hush fell over the loft, the guys eyeing each other. Leaving him when he was wounded, when clear and present danger still existed . . .

"I mean it." Tox frowned. "Go. They need you. I'm fine. Safe."

Ram could guarantee that in a limited fashion. But he didn't like how readily Tox shoved everyone out the door. They were a team. They worked together. Worked toward the same end goal, armed with the same information.

Haven shifted on her barstool at the counter, and Tox gave her a pointed glare, silencing her. She'd probably noticed him giving silent, unconscious signals that he didn't believe his own words. Ram didn't need deception training to know his brother-in-arms wasn't buying his own bull. Which was good, because neither did Ram. Safe? There was no such thing when a shooter put a round through your chest, then disappeared like a ghost.

"I want to get word to Chiji," Tox said.

Ram nodded. "I can do that quietly."

"Thanks."

After complaining about being attacked on their own soil, the guys headed out, leaving Tox and Haven alone with Ram.

"You should head back to DC. Talk to Galen. Get some security," Tox said to her.

Ram slipped down the stairs and into his office, then closed the door. Dialing his phone, he crossed the room, flipped up a hidden panel in the desk, and punched a button. A screen sprang to life, revealing live security feeds of the entrance, exit, upstairs, and downstairs.

"Go ahead." A calm, monotone voice drifted through the phone.

"I need a favor."

"Go on."

"A friend was shot on a beach. I want satellite images and/or chatter transcripts searched for anything that might connect." Silence anchored him in the room. He slid out a secure laptop and powered it up, trying not to overthink the lingering quiet.

The line clicked, and more silence gaped before a noise crackled.

"This isn't standard protocol," said a new voice. A familiar voice. "And you've compromised one of our sites."

"I know," Ram said quietly. "There was no choice. Someone just tried to kill Tox Russell in broad daylight."

"We'll see what we can do."

4

It'd been a week since lead had pierced his shoulder, leaving an ugly red mess. The skin around the healing wounds itched. He craned his neck to look at the one near his shoulder blade and winced—that scar wouldn't be pretty.

Dawn had yet to crack the day, but Tox had been up for an hour, doing physical therapy to get his shoulder and mind back in the game. Fifteen minutes later, when he emerged from the shower, he heard clanking in the kitchen. Ram was probably preparing another gourmet breakfast.

Tox slid his arms through the sleeves of a tactical shirt, then hooked it over his head with only a few grunts and grimaces. Tac shirts were comfortable, and the familiarity went a long way in an unfamiliar setting toward making him at ease.

He stepped out of his room to the drone of the news and the sizzling sound of bacon in the kitchen.

"Eggs and toast?" Ram called.

"Sounds good." This early in the day, when darkness still reigned and he needed a good jolt to his brain, Tox had priorities. Number

32

one was coffee. Thankfully, a fresh pot awaited. He poured a cup. "Heard anything from your sources?"

Ram, curly head looking like a bird's nest, grunted. "Nothing. Whoever hit you was good."

"We already know that." Sipping the piping hot coffee, Tox half listened to the news as he parked himself on a stool.

"Got another top tenner," Ram said, nodding to the wall-mounted TV while he scooped eggs onto plates.

Top tenners went back—and beyond, really—to the days of Iraq One, when the military issued decks of cards printed with the Top Ten Most Wanted so military personnel knew who to keep eyes out for.

"They seem as endless as grains of sand," Ram continued. "Take one down, another slides into his slot."

Tox slurped his coffee, his gaze hitting the TV. "But at least we're taking the fight to them." A reporter droned on about the details of a— "Wait." He pushed to his feet, setting aside the coffee. That picture. "Holy . . ." Couldn't be.

"What?"

Tox eyed the name below the photo of a graying Iraqi. His heart kicked his ribs, vaulting the past to the present. A dank, dark night. Small Iraqi village on the outskirts of An Najaf. Surroundings awash in green as he eyeballed a handful of tangos.

"Know him?"

"Command, target in sight," he'd reported.

"Tox."

He blinked. Looked at Ram. Then back to the TV. "Remote," he said, surging toward the living room. "Where's the remote?"

"Here." Ram lifted it from the island and handed it to him.

Tox aimed the remote at the screen, mashed the volume button.

". . . according to multiple sources. Again, U.S. Joint Special Operations Command is denying involvement in the killing of known terrorist Gabir Karim, wanted in connection with multiple attacks against Coalition forces and the deaths of Sergeant Luke Pappas, Sergeant Tristan Laine, and Staff Sergeant Guy Jefferies."

Icy fingers of the past clawed at Tox.

"You know—"

"Quiet." He cranked the volume again.

". . . time, little is known other than that Gabir Karim was targeted and killed as he left this hospital in Baghdad. It is confirmed that Karim was the mastermind behind multiple attacks that left more than two dozen American and British soldiers dead."

"Finally," Tox muttered, relief swift and strong. "Someone finally killed him."

"Tox?"

He unplugged his mind from the news and returned to the island. A few gulps of coffee warmed him, but not nearly as much as the victory delivered in the news. "Seven years ago, I got pulled into a mission to hunt Karim." He expelled a breath as if he could shake off the failure of that mission.

"Got away, huh? But"—Ram raised his eyebrows and nodded toward the TV—"like I said, another one down."

"Six years too late, but . . . yeah."

Ram's phone rang, and he answered it. Tucking toast in his mouth, he nodded, muttered "okay," then hung up. "Cell and Thor are ten minutes out with Wallace. Maangi and Keogh are close behind with Haven. I'll be back."

Alone in the kitchen, Tox downed the eggs, then his coffee, finishing it as the security system detected movement outside. He started for the stairs to alert Ram. "Someone's here."

Ram appeared on the top step. Aware. Ready.

"But you already knew that."

"Cell and Thor with Wallace."

Tox glanced back to the bank of security screens at the makeshift conference table. He shrugged, shaking his head. "Don't know why we need Wallace. He's just looking for a way to get her back. And after what he did to her in Israel . . . "

"Murder's still illegal in the U.S."

"Then let's take him overseas," Tox muttered, palms on the table as he bent toward the security feeds. In the small garage, a sleek gray Dodge Ram pickup with a king cab disemboweled itself of Thor and Cell, who opened the rear passenger door and reached in. He guided a man out of the vehicle and led him around the front toward the iron steps up to the loft entrance.

Tox eased forward, squinting at the grainy images. "What is he wearing?" He shifted his attention to the front of the loft.

Beeping announced Ram releasing the security measures. The main door slid open. Thor and Cell, cuffing the arms of Wallace, escorted him to the living room.

"What—"

Cell held up a hand. "Had him change. Ya know," he said around a poorly concealed smile, "to make sure he didn't have trackers or something. Couldn't give away your location."

"I had no intention of doing that," Levi Wallace growled, his gaze blocked by a blindfold.

"Yeah, but what you intended and what someone else in the FBI intended could be two different things." Cell winked at Tox, enjoying what he'd done to the agent far too much. He crossed the floor and stood beside Tox while Thor hung back, rubbing his jaw. More like trying to rub away his smile.

"Wallace—it's clear now."

At that moment, Haven walked in with Maangi, Drew Keogh, and VVolt, who trotted around the condo, sniffing everyone. The team wisely gave him room to secure the area and feel comfortable.

"What are you wearing?" Haven blurted.

There was a taut band of repressed laughter as Levi removed his blindfold and automatically glanced down. And saw the pink sparkling ladies' T-shirt with a glittering tiara emblazoned across his chest. "Are you"—his gaze skipped to the purple tie-dyed sweat pants—"kidding me?" He shot a glare at Cell. "You said I had to change for security reasons, not some high school prank."

Dropping onto the couch, Cell threw his head back and laughed. Thor was chuckling, but working more to conceal it.

"The loft is equipped with technology that would have neutralized any bugs or tracking devices you might've had," Ram said.

Which was probably how Tox should see it too, but he had to admit it felt good to see Superman's clone take a hit.

"So I didn't have to change," Wallace muttered, his face a mask of red.

"You didn't have to change," Ram said, his voice dry and devoid of humor as he pointed to the conference table. "Have a seat."

Wallace hesitated, shoulders sagging as he stretched his jaw muscle.

Tox thumped Wallace's arm with his hand, then motioned him down the hall. He led him back to his room and pulled gray Army sweats and a black T-shirt from his dresser and handed them off to the agent. "Bathroom's behind you on the left."

After a look past the door, Wallace gave Tox a hesitant nod. "Thanks." He clearly hadn't expected Tox to offer some of his pride back.

"We'll wait."

When Wallace ducked into the bathroom, Tox returned to the main area, spearing Cell with a look.

"The dude needed some humble pie." Cell chuckled unrepentantly as he joined them at the long wooden table.

"We need him on our side," Tox said, lowering himself to a chair.

"Levi's loyalties aren't so easily moved that a prank would make him withhold evidence or the like." Haven sat beside Tox, but he could tell the joke annoyed her. "But I also don't think he's done anything to earn your disrespect."

Cell shook his head. "This isn't about disre—"

"Bag's right there." Ram indicated the table as Wallace emerged, changed and recovered of his dignity.

After skidding a glance between Thor and Cell, Wallace went to his satchel. "I do want my clothes back."

"Dude, we burned them—"

As Wallace's eyes widened, Ram popped Cell on the back of the head, and VVolt trotted around the table, growling, ready for some of his own fun.

Cell laughed. "All right, all right. They're in the trunk."

Tox had to get this day back on track. He jutted his jaw toward the papers and folders Wallace had drawn out of his satchel. "Said you found something?"

With a bob of his head, Wallace set the folders on the table. "A few things. Not sure how much is helpful . . . "

"Lay it on us," Maangi said.

"We were able to capture this image of a vehicle—a rental—leaving the area."

Tox looked up from the document. "Any—"

"ID provided was falsified. Probably the shooter, but no way to confirm it."

"Surveillance video at the rental site?"

"None," Wallace said. "One camera, and our guy kept his back to it the whole time." He slid grainy black-and-white images across the table. It showed a man from the shoulders up, wearing a ball cap. "Signatures on the documents are as different as if someone else signed them."

Tox scanned the three pages. Shook his head.

Haven leaned closer, her floral perfume sweet and distracting. "He doesn't want to be found."

"At least not yet," Tox said. "If he didn't want me to know—why tag me? Why hit but not kill me?"

"Agreed." Propped back in his chair, Ram nodded. "He wants you to know who he is." He arched an eyebrow and held up a pen. "Eventually."

"Why?"

Wallace sighed. "We found one thing we believe to be useful, but we've run it through every database and haven't come up with anything."

Hungry for answers, Tox edged forward as Wallace handed him a glossy photograph.

"What is that?" Ram asked.

"The bullet?" Cell muttered.

"A close-up of the one used to try to kill Tox."

As he stared at the image of a bullet lying next to a ruler, Tox froze. Nausea roiled, spreading dampness across the back of his neck and shoulders. Dread. Cold dread.

Not because it was a bullet from a sniper rifle.

Nor because it was a .338 Lapua.

But because of the etching. Crudely carved into the copper casing.

A crown. A distinctive crown with three dots and a crossbar.

Photo in hand, Tox pushed to his feet and walked away from the table.

5

Tox locked his bedroom door and dropped onto the corner of his bed. He pressed a fist against his lips, staring at the photo. It just couldn't . . . ?

But Gabir Karim.

And that distinctive crown. He remembered the man who'd tattooed that symbol on his bicep.

It had to be the same crown. For Tox to get shot, then Karim killed . . . He tugged out his cell phone. Opened a news app and scanned the headlines until he found an article on the incident. Doubts roiled as he refused to accept it. He read another article. Then another.

A rap on the door startled him.

"Cole?"

Tox ignored Haven's voice. Focused on the reports. Scanned them. All said Karim was dead. None said *how*. He opened his contacts and hit one, then put the phone to his ear.

"Rodriguez," came the commanding bark.

"Sir, Russell here."

A muttered curse hit the line. One of resignation and frustration. Which told him Rodriguez knew the purpose of the call.

"How'd he die?" Tox asked.

"You can see the news as well as I can."

"*How* did Karim die?" he repeated.

Rodriguez went silent.

Annoyance snaked around Tox's spine. "Was it a sniper?"

"How would you know that?" Both speculation and incredulity pitched the general's response, confirming Tox's suspicion.

No, not confirming. Lending credence. There was only one way to really confirm it. "Do you have control of the site where he was killed?"

"Tox—"

"Do we have control?"

Silence again, then, "Why?"

That was essentially an affirmation. "Find the bullet."

"Come again?"

"The bullet that killed him. Find it and compare the case to the one that hit me."

"You're kidding, right?"

"If the bullets are the same, call me back."

"Why would I do that?"

"Because I'll tell you who's responsible." Call ended, Tox pushed around his thoughts. Thoughts that should be ludicrous yet kept coming back with more believability.

What was the point? Why tag Tox then hit Karim? That question felt vital to any further answers. It was time to come to grips with the man responsible for these hits. A blast from his past, one he'd have preferred stayed buried.

But then, that was just like ghosts. Staying buried wasn't their thing. They liked to haunt, torment. And this ghost had special skills, tailored for haunting. Tox could only hope he was wrong. Oh, he wanted to be wrong. But the ache in his shoulder warned him about fantasizing.

His phone buzzed, and he answered. "That was fast."

"How in sam hill did you know there was something on that bullet?"

Tox didn't want to believe what he already knew. Chose not to believe it until the general spoke the words. Anything to cling to the ultra-thin thread of hope that words he'd uttered years ago had not come true. "What was it?"

A waste-of-breath question, but again—the thin thread.

Rodriguez sighed, muttering about whether Tox knew who was in charge. "It's a W or something—the copper is pretty bent."

Tox closed his eyes. Swallowed.

"Now, you said you could tell me who's behind this, and I'm waiting. All ears, Russell. And you better have one heckuva good reason for knowing who's behind this, or you're going—"

"It's not a W. It's a crown."

White-blond hair, a crooked nose, and eyes blazing with fury and bloodlust swam through his mind. Face marred from tense fights and a stray bullet. But also laughter, and one of the best soldiers he'd ever known, though a little—okay, a lot—on the edgy side. "The shooter's name is Alec Costas King." Adrenaline tremored through his veins. "Sergeant Alec Costas King of the 10th Special Forces Group."

"Your old group."

"Yessir. He was my right hand for two years."

* * * *

Arms wrapped around herself, Haven allowed Levi's comfort as the others talked and tried to sort out what had happened with Cole. They all agreed he had recognized something or knew something.

"I need to get going," Levi said, touching her back.

She nodded and sighed.

"You need a ride back into town?"

"I'm not leaving," she said, then flinched at the annoyance in her words. "Sorry."

"I understand."

But he didn't. Not really. And she wasn't sure he'd given up on her "coming around" and seeing how "dangerous" Cole was. Or at least, how dangerous Levi believed him to be. "Call if you need anything," he whispered, before turning toward Ram.

Several of the men shifted, their gazes dark and postures tense. Cell glowered openly at Levi, apparently feeling protective of Haven on Cole's behalf. She appreciated their reactions, but she couldn't be stolen from Cole.

"I'll—"

The door to Cole's room opened, and he emerged. Holding his head down didn't conceal the weight so clearly pressing on his shoulders. Every cell of his body screamed one word: *defeat*.

The team quieted. Though Ram watched Cole return to the table and sit at the head, the others hadn't looked up. Moods and men were saturated in defeat like their leader. They knew Tox was about to drop some bad news.

Avoiding their gazes, Cole slid a photo of a bullet across the table. "Shooter is Alec King." When Ram straightened, recognition glinting in his eyes, Cole nodded. "He's one of us. I worked with him for nearly eighteen months. He was tough as nails. Cut it straight. He was a brother."

"How'd you figure out that he was the shooter?" Cell dragged the image closer.

Working his jaw muscle, Cole glanced at it. And some memory, some painful truth, slammed into his eyes. "Alec had this thing for etching a crown—for his last name—into his bullets. Always said he wanted the bad guys to know who was ruling the day." He rubbed the back of his neck, wincing and stretching his shoulder, then pointed at the photo. "Bullet that hit me had one, and so did Karim's."

"If he was like a brother, why'd he try to kill you?" Levi asked.

"Wasn't trying to kill me," Cole said, his expression grave. "He was tapping my shoulder. Giving me a heads-up." He folded his arms. "I think he wanted me to know he was responsible for finally taking down Gabir Karim."

Cell snickered. "Goober who?"

"Yesterday, a high-value target named Gabir Karim—a top tenner—was killed in Iraq. When I heard about that incident, and when Wallace showed us the bullet that hit me, I put two and two together."

To Cole's left, Ram adjusted his beanie. "News articles never said how Karim died."

"No," Cole said with a sigh. "But I took a stab in the dark and asked Rodriguez. He confirmed the kill, confirmed the bullet had a crown carved in it."

"What does Karim have to do with this?"

Rubbing his forehead, Cole sighed again. "Seven years ago while y'all were home, they put me on a team to track down a rising star in the terrorism game. A man with crazy-good connections who could put anyone in contact with just about any source. His resources supplied many attacks, IEDs, and suicide bombers. JSOC wanted him dead. We all did."

"But he got away," Maangi muttered.

Cole set his hands on his belt. "Alec and I tracked him to a remote village, where Karim was meeting with a supplier." His lips thinned and he cocked his head. "We had him in our sights—right there. So we radioed in, ready to level the place." His nostrils flared. "But Command reversed the order."

Ram sniffed. "Told you to stand down."

"They let Karim walk." Jaw muscle popping, Cole nodded. "Alec was livid. Insisted we disobey the order, say we never got it, finish Karim."

"But you obeyed the order," Levi said, then gave a firm nod. Though Haven saw from his expression what words would probably follow, he plowed ahead before she could stop him. "You did the right thing."

There it was. His black-and-white thinking forced upon the very gray world of combat.

Ferocity blazed through Cole as he locked onto Levi, eyes narrowed. "Six months later, Alec went out with another unit. Extended op. They got ambushed. Three of his six were brutally killed by insurgents. Alec collected some lead of his own but survived." He swung his gaze back to his team. "One of the 'terps betrayed them—to Karim."

Cell cursed. "No wonder he wanted Karim dead."

"Really," Thor said, "he's doing us all a favor, eliminating evil like that. There are thousands of 'em out there, plotting against innocents, anyone who doesn't believe what they believe or is just trying to have a decent life." He grunted, shaking his head, his lip curled. "I got so sick of seeing that, working patrol in the villages." His expression was weighted with dark, haunting memories. "Every freakin' day."

"Doesn't make killing them right," Levi said.

"Yeah," Thor barked, "tell that to the mother who died trying to protect her four-year-old son from monsters like him!"

Verbal sparring ensued, but Haven couldn't tear her gaze from Cole.

He'd gone rigid, the planes of his face like granite. His jaw muscle had stopped popping. What was that? What lurked in his expression? Anger? If so, at whom?

"Again," Levi said, terse and unrelenting, "doesn't make it right if he's acting outside the purview of the military."

"Nobody said it did." Cole's words were even and quiet. Cold. Icy cold.

Ram settled back in his chair. "What's King's endgame?"

Though Cole shook his head, it was a slight movement. Without conviction. "No clue."

But he did know. Or at least, he had a very good idea. And there was something else in his gaze that scared her. Despite her deception-detection skills, she wasn't sure what it was.

* * * *

— DAY 9 —
STUTTGART, GERMANY

The beautiful day, hand in hand with the events of the last few weeks, unknotted layers of tension that had built up over the years in Alec King's muscles. Guiding his Audi TTS Coupe along the busy streets, he was glad for a semblance of normalcy, far removed from dusty villages, Muslims trying to kill his friends, and baking sun.

He turned onto Heinestrasse and headed toward B27, ready to escape the city as well. As far as cities went, Stuttgart wasn't bad. Replete with history and having served as home to the U.S. military, he could appreciate it. Maybe even admire—

A car cut in front of him.

Swerving to avoid the guy's bumper, Alec laid on the horn with a curse.

The driver waved at him—not a hand. A finger.

His anger rose. This guy needed to learn that courtesy and kindness went a long way.

Alec accelerated, navigating quickly around another car to keep up with the Mercedes. A little kiss on the butt would—

A little hand rose from the rear seat—a child.

RONIE KENDIG

Letting off the gas, Alec mentally backtracked, his pulse slowing as the small arm wagged again, motioning to the driver. To the father.

Memories assaulted Alec. A pretty little round face with brown eyes and her mother's smile.

The driver might be an idiot, flinging his car through streets like a kamikaze, but the child in the backseat bought him some mercy. Alec would let this infraction go.

He slowed and eased away from the Mercedes's bumper as his phone rang. Alec answered. "Go ahead."

"They found it."

With a snort, he shook his head, eyeing the Mercedes again. "Took them long enough." He allowed a car between him and the Mercedes.

"Now that they are on to you, should we—"

"Change nothing."

"But—"

"Even if he figures out what we're doing, he cannot anticipate the order. Nor the lengths we will go to."

The Mercedes whipped in front of a red sedan, forcing it to swerve. But doing so threw the sedan into oncoming traffic. Two cars dove around the wrong-facing car before it could reclaim its lane.

Now the Mercedes driver had not only put the life of his child at risk, but everyone else's.

"Stay on track. I have to take care of something." Alec ended the call and put his skills to use. He accelerated and wove through traffic like a tactical breach. Bound and cover. Swerve and aim. Slow and accelerate. Within seconds, he regained the guy's tail.

Alec saw him look in the rearview—then look again. His high-end model was probably alerting him to the danger it had detected at the close proximity of Alec's car. "That's right," he muttered. "I'm back."

The Mercedes yanked into the left lane.

So did Alec.

Ahead, he sighted a lighted intersection. Saw the man checking it, then the mirror. Telegraphing his intention.

Alec nearly smiled. Anticipated the hard braking, which forced Alec to do the same. He allowed himself to smack the Mercedes's bumper. A jab in a fist fight—with cars.

45

The Mercedes turned hard right. Following, Alec found the side street less populated. Better suited for his purposes, especially with the overpass five hundred meters ahead.

Gunning it, the Mercedes driver probably thought to flee. But Alec's Audi handled the challenge with ease. As the gap between them and the overpass closed, Alec raced up alongside the silver sedan. The man wildly alternated between watching him and the road, driving more erratically, his panic controlling him.

Good. Loss of confidence meant mistakes.

Alec glanced at the car seat. If anything happened to that child because of this cretin . . . well, it wouldn't be the first time Alec had to deliver justice on behalf of injured or dead children. Wouldn't be the last, either.

The Audi purred, quiet against the nasally whine of the Mercedes. Alec angled out. As cars rode their horns and dove out of the way, he maintained his calm. Stayed focused. He nosed his left front bumper into the rear right tail of the Mercedes, who kept trying to edge away.

But Alec stayed the course. Eyed the vehicles ahead, his belief that they'd swerve to avoid him accurate. He checked the bricked curve of the old overpass. In three . . . two . . .

Lightning fast, he nudged the Mercedes's bumper. His Audi rebelled against the slight impact, but with a firm grip on the wheel, he evened out and nailed his own brakes.

The Mercedes wasn't so fortunate. It whipped to the right. Pitched its front end into the brick wall. The noise of steel and chrome crumpling in surrender roared through the overpass. The slight puff of the airbags deploying.

As the scene and car stilled, Alec verified that the rear half of the car was still intact. Tiny arms waved in frantic panic. Throaty screams told him the child was fine. Lethargy meant danger. Screaming fright was healthy.

Alec unbuckled, calmly glancing in his rear and side mirrors. When he stepped out, the Mercedes's driver was stumbling from his wrecked car and holding his nose, which spurted blood onto his light blue button-down shirt.

Alec strode toward him.

"You jerk! You piece of—"

He spun the fool toward his car. Hooked an arm around his neck, pinning him against his chest. Then he pushed the guy's head forward, cutting off his oxygen supply. He had to be careful. Too much pressure, and the man would die. The child would be fatherless.

When the driver went limp, Alec released him.

Drawing the KA-BAR from its sheath, Alec opened the rear passenger door of the Mercedes. Braced a knee against the seat and leaned inside.

Cherubic, with a round face and large blue eyes, the toddler froze. Confusion on its young face. The lower lip sucked into its mouth.

Alec hefted the knife.

6

"How's the shoulder?" Hands in the pockets of his navy slacks, Dru Iliescu waited on the other side of the security station, his dark brown hair cut short and slashed through with gray.

"Healing," Tox said as he endured the head-to-toe pat-down before stepping through the secure corridor of the Pentagon. He wasn't sure why he'd been summoned, but no doubt he'd find out soon enough.

"Saw the report on King—some piece of work."

"The man or the shot?"

Iliescu hiked an eyebrow as he guided Tox into a small conference room. "Both."

A half dozen uniforms and suits sat around a table. The man seated at the head kicked Tox's pulse up a couple notches—Major General Doran Savakis. Tox knew this general. Knew him to be tough as nails and willing to run a soldier up the flagpole without hesitation. He expected those under his command to operate with the highest level of respect to duty and country.

Savakis owned the room. Pressing shoulders with the CIA's Director of Special Activities Division Rick Hamer, he conversed in hushed, terse whispers. His iron-gray eyes never missed a thing, and they certainly hadn't missed Tox, following him all the way around the oval table to where he folded himself into a chair beside Rodriguez.

Ditching the general's stare, Tox scanned the others. To his right, a navy suit met his gaze and nodded. He had seen the guy before, but he wasn't sure where. To the suit's right sat a full-bird colonel, a woman with an expression as severe and tight as the ash brown bun at the back of her head. Her nameplate read: KAZAKOVA. The others were unknowns, which made Tox more tense. They were seeing a man who was supposed to be dead, but the clearance levels in this room were higher than his, so he wasn't going to borrow trouble.

Not only had he been summoned here for some unknown purpose—he was alone. No Wraith. No idea what was going on.

Not true. He had a decent guess: Alec King. But why bring Tox in alone?

Chairs squeaked down the line, snapping heads to the front of the room. To Savakis. "Sergeant Russell."

Tox shifted to make eye contact. "Sir."

"Good to see you again."

"Thank you, sir. Same."

"How're you holding up?" Savakis pointed at Tox's shoulder. "Hit by a sniper bullet." He glanced down and flipped open a manila folder, glaringly pale against the shiny black table. "Ten days ago, am I right?"

"The Fourth—yessir."

"Healing okay?" Savakis seemed genuinely concerned. That was another thing about Savakis that everyone knew—he cared about those under his command.

"As expected, sir."

"Good." He picked up a pair of silver-rimmed glasses. "Let's get introductions out of the way." He motioned toward the woman. "Beside you is Colonel Kalina Kazakova with CID, temporary oversight since Billings died."

"Ma'am." Tox nodded his greeting.

"Next to her, from the State Department—Conrad Dengler."

Another nod. State Department made sense because they monitored relations between the U.S. and other countries, so with Alec killing an Iraqi citizen, feathers needed to be smoothed. Army Criminal

Investigation Command—CID—also made sense, assuming Alec was still attached to 10th Group.

The general introduced the others—a couple of female officers and several more men. Names were lost to Tox as the litany continued. "Of course you know Hamer and Iliescu." Savakis dipped his head, more of that iron nature glinting in his short-cropped hair, and scanned the file again. "On 10 July, you contacted Major General Rodriguez with a critical piece of intel. You suggested he compare ballistics on the bullet that hit you and the one that killed Gabir Karim."

"Yessir."

"Explain what prompted you to make that call."

He hated this—recitation of facts everyone already knew. But this was the name of the game. "Shortly after I was shot, an FBI ASAC shared with me the image of the bullet that took out a chunk of my shoulder. That image clearly revealed a crown etched into the casing."

"And you recognized it." Kazakova lifted a pen, looking at him expectantly.

"Yes."

"*Ma'am*," she corrected. "I outrank you."

"Technically, *ma'am*," Tox said, skidding a glance around the table, "I don't exist. I'm not in any branch, so there's nothing to outrank."

"Russell, why'd you recognize the bullet?" Savakis asked.

"I'd seen it before. Six years ago, a soldier in the 10th had a fetish for carving a crown into"—he shrugged—"everything he could get his hands on. It was symbolic of his surname, King. It was funny—at the time. A way to blow off steam. To feel important when you're doing the same thing over and over, day in and day out, without any noticeable impact or change."

Holding up his own file, which looked eerily similar to the general's, Rodriguez said, "In one report, you called it 'annoying, possibly dangerous.'"

Tox nodded. "'Possibly' was right. If that symbol were traced, collected, whatever, the enemy could figure out who did it. Come after him."

Why did it feel like Tox was betraying his fellow brother-in-arms? It was stupid, he knew. But this whole thing . . .

Savakis sighed and looked at Hamer, then back to Tox. "Downright prophetic, Russell."

Tox held his peace.

Grunting, the general tossed down his glasses and sat back. "Conrad?"

The suit from the State Department threaded his hands over his folder and leaned forward. "The information you provided General Rodriguez was passed up line. Using it, we were able to determine that Gabir Karim is not Sergeant King's first or only victim."

The urge to shift in his seat pinched at Tox's focus.

"In fact, we believe Karim may have been his third victim."

"Third?" Tox glanced around. "You mean, including me."

"Poor choice of wording," Conrad Dengler said. "In our files, you were considered more of a friend—"

"*Friend?*" Tox snorted. "He shot me."

Dengler angled away from Tox.

"Russell, you yourself told Rodriguez you didn't think King was trying to kill you," Savakis said.

Heat climbed up Tox's neck as his gaze slid to the two-star. The words hadn't been said in confidence, but he also hadn't expected to hear them tossed back at him like this, surrounded by suits and uniforms who seemed ready to take him down.

"Are you changing your belief about Sergeant King's intentions?" Kazakova asked, her voice razor-edged.

"I'm not changing anything." Glare for glare, Tox refused to look away from the hard-nosed colonel.

"Easy," Savakis muttered. Whether to Tox or to Colonel Kazakova, Tox wasn't sure. But it pulled him up straight. He didn't know why the situation had made him angry.

Hamer sat forward. He probably only stood five nine, but he was a powerhouse presence, with his gray buzz cut and eyes perpetually narrowed in deep thought. "Tox, how would you classify your relationship with Alec King?"

"Alec and I worked together—six years ago. I haven't seen or communicated with him since, so I wouldn't say we even have a relationship, sir."

"Until he shot you," Dengler put in.

"Sorry. I didn't realize that classified as a relationship or communication." Tox ground his molars, fighting the agitation stabbing his spine.

"When you worked with him, did you trust him?" Hamer asked, his tone conciliatory. Kind, almost. He knew how to work people.

"I trusted Alec to get the job done. That trust was never broken."

"Did you have any misgivings about King?" Iliescu probed.

"I wouldn't have called them misgivings. We, all of us, have things about our character"—his gaze hit Dengler's—"others don't like or find annoying. But we work with it, because they're effective. I'm sure the men on my team might call me out on things."

"Things like . . . ?" Kazakova again.

"Annoying questions tick me off." He probably shouldn't have said that.

Her lips thinned. "Is this a game to you, Sergeant?"

"Okay, let's draw this down." Hand up, Savakis was studying the file again. "Using the information you"—without looking up, he pointed at Tox—"provided, we determined King was responsible for two other killings: Nasim Kazemi and Lufti Riyad."

Tox's heart crashed into his ribs. He heard himself curse under his breath. *Alec, what're you doing?*

Silence exploded in the room, the hum of the A/C and Dengler's pen tapping against the table the only sounds. All eyes bored into Tox. He hadn't wanted to believe it. Hoped there'd been another explanation so he could write all this off or sweep it under the proverbial carpet.

But there it was. Irrefutable proof.

"Serg—" When Kazakova fell silent, Tox could only assume someone had silenced her.

"Russell? You have something to add?"

He sat back and let out a thousand-pound sigh, feeling miserable. Finally he pushed his unwilling gaze to the four star. "Lufti Riyad was our interpreter."

"Why would he target the interpreter who helped your team?" Kazakova said.

"Because he betrayed Alec's team to Karim," Iliescu muttered.

Nodding, Tox was transported back to that day. Alec had returned to base covered in blood. Eyes wild, livid. Bodies of his men floated past beneath blood-soaked sheets as the medics delivered them to the morgue.

"*I'll kill him, Tox. If I ever get the chance, I'll do to him what he did to my guys.*"

"*Alec—*"

"*No way, man. I'm sick of this bureaucratic bull. They screw us, and we just walk away like we did something wrong.*" His nostrils flared beneath a thick, dust-and-blood-stained beard. "*No more. We should've double-tapped Karim when we had the chance. Now my men are dead! Maybe I'll add some brass to my hit list next time.*"

Tox scowled at the threat. "*Hey!*"

"*No.*" Alec gave him a small push and shook a finger. The shaking went beyond emphasis. Adrenaline-dumping. "*One day, Tox. One day you'll see. . . .*"

Tox's mind latched on to the words: "*Maybe I'll add some brass next time.*" Alec had meant those who had given the order to stand down. Which meant . . .

Tox's pulse sped up. "I need a phone."

IN DESERT MARCH OR BATTLE'S FLAME

Blood drenched the fields, changing them from the color of wheat and barley to a deep crimson. Cow and oxen carcasses littered the area as far as the eye could see. Buzzards lifted their heads from the plunder, blood marring their yellow faces and beaks. The smell brought back memories of the Holy City, but not as heavy. Of course, they were not standing ankle-deep in blood. At least here it had soaked into the ground, and bodies were not stacked as high as city walls.

"He has been here." Gripping the reins of his destrier tighter, Thefarie steeled himself. His mount shifted beneath the palpable tension and stomped his hooves against the dusty earth. The arid region offered little nourishment for the defiant scrubs and twigs that pushed up through the hard ground.

"You are sure?" Giraude Roussel asked, his accent dripping with the dread inherent in finding hundreds of cattle slaughtered for no reason other than a madman felt it necessary.

"There is no doubt." Prodding his horse forward, Thefarie had but one thought: to get ahead of this nightmare.

"In earnest, Thefarie—do not enter it."

Gaze still on the field of death, he drew his horse in a circle. "We must." His eyes rose to darkening skies. "If we were lured by the smell and the sight of the vultures, the Saracens will be, too. We must attempt to make contact. This battle cannot be won by our might alone, Giraude." He turned to the brother-knight he saw as closer than blood. "You know this. We have seen it."

Giraude stroked his slightly grayed beard. "But what you suggest—to align with our enemy against Gregorio . . ."

"If we do this," Ameus de Aldigeriis said through clenched teeth, "we are no better than the Saracens."

Thefarie nearly smiled. "Brother-knights, we are already no better than them."

"How can you—"

"Is it not one of our own who has done this"—he swept his hand over the field—"without provocation, without justification? He attempts to seize power, the greed of the crown possessing his better judgment. Gregorio must be stopped." He spoke the words with each beat of his heart. "Do you not agree? Were we not sent for this purpose, to stop him, to return the crown to its place in history?"

Giraude and Ameus sat stiff in their armor, a hot breeze tugging at their mantles.

Thefarie took no pleasure in chastising his brother-knights, but they could not afford to be wrongly focused in this endeavor. "The time has come," he said. "Spread out and take cover. We will wait."

"Have you confidence, brother, that they will come?"

"I have confidence," he said around the raw hope writhing in his heart, "that ad-Din wants Gregorio stopped as much as we do." Gregorio's path had been wild and unpredictable since he'd first placed that ancient crown on his head. He had defiled himself and the Code, murdering and pursuing wealth and fame. No longer was he worthy to wear the cross of the Lord Jesus Christ. But it was a vain hope that the Saracen ruler would come in pursuit. He would not dare walk among the dead. Even the knights were forbidden. But the mantle they carried went beyond the Grand Master. "Day surrenders to night. We must be quick."

"This is foul work, brother."

"Aye. So let us not waste breath in complaint and finish the task, so we may beg forgiveness sooner."

As they settled into hiding among the brambles and hills, darkness fell over them in a greedy rush.

"How is it you do not age?"

Thefarie maintained a steadfast gaze on the field, the opening between two hills where riders were most likely to come. But he also traced the outlines of the hills themselves, the probable route to deliver scouts a bird's-eye view of the small valley below.

"Years line my eyes and beard," Ameus said, "yet you are as spry as the day we met."

"It is your eyes that have aged, old friend, betraying your dwindling self-confidence," Thefarie taunted, then threw in, "Look at Giraude—as spry-looking as one without whiskers."

Giraude grunted but did not turn to them.

A shadow came up alongside them—a sergeant from Thefarie's unit. The black of his surcoat did well to conceal him and the red cross at night, but they were cruelly hot during the day. "My lord, a rider spotted on the eastern rise."

Sensing the time had come, Thefarie nodded. "Warn the others. The knights only."

The sergeant gave a sharp nod. "Of course, my lord." He hurried back along the ridge in the direction from which he'd come.

Thefarie shifted to Giraude. "Ready the torches."

"Aye."

Thefarie noted the movement between the two hills. The rider had searched the valley, and having seen neither enemy nor trouble, he was forced to venture farther in to investigate. His mission, no doubt, was to seek out the camp of Gregorio. But if sense could be made of the Italian's path to Sheol, Thefarie would have delivered him of this life long ago.

Thefarie, long cloak draped over his mantle to conceal his presence and movements in the darkness, removed himself from the brambles. He cast a quick glance to the heavens. The moon hid behind a haze of clouds, as if offering stealth and shelter to Thefarie and his brother-knights as they circled up on the lone rider.

When the perimeter of knights had been formed, the rider slowed, detecting their movement. Thefarie called out from behind the rider, "Peace, brother. We intend you no harm."

With slow precision, the rider turned. The moon escaped the captivity of the clouds and threw its full, bright light across the olive-skinned face of the Saracen. "If you mean no harm," he returned in Arabic, "why do you entrap me at night?"

"To make a point."

"What point?"

On the cue of those anticipated words, the brother-knights lit their torches. Only then did the Saracen see the bodies of the dead animals around him.

Wide eyes shot back to Thefarie, who, with a sweeping gesture of his gloved hands, threw back his heavy black cloak, revealing his white mantle and the red cross of the Poor Fellow-Soldiers of Christ and of the Temple of Solomon.

"Is that a threat?" the Saracen scout hissed.

"'Tis naught but who I am." Hand resting on his sword hilt, Thefarie stepped into the circle.

With a greedy whoosh, flames erupted, racing along the pile of carcasses, sealing Thefarie in with the scout. "Just as you are a Saracen soldier under Nur ad-Din."

"An entire army awaits my call. I have but to shout, and they will come," the Saracen growled, his lip curling beneath his thick beard. "And they will slaughter all of you just as you have these animals."

"And yet," Thefarie said, "you have not given that shout. I think because you are aware that had we wanted you dead, we would not be . . . talking."

"What do you want?"

"The same thing your general wants. The same thing everyone between Damascus and Cairo seeks."

The Saracen slowly took in the brother-knights surrounding him. Then he swung his full attention back to Thefarie. "Gregorio."

Thefarie inclined his head and motioned to the animals. "His handiwork. Madness claiming what was once a great brother-knight."

"Would that all of you would be infected with the same madness."

"I would have your name, Saracen."

The rider's nostrils flared beneath the glare of the moon. "Why?"

"When two men are about to strike a deal, it is common to know names. I am called—"

"Thefarie of Tveria." The Saracen's gaze was firm, but something in his features flickered. Some familiarity danced there, beckoned for a voice that was quickly denied. "You are known to us by another name." He paused, then lifted his chin as he spoke. *"Malaa'ikah."*

Nervous chuckles filtered beyond the fire.

"As you can see," Thefarie said with a rueful smile, "I do bring a message, but I am no messenger from the heavens."

"Aye," Giraude muttered, "I can attest—smell him after a hard battle."

More laughter helped ease the Saracen's tension, but only a portion. His wary gaze slid around the brother-knights and beyond, to the shadows of sergeants lurking at the far edge of the valley. "I am called Bahir."

"Thank you for your trust, Bahir."

"What of Gregorio?"

"I have information that will allow Nur's army to stop Gregorio in his tracks. It is perilous, but we will give you safe passage through Alexandria."

"Through *Dawiyya*-occupied territory?" Bahir's disbelief was palpable as he mentioned the Arabic term used for the brother-knights. "You must think me a fool."

"I think you as desperate to stop this as are we."

"Why? Why would you do this?" Bahir spat. "If you know where Gregorio is, why have you not stopped him?"

Thefarie hesitated. Surely Bahir was smart enough to know the answer to that question.

With a chuckle, the Saracen finally said, "Ah, if you kill one of your own—"

"He would not be killed." Thefarie squared his shoulders. "At most, he would be arrested and brought before the Grand Master."

"But you want him dead."

Thefarie walked the circle, hands behind his back. "Let us say that this—your swift action against Gregorio—is quicker, and his actions . . . they must be stopped." He faced the Saracen. "You would agree, would you not?"

Bahir said nothing.

"This path is necessary."

"So you want us to take care of your problem."

"I believe, Bahir, he is a problem of the Saracens as well. And with your general ill"—he watched the rider flinch—"it would seem that handing him an unexpected victory may improve his health." Thefarie drew in a breath. "Or perhaps position you to lead that army upon his eternal rest. So we will provide invaluable information on Gregorio's location. We simply require one thing."

Bahir grew wary again. "You have my ear."

"The crown he wears—deliver it to me, and you will not see me again."

Eyes rounding, Bahir froze.

"Yes, you will be rid of two thorns in Nur ad-Din's side: Gregorio and Thefarie of Tveria."

Hunger to appease his general and his people visibly plied Bahir. "I will do it."

Quick, long strides carried Thefarie to the Saracen. He moved forward until the flickering flames of the fire were blotted out in the scout's eyes. "Betray me, fail me, Bahir, and you will understand the full measure and meaning of the Lord's *Malaa'ikah*."

7

Savakis slid his folder aside. "Why do you need a phone?"

"We need to warn everyone involved in the stand-down order that stopped us from killing Gabir Karim six years ago." Determination cut a hard line through Tox. "Especially McKenna."

"McKenna's not with 10th anymore," Savakis said. "He's with 5th."

"You need to talk to him," Tox said. "Make him aware of Alec's . . . game."

"*Game?*" the colonel nearly shrieked, her thin eyebrows winging up. "Three men are dead."

"Three *terrorists*," Tox snapped. "And every one of us in this room knows the world is a better place with them gone."

"Are you—"

"No!" He knew she'd been about to ask if he condoned the killings. "I'm not." He took a stabilizing breath. "But right now, all we have is speculation that Alec's behind this. We owe it to McKenna and—" He froze, the name on the tip of his tongue pitching him back fifteen minutes. Suddenly, he couldn't breathe, his mind strangled by the thoughts pelting him.

"Son?"

Tox bounced back to Savakis. "Billings," he breathed.

Savakis nodded. "Mike Billings—former JSOC commander. He was killed in a car accident two weeks ago." He motioned with his eyes to the colonel. "Kazakova took his place, but it's not official yet."

"Mike Billings gave McKenna the order for us to stand down." Tox felt downright nauseated. "You're sure it was an accident, Billings's death?"

The room fell silent, their hesitation the same one screaming through his veins.

"It was investigated." Savakis's statement held no confidence.

"But that was ten days ago," Kazakova complained.

Tox held her gaze, wrestling his patience back under control. "Ten days ago, Alec was stateside, putting a .338 Lapua through me."

"And McKenna gave you the order," Savakis said as Iliescu, Dengler, and Kazakova started working their phones and jotting in their files. "King taps you with a bullet that says 'watch this,' then takes out Billings, Karim, Riyad, and Nasim Kazemi."

Sickened at the bald truth of that, Tox nodded.

"So King hasn't just gone rogue."

"He's cleaning the map," Tox said, daunted.

Savakis motioned to his left. "Get McKenna—"

"Already on it," Rodriguez said, raising a phone he was thumbing. Seconds later, he turned on the speakerphone and set it on the table. A ring tone rattled through the room.

"McKenna," the lieutenant colonel barked.

Savakis edged toward the phone. "McKenna, this is General Savakis."

"Sir. What can I do for you, sir?" The lieutenant colonel's tone had shifted from annoyance at the interruption to respect and contrition.

The general's gaze struck Tox's as he huffed. "There's no gentle way to say this, Colonel, but we believe there is a credible threat against your life."

Air conditioners and nerves thrummed in the expectant silence clogging the line and the small conference room.

"This is a new and ongoing investigation, but here with me are members of the CID, CIA, and State Department. At this time, we believe Sergeant First Class Alec King might be on a revenge-killing spree."

Hearing the words, the accusation, the disgust, conjured a man younger than him by a few years but older by decades with the weight he carried, the burden of protecting the innocent. Delivering justice to wrongdoers. Alec had always been ardent in his belief in what they were doing. And ticked off when held back. Yet he'd followed orders—with a mouthy spray of objection, but he'd obeyed.

What had changed? What shoved Alec off the beaten path?

"You're sure about this?" Wariness seeped through McKenna's question. The fear of being targeted, most likely, but also coming to grips with the reality that someone you trained, someone you commanded and knew, had put a bull's-eye on your head.

Savakis's expression wavered, shifting from the resolute confidence an officer should have in his men, to the awareness of the evil those same men were capable of, and finally, to wishing for any other possible answer. But there wasn't any. The evidence dangled before their eyes. "As much as we can be at this time, Colonel."

Pushing away from the table, Tox rested his elbows on his knees, listening. It was frustrating not to be able to enter the conversation with McKenna. To let him know he could trust what was being said. That it didn't make sense a man they knew could be responsible, but . . . it was true. He and McKenna had worked well together. Trusted each other. In fact, Tox would say they were friends. But since Tox was still dead to the rest of the world, he couldn't talk. Couldn't give his thoughts.

A nervous laugh crackled through the line. "I know you wouldn't have made this call without careful consideration, but I have to admit, this sounds far-fetched. Hard to believe about King. He was a fine soldier—intense, got the job done. One of the best. A little zealous, but not enough to justify this."

Tox found himself nodding. Alec had been intense—they'd fed off each other, determined to do violence on behalf of the innocent. If Tox hadn't been shot, he wouldn't believe this either.

"I think we all share that shock, Colonel. Base MPs should be there shortly to provide protection for you until we get this sorted and the threat neutralized."

"Understood, sir. I see them coming down the hall now."

As the security forces arrived at McKenna's office with a flurry of barked orders and banging doors, Savakis and McKenna promised to keep each other apprised of developments, then ended the call.

"What about Nasim Kazemi?" Dengler asked, flinging a near-accusation at Tox. "How does he fit into this cleaning up?"

Confused, Tox shrugged. "I don't know that name."

"We also have a possible fourth victim, Farouq Hassan, whom we haven't definitively tied to King, but we're working on it," Iliescu said. "Everything fits King's MO, though."

"Were Kazemi or Hassan involved with Karim?" Tox asked.

"Negative," Savakis said.

Rodriguez perked up. "Hassan is a top tenner, and Kazemi has been a pain in our backside since we got into A-stan, but they weren't connected, to our knowledge. And honestly, we had a difficult time getting information out of anyone at the bases there."

Tox squinted. "Same MO of attack? Sniper bullet with the crown mark?"

Iliescu nodded. "That's what landed their files on my desk."

Bewildered at the litany of kills, Tox roughed a hand over his face. "I have no idea why Alec would hit them. You said the bases aren't talking?"

"My guess?" Iliescu sighed. "A lot of frustrated soldiers are very glad King's quieting things down out there."

Tox could relate. War was exhausting, bone-sapping. And most of the SOCOM guys had multiple deployments. A few months on, a few months off. Away from family and friends. Sunk in the cesspool of terrorism. Tox tapped his finger on the table.

"I hate war as only a soldier who has lived it can, only as one who has seen its brutality, its futility, its stupidity." General Eisenhower had it right. Soldiers hated war more than anyone else. And yet dread, sick and reeling, coiled in Tox's gut. "Quieting things." The scenario made sense—remotely—if it was a retaliatory strike against Karim's organization, but outside that, it meant something Tox did not want

to entertain. A place he didn't want to go and desperately hoped his friend hadn't either.

Iliescu sat forward again, arms on the table. He oozed condescension, though it probably wasn't intentional, and a ton of sympathy slid down the table. "Tox, we think . . . " His gaze hit the general, who nodded. "We think Alec has turned vigilante."

"Vigilante." It hurt to say. Felt like coughing up a decade of combat experiences, as if the military code of honor had been wadded up and lodged in his throat. But even as he avoided choking on the brittle word, a new wave of dread hit him. Why had they brought him here? All this could've been delivered via phone. Most of it in an e-mail.

"You know him best." General Savakis seemed to read the question thumping through Tox's mind. "Would you say that's right, son?"

"No, sir," Tox ground out. He wasn't playing into their hands. Not against a friend. "That'd be his wife."

"*Late* wife," Iliescu corrected. "Divorce was finalized in August of last year, and three months later, she and their daughter died in a car accident."

Double whammy. One Tox thought might have an insinuation. "You think he killed his wife and kid?"

"Wouldn't be the first soldier to go off the rails after a divorce."

"No way," Tox said, snorting in disbelief. "Alec loved her. No way he would've killed her or their daughter." He was sinking, losing ground, losing hope that this was all just a really bad assumption. A bad dream.

"You spoke very highly of him in your AARs, Russell," Savakis said as he tugged off his glasses again. "Did you lie on them?"

"No." Tox had never lied on an after action review.

Savakis's hard eyes raked Tox. He aimed those thick shoulders and gold stars at him. "You worked together for two years."

Tox held his position. "Eighteen months." Night and day. Mission after mission. Together, they'd endured many a dark night.

"In fact," Rodriguez said, hoisting himself into the fray, "I have a report here from McKenna that says you and King were like brothers."

"Not *like*." Tox spoke evenly. "We *were*. Soldiers, the men I fight with, are my family. We eat, sleep, and breathe the same air, chaos, bloodshed, and war."

"Closer than your own brother, your biological brother?" Iliescu had a way of asking questions without the sharp, icy barbs. A technique born out of years working clandestine operations. He excelled at concealing his feelings behind a blank façade.

So did Tox, and he knew to expect it. And deflect. "Until this year, my brother and I hadn't spoken in nearly a decade."

"So that's a yes?"

Tox gave a sharp nod, anger and frustration writhing beneath his tenuous restraint. He knew what was coming. "With all due respect, sirs," he said carefully but forcefully, "why does this matter? Every soldier treats those fighting with him like a brother. We're close. We have to be, because we have to trust each other with our six when the crap hits the fan, as it always does. Alec and I worked well together. He was an excellent soldier." His gaze shifted. Might as well breach the door they were avoiding. "But that's not why we're here."

Rodriguez frowned.

"You want me to find Alec and bring him in."

"No." Savakis snapped his folder shut, the harsh sound silencing the room. Thick, meaty fingers folded over the file.

Blinking, Tox resisted the temptation to sit back, conceding ground. "Then what?"

"We want you to locate and neutralize him."

"*Kill* him?" Shock, then anger, shot through Tox's veins. "No." His pulse pounded in his ears. "I am *not* going to kill one of our own."

"He's murdering people."

"*Targets* on the Top Ten," Tox snapped. "They could be killed by any one of us, but Alec's getting there first. And we have nothing but a symbol tying him to these killings. What if it's not Alec?"

"Tox, this is naïve of you," Dengler growled. "And disappointing. King tried to kill you, and you're defending him? What about Billings?"

"You have no proof he tried to kill me. Or Billings."

Dengler stabbed a hand at his shoulder. "Have you forgotten nearly bleeding out on the beach?"

"I didn't nearly bleed out. The shot was clean, precise. Straight through, no peripheral damage. If he wanted to kill me, he would have."

"Is that supposed to reassure us?" Dengler barked a laugh. "That this AWOL Special Forces soldier is *hitting* people but not killing them? A few millimeters over, and it'd have been a different story. You'd be dead."

"Except that I'm not." Why couldn't they understand? But there was a bigger question—why *was* he arguing for a man who *had* taken a shot at him?

"He's leaving his calling card, for pity's sake," Savakis said. "He's autographing these killings, Russell. I know you might not agree with us, but—"

"You're right." Mortars detonated in his chest. "I don't agree."

"We have no choice but to end this before anyone else gets hurt or the media gets wind of what's happening."

Only when Savakis lifted his jaw to look up at him did Tox realize he'd come to his feet. He towered over the room. "I'm sorry, sir." He should probably take his seat, but that would lessen his vehemence. Reduce the potency of his response. "I don't agree that killing Alec is the only choice. If we follow that logic, every man in this room"—he noted Kazakova arching her eyebrow at him—"and every woman who has served this country could be rounded up and hung out to dry or killed. Including you and me."

Fury roiled through Savakis's molten eyes. But he wasn't shouting at Tox or calling down Hellfire missiles. That gave Tox the gumption to proceed.

"I will go after Alec." He touched the table. "But to *find* him, bring him back."

"You think he's redeemable," Savakis said with a grunt.

"If he's not, then"—a breath staggered through Tox's chest—"neither am I."

Shreek-shweep. Shreek-shweep. The noisy windshield wipers grated on Haven's last nerve, just like this conversation as she sat in her car. "I think you should show it to him."

"Absolutely not."

Shreek-shweep.

Flipping off the wipers, she eyed the restaurant where she'd meet Cole for dinner in a few minutes. "Galen, it would mean a lot to Cole, seeing how your parents took the news that the DoD officially cleared his name."

"It'll only make things worse."

"How?" she asked, her annoyance mingling with hurt for Cole. "To them, he's dead. He'll never get to see your mother or father again. He misses them—"

"Yes. Exactly. And if you show this to him, he'll miss them more, then try to rationalize a way to see them. It can't happen, Haven." Galen huffed. "Remember, this life is a choice he made. Don't let him get in your head."

"That's not even fair. You know he was forced into that decision." She couldn't fathom the courage it took to let everyone think you were dead so four men could have their lives back. "And he's not in my head, Galen. I understand people, especially Cole."

"Have you told him about this video?"

She sagged. "No." But she should have.

"Keep it that way. Because he's very adept at getting what he wants."

Her fight collapsed in defeat, and she deflated against the leather headrest. "I don't understand how you can be so callous about this. He's your brother."

"Yes, and this would only create a black hole of trouble. I know him, Haven. I know my brother, and seeing them now will gnaw at him until he breaks down and—"

"It's ludicrous that Pentagon officials and hospital staff can see him, but not his own parents."

"Haven—"

"No. Sorry. This is where you're wrong, Galen. He has every right—"

"What about my mom?" he growled. "She's been through a lot. You were there. You held her hand at the funeral. How do you think she'll fare, finding out he isn't dead, that he put her through that?"

"Charlotte will throw her arms around him and make up for all the hugs she's missed. He'd want to know about—"

"Don't be naïve. She'll be furious."

Thunk. Thunk.

Haven yelped, jerking away from the car window, where a shadowy figure loomed outside the driver's-side door. Light rain shrouded him in danger and mystery. But then she saw his face. The thudding in her heart slowed—then ramped. Had Cole heard any of this conversation?

"What's wrong?" Galen asked, concern heavy in his question.

She flashed a smile out the window. "Cole's here."

"Do *not* tell—"

With no remorse for Galen, she ended the call, dumped the phone in her purse, and opened the door. "You startled me."

"You should be more observant," Cole mumbled, scanning the darkened street. He took her hand and helped her from the car. "Who were you talking to?"

There was something in his tone, in that simple question, that made her hesitate. Protection. A hint of anger. It both unsettled and reassured her, and that made her hesitate, too. Mostly because she couldn't sort out what it meant. "Why?"

Cole's gaze, darkened by the night but also by something else, struck hers. She saw his annoyance. "I wasn't questioning *you*," she explained. "That was a question to understand what I heard in your voice."

His lips twitched. But instead of answering, he stepped back. "Let's go inside."

Trusting Cole was easy. Understanding his actions—like herding her through the door as if she were a cow—might take an eternity. He was hurrying. Irritated. This wasn't normal, even for the "Tox" version of Cole, terse and commanding.

"Any word from Chiji?" she asked. The Igbo man was a good balance for Tox, who needed him, especially while sorting out life after a near-assassination.

"Things are bad. He'll probably be there awhile longer."

Haven eyed Cole, wondering how he felt about that, since his voice betrayed nothing. "I'm sorry—for Chiji and for you."

He nodded. As he held on to her, moving toward the host station, where a man in a suit stared down his wide nose with a bored look, Haven couldn't help but notice how good Cole looked. From a strictly physical aspect. At nearly six three, though he wasn't a walking tank like some of his men, Cole filled out his pale blue button-down nicely, his biceps tugging at the material. Even when he was alert and scanning his surroundings, he had an easy movement that carried him through life with confidence. Men like Cole warned off most trouble. And attracted the truly aggressive ones. The way he held his broad shoulders said he was in charge, he could handle whatever got thrown at him.

"You okay?" she asked as they waited to speak with the host.

"It's crowded," he muttered.

Though they'd entered the restaurant, there was a lot about Cole that remained outside. His gaze. His mind, plotting an exit strategy, which he would no doubt update throughout dinner. This was life dating a hard-hitting soldier. A Special Forces soldier.

After putting their names on the list, he eased back to her, his gaze once more sweeping the foyer, the guests, then landing on her. "It'll be a minute."

Haven smiled.

And *there*. There was his near-smile. The one that melted her knees and heart. Hands on her waist, he tugged her closer, and the hard edges of his personality softened.

No. Not softened. There wasn't anything *soft* about Cole. But they lessened, enough to let her in without cutting her. This was what she waited for each time they met. This was what made being his girlfriend worth everything—the lessening of that tough exterior, which allowed her to exist within his tight perimeter.

When they were finally seated, Cole chose the chair that put his back to the wall, facing and eyeing the doors. Haven smiled as she slid in beneath the white polyester tablecloth, her own gaze skirting the restaurant. This had been her favorite spot to meet friends, but now . . . knowing how on edge the tightly packed environment made Cole, maybe she needed to find another place for them.

After the waiter took their drink orders and left them to mull over the menu, Cole angled closer. "Do me a favor?"

Haven peered up from the menu.

"Don't sit alone in your car on a dark street."

Confusion and annoyance clawed for dominance. On one hand, he had a point—it was dangerous. But she had training. She—

"I know you can handle yourself, but . . . " He roughed a hand over his jaw. "It's just not smart."

She winged up an eyebrow. "So I'm not smart?"

He frowned. "You know that's not what I meant. You are, but sitting in your car on a dark street with a phone screen lighting your face isn't the best move. Be strategic." Even as he said the words, Cole registered them. Drew his gaze down, then back to his menu.

Grateful for her ability to read people, Haven smiled, knowing Cole realized he'd treated her like one of his men instead of his girlfriend. Or maybe . . . maybe they were the same because in his mind, he was tasked with protecting both. That might offend some women. But Haven understood his wiring, his protector-guardian persona, carved out of more than a decade of military service. Yet

71

she had this nagging feeling something more was going on here. He was *too* tense.

He set his menu aside and scanned the restaurant, hands resting on his thighs. Alert. Coiled.

Still making her entree decision, and trying to be as casual as possible, she asked, "What's happened?"

Cole swung his gaze to her. "As in?"

She decided on the bow-tie pasta, which she'd have to run off tomorrow morning, and laid her menu over his. "You're on edge. More than normal."

The muscle in his jaw popped, and he flicked his gaze to the front door again.

"Can't talk about it?" She was used to that, with her own career and with Galen in their lives.

"Not really." He shifted, angling more toward her. "But I would like to talk about that phone call." His eyes sparked with that raw confidence he embodied.

"You heard us."

He neither agreed nor disagreed. Just stared, but his blue eyes revealed the answer.

Haven shook her head. "When I hoped for you back, I never imagined being caught between the two of you."

"So it *was* Galen."

Hesitation clapped its hand over her mouth. She'd thought . . .

"I heard you say I'd want to know, but I wasn't sure it was him."

Haven sighed. "I have to improve my resistance to blue-eyed torture."

A smile tugged at the corner of his lips as he played with the linen napkin beneath his hand.

Haven felt more like a translator than an active party to a decent conversation. Her guess was that he wanted to know what she and Galen had talked about, but he also wouldn't push her to talk about something she hadn't willingly offered. "You're not making this easy."

He snorted. "Sorry." Then he nodded. "I want to respect your relationship with Galen and the boundaries tied to that."

"But?"

A weighted grief rolled through the planes of his handsome face. "You mentioned my mom."

Haven swallowed, sagging at the reminder.

* * * *

Tox had never been good at conversation, and definitely not romantic dinner conversation, but he'd imagined this night going differently—better. Wining and dining Haven. Showing that he could fit in with civilians. That he could do this—be normal. Pursue this thing he felt toward her.

But he'd messed up twice since being seated. He was used to telling someone what to do, and they did it. Or giving enough respect to let them figure out the right thing to do. Which was why he drew back and restricted himself to ordering food, commenting on it, and staring as long as he could at Haven without her knowing. That last part was easy.

She was beautiful, with her dirty-blond hair and green eyes. Intelligent. Which begged the question of why she was here with him. But he wouldn't give her a chance to reconsider. He wanted her here, at his side. Wanted to hear her voice as she talked about agents at the office and their desperate attempts at dating the wrong women. Just the sound of her voice was soothing.

But Haven had a relationship with Galen tied up in the form of their thirteen-year-old niece, Evie. It gave them room to talk, to be connected. Which ticked Tox off for some reason. And now—again—Galen was holding something back from Tox.

Something that had to do with their mom. What if she was sick? "Just tell me—is she okay, my mom?" His gaze snagged on a man halfway across the packed restaurant. Their gazes collided. The man looked away, but Tox didn't.

"She's good," Haven said. "I haven't seen her since the Fourth, but she called a few nights ago."

"Yeah?" He checked again, certain the guy had been watching them, though he now sawed through a steak.

"She's taken on directorship of a charity, and it's given her new life—the Endeavor of Patriots event. I think it's her way of keeping you alive."

That pulled Tox's focus back to the table. "Yeah?"

Haven bobbed her head. "She's really excited about it and tackling it with fervor. Said she finally feels useful again." She rolled her eyes and laughed. "Charlotte Russell is so vital to so many, and honestly, she's the most amazing woman I know." Her words were sincere but surprising.

He studied Haven, who speared another bow tie pasta. She really meant what she'd said about his mom. And that did crazy things to his heart because, though his mom had been tough on him to keep him in line, she'd been the best.

"What caught me off guard was when she asked me to be a part of it."

"Why wouldn't she?" Sipping his water gave him another chance to check out the steak guy. Tox slid his gaze in that direction, but not all the way. Just enough to confirm the man was watching them again.

Haven shrugged, chewing then swallowing. "Because I've never done charity work, though my mom's always thrown money at causes like rice at a wedding." She gave a soft snort, then blotted her mouth with her napkin.

The uneasiness building in Tox made him scan the restaurant for an exfil strategy and others too interested in his business. The nearest door was behind them and led into the kitchen, which would provide an exit, but it'd be tricky.

"Still, it would get my mom off my back if I told her I was working with Charlotte Russell on the Endeavor of Patriots event."

The Linwoods and Russells were irrevocably yoked because of Galen and Brooke's marriage and daughter Evie. One family had tons of money—the Linwoods. The other—his family—had been embedded in power through politics and the military dating back to the Revolutionary War.

His mom and Haven working together. "That's good." He nodded. "You have a lot to give."

A shy smile made her soft skin glow. "Thank you. I haven't given her an answer yet, but—"

"Why?" He homed in on her, disappointed.

"Because . . ." Breathing through a laugh, she wilted a bit. Sipped some water. "I limit my interaction with her out of fear I'll acciden-tally mention you."

Tox hesitated. "Guess that would be a shock." He hated the thought of Haven not doing something she'd be good at because of him. That Haven was bound by an oath of silence. "I'm sorry."

She covered his hand. "I'm not. I love your mom, but I—" A flush snapped through her cheeks and she jerked her gaze to her half-eaten pasta.

I love you more.

He heard the unspoken words as clearly as if she'd said them aloud. Something in his chest ignited. He didn't deserve her unwavering devo-tion. Not with the things he'd done. Not with the truth that lurked in the void of the years they'd been apart. If she ever knew . . .

Haven nudged her plate aside, set her elbows on the table—in a very un-Linwood-like manner—and folded her arms. She leaned toward him, her light perfume coiling around his mind, and whispered, "In case you ever wonder, I'd rather spend time with you than twenty board members bickering over the best way to raise money and not get audited."

His gaze dipped to her lips, which were close enough for a kiss. "Good to know." He angled in. Stole that kiss.

"PDA," she said around a smile. "What's your CO going to say?"

Liking that she didn't pull away, he kissed her again, savoring her vitality. Her joy. Her soft lips that spoke gently and anchored him in the storm. As her breath skidded across his cheek, he embraced a painful truth. "He'll say I don't deserve you."

"Mm," she said, "I'd have to disagree with him. Report him for dereliction of duty for not recognizing the brilliance of the soldier under his command."

"Would you?"

"Yeah," she breathed, green eyes alive. "Because they say I'm pretty awesome, and I could never fall in love with someone who wasn't *at least* at the same level."

Grinning, Tox slid his arm up her back. "That right?"

With a breathy laugh, she nodded. "Absolutely."

But swift as storm clouds, he was struck again by that truth. He *didn't* deserve her. She was innocent, good. The light to his darkness. Being with her, letting this thing between them grow, scared him. He would never forgive himself if anything happened to her. And in the list of dangers to Haven, he included himself. In an effort to create distance, Tox brushed a few strands of hair from her face.

"Well, well, well." A nasally voice slithered into their conversation. "Isn't this cozy?"

Dread, hot and molten, poured into Tox's gut. He jerked. On his feet before he registered the move, one hand swinging out in front of Haven and the other reaching for his weapon, Tox had one mission: protect her. Breathing became a chore as anger rushed in, his veins feeling like they pumped sludge.

An unmistakable poke in his side stilled Tox. A muzzle. Pressed into the soft spot beneath his ribs. He froze, easing his hand from his own weapon and into view, so whoever held that gun behind him wouldn't shoot.

"Hello, Tox. Who's the beauty?" A golden beard and mussed hair rimmed the face of the man standing next to their table and grinning unabashedly at Haven.

"What do you want, Alec?"

9

It was good. Really good to see his brother-in-arms' protective instincts hadn't dulled. But seriously? Had Tox Russell gone soft for a woman? And the president's sister-in-law, no less?

Too good to be true.

Although Alec *could* see her allure. Blond, curvy, beautiful. And intelligent. She had to be intelligent for Tox to even be curious. He'd learned that years ago.

Tox's eyes darkened. "Why are you here, Alec?"

"A talk." He lifted his gaze to his brother, reading the raw fury there. The look a man got when what belonged to him was threatened. And clearly Tox considered this woman his. Good to know. For future reference, of course. It wasn't like Alec was bloodthirsty.

He motioned to the empty chairs at the table. "Shall we sit and talk?"

"Not here," Tox growled. "Outside."

Alec pursed his lips and shook his head. "No, we'll do it here." Tox tensed as Alec drew out a chair and speared him with a look. "I have four men in this room who will not hesitate to do whatever is necessary to protect me." Enough warning carried through his hissed words to make his intentions clear. Then he flashed another smile. "Shall we?" he repeated and sat down.

Though the beauty pulled in on herself, keeping her arms and legs as far from Alec as she could without being obvious, Tox wasn't moving. Rigidity held his arms to the side, ready for a fight.

"You'll crack a tooth grinding your teeth like that, Tox." Alec motioned to the chair behind his brother. "Sit."

Nostrils flaring, Tox balled his hands into fists but complied. "This isn't cool, Alec."

"Not cool?" Alec laughed. "Who's not cool, coming back from the grave after making all his friends think he's dead? Making his poor mother grieve." He clucked his tongue and let his gaze drift to the blonde again. "How did he ever convince an angel like you to—"

"Leave her out of this."

"Oh no," Alec said, moving aside plates, utensils, and glasses to lean in. "This isn't your game, Tox. You don't give the orders. Not this time." He breathed, so relieved to be calling the shots. "I'm here to recruit you."

* * * *

Struck by the absurdity, Tox bit back a laugh. "*Recruit* me?"

"Yes," Alec said, his expression laden with sincerity and determination. He shifted closer. Thankfully, his interest in Haven was momentarily abandoned. "A mission, Tox."

Was he serious? A mission? Tox had a feeling laughing in Alec's face wouldn't go over well. "The objective?"

Had Alec somehow been drawn into a black ops group that operated so far below the radar and purview of those Tox worked with that they didn't know? Iliescu said Alec had gone rogue. Was it possible Alec was legit and operating need-to-know?

Regardless, Tox had to get Haven out of here. "I'll talk, but let her leave."

Alec blinked, as if he'd forgotten Haven. "Oh no, I want her here." He touched her knee.

"Don't," Tox growled.

Alec smiled. "Good. Good to know you care about something,

because that little stunt, killing yourself off and vanishing?" He sat back, allowing a waiter to deliver a fresh glass of water. When the waiter stayed at the table, expecting an order, Alec waved him off. "That stunt worried me."

"Why does anything I do concern you?" Tox asked, sliding his hand into his pocket, where he kept his phone. He cursed the inventiveness of touch screens, lacking buttons to guide his fingers to dial for help.

"Because you and I are the same, Tox."

Another laugh caught in his throat. "How d'you figure?"

"I'm disappointed you have to ask. You knew it once. In fact, you once said to me that we were so much alike it scared our COs. That we were on the same mission."

"We *were* on the same mission." It wasn't figurative when Tox had said it.

"Gabir Karim."

Tox had walked right into that one and opened a quagmire.

Solidarity smeared through Alec, doused with pride. "Yes. You remember."

Touching his shoulder where a bandage still protected the wound site, Tox nodded. "You made me remember."

Alec rocked his head from side to side with a purse of his lips, as if shrugging off the incident. Shrugging off that he'd put crosshairs on Tox.

"There are easier, less painful ways to get my attention."

"But not as memorable. And this?" He gave a cockeyed nod and arched his eyebrow. "This needed heads-up, eyes-out, singularly focused attention."

"Is that why you killed Karim? For it to be memorable?"

"Not at all." Alec splayed his hands, as if the answer was obvious. "That was a life for a life—or rather, a half-dozen lives."

"Your men."

Alec nodded. "That never should have happened. Karim was supposed to be dead. They stopped us from answering evil."

"But answering evil with evil?"

"Evil?" Alec said around a laugh. "It was justice. I delivered God's judgment!"

"Judgment."

"Justice."

Inflaming Alec wouldn't help Tox figure out what had happened to his friend, how he'd fallen down this dark path. Time for distraction. "How'd you find me? How'd you know I was still alive?" He'd really like to know how Alec found them at this restaurant, but Alec wouldn't show his hand that far.

"You aren't the only soldier out there, Tox. And people know you. The people I know are the same ones you know. We walked the same mine fields, the same IED-infested roads with the same men." Waving a hand, Alec seemed to dismiss that train of thought and narrowed his gaze. "You weren't paying attention."

Though Tox focused on his friend, he also never let go of their surroundings. The steak guy he'd spotted earlier—he was one of Alec's men. "Paying attention to what?"

"To the evil, to the injustice soldiers are being forced to ignore. Look at Martland, threatened with a dishonorable discharge for delivering justice to an ANA colonel who kept a boy in sexual slavery." Alec's eyes blazed. "Does anyone do anything to the man repeatedly raping boys? No, they're more worried with the *political tenor*"—spittle foamed at the corner of his lips—"than with justice and honor being the hallmarks of our troops' presence. They want to throw the book at our guy, the one *stopping* the evil."

"Charges were dropped against Martland."

"Why were there even charges in the first place?" Alec railed, the veins in his temples straining against his outrage.

Tox knew the futility of the military code of justice. It wasn't flexible. Couldn't be. If it was, then men decided the rules, and the lines between right and wrong blurred.

"And Karim," Alec continued.

Tox tightened his jaw again.

"Evil won because so-called good guys *let* it win." Alec stabbed a finger against the table. "That has to stop." He shifted as if he could get closer to the table already pressed against his chest. "When we first met as grunts, what'd you tell me? Why'd you sign up?"

Answering that would feed his frenzy.

"You said 'to bring justice.'" Alec's lips thinned. "What did you tell our guys when we were breathing dirt and blood, fighting insurgents who couldn't give a crap if their tactics were cruel? Terrorists who played by no code book save the one that got them their virgins?" He craned his neck. "What did you say about them?"

"'Deliver justice and let God sort the rest,'" Tox muttered. He'd said it many times, a Band-Aid for the gaping wounds of their souls.

"'Deliver justice and let God sort the rest,'" Alec repeated breathlessly, rapping the table. "That's our mission. To deliver justice. Always has been. You and I. Fighting. Time and again. We made a good team."

They stared each other down. Tox, uncertain where this was going and wanting one thing: Haven out of the equation. And Alec, seeming to have made a point he was waiting for Tox to grasp.

"Each serving in our unique capacities," Alec continued. "Did you know that even the Bible says God gives us all different jobs?"

"I think God," Haven said, entering the conversation, "intended that to reference the function of each person within the body, for service in the church."

Tox flinched, all too aware of how her soft, firm voice drew Alec's gaze. His attention. Poised to respond, he watched his former friend, the blue eyes, the blond brows, searching for the rage. The anger. Slowly, Tox slid his hand over Haven's and gave it a slight squeeze, hoping she'd stay out of this. He didn't want Alec focusing on her.

"We *are* serving the church," Alec said to her, then met Tox's gaze again. "Living what you believe goes beyond a clapboard building and steeple. It's out there. We carry it into the world." His head swiveled as he emphasized his meaning. "In Ephesians, it says, 'Wherefore take unto you the whole armour of God, that ye may be able to withstand in the evil day, and having done all, to stand.'"

Tox swallowed, wishing for the wisdom of Chiji. Hating that Alec was quoting Scripture to him. From Chiji, even from Haven, he could deal with it. From Alec, it came across as sick, twisted.

"You and me?" Alec went on, "He made us warriors, to deliver justice—as you said—to resist in the evil day, to *stand*!"

Tox smoothed a hand over his mouth, not sure how to respond.

Haven shifted. "The Bible—"

"No," Tox said, more severe than intended. As an unspoken apology, he squeezed her hand again, then released it. He shouldered in, trying to block Alec's line of sight on her. "Let him talk." He didn't want Haven drawing herself into this any more than necessary. "Let's hear what he has to say. How he justifies killing people."

Alec smiled. "It's God's work, Tox." He tapped the table, the glasses clinking and ice rattling like Tox's nerves. "And it's up to us. They have to be stopped."

"Who?"

"The terrorists. The Top Ten. The DC machine. Once a bomber, it's now merely a prop plane, fumbling in the turbulence of war." Ferocity reddened Alec's face. "Fumbling and failing. They are *failing* our country and *failing* the innocent. No more! The jihadists claim it's a holy war, and they're right. It's time for us to acknowledge that and step up our game."

"You serious?" Tox asked with a nervous laugh.

"Dead serious. We need to go after them."

"Who decides which terrorists get hit?"

"They all get hit," Alec said with a devious grin. "Eventually."

Sickening realization churned through Tox. "Alec, one person isn't equipped to make that decision."

"Don't take this wrong, Tox, but evil is pretty easy to identify if you look carefully. And we can't keep letting them burn our country down around us while pacifists tell us we just need to talk to them, that understanding each other will quell wars."

"If we go off half cocked, we could kill an innocent."

"I'll give you that point. Yes, it's a possibility," Alec said, nodding but almost unaffected at the thought that innocents could die. "It's a risk I have to take. If we make ourselves sheep, the wolves eat us." Ferocity seeped into his leathered complexion. "I won't be the sheep. I'm going to be the wolf."

That Benjamin Franklin quote had been a favorite among the men, but the way Alec mentioned being the wolf . . .

"Join me, Tox. With your skills and mine, we can do this. Clean things up, and in the long run, protect more innocents. I know we can."

Alec had lost his mind. Yet Tox feared setting him off, angering him and having him turn his attention on Haven, who sat within striking distance.

"I know you aren't seeing things clearly right now," Alec said softly, condescendingly. "I know I've thrown things at you that might take time to think through, but I know you, Tox. You want the bad guy dead at the end of the day just as much as I do." He nodded forcefully. "Come work with me, and you'll see it's right."

Though Tox had absolutely no intention of working with Alec, he had to play this smart. "I'd have to give up a lot to do that."

Alec's head bobbed frenetically, as if he understood. "I get it." His gaze hit Haven. "But I'm sure an FBI agent understands that the evil in the world needs to be dealt with."

Over Alec's shoulder and through the darkened window, Tox spotted a black SUV sliding up to the curb beneath the street lamp and lurching to a stop. The glow of a phone washed over a face. Wallace. He sat at the wheel. Interesting. But why wasn't he coming in?

Waiting on backup.

Tox had to buy time. He leaned forward. "Understand *this*—she is off the table. You touch her, go anywhere near her, even mention her name again, and you'll wish you hadn't."

Alec grinned. "That's the Toxic Russell we need." He laughed. Came to his feet, bent across the table, and slapped Tox's shoulder. "So, you on the team?"

Tox rose, intentionally shifting to the left to draw Alec away from Haven and the windows, where he'd seen two more SUVs roll up. "I—"

Then, like someone had thrown a flashbang, things went crazy. Alec's men lunged into motion. Steak guy rushed up and muttered something to Alec, who looked at the newcomers.

"Seems we've got company." Annoyance slid along the lines of Alec's face as he met Tox's stare.

"Not our doing," Tox said.

Without warning, steak guy flung around.

Tox saw the fist, but not soon enough.

The fist connected with his jaw, spinning him around. Haven screamed. Chairs and china clinked. He jerked back, ready for a fight. Pulled up straight at the dark, primal look in Alec's eyes.

"Don't wait too long, Tox. Evil needs an answer." He glanced over his shoulder at Haven. "And we want to make sure our loved ones stay safe." He met Tox's gaze. "Don't we?"

Anger ruptured at the insinuation. "Alec—"

Glass shattered. Weapons fired.

Tox threw himself sideways. Right into Haven, taking her to the ground. He hooked an arm over her head, watching through a tangle of table and chair legs as agents stormed the restaurant. Behind him, he heard the back door flap. Flashbangs detonated. His ears rang.

Would Alec get out of this alive?

10

Pressed beneath Tox, Haven prayed. For their safety. For Alec. Thanked God her surreptitious attempt to call Levi had worked. The two men had been so intent on their private war, neither had noticed when she fished the phone from her purse.

"Russell!"

"Here," Cole said, easing off her. He had his weapon to the side, ready, pulling her to her feet and toward himself. Instinctive. Protective.

Face awash in worry, Levi navigated the maze of tables. "Either of you hurt?"

"No." Cole snaked his arm around her waist, but he was focused on the windows, the doors, the agents. "Did you get him?"

Levi searched her face. "You okay, Kasey?"

Kasey. It was strange hearing that name, as she'd mostly given it up since she started dating Cole.

"Hey," Cole barked, his muscles tightening her in his hold. "Alec King—"

"Agents are in pursuit," Levi said evenly. "We know how to do our job."

"Do you?" Cole growled. "Because I see you wasting time when I've already told you we're fine. That man is a wanted—"

"I know who he is."

"Special Agent Wallace?"

Cole stiffened at the voice intruding, and Haven saw a man in a suit approaching. She hadn't seen him since they'd returned from Spain months ago after stopping a deadly plague, but she recognized Dru Iliescu.

Levi turned and went rigid, too. "Deputy Director."

Well-muscled but lean, athletic like Cole, the deputy director strode toward them, tucking an ID wallet into his suit's breast pocket. "How are we doing here?"

Levi skated a look to them, then nodded. "Good. My agents have given chase—"

"They lost him, Agent Wallace." The deputy director's voice was flat, void of emotion. "Mr. Russell, Ms. Cortes." He motioned for Cole to follow him.

"Let's get you to safety," Levi said, relief in his voice.

Cole clasped Haven's hand and drew her past Levi, who fell into step behind them. She whispered her thanks.

"Sorry I didn't get here faster," Levi said as they walked out into the misty evening.

Cole opened the door to a silver SUV with blacker-than-black tinted windows and motioned her into the rear seat. He shook Levi's hand, mumbling something Haven couldn't hear. But Levi's look turned dark, pensive.

Cole slid in next to her and shut the door, watching through the window as the deputy director spoke with Levi and other agents huddled beneath the red-and-black awning of the restaurant. "You okay?" he asked.

Weak from the adrenaline dump, she sagged against him, grateful for his warmth and concern. "No, but I'll be okay. You?"

"Ticked." He tucked his arm around her, cinching her into his hold.

The deputy director climbed behind the wheel, and the SUV pulled away from the curb, leaving the authorities to sort out the mess. He glanced in the rearview mirror. "We'll have your cars towed."

Cole nodded.

"I'll take you to a safe house."

"Not necessary," Cole said. "Alec doesn't want me dead. Take us to my house."

"And her?"

"He knows what I'll do if he tries to hurt Haven."

His words should be a comfort, but they proved disconcerting. And maybe a bit alarming, because Cole would make good on that threat if King made an attempt.

"You said Alec wouldn't come after you—why?"

"Because he wants me to join his team."

Silence stretched with the miles to Cole's condo.

"How'd you and the FBI know to come?" Cole asked, his tone direct and authoritative.

"Got a tip called in."

"A tip?" Cole shook his head, glancing out at the city sliding by in a glare of lights and frenetic merriment.

Iliescu's eyes glowed in the rearview mirror. "An informant with hands on the situation." He grinned and shifted his gaze to Haven. "Or rather, on one of our assets."

Haven felt the heat creeping into her cheeks even as Cole finally swung his gaze down to her. She shrugged sheepishly. "You and Alec were in a verbal war, which gave me time to text Levi."

Cole hesitated, then squeezed her shoulder and kissed the top of her head. "Smart."

The deputy director lifted his chin. "So he wanted you to join his team?"

"Yeah," Cole said. "Believes it's some God mission."

"God mission? Since when was he religious?"

"Never, to my knowledge."

"So he's whacked?"

"I think it's worse than that," Haven heard herself saying. She twitched, realizing they were both looking at her now, that she hadn't been intended as a participant.

"What do you know, Agent Cortes?" Iliescu asked.

"It's more what I saw." Haven appreciated Cole's firm grip around her shoulders to keep her steady. "Alec King truly believes he's on a mission from God. That wasn't just talk, some fancy spiel to justify his actions. I mean, it might have started that way, but he had conviction in his eyes—his gaze became distant, unfocused—and his voice. Spittle in the corner of his mouth as he talked. There were no lie tells, not that I saw."

"So he believes what he's selling," Iliescu muttered. Shook his head. "Great. Nothing worse to fight than a religious zealot."

"They're more dangerous." Cole rubbed her arm, and she glanced at him, but he was watching the windows. When she cocked her head, he gave the slightest shake of his. Was he telling her not to say more? Why would he do that?

The vehicle glided around a corner and up to the curb of Cole's home. He climbed out, then opened Haven's door and assisted her. "Thanks, Director."

"Sure thing. We'll be in touch."

Cole led her up onto the front porch, a sensor throwing light into the darkness. After unlocking the door, he drew her inside, secured the locks, and strode down the hall to the right, to the keypad on the silent alarm.

"So what was that about in the SUV?"

Cole reappeared and considered her for a moment, then with a sigh, he headed for the kitchen.

"I thought you trusted Iliescu."

"I trust my instincts more." He stood at the fridge with orange juice in hand and guzzled straight out of the carton.

Haven made her way around the island to him.

Cole abandoned the OJ and folded her into his arms again. Then he lifted his phone, keyed in a code, and set it on the table. "How are you really?"

"I'll admit—hearing his words, hearing Scripture twisted for his . . . mission—that was disconcerting and maddening, but I'm okay," she said. "He's serious. He really believes this is a mission from God." Arms encircling his waist, she looked up at Cole. "How are you?"

"Same." His eyes raked the shadows of the home. "That's not the Alec I knew. The intensity is the same, but there was something else."

"Do you think he's crazy?"

"Strangely, I don't. Everything he's doing is crazy, but . . ."

"Then what?"

Jaw muscle working, Cole again looked around his home, but he wasn't really seeing anything. From his distant gaze, he might even be peering into the past. "I don't know," he whispered.

This was the way Cole hid himself. "You do, though."

His gaze struck hers, fierce. Then waxed clear. "It's just . . . hard." He leaned back against the granite countertop.

"What?"

"Hearing him talk like that and . . . understanding."

Haven couldn't hide her surprise. "Understanding?"

A storm moved into Cole's expression, pushing aside his thoughtfulness, his confusion. He met her look evenly and with frustration. "Yeah, I get it." The way he said those words came out like a challenge, a dare. "I get where he's coming from. What he said makes sense."

She drew back, though she tried not to because this was a test. Whatever had flashed through his features just now wasn't the Cole she knew. Six months ago, Levi would have said it was because she didn't know Cole. But she'd spent the last one hundred and eighty days with him, renewing their friendship and more. This storm, this defiance was new. And her reaction seemed to fuel the fire.

"Until you've been there, holding a child bleeding out from an IED . . . " Antagonism, defensiveness, and anger all roiled through his words and brow. "Or a disemboweled grandfather, or until you've gathered evidence—the pieces of a buddy off the road after an RPG— you can't understand what it's like."

"Whoa." Haven held up her hands. "Okay, I understand—"

"That's just it. You can't, Haven." His blue eyes blazed. "You've been protected from that. You haven't had to gun down men because they'd kill you given the chance. You haven't had to walk away from neutralizing murderous scum because someone on the Potomac felt it was too divisive or might derail their career, yet knowing—*knowing*—the scum would kill again."

"Cole," she said firmly, quietly, "I hear you. I do."

His chest heaved and his nostrils flared in and out. But he didn't sag. He was still poised in defense. In disquiet.

"It makes sense that you can relate to King's words. He made sense, twisting things just enough to bend them from truth."

"You think he's a monster."

Hesitation held her fast, not at his words, but at the confrontation in how he said it. The anticipation of her agreement. And his expectation. "No, I never said that."

The doorbell rang.

Tox was already headed down the hall before she could react. "Hey. Thanks for coming."

Thanks for coming? Who had he called and when? He hadn't—

Wait. Her gaze hit his phone on the counter, remembered him thumbing the screen before setting it aside. Had he called someone? She'd assumed he'd set some app that would fry listening devices. When she realized he hadn't come back to the kitchen, she peeked into the hall. He and another person chatted in hushed tones.

Ram Khalon lifted his chin to her. "Cortes."

Arms wrapped around herself, Haven managed a smile. "Hello, Ram."

Cole ran a hand down the back of his neck. "Ram's going to take you home."

Take me home? Insult steeled her spine. "Oh." She felt like a child waiting at the principal's office, but she hadn't done anything wrong. Had she? "Okay."

Ram's expression flickered.

Cole was all motion and little talk. He turned back to the door and opened it. "Text me when you get into your condo."

What on earth . . . ? But his expression severed her objection. Pangs darted through her chest as she returned to the island for her purse. She clenched her eyes, wondering where she'd gone wrong. What had upset Cole so much? It took several painful moments to temper her indignation, her anger at this treatment.

"Haven." His voice was quiet and close.

She didn't trust herself to look at him. "I might not get combat, I might not have killed someone, but I do get you, Cole." Strength coursed through her. "And you don't have to throw me out because you're upset."

"Haven." He held her shoulders. "I'm not—"

"You are. That's why you summoned Ram to *retrieve* me."

Surrendering, Cole rubbed a hand over his forehead. "You're right." He slowly shook his head, his internal confusion clear. "And I shouldn't have done that. I'm sorry. It wasn't done to hurt you."

"And yet you still want me to leave."

"I . . ."

"Got it." Eyes stinging, she started for the hall, then stopped. Glanced over her shoulder. "For the record—*your* record, since it's playing so loud in your head already—I don't think he's a monster. And I don't think you are either."

Cole faced her, his blue eyes holding a strange, desperate hope. One that gave her pause. What was going on behind that look?

"What concerns me," she said, "is that he's treading a fine line between fighting evil and becoming it."

11

The aggravating buzz of her cell phone dragged Tzivia Khalon from a dead sleep. With a groan, she rolled onto her side, the weight of slumber pinning her to the lumpy mattress. Light from her screen splashed over the wall and ceiling of her small flat in the Holy City. Squinting, she lifted her head and reached for the phone, once more feeling that weight. Resisting her. Holding her—

She looked down at her waist and saw the arm slung across her body.

Another groan, this one in frustration at herself, sifted her drowsiness. And her foolishness. Ram would kill her. And the man with her.

Whatever. Ram had judged her for everything else, so why not this?

She picked up the phone and glanced at the screen. Dr. Cathey. At five in the morning. She silenced the call. Dropped back against her pillow and closed her eyes.

The arm tugged her closer, warmth bidding her to surrender. The soft scruffiness of a beard tickled her shoulder and neck.

More buzzing. Insistent. Just like Dr. C.

Tzivia slipped from between the sheets and slid into a thick terry robe. Lifting her phone, she hit Accept, then eased out of the bedroom.

"Tzivia! Finally you answer!" Dr. Cathey's voice clapped through the line.

Door shut, she rolled her eyes. "Do you know what time it is?" She plodded to the kitchen and took a mug from the cupboard.

"Of course I do! It's five o'clock there—plenty reasonable for you to be up and having your first cup."

Staring at the gray mug, she sighed. "Yes, but it's too early, especially on a Saturday. It also means it's three in London." She stuffed a pod in the Keurig machine, which had traveled the world with her. "So what are *you* doing up at this hour?"

"You won't believe what I've learned."

She probably wouldn't. Not because he wasn't believable, but because Dr. Cathey had a penchant for getting himself into precarious predicaments. Just like with the Mace of Death. Or the ancient Aleppo Codex, which nearly helped unleash a plague. Did she really want to know what he'd learned?

"Are you there, Tzi?"

Pinching the bridge of her nose, she leaned her hip against the counter and closed her eyes. "I'm here."

"Do you know where I am?"

She lifted a hand at the obvious answer—where he lived. "London?"

"Mosul!"

Tzivia raised her head and opened her eyes. "*What* are you doing there?" Anxiety and dread choked her. Anxiety for the trouble the seventy-one-year-old had gotten himself into. And dread that he might drag her into said trouble. "You know what, never mind. I don't want to know."

"What?" He sounded affronted. "How can you say such a thing?"

"Because six months ago, my reputation was nearly ruined."

"But it wasn't. It was restored—even *enhanced*!"

That she could not argue, though it'd come at a brutal price—her friend Noel's death. "But only for a few months until the antiquities world discovered what we destroyed." She could still feel the fire of the cauldron that incinerated the plague-infested miktereths.

However, the outcome of her excavations at Jebel el-Lawz had lofted her to notoriety. She was now working with the Israel Museum and the Ministry of Antiquities to log the remnants of that excavation. Her name took her places, opened doors. She wasn't going to endanger that. Not even for Dr. Cathey. "I should go—"

"But you can't. Listen to me, Tzivia. I have good news! You won't believe what they say was recovered here."

She felt it, the sinking sand beneath her feet. Just like the sand that had dropped her into the miktereth nightmare.

"Remember how ISIL bulldozed Mosul?"

How could she forget? Every archaeologist and historian in the world had grieved the egregious acts of extremists who demolished significant pieces of history.

"It was good."

"*Good?*" Straightening, she huffed. "How can you say that? It was disastrous! Irreplaceable artifacts reduced to rubble. Centuries-old murals destroyed!"

Warmth cocooned her as strong arms came around her waist from behind. A soft, tickling kiss at her nape made her twitch. She drew in a shaky breath at the thrill of his touch. *This.* This was what she wanted—to be normal. To have a life. A love. Not more insanity.

"I have to go," she murmured and ended the call, ignoring the remnant of guilt at hanging up on Dr. Cathey. She breathed it away and nestled back against the strength of Omar Kastan.

"You are up early," he said, his deep voice rumbling against her spine.

She sighed wearily when he broke away and retrieved his own mug. A pair of sweats hung from his trim waist. Gaze traveling up his bare back, she smiled at the way his torso fanned out into broad shoulders. The tattoos scrawling a detailed history of his life and loyalties across his deltoids and biceps taunted her. "Too early. But I don't mind the view."

Omar removed her cup from the Keurig and handed it to her. "Cathey, eh?" He placed his mug beneath the spout.

She shouldn't be surprised Omar had figured out who had called. He was good like that. It came with being an agent of the Mossad. Cradling her steaming cup in both hands, she sighed and took a sip.

"What did he want?"

"I didn't say it was him."

"And you didn't say it wasn't."

She watched as he moved around the kitchen, pulling pans from hooks and eggs from the small fridge, then set about making breakfast. This she could get used to, though everyone in this narrow sliver of a country would call them immoral. She hated herself for sinking this low. Life felt fake, so why didn't she deserve a bit of happiness?

"He hasn't been in the Old City since the codex," Omar said.

That he knew Dr. Cathey's movements was unsettling. "He's too busy to make trouble twice in the same place."

"Perhaps, but he is eccentric enough not to make that a rule or habit." His dark eyes smiled as he whisked eggs, then added tomatoes and peppers for an omelet. Dimples hid behind his beard. And his skin was a creamy latte color. Everything about him was delicious.

He'd been around the world enough to pick up Western customs, as well as many European and Asian ones. She hadn't figured out his position in Mossad, but she would. One day. And that would prove to her advantage, give her what she wanted. Needed. For that, she'd sell her soul.

Until then, she could endure watching him a little longer.

"Does he need you to go somewhere?" Omar asked as he turned the first omelet onto a plate. Amazing how hands so skilled at death were also so good at cooking.

Annoyance prickled the back of her neck. He was plying her for information. "I don't know."

He gave her a long look as he started the second omelet.

She shrugged. "I hung up before he could entangle me. I like it here too much to draw attention again."

His smile was crooked as he stepped sideways and kissed her. "You got my attention."

He'd been on the unit tasked with overwatch of Tox's team while they were in country several months ago during the codex business, and that was when he'd fallen for her. At least, that was what he said.

"Don't play me. I know you're milking me for information about Tox and Dr. C."

"As much as you milk me about your brother and family."

She gave him a one-shouldered shrug. "Can't blame a girl for trying."

"I hope you never stop." He kissed the warm spot beneath her earlobe.

"Even though your father would call you wicked?" As would Ram.

"He has done that since I was four." Omar worked the second omelet onto a plate. "Besides, I hope to make an honest wife out of you one day."

"Sheol will freeze over first."

"Then I'll buy a parka." He delivered both plates to her small table.

Even with the easy, flirtatious banter, Tzivia knew he had a reason for asking about Dr. Cathey. "Do you know where Dr. C is?"

His mahogany eyes fastened onto her, but he said nothing as he ate.

"I'll take that as a yes."

"I heard from your brother last night."

Had Ram heard about them? "Nice change of topic." She fought the urge to ask for as long as she could. "What's he up to?"

"Saving Russell's life."

"Again?" She sighed, tossing down a wadded napkin, and reached for a different direction to this conversation. "I got a call from Mehdi Jaro. He's pretty sure they're on to something out in Kalhu."

"Yeah?" Omar put their plates in the sink, then returned, his gaze pensive. Wary. "Are you going out there?"

She shrugged. "I'll wait. See if he can verify more first. Might be nothing."

Omar had the most lively eyes, as if stars lived there, and they glinted more than usual just now. But then his expression turned serious. What slid into those starry eyes had nothing to do with Mehdi or a trip or Ram.

Tzivia's stomach squeezed. "Don't say it," she whispered around a raw throat.

He tossed down a chunk of bread he'd torn from their last loaf. "I can't keep doing this, Tzi. I love you, but—"

"You accepted my terms. You *promised*." Her chest heaved. "Don't do this. Not now."

"It's wrong. It violates everything I believe in—"

"Yet you're here," she snapped. "With me. In my bed." It was easier this way. Easier with no entanglements. No commitments. No fears.

Omar looked down with a shake of his head. "Ram will kill me if he finds out—"

"Then make sure he doesn't."

* * * *

— DAY 15 —
WASHINGTON, DC

Nothing cleared his head like a good run, and equal to none was the trail around the inspiring National Mall, dotted with memorials of American history. Hundreds of runners were doing the same, hitting the smooth paths early in the morning. It helped them avoid the hundreds of thousands of visitors that flocked to the Capitol.

Tox let the tension roll off of him with each step as he made his way along the Tidal Basin. Always safety conscious, he executed switchbacks. Cut across streets when openings presented themselves. Anything to keep the pattern random.

It was during one of those switchbacks that he'd picked up a tail near the Jefferson Memorial. Wearing a gray windbreaker, the man kept pace with Tox no matter the technique employed to lose him.

As he plotted an exit strategy, Tox wondered who was stupid enough to try this. Was it protective, meant to watch out for him? Or was this a threat? Alec? Wouldn't it be easier to just shoot him . . . again?

Too many innocents. Too many witnesses.

With his Bluetooth in, he keyed his mic and called Rodriguez. "You have someone tailing me?"

"You have a tail?"

Jogging along the route of the cherry blossom trees, a gift from Mayor Yukio Ozaki of Tokyo City to Washington in 1912, he lifted his phone from his pocket. "That would be why I asked. Is it you?" Beneath the tree limbs, he opened the camera and used it to check his six.

"Negative. We have no reason to track you like that."

Like that—so they tracked him another way. "Someone does."

"You want help?"

Tox considered the offer. "Could this be Iliescu?" He eyed the bridge ahead. Good spot—dark, out of sight. But the water . . . He crossed the narrow street and headed back toward the jogging path along the basin.

"Why would he tail you?"

"I'm asking you."

"We work with him. Your team is tasked under him."

"All the more reason to make sure I'm playing nice."

"Nah, that's not . . . doesn't make sense."

"Welcome to my world, Rod."

"You want me to send interference?"

Wouldn't be here in time. "I think I can handle him." Tox did another switchback, returning to the Jefferson Memorial. Straight into the path of the tail.

The guy staggered—a small misstep but enough to tip his hand that Tox's maneuver caught him off guard.

"Keep me updated."

"Will do." Tox ended the call.

Ten feet.

Tox kept his gaze straight ahead.

He plotted his attack. Stayed loose, relaxed.

Five feet.

The target swallowed.

Two.

Tox jogged one step past the man. Snapped out a knife-hand strike. Caught the back of the target's neck.

The tail pitched forward but didn't go down. He must've anticipated something, because he wheeled around. Came up with a right hook.

Tox swerved, feeling the air stir beneath the punch, and shot upward with an uppercut. Another knife-hand into the soft spot beneath his ribs.

A female runner yelped and dodged them, shouting for them to chill out, but kept going.

The tail grunted. Pitched himself into Tox's gut.

Holding him to keep control, Tox stumbled back, all too aware of the glimmering reservoir behind him. Too close. He braced to stop the momentum, then slammed his knee into the man's face.

Something cracked. The guy howled, pulling away. Tripped backward.

Tox drove his heel into the man's chest, sending him into the water. Another shout went up from a nearby jogger.

Tox pivoted and sprinted up the hill, determined to get lost in the throng of visitors beginning to fill the city. Tourism was always heavy, even long past summer, and he worked that to his advantage as he jogged toward the World War II Memorial. He steadied his breathing and settled into a normal pace to blend, aiming toward Capitol Hill.

His phone rang. Expecting Rodriguez again, he keyed the mic on his Bluetooth. "Hey."

"Very nice, Tox."

He drew up short, ears burning at Alec's voice.

"That was one of my best men you just threw into the basin."

Tox couldn't stop the urge to look around. He had to be close to see what Tox had done, right? He scanned the World War II Memorial, then turned and glanced across the street toward the Washington Monument and the National Museum of African American History and Culture. Tourists littered the space in between. Too many to home in on Alec. "Stop hiding. Face me."

"So you can have your spook friends come out and play, like you did at the restaurant?"

"Told you, that wasn't me."

"Yes, you did. But amazing how they knew you were there, and knew I was, too."

"I have no answers for you about that." There were answers. But no way would Tox drag Haven into this again.

"Might want to look into that."

Tox eyed the people around him. Maneuvered crazily through the joggers, but saw no one suspicious. He had to get out of sight, out of danger. He made several random turns and mashed the WALK button at an intersection.

"Wouldn't go that way, if I were you," Alec said. "I hear your brother is preparing to leave for the day."

Tox's hand froze over the button. His gaze rose. To the small camera on the pole.

"Ah, we finally see eye to eye, do we?"

"What do you want, Alec?"

"I want you to join me."

Anxious to make this difficult for the man spying on him, Tox sprinted through the intersection, not caring about the red signal. He dodged kamikaze taxis blaring their horns, hopped onto the sidewalk, and kept moving.

"I understand my invitation at the restaurant was a little . . . unexpected, but it is sincere, nonetheless."

"Why? Why me?"

Alec's sigh came through heavy against Tox's ears, despite the foot traffic and wind noise. "I explained all this."

"Explain it again, because like you said—it was unexpected."

"Do not toy with me, Tox."

"Then I expect the same respect."

Silence yawned for several long seconds. Tox turned his head to the side and up, listening carefully.

"Fair enough," Alec finally said. "My reasons are simple—we're the same, you and I. Your own government gave you up, sold you out. More than anyone else, you can appreciate the desire for justice. And, of course, there are your valuable skills."

"Are you doing this because of Rachel?"

"*Don't* mention her."

The growl in his friend's voice told Tox he'd hit a nerve. "What happened, Alec?" He wouldn't give an inch, not when Alec was hunting him. Not when Alec made veiled threats about Haven. Besides, Tox knew Alec. Knew sometimes he needed to be slapped with cold, hard reality to get back on track. "How'd you screw that one up? She was the best thing that ever happened to you—your words, remember? Divorce, and then she's dead?"

"Remember how you felt when I mentioned your girlfriend? Remember that primal instinct at the restaurant that made you want to rip my throat out? That's how I feel when you mention Rachel. Leave her out of it, and I leave your girl alone."

Something in Tox squirmed and writhed. "You're avoiding the question. Why did she divorce you—didn't agree with your left-of-center mission?"

"Tox . . ."

"Rachel put up with your crap, Alec. Not many did."

"Let's see . . ." Alec's tone was light. Casual. "Ah, here she is. Tell me, should I change the traffic light so your beauty drives that compact head-on into the trash truck barreling toward the intersection?"

Crap. "Okay." Tox lifted his hands. "I hear you, Alec." His heart thudded, imagining Haven critically injured or dead.

"Good. Let's not repeat that stupidity. We're bigger than that, aren't we?"

"I would hope." Tox sighed. "So is this vengeance? Is that what this is about for you?"

"Vengeance is personal. I have no *personal* vendetta against these people. They've committed atrocities. I'm a warrior, tasked with stopping them. They must be stopped—you see that, right? We must fight evil. It's a holy—"

"A holy mission. Yeah, you said that two nights ago. But there's a fine line between fighting evil and becoming it." Haven's words had haunted him, infected his thoughts.

"Exactly! And doing nothing makes us evil, Tox. All it takes for evil to triumph is for good men to do nothing."

Tox shook his head, seeing how neatly he'd twisted that saying.

"You're a good man, Tox. Will you do nothing?"

"This *is* personal, Alec. Not a holy mission. It's vengeance," Tox challenged. "You went after Karim."

"I'll give you that one," Alec said. "Karim *was* personal, but once I completed that mission, I saw that this was my purpose in life. Not everyone can do what we do. Some are too weak and cave to fear and pressure. We should've killed Gabir Karim when he was in our sights."

"We were told to stand down."

"Yes, and when McKenna did that, he killed six of my men."

"No, Karim killed them."

"And had the colonel not given that order, my men would still be alive."

"You can't know that."

"But I can—Reiss was heading home the next day. His wife had a healthy baby boy two days after burying her soldier. That should not have happened."

Tox dropped onto a bench, cradling his head in his hand. He'd met Reiss. Knew him. He'd been stoked about that baby.

"I know you get it, Tox. You were the best team leader I've known. You *get* this."

Nauseated that he did get it, that he understood, Tox tried to climb out of the cesspool. "We operated by the code—"

"No, we didn't." Vehemence laced Alec's words. "We operated by the whim of an armchair general who wanted another election victory for his candidate."

Tox stood, shaking his head, pacing. "This is wrong. It's vigilantism."

"They gave you your team back. Now they send you on missions."

How on earth did Alec know that?

"It's in you, Tox. The need to silence evil. To fight it, to destroy it."

Alec was reading from the diary of Tox's life. He pressed the heel of his hand to his temple. "If you know anything about me, Alec, you know I play by the rules. We have the Uniform Code of Military Justice—"

"And how well did that serve you, set up to take the blame for Kafr al-Ayn?" Alec sniffed. "It didn't. And listening to McKenna six years ago didn't serve Jed, Reiss, Whiskey, Holden, Matt, or Fiji."

"Nobody could've known what would happen."

"It's time, Tox. Time to deliver justice."

Tox stilled. Looked around, searching for cameras. For snipers. "Wh-what do you mean?"

Silence gaped.

"Alec?" Fire seared the back of his neck, and he turned a slow circle. Nothing.

A noise came through the connection. It was still hot. What was—

Crack!

IN FORTRESS AND IN FIELD

— 1171 AD —

EGYPT

The crown, gleaming the color of sunshine, sat atop Gregorio's unruly mop of hair as the Saracens set upon him and his contingent of guards. The battle was bloody, more than a hundred Saracens falling dead on the road as they followed the command of their new vizier, General An-Nasir Salah ad-Din Yusuf ibn Ayyub. Most knew him as Saladin, a Sunni, which made his nomination to the Shia-led caliphate rare and notable. The nephew of the great general Nur ad-Din was relentless in his pursuit to unite the Arab countries and wipe out the Christians. Especially the *Dawiyya*—the knights of Christ.

Outside the city, Thefarie sat atop his destrier, watching. Grateful for the clear view and confident the Saracens would end the scourge that was Gregorio.

It must be done.

A heaviness in the air disturbed him. Left him restless. As the last of Gregorio's guards were felled, Saladin had little hesitation in beheading the knight. He lifted the still-crowned head and shouted his victory. The Saracens crowed with him.

Grieved at the death of so many, including one of their own, Thefarie lowered his gaze. Offered a futile prayer of forgiveness. Gregorio had become a blight on the Order, on the Holy Lord. The Grand Master, though he had not sanctioned this endeavor, was aware of the strident actions that bloodied this field.

"He's removing the crown," Ameus muttered.

Thefarie's attention flew back to the battleground. The Crown of Souls was not like any other crown. Though it rose from the head, its invisible tendrils snaked beneath flesh and bone, as if fingers of some invisible god held the wearer's mind.

A chill raced up his spine, thinking of it.

Saladin held up the diadem, again shouting his victory. A nearby Saracen took the crown and placed it on the vizier's head.

"No," Giraude moaned.

Another chorus of cheers went up among the Saracens, as did an aura that made the Crown of Souls an ethereal blue.

Disappointment pulled at Thefarie, pulsing into a pure, hot anger. He tightened his gloved hand on the reins. "Fool," he growled.

It had begun. Again. The greed of man coupled with the lure of the crown's innate power. Saladin would have no choice now. Neither did Thefarie.

"He will betray us," Giraude hissed.

Ameus gave him a long look. "And you thought it would end differently this time?"

"We must intercept it before the crown seizes him." Thefarie drew his horse around and headed down the steep embankment, aiming for the road. By the time they had navigated the terrain, the Saracens were fleeing to the safety of the main army.

Riding hard, Thefarie resolved to stop the crown's destruction this day. No matter the cost. Already too much had been paid, too much blood spilled, beneath the subtle control and power of that accursed ornament.

As they gained on the band of fighters, Thefarie and his fifty engaged the closest Saracens. Like ants climbing over each other to get to the first, they fought Thefarie's advance on their leader. On Saladin. The crown.

Swerving to avoid a knight and a Saracen who had tumbled into the road, Thefarie guided his war-horse around one of his sergeants, who stood over a slain body. Another drove his sword into the heart of a fighter. And another did the same. On and on, protecting Thefarie's path until he and Giraude had closed the gap and descended upon the Saracen officers.

Giraude surged against the lesser general racing immediately behind Saladin, who rode ahead with another officer.

Thefarie went for his dagger but thought better of it, considering the leather armor the Saracen general wore. A bulging satchel on Saladin's mount caught his eye. The crown!

He glanced to his left, where Ameus rode hard. He pointed to the officer alongside Saladin, and Ameus nodded. But Thefarie remained focused on Saladin and the crown. He urged his destrier a little harder and eased up alongside Nur's nephew. With his sword, he sliced at the ropes tethering the crown to the back of the mount. The saddle, mercifully, protected the horse's flank, but the great beast still surged at the glancing blow.

Saladin jerked his gaze to Thefarie. Then to the box, precariously dangling by a single rope.

Thefarie reared his sword back and swung again, lancing the rope.

When the box fell away, Thefarie reined his horse around and galloped to the ravine down which it had tumbled. He threw himself from his mount and landed hard. Then slid and slipped down . . . down. Crashed into a ditch. He blinked, taking inventory of his pains.

Before him lay the satchel. Flat. The lip flayed open. The crown gleamed in the mud. *Thank the Lord!* Thefarie reached for it.

A weight plowed into him.

He pitched forward, crumpling into the ground. Water and muck smothered his face. Pressure pushed his mouth and nose into the sludge. Holding his breath, he flipped his legs and managed to throw the man from his back. Groping hard for air, he heaved thick breaths, expanding his lungs. He had only seconds.

He saw the face of his attacker—Bahir. The Saracen lunged.

Thefarie caught him, twisting his back and landing on top of the Saracen. The air was knocked from Bahir, and he gasped but flailed and fought. It took everything in Thefarie's might to keep him pinned as he struggled for his dagger.

Pain exploded through his jaw.

Dazed, he blinked and freed the blade.

Bahir knocked it free.

Three hard punches slowed the Saracen, made him sluggish. Straddling him, Thefarie drew his sword. Raised it with both hands to drive it through the man's heart.

"Wait!" Giraude shouted. "It's not the crown!"

Thefarie jerked toward his brother-knight. Saw the crown—broken into several pieces. While it indeed looked like the crown on the surface, this was made of wood. Painted.

Laughing, Bahir used his sleeve to wipe the blood from his beard, then shook his head, jeering. "You will never find it." His sleeve rode up, revealing a strange tattoo of perhaps a tiger, the black lines too scripted for Thefarie to be certain. Bahir noticed Thefarie's gaze on the inked mark and dropped his arm.

Rage tore at Thefarie. Betrayal. "For breaking your word and betraying me and my brother-knights, you will forever bear the mark of Thefarie." He drove his sword into the Saracen's chest.

Arching his back, Bahir howled as blood bubbled over his shoulder.

Extracting the blade, Thefarie glared down at the Saracen. "You will not die, nor have peace until the crown is returned to me." He placed his hand on the wound, and again the Saracen howled and then fell away into darkness. "Torment will be your name."

12

At the report of a weapon, Tox ducked, heart jammed in his throat. Only as he let out a trapped breath did he realize the sound had come from the phone. His brain re-engaged.

"Alec!" he shouted, turning a useless circle. When there was no answer, he yanked out the Bluetooth and checked it. No signal. He bit back a curse, glancing up the green toward Capitol Hill, then back toward the Mall. "Alec, what'd you do?"

Tox jogged a fast clip back to his car, mind reeling. Gut churning. He should call Iliescu. Or Rodriguez. But he couldn't. He couldn't think. Couldn't process. Didn't want to. Didn't want to believe a man he had considered one of his closest friends could fall so far, so hard.

He used the thirty-minute route back to his car to clear his thoughts. Only they became more tangled. More confused.

Was it a gunshot? Who had Alec killed? Or was it something else, the connection distorting the sound?

Distorting the truth was more like it. Alec had become good at that.

There's a fine line between confronting evil and becoming it. Again,

107

Haven's words were haunting him, pursuing him across DC. *Was he becoming evil? Or worse—was he already?*

Haven. She'd been upset with him. He'd hurt her. Pushed her away. He hadn't meant to, but if she was appalled by Alec's actions, how would she respond to what Tox had done to clear his men? She knew half the story. If she discovered the rest, would *he* be the monster that terrified her, instead of Alec?

It was stupid to pretend it hadn't happened. Date her. Get in deep with her. And not be held accountable for that . . . nightmare.

Tox had rounded the corner, aiming toward his Audi, when he spotted three black SUVs blocking in his car. He slowed. Let out a long sigh as he erased the last fifty feet to his vehicle.

A man emerged from the lead SUV. In a black suit and power tie, he wore his hair closely cropped. High and tight. Military bearing and experience, most likely. And a willingness to do violence. "Mr. Russell."

As Tox considered him, the other men formed up around him. In the middle of DC. They weren't worried about being seen or stopped. They were worried about *him*.

"The director would like to speak with you, sir."

Director. Iliescu, then. With a sigh, Tox slid into the armored vehicle, and it veered away from the Tidal Basin and any hope he had of evading this nightmare.

＊　＊　＊　＊

RUSSELL ESTATE, MARYLAND

Power, prestige, propriety. All three were embodied in the petite form of Charlotte Russell. She strode down the staircase with a smile that lit the open foyer brighter than its sparkling chandelier.

"Ah, Haven. What a nice surprise." Charlotte glided over and embraced her in a swirling haze of light floral perfume.

"I'm sorry to intrude."

"You never intrude, my dear!" Charlotte nodded toward the rear of the house. "Come join me for lemonade on the back porch."

Haven smoothed a hand down her linen pants as they made their way past the formal dining room. In the family living area, which abutted the kitchen and dinette, they made their way across the marble floor to the three sets of French doors that opened onto the wide, wraparound porch encompassing the rear of the house. Haven stopped short when a pair of familiar blue eyes glowed back at her from the living room.

Charlotte's laugh was delightful. "I had to put his picture back up after that decision came down."

"Decision?" Haven was too stunned to find the portrait of Cole hanging on the far wall to understand the context.

"Yes, clearing him of all charges." Charlotte waved a hand dismissively. "Of course, he was cleared after he died, so it doesn't do him much good." She huffed, smiling at the portrait. "I miss that boy so much."

Tears burned Haven's eyes.

"But ignore me. I'm not going to rain on our visit." Charlotte whirled and headed for the patio. "I'm so glad you reconsidered working on Endeavor with me."

Prying herself from Cole's soulful gaze, even if it was merely oil and pigment, Haven felt his stinging condemnation. He wanted his mom to know he was alive. But Galen . . .

Leave it alone. Leave it alone, Haven.

Even as she walked to the stone patio, his gaze followed her. Staring at her. Demanding she be his voice.

"Horace, could you bring the sandwiches and fruit?" Charlotte smiled at the butler, then turned that endearing expression to Haven. "What on earth is that look for?"

Haven started.

"You look like you lost your best friend," Charlotte said around a laugh.

Maybe she had. Cole hadn't talked to her for three days. Not since she'd messed up the night that psychotic man interrupted their date. "Sorry. Long day at work."

"You're a brave soul, working cases for the FBI." Charlotte clucked her tongue. "Too much violence for me." After the butler brought the lemonade, she sipped some, then crossed her ankles. "Now tell me what changed your mind about working on Endeavor?"

Haven breathed her smile. "A friend."

Charlotte laughed once more. She had a laugh for everything. A condescending laugh. A contrite laugh. And in this instance, a knowing laugh. "That friend sounds like more than a *friend*." She switched seats, moving closer and taking Haven's hand. "Ever since your husband died, I've just ached for you to find true love again."

Haven's heart sputtered.

"Tell me about him! Tell me everything. Don't leave anything out."

Heat flushed her cheeks. "I . . . I . . ." Haven cleared her throat. "Aren't we here to talk about Endeavor?"

Charlotte waved her manicured hands. "Who cares? I see love in your eyes. I want to know all about this man."

Haven struggled to breathe past the collision of reality and her hopes, against her future and Charlotte's past. "Honestly, I'm not sure where I stand with him right now."

"But you want to stand very close?" Insinuation clung to those words like a silk suit.

Haven laughed. Then nodded. "I do. He's . . . besides Duarte, I think he's the best man I've ever known."

Charlotte's eyes widened, and Haven realized Cole had inherited his mother's blues. "That's saying a lot."

"It is," Haven admitted. "But we had a . . . misunderstanding the other night." Remembering it, she winced. "I think it might take some time to work out."

"Was he with someone else?"

"No, he's not like that. It's just . . . sometimes he can't talk about"— *anything*—"his job. Or his life."

"Military man again?"

Haven tucked her chin.

"You know how to pick them, dear."

Wrinkling her nose, Haven sighed. "I know. He's so intense and focused. So rigid in his thinking that sometimes it gets . . ."

Charlotte groaned, sagging against her chair as she rolled her eyes. "Exhausting!"

"Yes!"

Charlotte sniffed. "Exactly the way my Cole was. Made his dad so angry all the blessed time. Infuriated his brother. And just plumb wore me out." A serene smile plied the older woman's features. "But there was no one like him."

Tell her. Tell her he's alive. "I . . . remember."

"What I wouldn't do to have that boy back, strong-willed and all." She gave a heartbroken sigh and reached for the crystal glass. "But the Good Lord saw fit to take him home."

Irritation wormed through Haven. Charlotte Russell had every right to know her son was alive and well. That he was here. "Charlotte."

Sipping her lemonade again, she raised her eyebrows. "Mm?"

"You should—"

"Excuse me, ma'am," a voice—the butler's—broke in. "There is a call."

"Oh." Charlotte scooted out of the padded chair.

"No, ma'am." He angled a hand toward Haven. "For Ms. Cortes."

Haven jerked around. "Me?" Who would know to call her here? She hadn't told anyone she was coming. "I have no idea who it could be. Please excuse me."

"Of course, dear."

In the kitchen, she accepted the phone from the butler. "Hello?"

"Kasey, you're—"

"Levi?"

"—needed at the Pentagon."

"How did you know where I was?"

"They pinged your phone when you didn't answer." His tone was hard, cold. Unlike him.

"Why is anyone pinging my phone just because I didn't answer?"

"Come in. You'll understand."

Her gaze turned to the window and the splendid view of Catoctin Mountain. "I'm not done here. I'll finish up—"

"Sorry. Head back now. You're needed."

"For what?"

"King struck again."

* * * *

111

CIA HEADQUARTERS, FAIRFAX COUNTY, VIRGINIA

One of Tox's favorite quotes by Mark Twain was, "Everyone is a moon and has a dark side which he never shows to anybody."

They all had dark sides. But they fought it. God knew Tox sure had. And glancing around the conference room, which was shaping up to look like a complete do-over of Syria, Tox wondered what demons would prowl the nightmare of this new assignment.

Because that was what this was. He felt it. Read the signs in those gathered, the tension weighting the room and moods.

They were going after Alec. Officially.

His phone buzzed in his pocket, and Tox drew it out. Recognized the long-distance number. He hit the accept button. "Hey."

"*Ihe ehi ḥụrụ gbalaba oso ka okuku huru na-atụ onu.*"

The Igbo proverb—*fools rush in where angels fear to tread*—could not be more true than now. Tox chuckled, amazed yet not amazed that Chiji knew he needed some sage advice right now.

Smiling, Tox replied, "*A tuoro omara, o mara, a tuoro ofeke, o fenye ishi n'ohia.*"

The words simply meant, *if you tell a wise one, he understands; tell a dunce, he runs into the bush.* In other words, Tox had tried to tell them—FBI, CIA—that this wasn't a good idea. But they weren't listening. Instead, they were rushing into the bush. Into danger.

Chiji had taught Tox many Igbo proverbs in the years he'd spent with the Okorie family, hiding from the government and life. Nearly dead, Tox had endured Chiji's Scripture readings while recovering. After that, he'd tried more than once to get away from the God-fearing family, but Chiji had followed him. Always. A shadow that never left him. A conscience that never abandoned him.

"I have missed you," Tox said.

"And I you."

"How is *Nne*?" Though Chiji's mom was not his own, Tox viewed her that way. She had insisted he call her *nne*, since he lived beneath her roof—sort of. He'd lived in a hut behind the main house because he feared a night that never came, one in which his troubled past brought death to those who'd become family.

"Sad, but good," Chiji said. "She said it has been a long time since you came to her."

Tox nodded. "A trip back is long overdue." It was, but the words and conversation made him think of his own mom. A new grief wove through him. His mom. Nne. Haven. Alec's threat at the restaurant made him fear for the safety of all three women. Even if two of them didn't know where he was right now.

The door opened, grabbing Tox's attention, and in walked Robbie Almstedt of the CIA's Special Activities Artifact Recovery & Containment Division. A klaxon sounded in Tox's head. What was SAARC doing here? He and Ram exchanged tight glances.

"I have to go, Chiji. Any idea when you'll return?"

"When it is right."

Tox snorted. "Of course. Later, brother." He hung up and slid the phone back into his pocket.

"Did we miss something?" Ram asked, adjusting his beanie as he lowered into the seat beside Tox.

"Only what they kept from us," Tox bit out.

"Ah, good," Iliescu said, motioning to the door. "Almost ready to start."

Two more people entered, Agent Wallace and—

"Haven." Tox scowled, not liking that she had come with Superman. That she was anywhere near this insanity.

She started toward him but was diverted when Iliescu pointed her to a seat. A flush colored her cheeks as she sat down.

"Son of a biscuit," Cell muttered as he and Thor sighed heavily, mirroring the tension that had just flooded the room.

With SAARC here, the meeting had gone from a mission to find Alec to something far more . . . unsettling. The entire alphabet soup was represented now, from the DoD, the CIA, and the Defense Intelligence Agency. SAARC would be involved only if—

"There's an artifact?" Ram demanded.

"Please, Mr. Khalon, give us a minute."

Tox scrubbed a hand over his mouth and jaw, doing his best not to shake his head or show his complete disgust with the fact that they were throwing Wraith under the artifact bus.

But that was what Wraith did. And they did it well. Somehow.

"What are we after this time?" Cell asked, chin and eyes down. "The holy grail? 'Cause last I checked, my last name isn't Jones."

Thor and Maangi snickered, and Tox bit back a laugh.

"Okay," Iliescu said, nodding to Almstedt. "You ready?"

"As I'll ever be," Robbie said with a long-suffering sigh.

"Gentlemen," Iliescu started, "as you can guess, we're sending you out."

"What?" Cell spouted off. "I thought we were here for free barbecue."

"In the last forty-eight hours, we've learned about two additional incidents involving Alec King." As Iliescu pointed to a screen on the back wall, Tox swiveled in his seat and saw Alec's service photo. "Ryan McKenna was shot and killed today. He was on vacation at Chesapeake Bay with his wife and kids."

Tox stilled. "His protection detail?"

Iliescu glanced down. "Ineffective against a sniper shot."

Nauseated at the idea of the man being killed in front of his family, Tox tried to cover his mouth. His eyes. But it wouldn't do any good. His need to believe that Alec hadn't gone beyond the grasp of rehabilitation slipped a notch.

"Tox, it appears you were on a call with King this morning when he took the shot," Iliescu said.

Tox hadn't wanted to believe he'd heard a shot. He nodded. Focused tightly on not betraying the chaos throwing his life, hope, and desperation around his gut like some category-five hurricane. "Alec said justice had to be served."

Rubbing a knuckle over his lower lip, Tox struggled. How could Alec do this? He'd wanted to believe his friend and brother-in-arms would come around, see that he was wrong.

"He wanted you to join him," Almstedt said.

Join him. Weren't they essentially the same man? Hadn't they all warred and taken lives in combat? Neutralized threats and shed blood? How was he any different? How were any of them different?

"Mr. Russell?"

Tox blinked. Looked at Almstedt. Her question—she'd asked—
"No, ma'am." His heart thudded. "Not wanted. *Wants*. He wants
me on his team."

"I seriously hope you've told him no."

He hadn't. Mostly because there'd been a veiled threat against
Haven. "I felt it smarter to keep him talking."

"Well, that's not all he's done," Almstedt said, with more than a
little revulsion as she nodded to Iliescu. "Run it."

A grainy image splashed across the walls. The video was spotty
and jumpy.

"This is CCTV footage from Stuttgart." Almstedt threaded her
fingers over the folder resting on the table in front of her.

"Why are we watching this?" Ram asked.

"Follow the silver and black sedans," she instructed.

Two cars were trailed through several intersections. The footage
jumped as the cars rounded a corner. The silver on the tail of the black
one now. Bumper to bumper, growing more aggressive.

"The black sedan belongs to Gunther Albrect, husband to Hilma
and father to fifteen-month-old Elsie."

The footage again flickered. The vehicles darted in and out of traffic, until they were racing straight toward the cameras. The two cars
slipped under an overpass. Though it was dark beneath the bridge,
light from the other side made it possible to see the silver sedan nip
the back end of the black car. It swerved. Slammed right into a brick
wall. Smoke from the engine and airbags hazed the air.

A man staggered from the black car.

Another climbed confidently, almost gracefully, from the silver.

"Alec," Tox whispered.

"Yes, Alec King forced Mr. Albrect into an accident along this stretch
of road." Almstedt paused, allowing them to watch, to take it in as
Alec punched the man hard. Then stood over him, doing something
the camera didn't pick up.

"Did he just kill him?"

Alec turned to the black sedan. He opened the rear passenger
door.

Haven gasped. "There's a child!"

Curses and mutters peppered the room, an uneasy tension coiling in the chest of each person seated at the table.

"Tell me he doesn't kill that kid," Thor growled. "I will beat him ugly. . . ."

Haven covered her eyes. Tox didn't want to look, but a part of him wouldn't let himself look away either. He'd face it.

"King knocked the father out, gave him a concussion," Almstedt said, ice in her tone. "Then he cut the car seat's belt away, removed the screaming child. He strode up to the nearest flat, where he deposited the baby on the stoop and rang the bell before vanishing in his car."

"The dude is *messed up*," Cell hissed.

"If he's killed everyone else, why didn't he kill this guy and the kid?" Maangi asked. "Easier to run them into a pylon or a river."

"Because he was *saving* the kid," Tox said, more to himself than anyone else. And it bothered him. Bothered him that he understood what Alec was doing. Bothered him even more that it made sense.

"Yes," Almstedt said, annoyance and surprise in her words. "That's what we believe. We think when Mr. Albrect cut him off the first time, King probably saw the car seat and let him off for the child's sake. But when Albrect continued to drive erratically, King took things into his own hands."

"Why?"

"Vengeance? Anger problems?" The laugh in Almstedt's tone hinted that she didn't care why Alec was doing this. "Who knows?"

"Protect the flock, Tox." He flinched, the memory so vivid he could've sworn Alec was right there. But he wasn't. That had been years ago, sitting in a freezing hut as their team waited out a terrorist. It'd been Alec's mantra, because he believed himself to be a sheepdog protecting innocent, vulnerable—stupid, he'd said—sheep.

"But a guy goes all whack in Stuttgart traffic? How is that vengeance?"

"He wanted to protect the kid—that wasn't vengeance. That was doing what he couldn't do for his own daughter," Tox said, irritation cutting through his words.

Curious expressions turned to him, the whir of laptops the only noise in the cramped room.

"Alec saw himself as the sheepdog, protecting the sheep from the wolves." Tox pointed to the screen. "He wasn't there to protect his own wife and kid, so he stepped in to protect that one."

"Running a car off the road into a brick wall to *protect* the kid?" Cell said. "Yeah, that makes so much sense."

"To Alec, it was better than if the distracted father drove the car off the highway going ninety and killed the kid, and who knows how many others. There, on the street, he controlled the speed, controlled the accident. At least, he thought he did." Tox had to get back on task. Understanding Alec so well felt like poison trickling through his veins.

"Dude," Cell said with a snort. "How d'you know what this guy is doing and thinking?"

"It was a probable scenario."

"No," Cell grunted. "There was *nothing* probable about what he did."

"We're all sheepdogs." Tox looked around the room, at his team. Searching their eyes, expressions, body posture. "We protect the innocent, the sheep. The flock. That's what Alec is doing."

"Bull," Cell snapped. "He killed McKenna."

"He or one of his men," Almstedt said.

"He has guys?" Thor asked, scratching his shaggy blond hair.

"He does—three, as far as we can tell."

"So he could've sent someone to kill McKenna?"

"No," Tox countered, nausea churning in his stomach. "The hits—those are his."

"Again," Cell bit out, "*why* do you know what this guy is thinking or doing?"

"Because," Tox said, nailing Cell with a look, "to Alec, he's bringing justice. It's personal. It's his mission. Protect the flock. The men working with him are just there to further his cause, not lead it." He hated the way even Almstedt and Iliescu were watching him now. Weighing and considering. But wasn't this why they'd assigned him to this mission, because he knew Alec?

"Anyone besides me bothered that Tox knows—"

Tox jerked toward Cell. "To find Alec, we have to *know* Alec." *Easy, easy. Calm down.* "I *know* him. That's why they want me here.

I've worked with this guy. Just as you can anticipate how I operate because you've worked with me, I know I can anticipate his moves." *I hope.* "Got it?"

Cell cocked his head, considering. Thinking. "Okay, Sarge. Lead the way."

Huffing out a breath, Tox lowered his gaze. Pulled it together, which brought him back to an earlier question. He looked at Almstedt. "Why are *you* here? There's no artifact."

Her gray-blue eyes glinted with annoyance. She probably wasn't used to someone talking to her so bluntly. Tox had nothing to lose, though—save the men around this table. And he'd go down screaming and shooting for them.

"Because you're tasked under me," Robbie said.

If she wouldn't come clean with him, it meant she was hiding something. "What aren't you telling us?"

13

"Go ahead, Robbie." Iliescu held up a phone and nodded. "It's cleared."

"Please. Just tell me there hasn't been another arrow," Cell said, rubbing his shoulder where, six months ago, a terrorist had shot him with a blue phosphorus arrow. A tool as symbolic as it was painful—the mark of the Arrow & Flame Order. "Because I can deal with a lot of things—"

"Except wax figures."

Cell glowered at Thor. "They were *animated*. It changes things."

Tox shook his head, remembering how freaked Cell had become over the animatronics at an Indian temple they'd infiltrated.

"It's not the AFO," Almstedt said with a grunt. "At least not as far as we can tell." She tapped a handheld device, and a grainy image sprang onto the wall. "Yesterday, an asset sent us this footage from Egypt."

Two luxury SUVs swept past the camera, blurring the view in a swirl of dust and action. The camera bounced, its holder running after the convoy, which pushed through a crowded village. One vehicle broke off and stopped, blocking anyone from following the others down a steep path to a smaller village. Whoever was filming

119

sprinted to a jagged outcropping that overlooked the valley for a distant, bird's-eye view.

Six men emerged from the vehicles. Most seemed native, but there were a few in black tactical gear. The locals stormed a dwelling, leaving four men outside.

"Dude," Cell said, "is that a—"

"Can we zoom?" Maangi asked.

"Negatory," Cell replied before Almstedt could. "The footage is already low quality. You zoom, quality will collapse."

"This is as good as it gets, gentlemen," Almstedt confirmed. "We've tried but—as Mr. Purcell stated—it degrades quickly."

"Smart phone videos are only so good."

"Is that what this is from? A phone?" Tox asked. "That's all your asset had, a smart phone?"

Thor snickered.

"The person filming is not our asset."

"But you said—"

"That our asset *sent* the video."

The locals dragged someone from the house and pitched him to the ground in front of the vehicles. Two other men were tossed behind the first. The rear passenger door of the middle vehicle opened. Sun sparked off the SUV's silver paint job as a man stepped out.

"That's King," Ram announced.

Dressed in black kit as well, Alec had the unmistakable bearing of one in charge. Confident. *Too confident.* What was he doing?

"It's a mission from God, Tox . . . join me . . . a holy mission . . ."

Alec turned back to the vehicle and drew something out. It glinted, but not brightly. Not like the SUV doors. More like aged metal. Not polished. He set it on his head and started toward the group of men.

"What is that?" Maangi asked.

"A crown?" Cell offered, then snickered. "Is he wearing a crown? He's crowned himself king." He snorted. "Get it? King—crown."

"Quiet," Tox growled.

Alec stood before the first man brought out, who knelt before him.

Suddenly, one of the other kneeling men lunged, snatched a weapon from a local guard, aimed it at the first man, and fired.

"What just happened there?" Cell demanded. "What was that?"

"The man killed was Sherif Makram Elarabi," Almstedt said.

"And the one who shot him?" Tox asked.

Almstedt's gaze went stony. "His brother."

"What? Was it an honor killing?" Maangi asked, elbows on the table as he waved his hands in confusion. "To . . . ?"

"Protect the rest of the family?" Thor suggested with a shrug.

The reason brother would turn against brother worried them all. Especially when it seemed to be in response to Alec's presence.

"No, not an honor killing," Almstedt said. "At least not as far as we can tell. There was no shame. No reason for one brother to kill the other."

Something tugged at Tox's mind. He adjusted in his seat, eyeballing the grainy image of the family-inflicted murder. Alec with the strange object. "We're asking the wrong questions." He avoided Haven's gaze, which he felt boring into his soul. "What did Alec put on his head?"

Almstedt let out a long, heavy sigh. "That's what we want to know."

Tox rubbed his jaw. "That's why SAARC's involved."

"And why we're sending you."

Tox swallowed the curse, but Cell didn't.

"It's an artifact?" Cell's voice pitched. "It looks like something from a bad sci-fi show. Some medieval head-thing."

"We don't know what it is," Almstedt said. "And this is the first we've seen of it. Might be an artifact. Might be entirely contemporary."

"Did Alec say something to the guy?"

"Unknown. Distance was too great to pick it up," Iliescu said.

"Am I seeing this right?" Ram pointed at the frozen images hovering on the wall. "He put that thing on, and brother turned against brother."

"Ram," Thor taunted, "you're always seeing supernatural things in these missions."

"Yeah, but he's not always wrong," Cell said.

"We don't know that's what happened," Iliescu said, his annoyance plain.

"Really?" Cell snorted a laugh. "Because I just saw that guy double-tap his own brother."

"But the *motivation* is not clear," Iliescu said. "We have a two-dimensional view of what happened. Until we know what that object is and why King is using it, we cannot throw around random guesses."

Tox threaded his fingers, pressing his mouth against them as he studied Alec's strange visage. "Perhaps the motivation is not clear, but it is suspected. *You* suspect something . . ."

Again, Iliescu and Almstedt exchanged glances.

Almstedt bunched her shoulders. "Yes. We do. But what?" She shrugged. "No idea. This"—she lifted a hand to the video wall—"is completely out of left field. He's killed at least a half dozen people, sniper-shot your sergeant here, probably hit Billings, and now he shows up wearing a crown. Who knows what he's using that thing for—to control people—"

"You think he's using it to control people's minds?" Cell yelped.

A barked laugh snapped through the room.

For the first time Tox remembered Levi Wallace was in the meeting and pierced him with a look.

"Right." Cell slapped the table. "Laugh, Superman. Because it's not like we had censers that unleashed a plague, arrows that boiled people from the inside out, or a mace of destruction that decimated villages."

Wallace's face went crimson.

"If you had let me finish, Mr. Purcell," Almstedt said, "you would have heard me say to control people through *manipulation*. No, we don't believe that thing enables him to control minds, but it does seem to have some sort of influence." She heaved a sigh. "We need it identified, and we need King stopped."

Tox raised his eyebrows and indicated the wall where the murder was still displayed. "Your asset—the one who got the video from a local?" When Almstedt and Iliescu didn't move, Tox knew he was onto something. "I want to meet the asset. I want to see that village, talk to that brother."

* * * *

— DAY 16 —
CHESAPEAKE BAY, MARYLAND

Located on six acres of prime waterfront property, the five-bedroom farm-style home with wraparound porch epitomized luxury living. The in-ground pool, tucked close to the home and secured with a white picket fence, seemed like overkill when a five-minute walk led to sandy beaches and the cool waters of the bay. Dense greens, saturated from an unusually heavy rainfall, reflected off the water. The setting stole Tox's breath.

"How did he get this on an LTC's pay?" Before deploying, Tox had wanted to see where McKenna was killed. What he expected to find, why he felt drawn to come, he didn't know. Just that it had to be done.

"Wife was in luxury real estate," Iliescu said as they trekked out to the Adirondack chairs clustered around a stone fire pit near the beach. "He was sitting out here with his son. Kid went back to the house for a soda. When he returned, he found his dad dead."

Tox swallowed. "How old?"

"Thirteen."

"At least his dad wasn't shot right in front of him." Jaw tight, Tox folded his arms. Stared at the weathered gray chairs. One covered in the dark stain of murder. He imagined the teenager finding his dad like that, dead.

Watching Keogh and VVolt doing a light recon to the edge of the manicured lawn, Tox swiped a hand along his jaw. Trudged out to the water. Scanned the area, searching for a sniper nest, a place where Alec could have a vantage and take the shot without being seen, without getting caught as he left. Adjusting his ball cap, Tox squinted at a location across the bay. Not half a klick off, the inlet arced out toward the bay. And there, in a copse of light and dark greens, peeked a roofline.

"That's what I was thinking, Sarge." Thor came up beside him, hands in the pocket of his hoodie. "Hidden but open. High enough. Close enough."

"It's a boathouse for another property—water on the north side," Iliescu explained.

"Perfect nest. Take the shot," Maangi said, nodding toward the water, "boat out." With the team members cross-trained in all aspects of warfare—medic, sniper, tactics—it provided redundancy and options, like having all of them able to assess the best sniper position.

"That's what authorities thought, but they found nothing."

Nothing had been found where Tox had been shot either. He studied the terrain, the canopies, the vegetation, the water, the sloping sandbar. Alec was good, one of the best. Just because authorities hadn't found something didn't mean he hadn't been here.

"I'll check it out," Thor said.

"We'll go with him," Keogh said, calling VVolt with a click of his tongue.

Iliescu hiked a thumb over his shoulder. "Sheriff's up at the house. He can—"

"Prefer to walk it," Thor said. "Get a feel for the layout."

Iliescu nodded. "Just don't disturb anything."

Alec had been here. Killed the colonel. And fled. Where was the honor in that? If the killings were justified, why flee? Why hide like a criminal?

"How's the family?" Haven's soft voice drifted from his six. She was probably standing near the chairs, near the tangible reminder of Alec's mission.

It's a holy mission.

Nauseating reality tugged him around, and he studied those grouped up near the pit.

"The wife and daughter are having a rough time, but the son"—Iliescu shook his head—"isn't talking."

"To anyone?" A cool breeze rushed up off the bay and tousled Haven's dark blond hair. She secured the rogue strands behind her ear, squinting.

Just over her shoulder, Tox spotted a woman. Classy. Short hair, stylishly colored. Business suit. Homing beacon of a wedding ring. Her expression was wary, maybe even angry.

He started toward her. But Iliescu held out a staying hand, then hustled up to where she stood on the driveway that led to the gray-sided and red-shuttered beachfront property.

Tox wanted—needed—to hear the conversation, to get her take on things, so he edged closer.

"Mrs. McKenna, I'm Deputy Director Iliescu. Thank you for allowing us on-site."

A half-acknowledging, half-annoyed nod was all he got, but her eyes skidded to Tox again. She frowned.

"We won't be here much longer, ma'am," Iliescu reassured her.

"These . . . people—they're looking for Ryan's killer?"

"They are."

Speculative and discerning, her gaze slid over the team. "They're CID?"

Tox navigated out of her line of sight, realizing she was too perceptive. Too aware. Being the colonel's wife, she'd no doubt learned to listen well, gather information. She certainly didn't need intel on a man who was supposed to be dead. Had McKenna ever mentioned Tox during the trial?

That could get messy fast. He banked toward the beach, pushing through a thick tangle of brush. A blue plaid shirt caught his eye before vanishing around a sharp curve. In a hurry? Maybe they hadn't noticed his approach.

Tox followed, curious who was on scene. As he spotted the person again, he assessed. Clothes were casual. Movements seemed young. Slumped shoulders. Head down. Attitude thick.

He rounded the corner and set eyes on the boy at the same time his mind made the connection—McKenna's son. Same tall, lanky build. Same dark hair.

Tox stopped, sand and rocks grinding beneath his shoes. He lowered his gaze, feeling wrong for intruding.

"Did you know my dad?" the boy asked.

Tox flinched, looking across the twenty feet that separated them. McKenna's son stood on a small dock, something in his hand. He twisted it between his thumb and middle finger.

Swallowing, Tox nodded. "He was my CO for a while."

The boy smiled. "Thought so."

"You did?" That was interesting, since Tox wasn't wearing a kit or uniform. "How's that?"

He shrugged. "You look military, is all. That's why I asked."

"Pretty smart," Tox said, impressed with the kid's perception.

"You live it long enough, you can see it," the boy said.

That sounded a lot like McKenna. "What's your name?"

"Jared."

Tox braved a few steps closer. "Heard you found your dad."

A pained expression smeared the young face before Jared turned and looked out at the water.

Tox hesitated. He didn't want to push and lose the chance to talk to the best witness.

"We were arguing," Jared finally said. "He wanted me to stay in private school. I wanted to go to the military academy, be like him." A lazy shrug that said plenty.

"But he didn't want that life for you." Tox could relate. He didn't want it for anyone else, either.

Jared snorted. "He's been my hero all my life."

It was strange. Tox's father had wanted him in the military. He really didn't care where he went as long as it was out of the house. Tox had been a royal pain in the backside. When Tox joined the Army, his dad said it'd be good for him. Maybe it'd teach him discipline. There was a small piece of the young Tox that wanted to be like his father—a political powerhouse. But there was a bigger part that just wanted to thumb his nose at his old man.

"Your father saw combat. Knew what it meant, what it does to the soul."

Jared's brown eyes struck him. "Have you? Seen combat, I mean."

"Yeah," Tox said with a tight breath. "Jared, no matter what the argument was about, you know your father loved you. Right?"

"Yeah, sure." Another lazy shrug. "I just—our last words were angry. Then I said I wanted a soda so I could leave. When I came back . . ."

Tox couldn't even remember the last words he'd spoken to his father. This kid was seriously well adjusted. Better than Tox had expected after finding his father dead and having gone silent. He wasn't being silent now.

"He came out of the woods, right there," Jared muttered.

Tox frowned. "Who?"

"The shooter."

His pulse misfired. "You saw him?"

The muscles in the kid's faced worked hard to keep a bevy of emotions at bay. "When I saw . . . when the blood . . ."

Startled at the comment, wrecked at what the boy couldn't come out and say, Tox moved forward. "You don't have to talk about this, son."

"Yeah." He swiped beneath his eyes, voice cracking. "I do." He shifted, eyeing Tox. "He said you'd come."

"Your dad?"

Jared shook his head, brown hair dangling over his brow.

Alec. Cold snapped through Tox's veins. He twitched, angry. This . . . this was crossing the line. "He talked to you. That's how you knew who I was."

Jared nodded. "I ran when I realized Dad was dead. Ran right into him as he came out of the bushes."

"Son of—" He bit off the curse. Wanted to punch something— no, someone. Alec. "Jared, I'm—"

Tears streamed down the kid's face. "He said you knew Dad, that you'd come." He held out his hand. On his palm lay a medallion. "He said to give this to you when you came."

Fury coursing through him, Tox braced himself and met the boy's gaze with an apologetic shake of his head. Instead of taking the medallion, he grabbed the kid's arm, pulled him into a hug, and held him. Staggered through a breath. Then another. *Sorry, McKenna.* "I'm sorry, Jared. He had no right . . ."

Jared's tears broke free.

Tox's thoughts ricocheted between anger and grief. Disbelief and . . . he didn't know what. When the boy's shoulders shook, Tox crushed him tighter. *Too far, Alec. Too far.* "I will find him."

The boy clung to him, sobs wracking his frame. Voices and shouts came from the path. Rushed up behind them.

"Jared!" his mother shrieked. "Jared, are you okay?"

Tox turned and urged the boy into his mother's arms, slipping the medallion from Jared's hand and loading his expression with a hefty dose of apology and sympathy. Once Mrs. McKenna took her son into her arms, she gave Tox a look, then headed back up the path.

Tox watched. Forced himself to memorize that picture. For McKenna's sake. So he would never forget what Alec had done. He had to stop him before he . . .

Before he what?

Crossed a line?

Done.

Killed?

Too many times.

Tox stomped down the path to the car, the others trailing him and talking quietly.

"What happened?" Iliescu asked as he fell into step beside him.

"Too much." Tox tugged out his phone, then dialed Thor. "We're heading out."

"Almost there," Thor said, stepping out of the brush. Probably just like Alec had yesterday morning.

"Tox."

He skated a look at the deputy director but kept moving toward the SUVs.

"What happened with the kid?" Iliescu demanded.

What was he supposed to say? They all had a bloodlust, a thirst for Alec's body in a bag. If he told them, it'd feed the frenzy.

"Tox!" Ram caught his arm, spun him around.

Instinct drew up Tox's fist.

Ram's eyebrows winged up.

Reeling it in, Tox tucked his chin. "Alec talked to him."

"The kid?" Ram asked, his tone absurdly even, as if he knew Tox was on edge. He probably did.

He handed over the medallion. "Killed the dad, then went to the boy. Gave him this. Said I'd be coming."

Ram turned it back to front, inspecting it.

"It's a challenge coin," Cell muttered.

"From our unit—the Spartan helmet with a scar and lightning bolt." Tox swiped the back of his hand along his mouth, ignoring the grief and concern from Haven.

"Dude, that?" Cell said, pointing to the coin. "That is whack."

"He carved his symbol into it." Ram angled the coin, showing the men the crown etched into the back.

Just as he's carved me into this nightmare.

"And *this* is the guy you just want to *bring back*? The guy you said you understand?" Cell demanded.

"This guy"—Tox tapped the coin—"could be each one of us. Has done what everyone here has done." His heart thudded. "So yeah—I want him brought back. Alive."

"I say double-tap him and leave him in the dirt."

"Is that what you'd do to me?"

"If you went all *Silence of the Lambs* psycho like him?" Cell's face contorted in a mix of rage and incredulity. "Heck yeah."

Shock pushed the breath back down his throat. Tox considered Cell. Saw that he was dead serious. Then Thor—same. Maangi looked penitent but serious.

Nodding, Tox struggled to breathe around the storm raging in his chest. "Noted." He strode to the vehicles, slid into the front passenger seat, and rode back to the city in silence. Though he was with his men and Haven, he was alone.

In his thoughts.

In his beliefs.

In his fears.

14

The storm in Cole had hit catastrophic levels.

They'd been doing so well the last few months, dating and figuring each other out. But this whole nightmare with Alec turned the world—and Cole—upside down. After the team's visit to the McKenna property, he'd given her a quick kiss, said he'd call, then vanished.

Being far too skilled at reading deception, Haven knew he didn't intend to call. She got it. He needed space to work through recent events. It wouldn't be the first time he'd done that. She'd often given him the room to do it.

This time, it felt . . . different. And he didn't have Chiji to bat him into line with a kali stick or a well-placed remonstration.

Haven licked the cookie dough off her thumb, then slid the sheet into the oven. She set the timer and washed her hands. Her roommate, Emilie, had gone to California to visit her family for the week. A nice respite for Haven, but perhaps a little too quiet. She headed to the TV and turned on recorded episodes of her favorite show to smooth the tension from her shoulders.

As she sank into the sofa, sighing in relief at being off her feet, she glanced at her phone. Why she thought Cole might've called in the last two minutes, she didn't know. She squinted at the TV, trying to get back into the show, and her doorbell rang.

"Seriously?" she groused, then pushed off the cushions and hit the pause button. "You couldn't ring the bell while I was still on my feet?"

A quick glance out the front window and the sight of a black Lexus stopped her. What was he doing here? She unlocked the door and swung it open. "Levi. What—" The question fell away when she saw the people behind him. "Robbie. Deputy Director."

"Can we come in?" Robbie was already pushing into the townhome.

"Um, sure." She forced a smile for the deputy director and Levi. Though she knew what folded arms meant at times like this, she couldn't resist. "Sorry you missed dinner. Chocolate chip cookies are baking."

"We only need a minute," Iliescu said. "And I am sorry for the unannounced visit. We thought it better this way."

"What was better this way?" Irritation skittered up her spine, especially that Levi was involved.

"Why don't you have a seat?" Robbie planted herself on the sofa. As if this were her home.

Something was off. And it brought Haven's Irish side to bear, made her want to rebel. Instead, she perched on the edge of the armchair and motioned to the oven as an excuse. "Timer will go off soon."

Her nerves rattled, she could only think of one reason they were all here. It had to be Cole. But she couldn't bring herself to ask if he was okay. He wasn't. She'd known that when he drove off last night. "Has the team left yet?"

Robbie and Iliescu looked at each other.

And there it was—her confirmation that things were wrong. With Cole.

"Soon," Iliescu said.

Haven nodded. They wouldn't talk details, not in an unsecure setting. So that they told her this . . .

The timer blared from the kitchen, giving her an escape to think. "Excuse me." She hurried to the oven, removed the cookies, and set them on the granite countertop. If she left them on the pan, they'd overcook.

But then, *she* felt overcooked by the tension that had just walked into her townhome. They were here. It was about Cole. No other viable scenarios presented themselves. But standing in here thinking wouldn't get her answers.

Abandoning the cookies, she turned off the oven and returned. "Okay, just give it to me. I know this is about Cole."

"I think the visit to the McKenna home shook him up pretty badly, seeing the family and talking to the kid," Robbie said with a sigh.

Haven nodded. "I agree." His stoic façade had turned to granite there.

"Can you explain what you know?" Iliescu asked.

Oddly, Levi was silent. He sat with his elbows on his knees, his expression all concern and worry. Which in turn worried her.

"What *I* know? I don't know anything you don't." It was mostly true. "Really, just tell me. I can't take this beating around the bush."

"Kasey," Robbie said with a soft, maternal tone, "Tox has formally requested you be removed from the team."

The words slapped her. Breath trapped in her lungs, Haven stared at her boss. Yet somehow her heart was thundering. In pain. In hurt. He'd requested she be removed? Her eyes burned. An ache bloomed in her breast, yearning that he'd trust her, include her instead of shutting her out.

Well. She swallowed, looking down. She wasn't surprised, not really. "He's afraid I'll get hurt."

The director nodded. "He said as much—that Alec would make good on his threat at the restaurant."

Haven closed her eyes to the grief, to the truth that Cole hadn't even talked to her about this. That he'd just made the decision. That was why he wouldn't talk to her, return her calls or texts. The coward.

"Kase?" Levi shifted forward, laying a hand over hers.

No matter what Cole had done, she didn't want Levi trying to wedge in. She shifted her hand, but her shoulders sagged. It made sense. All of it. His retreating. His concern. The danger *was* real. This wasn't just a silly protective instinct. Legitimate concern existed.

But he hadn't talked to her about it. He'd just . . . decided.

Levi insisted on touching her again. "Kasey, you okay?" His light blue eyes probed hers.

"So I'm off the team." She looked at Robbie and Director Iliescu, feeling the burn at the back of her throat and her eyes.

"No."

She started at the deputy director's firm, snapped reply. "I'm not?"

"Well," he said, with a cockeyed nod, "we'll leave that decision up to you, but that's why we're here."

"Russell wants you off the team," Robbie said, "and yes—because he's concerned for your safety."

"Okay . . ."

"But we're concerned for *his* safety."

Haven snorted.

"His mental safety."

"Mental?" What were they saying? "Cole's not crazy."

"No, but we think this situation with Alec King is impeding his ability to act with the decisiveness we need from him," Iliescu said. "There is no operator better suited to pursue King. We need Tox in this hunt. We need his entire skillset. But he's shaken and fighting us on the end goal. We've all seen his anger, his reaction to this."

The conversation had shifted from his asking for her removal to his "instability." Haven had a bad feeling about where this conversation was heading.

"Why do you think Russell is reacting so strongly?" Robbie asked.

The question was a tactic to draw Haven in, get her to empathize and side with their purpose. "Cole sees himself in Alec."

"I think it goes further than that," Iliescu said. "I think Russell sees himself as no different than King."

"That's insane. King has killed. He's murdering people."

"Yes," Iliescu said. "And that's why we need you to go on this mission."

"Me?" Haven pressed a hand to her chest, startled at the way they'd included her in this. "Why? I'm not an operator."

"No, but you *operate* well with Russell. He listens to you."

"Yes, because I'm his girlfriend—"

"No," Robbie said. "No, Russell listened to your counsel before

133

you two started dating. You're balanced. You read people. You see through lies."

"You see through *his* lies," Levi said.

"'His lies'?"

"To himself," Levi clarified with upheld palms.

"I don't understand." They wanted her to help Tox see through lies, his own lies, but what did that have to do with his mission? "Wait." Her heart had a head-on collision with the truth. "You're afraid he's going to join Alec."

"We want you to be there for him. Let us know how he's doing. If you see anything that concerns you—"

"You want me to *spy* on him?" Her shriek mirrored the one in her heart. "Absolutely not!"

"Haven, we need you there. *He* needs you there, even though he doesn't think so."

"For good reason—I was threatened by the man you're sending him after."

"And King found you here," Iliescu said, his gaze steady. Boring through her justifications. "I don't mean to be insensitive, but Alec King will not be put off by holding you stateside. In fact, keeping you on the move will make it harder for him to locate you. Russell knows this, if he'd think about it."

Breathing became impossible. "I cannot believe you seriously think I would do this—betray him."

"It's not a betrayal," Robbie said. "He asked for you to be removed, and I told him no, because you were—*are*—necessary."

"But you want me to report on him. I won't." She heaved a breath. "I won't do that to him."

"I think you misunderstand," the deputy director said, his expression washed of the former intensity. He glanced at Robbie, then Levi. "Nobody wants you to spy. We want you to be there. Monitor the situation as well as Tox. Do what you already do with him on a daily basis. He trusts you, listens to you. That's all we need—a voice of reason." He shifted to the edge of the sofa. "Ms. Cortes, I believe you're the type of person who will do whatever it takes to protect those you love."

She held his gaze. He was manipulating her.

"True?"

Swallowing around her unwillingness to be a pawn, she forced herself to speak. "True."

"That's all we're asking. And I believe if you felt he was in trouble, you'd do whatever it took to help him, even if that meant communicating that concern to one of us."

It was too easy. They'd switched tactics. But if she could go on this mission, if she could stay with Cole and not betray him . . . she wanted to go. She'd never been one to back down from danger or a threat. In fact, a threat, being manipulated—as they were trying to do here—seemed to slide a steel rod down her spine.

"Can we count on you?"

"I do not work well under manipulation, Deputy Director." Her words were firm. "But I'll go. Not for you. Or even for me." Maybe that was only a half-truth. "But for Cole."

Because she *was* concerned for him. Worried, honestly. This thing with Alec was tearing Cole up inside. And that, in turn, ate at her. But if he ever found out they'd asked this of her, even though she refused to spy, he would never forgive her.

* * * *

— DAY 19 —

RESTON, VIRGINIA

Tox stormed into the newly minted SAARC headquarters. The clandestine center was tucked into the basement of an office building with a lot of foot traffic and enough distance from DC to have breathable air. He stalked to the command center, where he found Robbie Almstedt in the main hub, bending over a console. "If you're convinced this is an artifact we're dealing with, why haven't you called in field experts?"

"What experts?" Robbie Almstedt asked as she straightened. "We don't know what it is, so how do we determine who to call?"

Disgusted, Tox tossed the mission briefing on the table. "I hate this."

"You and me both, Mr. Russell." She came around the six-foot table and crossed her arms. "But we operate with the cards we're dealt."

"No, I hate *this*." He slapped the brief, flipped it open, and pointed. "Why is she listed under personnel?"

Almstedt lifted her chin.

"I told you—"

"Regardless of coming back from the dead, Mr. Russell, you aren't a god. You don't speak and we obey."

Tox stared at her. "She's not field qualified."

"Cortes is trained in exactly what we need her trained in. The joint task force decided she'd be on the mission, so she is."

"This is wrong." How could he make his point? "Alec's made it very clear that he will take his vengeance out on her if I screw up."

"And having her sit in her apartment here, exactly where he knows she lives, is the smartest way to keep her safe?" Raising an eyebrow, she leaned back against the table. "And to address your concern, I guess the best thing, since Ms. Cortes is on the team, is to *get* her field qualified."

"What?" His heart stalled. "No!"

"Kasey Cortes is attached to the Wraith team—that was your doing, remember—so she will be going with the team. Her ability to read people and situations is uncanny. Even you can't deny that. She read you. Called you on things during the codex mission and saved your life."

"That isn't . . . this mission—it's different. Alec is *targeting* her."

"No." Almstedt pushed off the table and crossed the iron grating of the floor, taking the four steps to the lower section where the offices huddled. "Alec King is targeting our Top Ten. Plus a few extras."

"But he—"

"He also wants you on his team, and that's where the danger led to Ms. Cortes. So if I follow your logic, Mr. Russell, then in fact—aren't *you* a threat to her?"

"Don't go there."

After a shrug, Almstedt entered her office and sat behind her desk, where she flung another eyebrow at him. "Should I remove *you* from the mission?"

"You won't do that." He forced as much confidence into his words as possible, sickened at the thought of being cut. If Almstedt benched him, the team would go after Alec as hard as they could. Kill him first chance they got. "SAARC needs me because of my history with Alec. You won't cut me."

After a glowering look, she sighed. "No, we won't."

He let out a breath he hadn't realized he'd held hostage.

"But we also won't be removing Cortes, so don't ask again. She's in. She's an asset." Almstedt nodded her dyed head toward the brief on the table. "Might want to get familiar with that, you and your team. Wheels up at 0400."

"If she gets hurt, I'm coming for you." Tox snatched up the file and stalked back to the main command center, banked left to where his five-by-six module linked up to the hub, and pitched the file onto his desk. Pinching the bridge of his nose did nothing to temper the stench of this nightmare.

His phone rang. Relief hit him when he saw the familiar international number. "Chiji, my brother."

A deep laugh rumbled through the line. "That is a desperate greeting."

"You have no idea. I've never needed you more." Tox folded himself onto the chair. Elbow on the desk, he cradled his head. "How's Nne, the family?"

"It will take time."

Time. Tox's gut twisted. "You're not coming back."

"Not yet. I must finish this and be here for her. This has been very hard for her, to lose a child."

"And you—he was your brother."

"God gives me peace. Now, what is it that weighs on your heart so much, Ndidi?"

After a snort of disbelief—how did Chiji always know?—Tox explained the situation, the infuriating decision by SAARC.

"She is safer with you, would you not agree, Ndidi?" Chiji sounded calm. Serene. Curse the man.

"No. I don't," Tox huffed out. "Because Alec's going to anticipate my moves, he'll know where I'll go, what we investigate. The very nature of this investigation means we're one step behind him, walking in *his* footsteps. If she's with me, he knows where she is." He ran a hand down the back of his neck, remembering Jared McKenna. Remembering the daunting truth. "He knew, Chiji. He *knew* I'd visit McKenna's kid."

"What you are struggling with, I think, is not fear about protecting Haven."

"Of course—"

"But fear of facing this man. Facing the truth about him."

"What truth?"

"That he is more like you than you want to admit." Chiji had a way of cutting through the muck and mire to get to the bald truth. "But perhaps you know that. Perhaps what you fear is learning that he is not redeemable."

"He is!" Tox hated the way his voice bounced back at him, throwing the words in his face.

A rap on the door jerked Tox away from the conversation. "Hang on," he said to Chiji.

"Hey, Sarge," Cell said. "Thor wanted me to let you know he's running behind—but he'll be here."

Shaking off the haunting words of his Igbo brother, Tox gave a half shrug, half nod. "No problem. You got the equipment checked and tested?"

"Roger that." Cell pointed to a pile near the far wall. "Packing it up now."

"Good. We'll—" Tox spotted two figures near the far door and froze. Haven and Wallace. Why was she with him?

Her gaze hit his, and he saw it. The clear message that she knew he'd requested her removal from the team. While he didn't regret the request, he did regret how he'd handled it.

"I'll be getting that packed up," Cell said, his expression telegraphing his confusion and dislike that Haven had arrived with the agent. "You go . . . take care of things."

Tox looked down and returned to his phone call. "Chiji, I'm back."

"Remember, *Otu onye tuo izu, o gbue ochu*," Chiji said.

"But this isn't about knowledge, about two heads being better than one. This is about keeping her safe." Tox gritted his teeth, allowing himself to look toward where she stood talking with Wallace and rubbing her arms.

"*Gidi gidi bụ ugwu eze*," Chiji insisted.

Unity is strength.

"There will not always be a mission, and she calls to your soul, Ndidi. There is no room for silence or justification."

Her green eyes came to his, and Tox knew Chiji was right. Not about the justification. His reasons and the danger were legitimate. But after the mission, after things settled, what would be left of their lives, of their relationship? The thought made him wince.

Maybe it was better for her to be with Wallace. He'd thought that before they'd started dating. But maybe it was time to push her into Superman's arms.

"Before you leave for this mission, you must talk with her."

When they had first met in that underground facility, him handcuffed and chained to the floor, he knew she was too good for him. But fool that he was, he'd been intrigued by her. "Some things are better left alone."

He lifted the file, opened it, and scanned the details of the mission. Realized Chiji hadn't responded. "What?"

"You will go into a trap in the middle of the jungle. You will save a man from a plague-infested tunnel, but you will not face the woman you love." His tongue clucked. "I must go, Ndidi. Seek Him. Listen to Him. Trust Him." Chiji hung up, leaving him alone with his thoughts, guilt, and cowardice.

"Some fires burn less," Tox muttered to himself as he dropped into his chair and rubbed his face.

"Just promise me one thing." Her voice was quiet, plying. It pulled his gaze to where she hesitated in the doorway. Hurt marred her beautiful features, yet she stood there in that raw confidence he admired so much.

Tox didn't trust himself to talk. To offer the apology he knew she wanted to hear. He came to his feet.

"I know you won't apologize," she said softly as she edged into his module, "because you believe so wholly in what you're doing."

She got that? Did she honestly understand that was why he did what he'd done?

"Just like Alec."

Heat shot down his spine at the implication and comparison. "Hey, now."

"But promise—next time, at least show me some respect and talk to me first." Her brow knotted. "Don't go behind my back when I have held *your* back and trusted you with my life."

He moved toward her. "Then trust me again."

"How?" Her eyes pleaded for an answer. "How can I trust you when you won't talk to me? When you go around me—"

"That's not—it wasn't like that." *There is no room for silence or justification.* "I went up the chain of command, as I'm supposed to do."

Her eyes swam with unshed tears. "Does that really assuage your guilt, Cole? Do you really believe that?"

"I do."

She snorted, lifted her hands. Maybe in frustration, defeat, or giving up on him. "Cole . . ."

He closed the short distance between them. "You're right—I won't apologize, because I did the right thing." He cupped her shoulders. "I don't want you to get hurt, and that's exactly what Alec threatened." He rubbed a thumb over the bony part of her shoulder. "Okay, yes, I guess I could've handled it differently." He felt the frayed ends of his heartstrings twisting into a knot. "I . . ."

"You didn't want to face me."

Surprise tightened the knot. A smile tried to twitch his cheek that she'd nailed him so perfectly. "Guess so." He shrugged. "But—"

"No 'but.'" Haven drew in a breath. "No excuses, Cole. I don't need to hear them. I don't *want* to hear them. Fairness and respect—that's what I need. That same package you dish out to your men is what I want."

Did she understand that she'd just asked for exactly what he'd done? Because this was what he'd do to the guys, if he felt it would keep them alive. He wouldn't hesitate. Ever.

"If we're going to date, if we're going to pursue whatever this is between us, then we have to be honest."

"If?" That caught him off guard. He thought they *were* dating.

She raised an eyebrow. "Dating requires honesty."

"I haven't been dishonest, Haven. I just . . . I'm not used to having to run every play by someone."

"Not true," she said. "You run everything past Ram."

"When the mission requires it, but only after I have initial intel and a preliminary plan. It's the way the chain of command works." He never thought someone nearly ten years his junior with no field or military experience could get him by the scruff of his collar like this. But then again, he'd never met anyone like Haven. "I will work to include you more, but Haven . . ." She wouldn't like this part. "I can't—*won't*—promise to always tell you everything. My job, what I do—I can't."

"Then maybe we should step back until we can figure this out."

Nauseated, he pulled out the invisible dagger she'd just thrust into his heart. "I guess until we both understand a few things, maybe it's best."

15

With his ruck over his shoulder, Tox hopped off the Black Hawk and made his way toward the hangar, as much for cover from bullets as from the brutal Egyptian sun that seemed as angry as some of the terrorists.

"Hottest freakin' month of the year in Egypt, and that's when we have to be here," Cell groused as they stalked toward the small building.

The Multinational Force & Observers' Forward Operating Base-North was home to an array of soldiers from Australia, Colombia, the Czech Republic, France, Canada, the United States, and more. Nearly a dozen countries served as peacekeepers in the Sinai and were split between the FOB-N, which served as the MFO's Sinai headquarters, and the Sharm El Sheikh base in the south that also served as the naval coastal patrol camp.

Though the MFO was authorized for several thousand peacekeepers, the numbers had dwindled in recent years. The U.S. had roughly seven hundred soldiers in the region, half the number from the early '80s. Tox wasn't sure if that was good or bad in the scheme of things. For now, it meant fewer resources if he and his team got in trouble out here.

A guy in a flight suit jogged out of the building toward them. "Sergeant Russell?"

"That's me," Tox said, stepping around his men, Haven, and Wallace. "You are?"

Though he wore a head cover that shaded his face, the kid's blue eyes were especially bright in the glaring sun. "Oh. I'm nobody," he said with a goofy grin as he tugged the brim of his hat. He hooked a thumb over his shoulder. "I was asked to bring you inside." He took in the team. "But, uh, there are more of you than I was told."

"That a problem?" Tox asked, an edge to his voice.

The kid scratched his head. "Only if y'all have a problem doubling up."

Doubling up? On bunks? Was the kid serious? Tox considered the others, the same disgust on their faces that he felt.

"I'll double with Cortes," Cell volunteered.

"And it'll be the last thing you do," Tox said, knowing Cell was teasing. He turned back to their welcome committee. "I need to talk to whoever's in charge."

The kid busted out laughing. "Just kidding. Sorry. Thought y'all looked a bit uptight and needed a laugh."

"I'm about to show you a laugh that looks a lot like a cry," Thor threatened.

He waved them down the road. "C'mon. Let's get you settled."

Inside the long portable building, where air conditioning struggled to keep the heat at bay, the kid loped down a hall and banked right. "All right. Y'all are in here. Bathrooms are farther on"—he slapped the air to his left—"right next to the showers. Which are more like rust-dumping conduits, but it'll get you clean. Eventually."

Tox glanced into a room that held twenty bunks. "We have to meet up with—"

"I'm to drive y'all out to the village at 1420 hours," the kid said. "Y'all be ready then?"

"We were supposed to meet a contact."

"Yeah, sometimes this happens. But don't worry. You came to see the village. You'll see it."

Tox huffed, and the guy vanished down the hall.

"He looked fifteen," Ram said, shouldering past him.

"If that."

An hour later, they were heading back out into the heat and sun. Dressed in jeans and a T-shirt with a keffiyeh twisted around his neck, the kid stood beside two vehicles that didn't look like they'd get off the base, let alone across the terrain to a remote village.

"What happens when these things break down?" Thor asked.

"We fix them," the kid said. "You know how to fix a car, right?"

His taunts were annoying. They loaded up. The trip out was like trying to ride a bucking bronco. Not much different than Afghanistan. Except hotter, if that was possible. The heat here seemed drier, meaner.

"You're American," Tox said to their guide as the vehicle pitched them across the miles.

"Accent gave me away, huh?"

"Army?"

The kid nodded.

"You're not in uniform."

He grinned, pinching wrinkles into his sun-darkened face. "Keeps me alive longer."

When Tox frowned—he was clearly a Westerner, so uniform or not, he wouldn't be confused with a local—the kid went on.

"I speak French, so I can pass myself off as that out there. Not as evil as being American, according to the locals."

Tox nodded. When people got in trouble, they wanted America to help, send money and resources. When things normalized, America again became demon spawn.

"Got a name?"

"Quite a few. Most just call me Runt."

"Runt?" Tox scowled at him.

"Youngest in the family. Military brothers. They made sure the name carried." He lifted a shoulder. "Makes people underestimate me. Gives me the advantage, like home turf."

"D'you know anything about the family of the guy who got killed?"

"Not much," Runt said with another shrug. He navigated the desert with a lazy confidence that warned his home-turf advantage was true.

Runt *was* at home here. "Most people here don't care much about politics. They're just trying to survive in the desert. Sometimes the kids leave and find jobs. They either bring money home or send it home. Little in the way of commerce out this way. Lots of rock farmers, but not much else." That was a joke. Had to be. "Unless you're into terrorizing people, and then there's money, drugs, skin trade . . ."

Ten minutes later, they pulled through the village, and Tox noticed a vehicle behind them. Tension knotted his shoulders.

"Easy," Runt said without glancing back. "They're friendly."

"You know them?"

Another lazy shrug, his gaze on the road. "Know is a relative term."

They slowed through a couple of switchbacks and aimed down into the lower valley. There was no difference between the grainy images he'd seen four days ago and the brick dwellings in the same shade of dried mud. He recognized the steep incline that had him bracing his weight as the vehicle tilted down the slope. They evened out and slid beneath what was left of an arched gate. Drawing up to the house, Tox had to shut off the video playing in his head of Alec getting out of his vehicle. Of the brother shooting Sherif.

"Wait here," Runt said as he parked the beat-up Jeep. Only as the kid approached the two-story structure with curtains for windows did Tox see the bulge at Runt's back. The shoulders that had not seemed broad before.

The stance.

Runt wasn't a runt. He was—Tox snorted—underestimated.

A stream of Arabic flew into the air as Runt rapped on the wall beside the draped door. It shouldn't be a surprise Runt knew the language, but it was. Tox scanned the buildings around them, catching more than one shower-curtain door flipping back. Too many eyes.

The flimsy barrier flapped aside. A man, bent with age, appeared. Face wrought, he shouted at Runt.

Tox eased his hand toward his leg-holstered Glock 22, suddenly wishing they had more than just handguns. But this was a peaceful mission, talking with the locals. Besides, Western soldiers walking into a village armed to the teeth would not only give the wrong message but would have trouble breathing down their necks. At least he had his Glock.

Runt stepped back, lifting his palms in a plaintive gesture.

Gun in hand, Tox reached for the door handle. He didn't know what—

More Arabic swam between the two, then Runt was leading the old man toward the rear vehicle. Toward the rest of the team.

"No no no," Tox muttered, heart rapid-firing. He stepped out, weapon cradled down and to the side. He stopped when Runt put his arm around the old man's shoulder and indicated the last vehicle—not the one carrying the team. A goat shifted in the bed of the truck.

Face alight, the old man clapped Runt's shoulders. Kissed both of his cheeks. Runt laughed.

And Tox stood stunned, confused as Runt trudged back toward him, wiping something from his eyes. He swept past Tox without even looking at him. "Might put that away if you want them to actually talk to you," he muttered without hesitation, then flew into Arabic again. A greeting. One Tox knew from his days in A-stan.

At the door stood the brother who'd killed Sherif. Swallowing, unsettled by the fact that Runt had bought favors from this family, Tox holstered his Glock. When he heard creaking doors, he looked back as two men in brown pants and shirts followed the old man around the side of the home with the goat.

"What's going on?" Ram asked.

"Goodwill gesture."

"No," Ram said, nodding to the men at the door. "I'm talking about fly-boy."

Tox considered Runt. Thought of the conversation. Thought of the nickname. Why he liked it. Tox smirked. "I think he's our asset."

* * * *

Since the Elarabi home was too small to accommodate all eight of them plus Runt, at Cole's instruction, the team split up. Cole, Ram, and Thor stayed with the family, while the rest ventured back to the "higher" village to find the man who'd filmed the incident.

Perched on the hill, Haven stood back as the guy Cole called Runt walked up to a group of men loitering at the corner. They'd gathered as the convoy made its way down to the lower area. As Cell and Maangi flanked Runt, the group grew animated.

Runt's expression and tone darkened, firmed.

Two of the men shifted back. Snapped hands at him, as if telling him to back off.

"That doesn't look good," Levi whispered.

But she'd read the body language. The facial expressions. The men weren't angry. They were . . . bargaining. But for what? "It's okay," she said quietly. "I think they're just trying to get something out of him."

"Like the old man and the goat?"

Haven nodded. It shouldn't surprise her. Making wages out here couldn't be easy. Many African countries were embroiled in corruption, bribery as much a currency as any bill or coin.

"Okay, okay," Runt said, going for his wallet. He opened it.

The arguments died and hands stretched toward him. Runt handed out colorful paper bills, and finally the crowd parted to reveal a gap-toothed man with a scar across his nose. Shaking his head, dismayed— but not really—Runt handed him several bills.

When the gap-toothed man led the team back toward her, Runt came straight to Haven. "Stay close."

At his warning tone, her pulse skipped a beat, and she fell into step with him. "What's wrong?"

"You're white. You're a woman, beautiful. They're interested."

"In what?"

"Buying you. Renting you." He shrugged. "Whatever they can get."

Haven felt more than saw Levi's presence behind her. She'd never been more glad to have him hover.

"I'm afraid her boyfriend would slaughter anyone who touched her," Cell muttered, his brown eyes skating to Wallace.

Probably not a good idea to mention right now that she and Cole were at odds. Even she didn't want to admit she'd broken up with him. A threat she'd tossed at him, not expecting him to agree. But he had—and so coolly.

"Which is why I told her to stay close," Runt said as he kept stride with the local, who pointed ahead. "We don't need any incidents."

"Where are we going?" Haven asked, anxious to change the subject.

Runt nodded down the road at two structures. "There. Between the homes. That's where he stood to take the video."

Cell shouldered out of his ruck as they stepped into the alley created by the buildings, dousing them in shade and an instant relief of at least ten degrees. Automatically, all eyes swept toward the rooftops. Haven couldn't resist following their lead, knowing they were in a barrel, as Cole had once called it. Shade or not, they were all relieved to be back in the open. Perched atop the hill, the local man explained something to Runt, indicating the lower village.

Squatting, Cell dug something out of his pack.

Haven was more interested in the two men talking. The local seemed animated. Now so did Runt.

When he returned, she asked, "What's wrong?"

"He said something about ghosts," Runt said, shaking his head. "Probably just superstition."

But there was more. Something that concerned him. The two men fell into heavy conversation, the gap-toothed man pointing over the village, then to the Elarabi home.

"What?" Haven insisted on being updated.

"He says Sherif's brother has not been the same since the man with the crown came."

"Crown?" Haven thought of the object Alec King had put on his head.

Runt nodded. "That's what the people here are calling it. And they say that it took Makram Elarabi's *ba*."

"His what?" Cell asked from where he worked on his equipment.

"What are you doing?" Runt demanded.

"Tox wanted a video. I'm getting him a video." His voice was eerily calm as he scanned the village, then aimed the camera down the embankment to the lower village, where Cole, Ram, and Thor were entering the Elarabi home.

"Do it quickly. The villagers won't like you recording their homes."

Haven shifted back to Runt and focused on the words he'd said earlier. "You said ba?"

"Ba and *ka*. Ancient Egyptians believed the spirit or soul of a person exists in three parts: the ba, the ka and the *akh*. Sometimes, those beliefs weave their way back to life when things happen they can't explain. Thus"—he bobbed his head toward the Elarabi home—"they think Makram's ba has been stolen."

"But he's still alive. If his ba was gone, wouldn't he be dead?"

"No, only if his ka is gone, too."

"I thought these people were Muslim, how—"

"Ninety percent of Egypt is populated by Muslims, but in remote villages like this, some Egyptians still hold to the old superstitions." Eyes the same color as the clear sky, Runt squinted down at the lower part of the village. "Makram is changed, they say. Which would explain why his grandfather answered when I knocked and tried to get me to leave."

"They think that thing Mr. King put on his head is a crown?"

"That's what they say," Runt said with a hint of a smile. "Your friend is called Mr. King? And he wears a crown."

"Not our friend, dude. He tried to kill the sarge." Cell lifted a handheld radio and adjusted dials. "Putting him down as soon as we find him."

The radio crackled.

Cell frowned. Adjusted a dial, muttering.

"So," Runt said, "he said your boyfriend would slaughter anyone who touched you. Tox your boyfriend?"

Haven almost smiled. "Why'd you guess him?"

"You're attentive to him. And he's the only one here I can't get an angle on."

"Which means?"

"I trust him the least."

Haven grunted. "You should trust him the most."

A howl shot through the air. Then a gust of wind carried a strange, haunting voice, like the whispers that pervade horror movies. It crawled up the back of Haven's neck and pinched her nerves.

She whipped around, the unnerving sound coiling through her mind.

Eyes bulging, Cell threw the radio down. Hopped back. Cursed. He stared at the radio as if it had come to life. Wide, panicked eyes rose to hers. "Did you *hear* that?"

16

Sweat trickled down his spine as Tox sat cross-legged on the floor between Ram and Makram Elarabi's grandfather. In front of him, Makram and his uncles stared back impassively, oblivious to the ninety-eight-degree weather and cramped quarters. The heat, insufferable in the mud-brick home, baked Tox from the inside out. But he sat. And listened. Talked with Makram.

Correction: he talked with the grandfather and mother. Makram hadn't spoken since saying in a very robotic tone that he didn't know what came over him. That one moment he was ready to defend Sherif. The next, he was killing him.

And they were supposed to believe him.

Ram conversed with the family while Tox waited. There were formalities. Customs. Respect to be shown. But had Makram really not known what he was doing, aiming that gun at his brother's head? Had he checked out, mentally?

Tox considered Makram, noticing once more that he glanced to the window, the tattered fabric hanging over it rustling in a hot wind. He'd looked that direction a few times already. Restless as a kid wanting to play outside while the adults talked.

But his eyes weren't vacant. They were focused.

The uncle slapped Makram's side, saying something that caused the room to burst into laughter.

Save Makram. He skidded a look around the room, a smile wobbling on his lips, before he once more turned those dark eyes to the window. Tox saw a dangerous gleam in his gaze. This wasn't insanity. This was anticipation.

Alarm twitching through his veins, Tox extricated himself from the conversation and pushed to his feet, catching frowns from the others. He slowly worked his way to where he could get a similar line of sight out that window. He saw nothing but courtyard and vehicles. *But I'm standing. The angle is wrong.*

He kept moving. Slid in front of the window, squatted. Squinting, he scanned the windows and doors of the other buildings. Nothing. What was so important—

A kid sprinted across the courtyard. Right toward a home where a man waved him in, urgency carved into his features. The man glanced up the hill, then ducked into the house.

Not good. Dread in his gut, Tox slid his gaze up the incline. Sighted his team—Haven and Cell at the edge of the overlook, examining something. Wallace and Maangi talking with Runt and a local.

From this vantage, Tox was far enough from the incline to see the road leading into the village. Cell jumped back, motioning to his equipment in frustration. Tox bounced his gaze back to the road. Clouds—dust plumes. Big and crawling closer to the village. Vehicles racing down the road straight toward the team. From their position shielded by mud houses, they probably couldn't see the trouble coming.

Tox keyed his mic. "Cell," he hissed.

No response.

"Cell, report."

The plumes were growing. Trouble coming fast.

No no no. "Wraith Three, report!" Throwing aside the thick tarp door, Tox dove out of the Elarabi home. Hurried toward the incline. "Get down! Get down!"

Gunshots warred with his words.

"Go, go," Ram shouted behind him.

Sprinting, Tox ignored his Glock 22, knowing the distance was too great. Wished for his M4 to even the odds.

More shots ruptured the hollow moment.

As Tox ran, he saw Maangi snap up his weapon. Wallace did the same. Both diving for cover as they returned fire. Cell crouched with his equipment.

Haven stumbled. Dropped to the ground, as if sitting. But she wasn't sitting. She'd been hit.

Rage detonated. "No!"

Tox threw himself at the near-cliff face. Futility and rage propelled him up the steep incline. Shoving himself up, left and right, in a concerted, determined effort, exhausted him quickly. Sprinting the hill felt like trying to climb a wall at a full run. With each plant of his foot, each claw with his fingers, he ignored the shots. Ignored how ill-equipped they were. Only one thing mattered: getting to Haven.

His breaths came in heaving gulps. He finally clawed over the ledge and flattened himself, knowing he lay in full view of the gunmen. He shifted to his left. Three buildings stood between him and Haven. If he could just get to the first one without being seen . . .

Gut to the ground, Tox low-crawled toward the one-story structure, careful not to disturb dirt or shrubs or anything else that might draw attention or bullets.

It was excruciating—the seconds it took to drag himself to cover. Once out of sight, he came up and crouch-ran to the sun-warmed spine of the building. Glock out and ready, he eased to the corner. Took a breath. Whipped around for a split-second assessment, then snapped back. He saw the second truck, but they hadn't spotted him.

He peered toward the outcropping, where he'd last seen Haven. She wasn't there. Confusion choked him. Panicked him.

But then he noted a blur of blue amid the grays and browns. Her leg slid out of sight, but she shifted and their eyes met. Hers, round and watery. He telegraphed every bit of confidence and reassurance he could into his, anything to let her know he was coming.

Tox checked the alley between the houses again, then pitched himself at the next building. Hustled up to the far corner. Pressed against the plaster. A quick look and he'd almost be—

Rocks crunched.

Shoes ground dirt.

Tox recoiled. Froze, holding his position. Forcing himself to calm, his heart to slow. He waited for whoever was coming between the two buildings. Coming right up on him. With two puffed breaths, he prepared. Firmed his grip on the Glock.

The muzzle of a Russian Kalashnikov slid past his shoulder. He waited . . . waited . . .

Stepped to the side. Grabbed the stock. Yanked it toward himself, pulling the shooter's face straight into his fist and freeing him of the weapon. Stumbling, the man grunted but kept his feet. Tox rammed the butt of the rifle into the man's nose.

A rush of air behind him warned him of a second fighter.

Pain exploded in his side.

Tox groaned and drove his boot into the first man's knee. A loud crunch preceded a howl. Then an arm hooked around his neck, strangling him. Dropping the rifle, Tox thrust his elbow into a soft gut. When the second man doubled, Tox threw a back fist into his face.

The second attacker gargled a scream and released him.

Tox pivoted. Coldcocked the man, which drove his broken nose into his skull. He crumpled, moaning but not moving. Good enough. Tox snatched up the rifle and turned just in time to see the first attacker, barely stable on a broken leg, coming at him again.

Tox fired three shots into the man's chest. Before the attacker hit the ground, Tox was scurrying to the next building. He hesitated for only a second, then sprinted across the open area. Bullets chased him across the dirt as he threw himself toward Haven. He rolled and came up, slamming against the east wall.

There, dusty and bloody, Haven wilted. Her eyes morphed from sheer panic to desperate relief. Hair dirty and caked with sweat, she managed to smile around shaky breaths. But the dark stain spreading over the bottom of her shirt snagged his attention. She grimaced, holding her side. He went to a knee.

Haven grabbed his tactical shirt and pulled him closer. Her left arm snaked around his neck, her thin frame quivering, as she buried her face in his shoulder.

"Easy, easy," he whispered, realizing how hard and fast his heart pumped. Around them railed a fierce firefight. The team, even with limited weapons, was pushing back the enemy.

"I'm okay. I'm okay." Her breathing shuddered. "I'm okay."

He wasn't sure if she was saying it to reassure herself or him. But it would take more than words to convince him they were okay. That wouldn't happen until they were out of here and in a secure environment.

"Lie back. Let me see." He disentangled himself. "Maangi," he shouted.

Swallowing, she grimaced and eased onto her back. She lifted her hand, bloody and trembling, from the wound.

"What," he said as he drew up her shirt and inspected her wound, "are we taking turns getting shot now?" Relief knifed him. The injury was superficial. Just a graze—a long, angry one that might need stitches, but not life-threatening.

"Couldn't let you get all the glory," she teased.

The thud of approaching boots jerked Tox around, his weapon up. He angled to protect her.

Two men rounded the corner.

"Friendly, friendly," Cell said.

Maangi went to Haven and slid to his knees. "What's the word?"

"Graze," Tox said, moving back so the combat medic could work. Palms bloodied, watching Haven's pallor return to normal, his anger and adrenaline combusted. He punched to his feet. Pivoted to Cell. "How did you *not* see them?"

"Dude—"

"If you were paying attention, doing your job—"

"I was doing my job! Which, I might remind you"—Cell's face went red—"is *communications*. And if we hadn't been stripped of weapons, we might have had this solved in minutes!"

"We should clear out," injected Ram in a calm, reasoned voice as he joined them, sporting a rifle he'd obviously confiscated from a body. "Before more excitement arrives."

"Chopper's inbound. Five minutes," Runt said. "Rendezvous outside the village."

Tox rounded on him. "D'you know who did this? Have you seen their vehicles or faces?"

With a snort, Runt raised his hands. "There are a million terrorists out there ready to kill sunburned Westerners, and they all drive beat-up pickup trucks. If I had every one in my Contacts list, we might actually be turning the tide rather than losing so heinously. We—"

"We should get mobile," Ram snapped.

Prying his glare from Runt, Tox shifted to the scene at his feet. Haven draped an arm over her face as the medic applied a bandage over liquid stitches. "Maangi, we need to get moving."

"Not a problem," Maangi said, snapping off gloves and closing up his kit. "She'll need to get checked out at the base, but she's good for now."

Tox faced the team. "Move out!"

"Cole."

"Yeah?" He turned to her, hooking an arm around her waist as she stood.

She shuffled forward, wincing. "Look." She pointed down to the Elarabi home. The place that had put him too far away to protect her.

"What?"

"*Look.*"

This time, not only did he look, but he saw. A reminder. Maybe even a taunt. The crude symbol carved into the side of the home. Alec's symbol, the crown.

* * * *

SOMEWHERE OVER THE MEDITERRANEAN

She might as well be wearing a girdle, the way the bandage forced her to sit erect. Seated on a jet and flying to Baghdad, Haven felt the ache of every move and the twitch of every muscle. She'd only had some skin seared off, but it felt like she was dying. Cole had been shot through and through nearly three weeks ago and never complained. She didn't know how he did it.

Vigilant. Ever-ready. Always planning, thinking five steps ahead. Yet he'd tell her it wasn't enough. So it didn't surprise her that he refused to allow the team to remain in Egypt after being attacked in broad daylight.

"If they knew we were in that village, then they know we're at El Gorah," he'd insisted.

The others were sleeping as the jet raced through the night. But the burn in her side kept nudging Haven from a sound sleep.

Cole strode down the gangway and stopped, hands on the two aisle seats on the row in front of her. "You get it now, why I didn't want you here, right?"

Furious yet contrite, she met his gaze. Gave a nod.

"Things change in a split second. And I wasn't there. I couldn't protect you." Rawness thickened his words. "Having you removed from the team in light of Alec's threat *wasn't* personal."

"Wasn't it?" she asked. "Do you have any idea what it felt like to have Robbie and the deputy director come into my home and tell me you made a formal request to have me removed?"

He hung his head.

"You might as well have cut my heart out with a spoon and fed it to Alec."

"It was the only way I knew to protect you. To keep you from him." Cole swung around and lowered himself onto the seat beside her. He bent forward, elbows on his knees. "He threatened you."

"And he found me—us. While we were having dinner, Cole. What makes you think forcing me to stay in DC would be safe?"

"I could ask Galen to have you locked up in a bunker."

Haven stared at him, her mouth falling open.

"It was a joke."

"No," she said, breathing hard, her mind reeling. "You know I study biblical deception—Proverbs 26:18-19: 'Just as damaging as a madman shooting a deadly weapon is someone who lies to a friend and then says, "I was only joking."'" A lie—saying he was joking—to cover the truth. "Cole, you thought about it."

"Past tense. Two days ago. But I knew you'd never speak to me again."

Was that supposed to make it better? Make her less angry? "Among other things."

He raised his eyebrows, then sagged. "You've been in danger ever since I came back."

"I've also never been happier." Her heart stumbled over the words—but more so, his reaction. The way his gaze popped to hers, surprise etched in his blue irises. Did he have a single clue how gorgeous he was? Even when trying to be Sir Galahad and coming to her rescue. She might have never said the words out loud before, but she'd felt them all along. Even in the moments when she wanted to strangle his heroic self. "But never mind that—I'm angry with you right now."

Bent forward, Cole threaded his fingers. Stared at the industrial carpeting on the SAARC jet. "You're right—Almstedt's right."

"Hold on," she said, watching the way his jaw muscle worked as he stared at the floor. "Can I get my journal and write this down, Cole admitting I'm actually right this time?"

He breathed around a laugh, shaking his head. "And I don't want to take that break." He lifted his blue eyes up to hers. "And maybe it is smarter to have you here with me."

"Wait—let's be clear. You're saying I'm smarter?"

He gave a breathless laugh and sat back, swiping a hand over his face. "I think we all know that much is true."

The sound of hissing and a weird howl cut through the plane.

"Would you turn that thing off?" Maangi said, hitting Cell with a small pillow. "Some of us are trying to sleep."

"And some of us are trying to get clues on the mission, so we don't end up drilled full of holes like Gorgeous back there."

Cole's head came up. "Hey."

"I know—she's yours," Cell called back.

Haven couldn't help her smile.

"But, Gorgeous, if you want someone with a sense of humor . . ."

"You're about to be someone with a broken nose," Cole threatened.

"See?" Cell lifted both hands. "No humor."

Haven laughed quietly, grateful for the banter. Was this what kept Cole sane during assignments? She'd never forget being upright and scared one second as those men barreled into the village, then shoved onto her backside with stinging pain the next.

How did he deal with it on a daily basis? She'd thought being an analyst with the FBI had been rough. Cole dealt with flying bullets, terrorists bent on his death, and danger at every corner. He wasn't a desk jockey at Command. He was out there every day, confronting the demons, the terrorists.

"You okay?"

"I'd ask you to stop trying to protect me, but that's in your blood. Just give me the benefit of the doubt."

"You got shot."

"So did you."

He snorted. Then reached over and threaded their fingers. "I don't want—"

"—me here." She nodded. *Be brave. Be strong.* "I know."

He lifted her hand to his lips. Kissed her knuckles. "No. I don't want to hurt you again."

Breath stolen by his correction, she eyed him and was lured into the vacuum of his presence, the one that tore her from a relatively happy existence and vaulted her into a wonderful one. She had been successful before him. Happy. But Cole brought something to her days, to her life, that hadn't been there previously. It was impossible to stay angry with him. He leaned over and caught her lips with his, lingered, then kissed her again.

When he was called back to the front by Ram, Haven saw it—saw how having her around, in the field with them, hurt him. Stressed him. Strained his focus. Though she knew she shouldn't worry—God would handle the fight, would protect him—she did.

Her phone buzzed. She frowned, tugging it out of her tactical pants pocket. She saw the ID and frowned again. "Hello?"

"Kasey, how are you?" Robbie asked.

Weariness tugged at her. "Fine. A little sore, but yeah"—the bandage tape pulled at her skin—"I'm okay."

"And Tox?"

Indignation wormed through Haven. This was it—they'd said she wouldn't have to spy, but what was this, if not spying? "Upset, naturally. I think we both are."

"He still focused?"

"Of course." She sounded defensive. "He's a soldier. Let's trust him to do what he does best, okay?" As she hung up, a large frame folded itself into the seat across the aisle, and she met Ram's contemplative expression.

"You're reporting on him?"

Her heart staggered. "I'm doing my job," she said. Again, defensive.

"They asked you to spy on him."

"They asked me to let them know how things were going with all of us."

Ram adjusted his beanie and his gaze traveled up the aisle to where Tox leaned on the bulkhead to the conference room. "Be careful with that. Tox needs you, and we can't have his focus screwed when he finds out you're ratting him out to your superiors."

"I am most certainly not ratting."

"I'm not going to say anything, because you defended him." Ram's gaze hit hers. "But if that changes, so does my decision."

17

First Egypt. Now Baghdad and sitting in a cramped, smelly van with Cell and Wallace.

Tox shifted on the hard stool. "Wraith Three, give me a sitrep."

At his nine, Haven glanced at him. Headphones fed her a long-range microphone feed of what was happening at the hotel, so she could monitor verbal tones against body language. They were also recording so she could analyze it later.

"Wraith Two in position," Thor said, his voice deep, subvocalized. "Weather is clear. No joy on package yet."

Nodding, Tox eyeballed the feed coming from the camera at the back of the van, providing a wide-angle view of the Grand Sultan Hotel, where Taweel bin Mufti held court. Gabir Karim's right-hand man had unilaterally seized control of Karim's empire, finances, and family after Karim's death. All in the name of protection, of course. SAARC wanted to find out if there might be more targets or if there were more threats. Subtler ways to probe Karim's dealings and connections had all failed. No intercepted phone calls. No overheard conversations.

Until Ram pulled strings and Mufti agreed to meet under the guise of Ram posing as someone out for vengeance against those who hit Karim. Sunlight off the Tigris River threw dagger-like glares at the black Land Rover driving up Karada Dakhil toward the hotel. That vehicle held their only hope at getting information on Gabir's connections and future possible targets.

"Wraith Three, tighten up on camera one," a monotone voice ordered from stateside, where CIA, DoD, and SAARC monitored the mission.

"Roger that," Cell muttered, reaching to the side and adjusting a dial without looking. He was too focused on something else, his brow furrowed.

"Problem?" Tox asked.

Cell jerked his head up. "Nah." But he frowned again. "Just . . . getting some weird interference." He flicked another button.

"Expected," Tox muttered. "Mufti's ape over security since Karim's death."

"Yeah." The communications specialist didn't sound convinced. Which unsettled Tox.

A curse hit Tox's earpiece. "Wraith Actual, I have a problem," Thor grumbled.

Tox fingered his comms bud, pressing it farther into his ear. "Go ahead."

"Old lady just hung laundry up here. I'm losing my vantage and visual."

"You have to be kidding me." Fisting his hand, Tox tensed. If Mufti or any of his sentries posted around the Grand Sultan saw Thor moving, this mission would be a bust. And they'd have no chance to save future lives. And yet, not having a sniper protecting Maangi and Ram, who were headed into the proverbial lion's den . . .

Tox studied the area map. Rubbed his chin, irritated that his man had to relocate, and determined the next-best nest. He huffed. "Keep your head down and relocate to Yellow Four."

"Roger that. Relocating."

As minutes ticked by, Tox eyed the feeds, searching for any sign of Thor. If Tox, who knew to look for him, saw Thor, then so would Mufti's men.

"Vehicle One is one klick out," stateside droned.

Tox tensed because Thor wasn't in place. Too dangerous. He keyed his mic. "Slow that vehicle."

"Vehicle One," a voice said through the feed, "reduce your speed by five."

By five? That wasn't near enough.

"Too fast, too fast," muttered Wallace in warning.

Feeling the reins of control slipping through his fingers, Tox clenched his teeth. Eyed the red dot gliding all too quickly toward the hotel. And no eyes on Thor yet. "Two, sitrep?"

"Reached . . . Yellow . . . Four . . ." came Thor's panting breaths. "Two mikes till—"

Silence strangled the line and Tox's hair-thin patience. "Two?"

"Actual," Thor breathed, "we got anyone else on-site?"

Alarm shot through Tox and pulled him toward the monitors. "What do you see?" His gut cinched when the black SUV delivered Ram and Maangi to the hotel.

"Caucasian male. Early thirties."

Caucasian, here? "What's your location?" Tox gulped the pulsing adrenaline as Ram shook hands with Mufti.

"They look tense," Haven said, shifting the headphones so she could hear, eyes on the scene unfolding. "Voices are tight."

Made sense. In light of Karim's assassination, Mufti probably didn't trust anyone, even the men approaching him now.

"Alley behind—" Thor's curse severed his position. "Hey!"

Crack!

Pop-pop-pop!

Tox punched to his feet, smacking his head against the hull of the van. "Two! Two, report!" Eyes glued to the monitor, anxious for eyes on Thor, he froze.

"Not good," Wallace said. "I think Mufti heard the gunfire."

"Taking fire!" Thor shouted.

Tox watched helplessly as the security detail dove in, separating Ram from Mufti and hurrying their boss to safety.

"In pursuit," Thor huffed, frantic. "It's them—it's one of King's men. He just . . . painted . . . the freakin' wall."

Cell jerked around, brown eyes wide.

"Stay on it," Tox growled to the communications expert as he did a press check on his weapon. "Two. What's your position?" When he didn't get an immediate reply, he said, "Command—you have eyes on Two?" They had satellite access nobody should know about.

"Working on it, Actual."

Wallace jerked forward and tapped a screen. "There."

Disbelief nearly choked Tox when he saw two men sprinting down Karade Dakil, weaving through traffic.

Not good.

"Looks like someone's down at the hotel."

Tox swung his gaze to that feed, powerless to effect change. To do anything.

"This is Vehicle One. Packages are secure and we are exfiling."

So Ram and Maangi had gotten out alive. One problem solved.

"They're coming right at us," Wallace said.

Lifting an M4A1 from the van's rack, Tox made his plan: nail Alec's man and get out of Dodge. He threw open the back door of the van and hopped out. Aimed the rifle at the target, who hadn't yet seen them.

Crack! Ping!

The van door swung violently at Tox. Knocked him sideways. It took a second for what had happened to register. "Sniper! Take cover!" he shouted, his voice mingling with the *ping-ping-thunk-ping* rain of fire on their armored vehicle. He threw himself back inside, angling toward Haven to protect her. Cell was clawing his way toward the driver's seat.

Glancing out the flapping door, Tox keyed his mic. "Command, we are under atta—"

Boom!

The van rocked beneath the concussion of an explosion. Debris and smoke churned through the street. Tox blinked rapidly. About to shout for Thor to report, he saw a large frame coalesce in the thick black smoke outside the van.

The engine revved, and Tox braced for them to peal away.

Thor flew out of the smoke and into the van. Wallace yanked the door shut.

"Command, we need emergency evac." Tox slumped against the steel-reinforced floor, sliding from one side to the next as Cell spirited them to safety. Defeat pushed his gaze to the ceiling. He banged his fist against the floor and growled out his frustration. "Mission: failed."

OUR WAR-CRY IS THY HOLY NAME

— 1172 AD —
SYRIA

It is never enough, will never be enough. He must wear it to sate the cruel, unending thirst that ripples through his very being, burrowing into his soul as maggots consume a dead host. Though Saladin is not yet dead in body, he is lost in soul. It has been three years; I cannot see that there is hope for his soul. I grieve for him, as he is revered and respected, intelligent, and a warrior to be both feared and admired.

Tucking aside his leather journal, Thefarie lay beneath the stars, watching their bright display. Remembering. Though Heaven and the one true God were not literally "up," the concept of looking heavenward lifted the eyes of the tormented from their earthly plight, from the striving and desperation, from the hopelessness. For far too long, he had gazed upward, aching for what he'd lost. What he'd thrown away. Desperate to be free of this punishment, this cruelty.

He had been a fool, greedy for what he did not have, ungrateful for what he had been given. The Poor Fellow-Soldiers of Christ had provided him with perspective, purpose, one he had not known before to this degree.

And now, on this very earth and soil, another strove beneath a similar desperation—Salah ad-Din had become a slave to the irresistible pull over his heart and mind. One moment of use demanded two more. Two days required a month longer. It would never be enough.

For nearly two years, the enemy had grown in power and province, seizing lands and kingdoms in an ever-widening attempt to spread his beliefs. At least, that was what he said. Saladin had lost himself to the Crown of Souls and served one purpose: to do its will.

Thefarie removed himself to his tent and gained his cot, weary that he must once more watch this happen. Witness another fall to the crown.

Though he would never find true rest, it must be enough to give rest to his limbs and back. He surrendered to the night, to the exhaustion that plied him.

Not far away there came the crunch of leaves and rocks.

Ears attuned to the telltale noise, Thefarie coiled his hand around his dagger. The steps drew nearer. He stilled his breathing, listening. Waiting.

A faint whistle alerted him.

He snapped up his blade and opened his eyes. In a split second, his dagger glinted beneath the chin of a bearded man. Thefarie became aware of the scimitar at his own throat.

"I told you," another said, shrouded in the night, "he never sleeps."

Fierce, formidable eyes stared down at him, the expression so resolute that it dawned on Thefarie that this man gave no care for the steel pressed against his neck. "I would have your ear, Thefarie of Tveria."

"At the expense of my life?" he growled beneath the pinch of the curved blade that swept too elegantly around his throat.

With a flourish, the blade was gone, and the man stepped back. Effortless. Swift.

Coming to his feet, Thefarie returned his dagger to its sheath. "You are either brave or foolish to enter our camp." His gaze slid to the first voice, recognition ringing through his head as he eyed the man. "You are familiar to me."

"I would have your help, knight," the man with the scimitar said, deliberately drawing attention from the younger.

Yielding to the tactic did not mean Thefarie surrendered the fight. "You are a Saracen. Since when do we ally ourselves?"

"Since we have a common enemy." The older man, hair as thick and gray-streaked as his beard, inclined his head.

"Am I to know the name of the man who comes to me at night with a scimitar and veiled threats?"

"It was not a threat—I knew you would awaken with dagger in hand. You speak violence, so I preempted in your language." He parted his hands and rolled them outward, the sleeve of his long tunic drawing up. The light of the dwindling fire illuminated black marks on his arm.

Thefarie's mind scrambled, registering the tattoo and recalling it from years past. At the time, it had meant little, save that it violated the rules for knights.

"You once struck a bargain with a Saracen, did you not?"

"And I was betrayed for that slip in judgment." Since that treacherous night when the crown had been lost, not a day passed that Thefarie did not search for it and the men who had ripped it from his hands.

"It was no slip." Guilt hung heavy on the younger man's shoulders. He pulled aside his tunic and revealed a glaring scar in his chest. "Your reminder, *Dawiyya*."

"Bahir," Thefarie breathed, assessing his reaction. "Traitor."

"The mark is unfortunate," the older man said. "Bahir was not a traitor—at least not to you. He has been among our number since he was but a youth. We worked him into the inner circle of Saladin once we noted Nur's favor upon his nephew. What you saw as betrayal was in fact Bahir's cunning."

"There will be no more words between us, old man, unless you give your name."

"Why give what is already known?"

Thefarie lifted his chin, confused. He thought of how the older man had stolen into the camp without alerting any of the other brother-knights, sergeants, or soldiers. Was he truly *that* Old Man?

"Let us sit and talk." The old man lowered himself to the ground, just far enough from the fire for the light to strain but fail to reach him. "As a knight of the Poor Fellow-Soldiers of Christ, you are limited in the action you can take."

Thefarie perched on his cot.

"Is it not frustrating when your hands are tied by the Grand Master?"

Tension rolled through Thefarie, but he gave no answer. He studied the long, thin face before him. Lined with age, but more with wisdom and cunning. He was as mysterious and slippery as mist.

"Is it not even more frustrating when the orders that restrain you are higher than that?" A smile listed beneath his ash beard. "Eh, *Malaa'ikah*?"

Alarm pinged, but Thefarie planted a hand on his thigh and considered his guests. "That name has oft been attached to my person, though there are little grounds or justification. But I *am* a messenger," he said, filling his words with menace. "A messenger to carry out the one true God's purpose of protecting the Holy City and His people. That mission is not so different from yours. Is it, *Old Man*?"

This time, a knowing smile parted his lips and revealed yellowed teeth. "Very good." He nodded yet again. "*Very* good." He took in a breath. "Now that we are past that, I would have your help against Saladin."

"What do you want?"

"Information. Bahir"—his brown eyes flicked to the younger man crouching at the edge of the tent and watching outward—"says you are well equipped with connections."

"Though some of us move with haste, I have long been in these lands." It was necessary to be among the people, speak their language, understand their customs.

"Know your enemy," the Old Man said with a nod. "If you are able to help us learn his location, we can free my country from Yusuf's iron grip."

It was strange, yet good, to hear the man refer to Saladin by his common name among the Saracens, because that told Thefarie there was no reverence, that the opportunity existed to end the warrior, not join him. "Once, two years ago, I struck a bargain with a Saracen," Thefarie said, looking at Bahir, "and I was soundly betrayed. Why would I do it again?"

"Because I do not want the crown."

"Yet you must take the crown from him to end this unnatural rise to power and fame." Thefarie sighed. "It took the crown but one heartbeat on Saladin's head for his mind to be changed. If you—"

"I will *not*." Ferocity bled through the Old Man's eyes. "I seek not power. I have seen its corruption and destruction on my people. My life is but to serve and protect Syria."

Thefarie rubbed his hands together, thinking. Considering.

"Together, *Dawiyya*, we can stop this plague sweeping our lands. You want it. I want it. Let us work together."

Did it violate his oath to enter this agreement?

Thefarie gave a soft snort. Had he forgotten that while he might serve the Order now, he had a much longer, more permanent oath to uphold? This moment, this unrelenting storm called Saladin, would prove to be no more than a blink on the map of humanity.

"I will do this," he finally agreed. "But know that there will be no end to my vengeance should I again be crossed."

The Old Man inclined his head, his expression inscrutable. "If Yusuf discovers you are in league with us to assassinate him, there will be no mercy, for you or any other knight."

"I do not fear death," Thefarie said. "The crown must be returned."

"Why do *you* want the crown, *Malaa'ikah*?"

"The same reason you want Yusuf."

"To stop what's happening."

"Thefarie?" came the gruff voice of Ameus from another tent. "Are you praying in your sleep again, brother?"

The Old Man's grin returned. "Prayers will not rectify the wrong you have done."

The *thwap* of a tent flap drew Thefarie around, and he spotted Ameus peeling from his cot, dressed as required in shirt and breeches, shoes and belt. The ever-burning candle glowed behind him. Hair askew, Ameus frowned, his gaze skating around the campsite. "Who were you talking to?"

Thefarie turned, surprised—and yet not—to find the Old Man and Bahir gone. It had been a thrill and a fright to sit with such company. "One of the Nizari Ismailis." It felt good to finally say the name.

Ameus barked a laugh. "You jest!"

Thefarie sensed his brother-knight's gaze, the anxious expectation that he would laugh off the anvil he'd dropped. "Nay, 'tis no jest," he said, squinting to where a shadow flitted over the land in the distance. "And no less than Rashid ad-Din sat at my feet."

"Rash—the Old Man of the Mountain?" Ameus stomped up to him. "You sat with the Grand Master of the Assassins?"

18

"That was some piece of work."

Tox kept his face neutral, his anger roiling beneath the surface.

"I haven't seen a royal screw-up like that in a long time, not from you, Tox."

"Beyond my control, sir."

"Was it?"

He gritted his teeth.

"Regardless," Iliescu said, leaning into the camera feed, "it can't happen again. Mufti's got everyone and their brother looking for you after his guys caught you on camera with an M4 bringing Thor in."

Not exactly what he'd been doing with that weapon, but the point was moot. And he'd already told Iliescu what really happened in his debrief, then repeated it in his AAR. Saying it now would be a waste of breath.

"Get your team back on track." Iliescu sat back with a grunt. "We have to get King shut down before he puts more heat on us."

"Yes, sir."

"I'll update Rodriguez and Almstedt. We'll be in touch."

The screen went dark, and so did Tox's mood. He shoved his hands over his face and scrubbed his scalp with a growl.

"Sarge!" Cell burst into the room, face animated, the team hovering in his wake. "You have to see this. I found it again. It's unbelievable."

Not the best timing, but Tox couldn't pass up any chance to turn this disaster around. "Explain."

"Explain?" Cell's voice cracked, shaking his pasty white face. "Dude, there's no explaining this." He hefted a case onto the table as the guys took chairs. "We need Ghostbusters or something."

Tox's patience had worn thin. "Try that again," he warned.

"I heard it."

"Heard *what*?"

"That . . . *noise*. Same one from Egypt, but . . . different. Louder." His forehead wrinkled and he rubbed the back of his neck. "Same freakin' thing. Listen." He flipped the locks on the case and sprung it open. A few knob adjustments and the push of a button later, the recording of the failed mission hissed to life.

Tox gritted his teeth. He did not need to relive that mission.

Cell stepped back, folding his arms. Bit the nail of his thumb.

The feeds were dull and grainy, taunting him over missed intel on Karim's organization. He scowled at Cell, shaking his head. "Why are we watching this?"

Cell frowned at the box. "It was there. I *heard* it." He stalked forward. "Let me try . . ." More knob adjustments. Consternation knotted his brow. "It was just like Egypt, Sarge."

"Cole didn't hear it there like we did," Haven said. "He was down the hill with the Elarabi family."

"Right," Cell muttered. "So he didn't hear the ghost—"

"Did you cross paths with a black cat?" Thor taunted.

"Or step on a crack?" Maangi suggested.

"Not funny." Cell didn't look up as he continued messing with the machine, then paused, thinking about something. "Sidewalk seams don't count," he muttered and went back to work amid the guys' laughter.

"Stop," Tox said, but the recording started again. He hung his head and let it play out. There was street noise. The loose chatter of Ram first encountering Mufti. But nothing else. "Cell. I just got chewed out by Iliescu. If this—"

"I'm telling you—"

"Cell," Tox growled.

He straightened. "I—"

Howling, low and ominous, creaked through the room, filling it with hollow, empty whispers.

A chill shot down Tox's spine.

Hands like blades, Cell jabbed them at the machine. "*That*. Tell me that was just in my mind."

Exhaustion plied Tox. Surrender forced him to say, "Play it again," as he unfolded his arms. He pushed his gaze down so he could concentrate. He shut away everything else, listening to see if he could make out what was said.

Were there even words?

The feed ended.

"Again." Tox came to his feet and moved away from the table, wondering if distance helped.

Howling . . . whispers . . .

"It's indecipherable." Ram sat beside the speaker.

"But there are voices," Tox said, as much for himself as the others.

"Definitely," Maangi said.

"Where did it come from, Cell? How'd you—"

"I don't know!" Cell shrugged. "I was getting that interference in the van"—he nodded to Tox—"remember? I told you about it. I couldn't figure it out, so as soon as we hit Stryker, I got the box out and starting going over it. That's when"—he wagged his fingers in the air—"I heard it. *Freaked. Me. Out.* I fell over my chair." He angled his elbow, where a scab was forming. "Took a chunk out of my arm."

Maangi snorted. "How did you make it out of Special Forces school?"

"I'm just glad I was recording." Cell shook his head. "There's got to be something to this. I heard it in Egypt. Now here."

"Coincidence?" Thor shrugged, not really believing his own suggestion.

"Possible," Tox admitted. Though very unlikely. But still . . . "We should notify SAARC about this."

"Agreed," Ram said.

An hour later, back in the conference room with the team, Tox had Cell explain what had happened with the noise to Iliescu, who wasn't amused or interested in it. Almstedt and Rodriguez seemed mildly fascinated, the way someone might inspect roadkill.

Rodriquez shifted and drew out a folder. "What about King? Is he done with Karim? Should we put assets there?"

"As far as I can tell," Tox said as they briefed again, "Alec's hit everyone connected to the Karim mission." A shrug filled the gap as he thought through who might be connected to that mess. "Besides me, I can't think of anyone left. Three of his team died, and the rest are working with him. Unless he goes after clerks and admins, he's run out of bodies to put in the ground."

Robbie Almstedt leaned toward her camera. "I hope you're right, Sergeant Russell, because we've racked up quite a bit of trouble with the people he's killed."

"He's made threats against me and Cortes, but those were intended for nothing other than persuasion."

"I'd call his method of persuasion rather violent," Robbie said. "And can you guarantee that he's done with this . . . vendetta, Sergeant?" It wasn't a question. It was a challenge.

"I can guarantee nothing, ma'am. I am not Alec King." Not technically. But he was Alec in that he was a soldier who had killed enemy combatants. Who'd been given orders to take out targets. Who'd complied. Who'd believed years ago God had gifted him . . .

"Then we must continue to act with caution, and in doing so, we will ask that your team remain in place for the next twenty-four hours."

"Remai—ma'am. To what end?"

"That I cannot divulge at this time, but as our team works the intel, we need you accessible."

"For what?" he asked at the same time as Ram and Cell.

"Moving on." Iliescu assumed control of the briefing. "We're looking into something."

"We rerouting?" Runt asked.

"Negative. Just limited information to share at this point. We've been trying to piece together why King was in Stuttgart when he got into that altercation with the German." An image splashed across the screen. "This man was seen with Alec in the Neue Staatsgalerie museum. Their meeting went undetected until we unearthed a selfie by a visitor. Today we identified the man as Frenchman Henri Barre."

"Is he important?" Ram asked.

"He's the CEO of a shipping conglomerate, Mattin Worldwide, which specializes in large luxury pieces."

"Artifacts?" Maangi asked.

"Possibly, but unproven. Our agency has long tried to prove that Mattin also controls—through threats and attacks—the shipping lanes in and out of the Middle East and Asia."

"Why haven't you intercepted him?" Tox asked.

"Barre is a face, that's all. The power players behind Mattin—they're hidden. He's their mask. We have to get under that mask before we can move. That Alec King met with Barre is . . . unsettling."

"Most everything he does is unsettling," Cell shot back.

"It may be," Almstedt interjected, "that King is looking to expand his empire. Whatever his purpose, we can't let him proceed, since he's lost his footing. Too many years as a soldier fighting bloody battles have taken their toll. He's a lost cause who needs to be put down before he can do more damage."

"Pardon, ma'am," Thor said, "but you're speaking to five grunts who've spent a decade or more fighting bloody battles. Does this make us lost causes, too?"

"Don't you turn this against me, Thorsen. You know full well what I mean," Almstedt bit out.

"Back to King." Like an attack dog that didn't stop until he fulfilled his last command, Iliescu lifted a paper. "We'll look into Mattin Worldwide, but until then, stay put. As Almstedt said, we may have something in Afghanistan that needs your attention."

"No," Almstedt hissed, with a glowering look. "I didn't mention that, Dru. Hasn't been cleared yet."

"Oh. Sorry." Iliescu might've apologized but there was no contrition in his expression. He'd dropped that information on purpose.

"Wha—"

Low and out of sight of the camera, Tox's hand flashed out. He silenced Cell, who wasn't keeping up.

Almstedt seethed. "Sergeant, we will be in contact within the next twenty-four to thirty-six hours. For now, stay low. Get some rest."

The feed ended.

"So, rest." Haven looked relieved.

Tox's smile never made it past his lips as he turned to Cell. "Power up your computer."

Cell's grin was a mile wide. "Afghanistan?" His fingers flew over the keyboard.

"Listen up," Tox said to the rest of the team. "I suggest that if you haven't had rack time in the last twenty-four, grab some now. Everyone else, shower up and eat."

"Should you—we be doing that?" Haven asked, bobbing her head toward Cell's quick fingers on the keyboard.

Behind her, Wallace waited. He'd been unusually quiet this mission. Tox wanted to be glad, but it unsettled him not to have the agent in his face every second.

"Iliescu said Afghanistan—"

"Yes, but Robbie—"

"Iliescu named it because he wanted us searching it." Tox admired her tenacity. Always had. He guessed that was how and why she was his now. "The sooner we get the 411 on a situation, the more time we have to plan and be intimately acquainted with it."

"What situation are we getting a handle on?" Haven asked.

"It'd be my guess that something's blowing up in A-stan," Tox said, noting Ram pecking away on his phone, searching—no doubt—for trouble. Tox wouldn't mention to Haven that if Iliescu wanted them digging now, that increased the likelihood of it being a very bad situation. For now, rest and relaxation. "Grab grub or a shower. Then rack time. We have no idea when they'll call us up." He nodded to Wallace, indicating he should rest up, too.

Once Haven and Wallace started out, Tox returned to Ram and Cell, who were bent over their devices. "Anything?" As he shouldered into the discovery process, he stole a peek at Haven, walking away with Wallace, who leaned in, smiling.

Cell huffed. "Nothing."

"I'll grab my tablet," Tox said. "More eyes on this, the sooner we'll figure out what's going on."

"Here."

Tox looked over his shoulder to where Haven stood, a small device extended toward him. Hesitantly, gaze bouncing to Wallace, who had a weary, *I give up* expression on his face, Tox took her phone. Glanced at the screen. Scanned the information. Then shrugged. "I don't . . ."

Haven moved closer, motioned to Cell's laptop. "Pull it up on yours."

With Tox calling off the URL, Cell input it. The screen filled with a news piece. Images scrolling across the top. Haven bent between them, reaching for the keyboard.

"Hey-hey-hey!" Cell growled like a dog protecting its bone. "Hands off."

Withdrawing with a smirk, Haven pointed to the laptop. "Play the video there at the top."

With a mock glare at her, Cell aimed the mouse at the arrow on the blackened video screen. This wasn't homemade like the Egypt video— this came from an Arab news service but had a British voiceover and captions.

Haven nodded. "A brutal murder was committed in this city not two hours ago at the hands of an American."

The video showed a small city of dirty shops and vendors. The camera crawled along the terrain, children chasing a ball down the pothole-laden space that served as the street. The voiceover switched to Arabic.

"Five men, believed to be American . . ." Fist near his mouth, Ram listened and translated. "Came in, shot an entire family, then"—he cocked his head and swallowed—"dismembered the father. They then left his limbs on the steps of four other homes."

"Son of a biscuit," Cell whispered.

But how had Haven known to show them this? "Why'd—"

"Back it up," she said, her color a little pale as she watched Cell draw the time bar backward. "There."

He released it, and the video started.

"Stop!"

At her command, Cell snapped a finger on the track pad.

"Look," Haven said, her voice thick with emotion.

Tox leaned in a little closer. "Is that blood on the stoop?"

"I have no idea," Haven said. "But look at the field."

His gaze hit the semi-green field. "Oh." The grass stamped—or cut—into the shape of Alec's symbol. Seeing it felt like the world collapsed in on him.

"I guess she found it," Ram said, patting Cell's shoulder. "Let's get the names—the dismembered man and those who got a limb."

"Right. Let's just bypass the insanely morbid reality of that horrific act and get right to work," Cell mumbled as he worked, shaking his head. "This guy is one sick puppy."

Ram edged closer, his hazel eyes tracking over the structures. "Why this house? Who was he?"

"I thought you would've figured this all out by now, what with your connections." Tox stared at the small city. *What the heck are you doing, Alec?*

With a sidelong look, Ram said nothing.

"Gotta be someone really bad to get hacked up like that," Cell said.

"Keep hunting for answers. I'll be back." Pivoting, Tox headed to the showers. He just needed time to think, sort this nightmare. He went to the gear and grabbed his ruck.

"Hey, Sarge." Cell trotted up to him. "Think we could . . . I wondered if we could, you know, get better equipment."

Tox frowned. "Like what?"

"I . . ." Cell glanced away. "I, uh, thought if I could get a more powerful amplifier and radio, I might be able to, you know, work out that crazy sound thing." He shrugged. "Whatever it was or is."

Tox shouldered his ruck. "If Cortes found the right feed, and I'm pretty sure she did, we'll be wheels-up by morning. No time for new equipment. Sorry."

"Could you just request it? I . . . I can't figure that thing out unless we get better equipment."

Tox strode toward the showers. What was Alec doing? Why wasn't he stopping? He'd killed enough, hadn't he? Equalized the balance of the world, or whatever he was trying to do with the Karim vendetta.

"Sarge? . . . 'kay. Thanks for listening."

Guilt harangued him as he stepped into the tiled shower room. He couldn't bring himself to talk anymore. His mind was worn out, his body exhausted. He stalked past the first two stalls, the middle occupied by Thor, and entered the last one. He lined up his shave kit, bringing some order to the chaos that engulfed this mission. But as he set out the razor, his mind slipped back to the feed.

Dismembered . . .

Was Alec really dismembering people? His gut roiled at the thought. That didn't make sense. Then again, had any of it?

Yeah, it had. Killing people who committed heinous acts but were somehow protected by some law or justice system . . . People got angry when they felt powerless to effect change.

But with his training and expertise, Alec wasn't powerless.

Neither was Tox.

They were skilled operators. Trained in tactics. Weapons. Krav Maga. Trained in a million different ways to kill someone—without a gun or knife. Trained to assess a situation and figure out the best solution. Trained in the art of warfare. Trained in death.

They were good at what they did. Alec, Tox, their men. They were deadly.

Did they come home with baggage? Absolutely. No sane person could witness what they saw every day in the field, or carry out the acts of violence they were tasked with, and not come away affected. It was what they did with said impact that made the difference.

There had been so many times Tox felt like he stood on the precipice of a thousand-foot cliff, the powerful claws of gravity, leaden with guilt, groping for his boots. For his life. So many times, he'd wanted to jump. Let it take him. Be free of it.

Hand on the wall, he braced himself. Against the memories. Against the torment. He didn't know what held him back, what kept him tethered to this life.

Haven.

He hadn't wanted to jump in the last six months—a long time.

179

It seemed like forever with her near him. She'd anchored him to . . . goodness. To light. To God.

Tox snorted. Since when was he anchored to God? Wasn't he farther from Him now that he saw the goodness in Haven? Heard the truth from Chiji? He'd sure felt farther from God. More aware of his failings. His shortcomings. His wickedness.

Am I so different from Alec?

Alec had gone off the deep end. Had he not processed some wound and let it eat through what good remained in him? Had something in him broken? Snapped?

His wife, Rachel.

They separated. Divorced. Then she died with their daughter in a senseless car accident. Was that the catalyst for this madness?

How would Alec justify this one? Alec had violated their code by killing like this. He'd willingly or unwillingly—didn't matter now, did it?—drawn a line in the sand. The Special Forces Creed.

My goal is to succeed in my mission—and live to succeed again.

They did that well—justifying actions. The mission. Sometimes, answers weren't clear. Sometimes, the line between right and wrong blurred. But they were soldiers. They followed orders.

Which could be a crutch. Rarely did they have all the pieces of a puzzle that required them to perform without question.

And then there were times a guy felt he had to do something that went against his own moral compass for the greater good. Like the mission Tox carried out that cleared the team. Expunged the charges related to the death of President Montrose.

Brooke.

Eyes closed, Tox fought the crush of memories. The lies. The justifications. Her blood on his hands. He slid down the wall and crouched, fighting the images. Her face. The vow she'd extracted.

"Cole?"

He punched to his feet, mind warping back to the present as he blinked at the person in front of him. "Haven." He checked the stall where Thor had been and found it empty. "What're you doing here?" At least he hadn't undressed yet.

"You looked lost a moment ago."

That was her counselor voice. She was reading him again. "Yeah," he said, knowing that trying to lie to her was futile. "Thinking."

"About Alec?"

Among other things and people. Instead, he managed a nod.

She drew closer, and awareness flared through him. "I'm worried about you."

He frowned. "Why?"

"You think you're like Alec."

"I am, in nearly every respect."

"Except your name, social security number, and . . . looks." Her smile was beguiling and distracting. Just as she'd intended, no doubt. "*You* are different, Cole. You know right from wrong, and you let it guide you. Friends like me and Chiji give you advice, and you listen."

"Chiji's not here." It surprised Tox how angry that made him.

"Maybe not in person, but he's here." She tapped her heart. "Even if you don't agree with our thoughts or advice, at least you think about it. Consider it. Weigh it."

Only as her gaze bounced to his chest did he realize he was missing his shirt.

"You even look to the Bible for guidance. Alec is looking to no one but himself. He's in a rage, driven by a thirst. We all have that thirst, but what we do with it, how we fill it—that's what makes the difference."

Thirst. Yes. There was a thirst. Deep in him. How had she known? Did she understand how powerfully it drove him? But . . . maybe she wasn't talking about the same one. "What thirst?"

Haven gave a small smile. "For God."

He sniffed and shook his head.

"Seems too easy, doesn't it?" She smiled again. "We argue against it or run from it. When we run, that's when the thirst grows. When we pour toxic"—he winced at the use of his moniker—"things in there instead of filling it up with healthy relationships with God and friends. God . . ." She sighed. "God isn't the way we've made Him out to be, some ambivalent god. We rip control of our lives from Him, demanding our way, but then we scream at Him when we screw it up or something goes wrong. It's hard." She nodded. "So hard to look inward, to admit there is a darkness in us that wants to be free, that wants our own way. To be honest with ourselves." The warmth of her fingertips against his arm was light. Yet fiery. "You're not him, Cole. Please stop thinking you are. Don't let him get in your head—he wants that. He wants to drag you down with him."

That was something he hadn't considered. Alec taking him down, but . . . "Why? Why'd he pick me?"

Haven shrugged and pursed her lips. "You were in the same unit?" He nodded.

"But he hasn't tried to kill you. Well, despite sniping you with expert precision"—her gaze dipped to his shoulder wound, still pink and fresh, as her fingers traced a path across his heart to the marred flesh—"which you believe was a message, not a kill shot. Yet you were part of keeping Gabir Karim alive, ultimately. Though you were in the trench with him and didn't like the stand-down order, you obeyed."

Did she realize it was hard to think with her touching him?

"What better way to get even than to destroy the hero *he* wanted to be. The hero you are."

"I'm no he—"

"To make you into himself." She hunched her shoulders. "I don't know. Maybe he's going through the inverse—believing *you* are the same because he sees the *good* in you."

Yes, he liked that better. It felt . . . positive. "He keeps calling it a mission from God."

"He's speaking to the good in you, because he knows that with you, he needs to say something that will resonate. And you have a high moral code."

"But what if he really believes that—that it's a mission from God? You even said he did."

Haven's fingers pressed against his face as she met his gaze. "What matters is what you believe."

Which was great. Because he had no idea right now what he believed.

"Is that what you believe? That God is having him chop people to pieces?"

"No." But . . . "Yes—maybe." Tox shook his head. "I don't know."

"Tox!" Ram shouted from the main area. "Incoming intel!"

"On my way," he called, his gaze on Haven. What must she think of him that he couldn't answer that question? That he couldn't outright condemn Alec? "Please . . ." He sighed, not sure what to ask or say, so he just grabbed his shirt. "I'm needed."

"Hey." Haven's fingers against his face firmed, pressed. "You're not him."

Hungry to believe that, he kissed her. "Maybe, but I am the only one who can help him. And I won't give up until I've tried." He spun and headed out, knowing full well that if Haven knew the truth about his dark side, she'd never speak to him again.

19

Cole was sliding down a dark hole of self-condemnation, especially after the failed mission in Baghdad, and wouldn't allow anyone to throw him a lifeline.

As they climbed out of their vehicles at the village where the man had been dismembered, the team took their time, preparing, planning for an effective mission to gather information. Find out what brought Alec King here.

Geared up, Cole slung his rifle over his shoulder so it straddled his pack and spine. Could she break through that stubborn wall that held his guilt and irrational beliefs intact? Before he surrendered and gave Alec King what he wanted?

He wouldn't do that, would he? He wouldn't give in to Alec's insistence and join him, right?

No, Haven didn't buy it. Cole was too torn up right now about seeing his friend go down this path.

"You okay?" Levi asked, touching her elbow as they stood back from the team, now conversing with locals.

"No." Haven sighed. Then shrugged. "He's the best man I know, but he believes himself to be the worst. He sees himself as some . . .

184

monster." She narrowed her eyes, watching Cole, thinking how best to help him. "I don't know how to change that."

"You don't," Levi said quietly. "That's something he has to figure out himself."

She knew that in her head, but getting the message to her heart was a different story.

"Incoming," Maangi shouted, and their gazes swung upward. A large plane rumbled overhead. Haven tipped her fingers to her forehead to block the morning sun and get a better look as a payload dropped.

Her heart tripped. "What is that?"

"Good favor points," Levi said loudly enough for her to hear over the droning engine, then started toward it. "Come on—check it out."

What did that mean? The large crate thudded to the ground. The small parachute attached to it sagged over the crate and road.

"Hold up," Cole said. "Keogh—bring VVolt. Sniff it out."

"It's from—" Levi started.

"Someone I don't know, and you just gave away our location to an unsecured—"

"He's with the DoD! I know—"

"Don't ever bring anything into my mission without going over it with me first."

The dog and handler were on it, the flaps of VVolt's snout waffling as he hauled in big draughts of scents around the equipment while the team held their collective breaths. After several seconds, VVolt turned in a circle and lay on the ground. Bored.

"Clear," Keogh said.

Cole exchanged a long look with Levi before finally nodding to Cell. The MWD handler moved toward the MRAP, where the dog got a reprieve from the heat and sun. It was a nice change to have a Mine-Resistant Ambush Protected vehicle as opposed to the beat-up trucks they'd had in Egypt.

Thor found a splintered corner on the crate and managed to pry open a side. They pulled out two large, black hard-sided cases. They were locked.

"What in James Bond is this?" Cell muttered.

Levi shouldered his way in to the group. "Excuse me." He entered a code on the first case, and the hard-sided top clicked open. Then he repeated it on the second. With a grin as big as Texas, he turned aside, facing their comms guy. "Will this work?"

Cell's eyes sparked with excitement. "How'd—yes! This is amazing! How'd you do this? Sarge couldn't—"

"I called in a favor. And I believe that noise you keep finding is important to figure out." Levi stood tall, pleased with his delivery and the response.

"What is it?" Thor asked.

"Spectrum analyzers," Cell said, his words tinged with awe. "This is some serious stuff—ten large at the bottom range." He shoved his hands through his short-cropped hair. "Dude! This is"—he shook his head—"sweet!"

"Power it up," Levi said. "Make sure that drop didn't kill them."

Cell did as told, his expression enlivened as colors danced before a green grid on a black background. He rubbed his palms together. "Come to me, weird ghost noises."

Tox and Ram stared at the equipment, disbelief in their reserved posture and expression. "I'm guessing you'll need time with this," Cole said to Cell.

"Yeah. Like, all afternoon time."

"You have fifteen." With that, Ram and Cole headed to a nearby house where a dark stain marred the wall and cement step.

"Dude, this is freakin' awesome," Cell said, crouched over the black cases. But then he closed them up. "Grab one," he said to Levi. "Help me get these back to the MRAP. I want to hook them up."

"Right now?"

"Yes. In fact, yesterday! Both those places where Whack Dude killed someone had that noise. I want to find it."

"You think it's here, too?" Haven hurried to keep up with their long strides.

"Dunno, but why not?" Cell climbed up into the back of the armored vehicle and set the cases on the seats. Soon, he was flipping switches and rolling dials. "Okay," he muttered, pressing a button, "we are recording"—he flicked a knob—"and searching."

186

Haven eased onto one of the seats, holding her knees. Part of her dreaded hearing that noise again, but another part was curious. What was it? Where was it coming from? Levi crowded in beside her. She gave him an appraising look.

"What?" he asked.

"Nice." She had to admit that much. "But how . . . ?"

"I know a guy who knows a guy," he said in a fake Italian accent.

With a shake of her head, she turned back to Cell. "You have a theory about what this is?"

Cell didn't bother to look up. "Yep."

"Care to share?"

"Uh," Cell droned as he adjusted the settings again. He flicked her a quick but apologetic glance. "Not yet."

For the better part of forty minutes, Cell worked without a word, scribbling notes, stuffing a pencil between his lips, then shifting back to the spectrum analyzers.

"Looks like time's up," Levi muttered as Cole and Ram headed their way. When Cole's gaze connected with hers, he motioned her out of the MRAP.

She met them halfway. "Everything okay?"

He pivoted and started back toward the villagers. "Yeah. I want you to come with us. There's a girl—nobody will let her talk. See if you can figure something out."

Haven skipped a step to keep up, her heart doing the same. "But I don't speak their language."

"But you do speak body language."

"But half of what I detect is done by comparing body language with spoken language."

"We'll get a 'terp who can help." Ram jogged ahead and pulled someone from the crowd.

Haven brushed loose strands of hair from her face, shoving aside her disquiet to focus on the task. "Do you have any more intel about the man Alec killed or his family?"

"Name only. Still no idea why he was targeted."

"Maybe someone in his family was the reason?"

"Unlikely. He was Alec's message, so he's responsible somehow."

She skirted a glance at the dilapidated structures around them. "And the homes that received a special delivery?"

"Extended family—we think."

Ram brought over a middle-aged man, who inclined his head. "This is Ismail."

Haven extended her hand. "Hello. I'm Haven."

He shook her hand, and they returned to the chattering group gathered around a stone-enclosed well.

Cole moved with confidence and determination, his blue eyes sparking with purpose. But then his brow crowded. "Look for a girl, somewhere between twelve and fifteen," he said in Haven's ear. "She's here somewhere. Possibly hiding or being hidden."

Ram, who stood even with Cole and had the same strong presence, asked questions of the group. There were at least a dozen men, maybe half that number of teen boys, and three women. All seemed anxious to tell their story.

"They say," Ismail began, leaning his head toward Haven as the men answered, "that since the Americans left, things were okay. Then a few months ago, things started getting worse."

A woman said something quickly, angrily.

"She says American soldiers treat their women bad."

His answer was short for how much the woman had said, and his grim expression betrayed his annoyance. "I think she said more than that," Haven suggested.

Curiosity ran thick and wide when Westerners were around, Haven knew, but this crowd seemed more . . . intense. There was an urgency.

A thirst.

Thirst for justice. Or a thirst for blood, she wasn't sure. But they wanted a response to what had happened here. At least, that was how it seemed to her. She thought of her conversation with Cole. This thirst, however, had a fervor rippling like a water moccasin beneath the smooth surface of a lake named Cooperation. It might seem docile and placid, but it could fly in their face in a split second.

A woman in a striped hijab started yelling at Cole and Ram. An older man thwapped her with the back of his hand as she ranted, then started talking over her. The woman got louder.

188

"What are they arguing about?" Haven asked the interpreter.

Ismail lifted his chin. "She says they are no good if they cannot stop their own soldiers from murdering. She says children are afraid at night, that they never should have let the soldiers come. He disagrees, says the Americans helped get rid of mujahideen and ISIL."

The confrontation continued, and another man joined in. But as she stood there, Haven had the uncanny feeling of being watched. Her gaze drifted around the crowd and then to a shadow lurking between two parked vehicles. A young girl. She wore a head covering, but she didn't seem old enough to have entered puberty, when girls were required to do so. They were covering girls younger and younger these days. The girl brazenly locked gazes with Haven for a long minute, then skated a look around before slowly coming back to Haven. Then a nod.

She wants to talk.

A man in the crowd barked, and Haven twitched, her attention momentarily snatched back to the arguing. The man, short and rotund, railed at the woman. They shouted, their bickering so fast and heated it made Haven's temples throb. Then the interpreter went to them. And gave her the perfect opportunity.

She moved to the vehicles and propped her hips against one, pretending to be tired and nursing a headache.

Cole glanced over and started toward her, brows knotted in concern, but Haven gave a quick, subtle shake of her head. He hesitated, confused, then he must have seen the girl. His shoulders squared, and he eased away.

Would the girl come forward? She had an eagerness about her, but it wasn't like most here. This was tinged with hope, maybe some fear.

"You American?"

Haven glanced over her shoulder, surprised at the English.

"No. No look," the girl snapped, but Haven had noted the terror in her eyes.

"Yes, I am American," Haven said, locking onto Cole, who had not stopped watching. He must've seen the tension, because he frowned. His gaze seemed to ask if she needed help. Surreptitiously, she held up a hand to stop him.

"They kill uncle because he hide ISIL."

"Who killed him?" Haven asked, considering the angry group a few yards away.

"A man, American soldier."

"How do you know?" How could the girl even speak English?

Haven felt something against her hand and stilled.

"He say give you."

Heart thudding, Haven curled her fingers around whatever the girl had passed on. Should she look at it now? Or wait until the girl had left? "Are you safe?"

But there was no answer.

"Do you need help? We can help you."

Only silence met her questions. She peeked to the side. Gone. The girl had fled. Haven turned a full circle, searching, but there was no sign of her.

"What'd she say?"

Haven jolted and spun.

"Easy," Cole said, bracing her. "She say anything about the dismembered man?"

"Yeah." She sighed, shrugging that gruesome word aside. "He was her uncle and harbored ISIL members."

Cole's gaze went hard. "You're sure?"

"That's what she said. And she ga—"

"Guys! Guys!"

Haven held out her hand, but Cole had already turned. He caught her sleeve and tugged her back toward the MRAP.

Cell's shout drew them on. "I got it—c'mere. It's here." His face and actions were animated. "The *ghost noise!*"

* * * *

Tox crowded the ramp of the MRAP with Maangi and Ram. "Go ahead."

With everyone's attention on him, Cell seemed entirely in his element. "I think I've figured out what the noise is, but first—give a listen. Then I'll explain."

Staticky noise rattled the interior, then a sinister voice gave chase. Two words were clear: *must pay.*

190

Ominous, considering a man had been dismembered.

"Whose voice is that?"

"How'd you catch that?"

"Who has to pay?"

"Pretty obvious, right? It's the dude they chopped up." Cell nearly smirked, glad he'd caught something they could decipher.

"Who's speaking?" Tox demanded. "What is it?"

"Yeah. Where'd it come from?" Ram probed.

"I think what we're catching is a variation or enhanced form of a ghost skip." Nodding, Cell folded his arms. Because that should answer all their questions, it seemed.

Thor scowled. "Okay, Einstein, pretend we're normal Special Forces soldiers, not an annoying know-it-all like you."

Cell sighed. "Okay." He held out his hands, apparently unable to talk without them. "A ghost skip is an echo-like signal that repeats only a portion of a radio signal."

"Radio signal? Whose radio signal?" Ram asked.

"Well . . ." Cell gave a nervous laugh. "That's a bit tricky, and I think I'd rather reserve speculation—"

"Just tell us what you're thinking, Purcell." Tox gave him a nod.

Cell blanched at the use of his full name. "I . . . I don't know. Not for sure." He slumped against the seat. "I have no idea where it's coming from or why it's there. I mean, I could guess, but that's all it'd be at this point. I've only had this equipment for, like, two hours."

Thor huffed.

"Easy," Tox said, then focused on the comms specialist. "Tell me more about this ghost skip."

Cell bounced his head from side to side. "Well, that gets tricky, too, because research is in its infancy. Theories—you technically shouldn't call them that yet either, because they're still forming—might explain one thing but not the other. And if I get something wrong, you'll be all up in my face like, 'Dude. Why'd you lie to us?'"

"Spill it," Maangi ordered with a growl.

"Just remember that you asked for it." With a shrug, Cell launched into his explanation. "Radio signals are sent out, and they might pass through the ionosphere, then be ducted in the magnetosphere.

That could be out to as far as several earth radii over to the opposite hemisphere. Then they're reflected on top of the ionosphere. Round-trip time varies with the geomagnetic latitude of the transmitter. But then there's also—"

"But why are we hearing them?"

"I'm guessing here, but maybe it's because they get"—he shrugged—"trapped in magnetic field-aligned ionization ducts. After being trapped, they can propagate to the opposite hemisphere and end up reflected in the topside ionosphere. That's when they run along the duct, leave it, and end up here, where we pick it back up."

"Cell, I'd ask you to repeat that in English, but I have a feeling I'd still be lost."

"You probably would," Cell snarked back to Thor.

"You think this signal is King's?" Ram asked.

"Yeah." Cell bounced his shoulders. "I guess. I mean, I can't know for sure. Not yet. Maybe not ever, technically, but—"

"So," Tox said with a heavy breath, "you're saying the signal, some signal Alec put out, got . . . caught or trapped"—he waved toward the sky—"up there, somewhere, and then . . . ?"

"Returned."

"That doesn't make sense," Maangi objected. "King was here two days ago. I pick up a radio and speak into it—you hear me. Right then."

"True." Cell seemed excited again. "Radio waves travel around the world many times. In one second, some can even circle the earth seven times. You know how sometimes when you're on a radio, only part of a signal or message comes through? What happens to the rest?" He raised his eyebrows for emphasis. "It gets trapped. So King sends out the signal two days ago, it gets trapped, then we're listening and get part of it back."

"But every time? Every time he hits a place?" Maangi scowled. "It doesn't make sense that he's sending a signal and part of it's getting lost every time, waiting to be found."

"Could something be interfering with the signal?" Thor suggested.

"Hey, look." Cell scratched the back of his head. "Like I said—it's new to me, too."

Tox rubbed a hand along his jaw, scruffy after a few days without a shave. "So he's sending a signal. But why? To who?"

"Beats me, man," Cell said. "I just read the signals."

"How do you even know this?"

"Well, it's not *known*," Cell reiterated. "It's *speculated*. The phenomena are fleeting and non-repeatable, so our understanding of how the magnetosphere interacts with solar wind is still evolving." He pointed to the devices. "But this, *this* is gold! When word about this gets out—"

"No!" Tox and Ram barked at the same time.

"No one talks." Tox scowled, meeting each and every gaze to make sure his meaning was clear. "Not to anyone about this ghost skip, or whatever it is. Not about our mission."

Tox headed away from the MRAP, scanning the city, and heard Ram join him. "Radio signals . . ."

"Yeah. Bugs me, too."

Tox slid on his ballistic Oakleys and scanned the road, spotting Keogh and VVolt working patrol. "Alec wouldn't use anything that could be traced. And why would he come *here* and use a radio? Who's he contacting?" He pointed to the people gathered by the old well. "They said he came in, went straight to the man's house, and killed him. Cut him up and went to four other houses. No hesitation. Alec knew exactly who he was after and where they lived."

"So . . . maybe he's contacting someone? Verifying targets?"

Tox mulled the thought. Unable to discount it wholly, he winced. "Could be." But he doubted it.

"Sarge, this could mean we're getting closer to him. And faster." Cell sounded hopeful as he came up behind them. "We're catching up."

That thought, that possibility thrummed through Tox. Alec had been here two days ago. . . . "How long do skips last?"

"Well, normally only three to six days, so I think the reason we were able to make out words is because the signal is newer, fresher."

"So you didn't need the equipment?" Wallace asked, the rest of the team grouping up again.

Cell snorted. "I definitely needed the equipment. I wouldn't have found it otherwise, and I probably couldn't have deciphered those words."

Tracking Alec, using a signal trapped in some invisible sphere . . .

"What's wrong?" Haven asked. "This is good news, right? Cell figured out the noise."

"I like this girl." Cell held up a finger. "And that should be *maybe* figured out the noise."

"But figuring out how to use that to track Alec . . ." Tox turned to the comms specialist. "Can you do that? Use it to find Alec?"

"Oh." Cell's expression fell. "That I don't . . . Track? Not so much, unless we find a way to do a wide—massively wide broadcast. At this point, all we can do is verify he's been somewhere." Wariness crowded his features as his brown eyes traced the equipment. "I'd have to pin down his signal, maybe even the source, and I'm not even sure that can be done, but then I'd have to find the frequency and—"

"So we're seriously buying this?" Thor asked with a disbelieving laugh.

Tox considered him. "You have another idea or explanation? Or a better idea to find Alec? Besides waiting for more bodies?"

Thor held Tox's gaze evenly, a twitch in his cheek saying he very much wanted to argue. But he held his tongue.

"And aren't we past blowing off unusual and supernatural explanations, what with the missions we've done?" Ram asked. "We just need to accept our purpose. We're working with SAARC. That means the unexpected and unexplained."

"Exactly—unexplained," Thor said. "Not supernatural."

"If that helps you sleep at night." Ram slid his gaze to Tox. "We have resources to help us with this stuff, experts we've worked with before."

"Wait." Cell gave a toothy grin. "Does this mean we're calling in the hottie archaeologist?"

Ram glowered. "That's my sister you're talking about."

"Right." Cell was unrepentant. "But she *is* hot." When Ram lunged, Cell leaped out of reach.

"Think he's right?" Maangi asked. "We *are* dealing with an artifact."

"It makes sense." Ram settled back, arms folded, eyes glinting with intensity. "SAARC got pictures of King wearing something."

"A crown," Cell muttered.

Maangi indicated the new equipment. "Then these signals . . ."

Tox didn't want to think about it, but there was no getting around the hard-boiled truth that they were dealing with another artifact. If all indications pointed north, no reason to go south. *Keep it simple, stupid.* He shared a long look with Ram, knowing that roping Dr. Cathey and Tzivia into this all but guaranteed a direction that, by Ram's conflicted expression, neither of them wanted.

"No coin," Tox said, muttering to himself, a lame attempt to believe that maybe things weren't . . . yeah. He couldn't even convince himself that Alec hadn't done this. But was there a real, legitimate reason? Harboring ISIL was bad, but kill-worthy?

"Maybe he ran out of time." Ram's answer was as flimsy as Tox's.

At the juncture where hard-packed earth became a footpath that arced in front of a half dozen homes, a man in a long kaftan trudged toward them, his arm draped around a young boy. Father and son? Both faces were dirty. Clothes grungy. Expressions wary.

Tox eased his hand to his leg holster.

"Uh—"

Silencing Haven, who'd seen the newcomers approaching, he scanned their clothing again—no strange bulges. Didn't look padded. Both were scrawny, garments too small. "Ram, Thor. On me," Tox said, moving toward the locals and noticing the father and son widen their eyes as Thor and Ram hefted their M4s at the ready.

Tox held out a palm. "Stop right there," he called in Arabic, lessons from his days as a Green Beret in A-stan and Iraq coming back hard.

"Just a kid," Wallace whispered behind them, most likely wanting to defuse the anxiety warbling like heat waves.

Tox didn't like holding a weapon on a child, but the kids in this region were raised differently. Some were given fully automatic weapons and IEDs instead of pencil and paper.

"'Just a kid'?" Maangi's soft mutter held frustration. "Had a cowboy friend whose team was blown up by a seven-year-old in a suicide vest."

A stream of fluent Arabic, unlike Tox's limited but effective ability, sailed off Ram's tongue, stilling the father-and-son duo. The father, his dusty beard shielding his mouth, replied quickly. Fervently.

Ram angled only his head toward Tox. "Says the boy drew something we need to see back there."

Behind the duo were shadows and broken buildings. Not exactly safe. "Thoughts?"

Ram's weapon hadn't lowered. "Not sure."

When the boy's hand lifted, Tox twitched. "Wait—"

A paper flapped on a rare, hot breeze that stirred dust and emotions. The simple offering seemed to mock their apprehension.

It's just a kid. Just a paper. Innocuous enough, distracting enough. But the reality existed: American soldiers were targets. They got bombed. With the murder of one of their people, it would make sense this village wanted retaliation. Revenge.

Reaching for the paper, Ram dragged his foot forward. Not a real step. He hadn't moved much, but he was within striking distance. Tox realized he held his breath. Their hunger to stop Alec was making them take risks.

Ram muttered his thanks as he stepped backward with the drawing. But they were still too close. If there was a bomb . . . they'd be shipped home in baggies.

A heavy huff made Tox skate a look at Ram, who handed him the paper, eyes on the father and son as he again thanked the boy.

The kid's brown eyes were on the drawing Tox held. Attention falling to the paper, Tox winced. His vain hope that this wasn't Alec, that he wasn't responsible, tripped and fell over the proof. Though there was a confused tangle of scribbling around it like any other child's chaotic depiction, the drawing revealed much. The boy had clearly sketched Alec's symbol in the middle.

Ram shouldered closer and tapped the page. "The father says this was on the outer wall of his house, painted by the guy who killed the victim. Villagers scrubbed it off."

"They didn't know about the field, I guess," Thor muttered.

"When your people are getting killed, you don't worry about grass," Ram growled.

"Show me," Tox demanded, then glanced over his shoulder. "Keogh."

The military working dog handler was waiting in the still-running MRAP, as VVolt needed cool shelter and water to avoid heat exhaustion.

"Show you what?" Ram hissed. "It's gone—washed off."

"The house."

Keogh and the Malinois trotted up, walnut eyes squinting in the sun with both pleasure and excitement.

"Take us farther in again." Tox nodded to the father and son.

"We'll patrol ahead," Keogh said, ready to be useful. He gave commands to VVolt and started after the father and son.

"Right back into the lion's den," Thor muttered.

Sweat dripped down Tox's temples and spine as he trudged through the town, scanning doors and windows, stealing glances at the MWD team. He found comfort in their presence, but it wasn't a foolproof guarantee. This entire situation, luring them away from their vehicle, was standard MO for an ambush. But he believed enough in this man's story to follow him. To take the risk.

So desperate for this not to be real, not to be Alec's doing.

"Cole," Haven called as she came up on his left.

Without stopping or answering, he sandwiched her between him and Ram, and away from a local.

"Look," she said softly.

He glanced in her direction. When he saw what was in her hand, he stopped short. A challenge coin. "Where—?"

"The little girl. She talked to me, remember?"

"Why didn't you tell me she gave you that?"

"I tried, but Cell called us away, and we got distracted with the ghost signals."

"Hold on to it," he muttered, unwilling to lower his weapon as they eased around a corner, scanning the narrowing path.

The building at the far end of the alley stood in a puddle, the result of the locals trying to scrub away Alec's presence. But like the stain Alec was, the symbol seeped through the plaster and glared back at them. Just like Alec had been doing.

"Why mark the field and the house?" Ram asked. "*And* leave a coin?"

Tox shrugged. "Overkill."

"Yeah, he does that well."

Keogh and VVolt had reached the house. The Malinois went up on his hind legs, his right front paw resting on the wall as he sniffed the mark, apparently drawn by the smell of the paint—an accelerant. He dropped back down, the sides of his snout flapping as he took in scents along the base of the hut. Long draughts. Short draughts. Long exhales and snorts. In, out. Taste, mull.

He veered right, nose all but buried in the sand.

Then switched left. Right. Left.

When Keogh snapped up a fist, signaling an all-stop, Tox's nerves screamed. He waited, motioning the others back. They kept eyes on VVolt as the Malinois did his thing. Anticipating an explosion. A concussion.

But VVolt lifted his head and trotted to the other side of the path, then hiked up his leg and relieved himself at the corner of another house. A nervous waft of chuckles evaporated the tension.

Keogh shrugged and motioned them forward.

Tox shook off his dread and started for the house. VVolt might not have gotten a hit, but he increased their chances of coming home alive. MWD and handler patrolled between buildings, toward a small field that looked like a dog with mange, grassy in one place, barren in another.

Turning to him, Ram sighed. "This—"

Boom!

Searing white exploded across Tox's field of vision.

20

Punched backward, Haven felt a superheated blast tear over her. Daylight winked out. Pain dragged her from the darkness. She lifted her head. Fire seared her corneas. She yelped, her own voice hollow, as if underwater. She blinked several times, trying to get her bearings. What had happened?

A shadow fell over her. Something clamped her upper arm.

She looked up. A shape shifted and blurred. Pain pricked her neck. The world again faded into oblivion.

* * * *

Attack!

They'd been attacked.

Slumped against a wall, Tox fought the effects. Struggling to clear his head, telling himself to get on his feet. Assess his injuries. The team. Hearing plugged, he squinted through the haze and staggered upward.

Haven.

Head and heart thundering, he climbed to a knee. Where was she? "Sound off!" he shouted to the team, his ears still ringing.

Thor and Maangi. Then Cell. Ram. What about Keogh?

"Wallace and Cortes are MIA," Ram called.

Tox scrambled to think, to find her. Where had she been? Behind him, right? Tensed beneath the pain pounding his skull, he scanned the smoky haze burning his eyes, making them gritty. "Haven!" His popped ears warped his shout.

What caused the explosion?

The bright light. Being flipped backward.

A bomb.

From where?

Thor and Maangi were rushing toward him, alarm plastered into their dirt-streaked faces. Half the buildings near the end of the alley had sustained heavy damage. The ones closer were missing chunks of wall, but nothing major. Good thing the villagers had been out near the well, arguing with each other, or Wraith would be dealing with casualties and fatalities.

Straightening, Tox lifted a hand to let them know he was fine. He spotted Cell hunched against a half-destroyed wall, blood seeping from his temple, with a glower that mirrored the fury roiling up through Tox. He worked to clear his hearing, nearly buckling when it did.

"Keogh," he said to Ram, whose left tactical sleeve was shredded. His arm looked like someone had taken a rake to it.

Ram was searching, too. No Wallace. No Haven. He turned, called out, "Keogh! Cortes!"

"Haven!" Tox swiveled his head. Scanned. Surged forward. Panic clawed at him. She wasn't where she'd last been. Where could she have gone? "Eyes out," he ordered. "Find Cortes and Keogh. Now!"

The five members of Wraith worked organically in a grid pattern, clearing the houses around them, then fanned out.

A curse seared the air. "Keogh!" Cell shouted. "Man down! Man down!"

Tox rushed forward, M4 pressed to his shoulder, unwilling to end up in a pine box on a C-130. As he climbed over a pile of cement, plaster, and rebar, he realized the debris had been the house marked by Alec's crown. When he stepped off the crumbled house, he saw the depression—several feet deep. Cell and Maangi stood at the perimeter. Dark spots stained the ground—blood.

Why weren't they helping? Tox hustled forward.

"Call off your dog," Cell bit out.

The dog's ears were angled back. Growling permeated the air. Bent over the mangled body of Drew Keogh, VVolt, haunches up, forepaws down, growled, daring Cell and Maangi to advance.

Keogh's chest rose and fell unevenly. His lips moved, but Tox didn't hear anything.

VVolt whimpered, then backed up to his handler, watching Wraith.

Cell and Maangi edged in carefully, slowly. They knelt.

Only as Tox cleared the rim did he see the extent of Keogh's injuries. Legs were gone. His left arm dangled by a tendon. Blood soaked into the unforgiving earth. He'd bleed out. Three limbs. Three men to apply tourniquets.

No time to waste.

Tox threw himself down into the pit, shrugging off his pack. His hand was already in his ruck, curling around his med kit, before his knees hit the ground.

Maangi and Cell hurried to apply tourniquets to the legs. The pain made Keogh thrash and howl, until he finally fell quiet and still. Alive, but barely. Unconscious.

"Keogh. Eyes open!" Tox barked as he worked on the arm. Tourniquet first. Then strap the arm to him so doctors could reattach it later.

"I'll look for his legs," Thor said.

Nauseated at the mutilated flesh, Tox continued working. Blood slicked his hands and gloves, making it difficult to twist the tourniquet tight. He gritted his teeth and closed his mind to the sweet, metallic scent that filled the air.

Ram was there, a strip of cloth tied around his own arm as he threaded a wide-bore IV.

Swiping the blood from his face, Cell shouted into his comms, "Wraith Three requesting immediate medevac to our location."

Blood squirted. Tox clamped his molars and twisted the tourniquet again, the torque cutting into his fingers. Finally the bleeding trickled off. Though Keogh was critical, Tox had seen soldiers survive injuries like this. It took a miracle, years of surgeries and therapy, but they survived. If VVolt hadn't patrolled off-lead and ahead of his handler, the Malinois would probably be dead.

"Losing his pulse," Maangi said.

Tox raced through options. "Keogh, stay with us."

His eyes fluttered. Rolled.

"Keogh!" Tox shouted.

"Thready. We have to get him out of here *now*," Maangi said.

Ram produced the stretcher. "Let's go."

As they loaded Keogh up to move him to an open area where the chopper could retrieve him, Thor returned. In his hands, he carried a bundle wrapped in a bag, dripping blood. "Only found one."

Then it hit Tox. "Haven and Wallace are still missing." His gut tightened. Would he find her in a ditch, too? Cell, Maangi, Thor, and Ram lifted the makeshift stretcher.

A local scurried up to help, then two more.

"Get him back to the MRAP," Tox ordered. "I'm going to find them."

"I'll help," Thor said, guiding one of the locals to take his place at the stretcher.

Tox nodded. "Don't wait for me." He keyed his mic. "Command, this is Wraith Six Actual."

"Go ahead, Actual. What is your situation?"

"We need that medevac—one critically injured. Two MIA."

"Copy that. Medevac en route. ETA in ten. Sending coordinates."

"Roger that. Team will rendezvous then circle back." Tox turned his attention to finding Haven and Wallace. "Ready?" he said to Thor.

Weapon up, anger blazing, he stalked back toward the passage that had blown. They climbed the mound of rubble. Up, over. They stuck close to the walls. Avoided doors. Ducked beneath windows. He didn't trust anyone right now. The damage was crazy, unpredictable, as evidenced by the demolished house next to another with chunks broken off yet stable. Then a third—a complete collapse, most likely from the concussion.

His gaze hit on something.

"Sarge!" Thor called, squatting at the very spot Tox eyed. A wall had folded in on itself. A boot stuck out from beneath it.

"Wallace."

"I'm here," the agent moaned, boot shifting. "I can't . . ."

"Easy, easy," Tox said, slinging his weapon over his back. "Any injuries that you can tell?"

"I . . . no, I don't think so. Just stuck."

Crouching, Tox grabbed the corner of the broken wall, grateful for the protection of his fingerless gloves. He nodded to Thor. "One . . . two . . . go." They lifted, the cement shifting in their hands. "Wallace, hurry. It's unstable."

Wallace shimmied out but stopped with a foot still beneath the wall. "Pants're caught!"

"Rip it!" Thor snapped through gritted teeth, his face crimson. Veins bulging.

"I can't. Won't give!"

"My knife," Tox said, shifting his right leg so Wallace could reach it. "Cut it free."

Wallace yanked out the KA-BAR and sawed at the material.

The wall trembled—so did Tox. A piece broke in his hand. The wall canted. Dropped. "Augh!" He caught it, but every muscle in his arms and shoulders shook. Still, he felt the grating cement in his hand, threatening, warning.

Wallace scrabbled backward. "Go!"

Thud! Whoosh!

Stunned, Wallace stared at the wall. Then his leg, which sported a nice gash but probably wouldn't even need stitches.

"Tox."

He pivoted to where Ram was jogging toward them, Keogh's blood staining his tac shirt and pants. "She's gone."

She. There was only one *she* with them. Ice shot through Tox's veins.

"Haven's gone."

203

21

Entirely disappointing. He had given Tox plenty of time to join him. To recognize that he was designed for this purpose, to be the blade of justice in a world gone horribly wrong.

How could Tox refuse? Why would he?

Alec rubbed his lower lip, studying the monitor.

"Sir."

He looked up at the burly frame filling the door. "What is it, Sagel?"

"It's done."

It wasn't what he'd wanted or intended. But it had become necessary. If men learned their lessons the first time, they would not have to suffer the wounds that came with relearning them. Being forced to learn them. Most men only needed the right motivation. The right trigger. But Tox was proving rigid and obstinate. Disappointingly arrogant.

"King," growled the diesel-engine voice of Jason Bollinger. "Check the news."

Alec's gaze flicked to the screen. A lovely journalist sat before the camera, prim and proper. Hair perfectly coiffed. Makeup expertly applied. He hit the volume button.

"—cre that took the lives of five local villagers. Among the dead is a man known to be connected to many ISIL attacks across the world. A man who publicly and brutally beheaded his own daughter for refusing to marry an ally.

"The man suspected in the death of Elarabi is also believed responsible for the killing of Gabir Karim and several top-level generals within the Afghan army. Men often deemed untouchable. While lawmakers and military personnel call this person a criminal and murderer, that is not the view of some on the street, some with boots on the ground." Her gaze turned to another camera. "Reporting from Kabul is Mel Caral. Mel?"

The screen switched to a man in a blue shirt with sweat stains. "That's right, Lila. Here at this forward operating base, this man, a purported Special Forces veteran gone rogue—"

"Hear that?" Bollinger said with a grin. "You're a rogue."

"—a hero. With me is a soldier, whom we'll call Shaw for the sake of this interview." Caral shifted toward the soldier as the camera panned, but they had concealed the man's identity by showing only his silhouette. "What do you think of this man who has gone outside the wire and confines of military code?"

"I say it's about"—*bleep!*—"time someone did something. Brass has us sitting on our hands, and we can't win the war sitting on our"—*bleep*—"and weapons."

"So you don't think he's gone beyond the law?"

"Sometimes in combat, the lines of right and wrong blur. It ain't pretty, but we can't let terrorists win. We can't play Russian roulette with the lives of our military or civvies, who are being heinously murdered while we stand by and play political cards."

The camera returned to Caral. "Earlier, I spoke with some Afghan villagers. Their sentiments are very similar. Frustration has built over the last few years as hands have been tied by political processes and government machinations. Ultimately, many feel politicians and armchair generals are playing games with their lives."

A woman in a pink hijab, face blurred, said, "He is a hero! He saved my family."

"We need more soldiers like this Soldier Savior," a man said, his face hidden as well.

"Soldier Savior? Why do you call him that?" Caral asked.

"He wears a crown," the man said, holding his hands above his head.

Satisfaction massaged Alec, and he muted the television. They got it. They understood what he was doing.

"Soldier Savior," Sagel chuckled. "Nice."

Still. Alec hadn't meant for word about the crown to get out. What if someone came after it? Tried to take it from him? Steal it?

His eyes drifted to the pedestal to his left. He let his gaze caress the amazing craftsmanship of the gold-overlaid crown. There were empty braces that at one time had held gems.

The genius of it. The brilliance. He felt it calling. He didn't need gems, didn't need it to be beautiful. It was *blessed*. He was blessed wearing it.

No, that was just the itch. To wear it. Use it. And the itch grew, because he hated sitting still. Hated being inactive. There was too much to do. Too much to change. And there was only one way that would happen.

"Their voices must be heard." He nodded, an idea forming. "From now on, make sure that journalist gets wind of what we do. If we can build support, they will be less likely to try to stop us."

"Anger the people, they get a riot," Sagel said, his head bobbing. "Smart."

Holstein stepped in from the other room. "Looks like one of Russell's men won't make it."

The momentary high of his fame and the support from the people faded as Alec came back—as he always did—to Tox. "Which one?"

"The dog handler."

Sadness pulled at Alec's mood. He frowned. "And the dog?"

"Fine, I guess."

"Good. I like that dog." But if Tox could not come to the light, Alec would be forced to make him take that journey. For his own good. "Sagel."

"Sir?"

"Send the message."

* * * *

206

NIMRUZ PROVINCE, AFGHANISTAN

"Augh!" Tox punched the air, wishing it was Alec's face. Keogh was fighting for his life. Haven was missing!

He gripped his head and paced. Harnessed the anger and frustration. He was going out of his mind. They'd spent the last several hours searching the small city, knowing the villagers could be rerouting Haven. Moving her from one place to another.

His vision jounced. He needed water and food.

No, he *needed* to find Haven.

Futility tightened his muscles. Poked at his nerves. "God . . ." Throat dry, he tried to swallow. Couldn't. Where was Chiji when he needed him most? A smooth insertion of Scriptures and a poignant Igbo phrase would help Tox get his head on straight.

One admonishment that Chiji constantly dished out came rushing back to him: *"Do not turn away from Him in your greatest need, Ndidi."* They'd been on a cliff, staring into the silent night. Chiji's dark eyes had practically glowed beneath the moonlight. *"Turn to Him."*

"I have no idea how to do that."

Tox snorted. Pathetic. That'd been two years ago, and he still didn't know how.

"In Exodus, it says God will fight for you. That you must only be still." Chiji smiled. *"Get out of His way, so He can work."*

"But will He?"

Or the time they'd been practicing kali beneath the unrelenting sun and Tox had been struggling—yet again—with his circumstances. His mistakes.

"We may suffer the consequences of our actions, but God does not have a giant stick waiting to strike you over the head."

"Sometimes I wish He would."

"You and me both."

A smile pulled at Tox's stubbornness. But this . . . what was he supposed to do? Two missions—Egypt and this village—and they'd both failed. The first one ended in nothing but Haven getting hurt. This one ended with Haven being taken, and Keogh in critical condition.

Should've listened to my gut instinct and made her stay stateside.

Now she was out there, God only knew where. Was she alive? "God, please . . ."

Ram rounded a corner. "Anything?"

"Nothing. You?"

"Negative." His sleeves were shoved up, probably to push the blood stains out of sight as he worked.

Other than Keogh, they'd been lucky to come out pretty much unscathed. Had Alec intended that, or was God watching over them? Either way . . . "I'm going to kill Alec."

His secure phone beeped, and he tugged it out. Glanced at it. Numbers spilled over the screen. *What?* Confusion struck him, but then his breath caught. The numbers weren't random. They were structured.

"What is it?" Ram asked.

"I think . . ." He thumbed the numbers into an app on his phone. Ram shouldered in.

When a map pulled up and started isolating a location, Tox's hope sprouted. "GPS coordinates."

"Haven? But how? Who?"

"Who else is playing roulette with our lives?" He studied the coordinates. "Less than an hour north."

"Ambush?"

"Probably." Tox clenched his fist. They only had one vehicle. He keyed his mic as he stalked back to the MRAP. "Wraith, RTB."

* * * *

A sharp cry snapped Haven awake. Darkness pressed in on her, and a sudden gust of air slapped her with a foul, acrid odor. Her stomach churned, and she felt bile rise. With a groan, she covered her mouth and blinked rapidly, trying to see in the darkness.

Large and hazy, a full moon hovered overhead. Just a little more of its glow would reveal her surroundings. As she sat up, her vision adjusting, she struggled for clarity. Where was she? Why was she here?

Grass. There was grass beneath her. Why was that strange?

Head throbbing, she pressed her fingertips to her forehead. Grass was strange because . . . there hadn't been any grass between the buildings. That was the last thing she remembered. Buildings. On all sides. But with the breeze wafting that horrible smell over her, she knew there wasn't a building nearby. There was something else, an impression that tugged at her consciousness.

Something terrible. Warning. Fear.

Explosion.

There'd been an explosion as Cole—

"Cole!" she cried out, the sound hammering her skull.

A loud squawk came from her right, startling her. Haven twitched and only then noticed large shapes, like people on their knees, shifting nearby. She scrabbled aside, heart ramming into her throat, strangling her cries.

Body drenched in fear and warmth sliding down her spine, she murmured, "'God has not given us a spirit of fear. . . .'" The verse had been as automatic on her lips as breathing. Still, she swallowed, straining. Discerning.

But that smell! Lord of heaven, it would not leave her. Haven shifted to her knees.

One of the shapes expanded.

Surprise choked her.

Wings spread. The creature shrieked at her, flapping briefly into the air.

A bird.

No, a vulture! An angry one. Challenging. Its ardent protests drew others. Two joined it. Then three.

She clambered to her feet, trying to put more distance between them. Half afraid the vultures would attack her. She stumbled back, placating as much as one could a bird protecting its kill.

What kill?

A large rock clipped her calves. Haven pitched backward. But where she expected hard rock, she found a misshapen, uneven mound. Soft. Furry.

A vulture screeched in her ear. Wings batted her head, like being struck with cardboard. She scrambled onto all fours—and froze. Blind panic at meeting the mutilated, partially eaten face of a cow shoved her sideways.

Vultures screamed and shrieked.

Haven threw herself away from the dead animal and the torrent of flapping wings. Tears blurring her vision, she rushed forward. Only to stumble over a pile of branches.

Fingers grazing the wood—she screamed. Legs. Not branches. She stumbled off, the birds slowing their pursuit.

Slowly, step by step, Haven gained her balance. Her presence of mind. Saw the snaking curve of a road. Between her and that path lay dozens of dead cows. She ran, sobbing.

* * * *

In the vehicle, he and Ram waited an excruciating ten minutes for the guys to make it back, so they could head out. A weight had settled on the team with Keogh fighting for his life. With this ambush. And Tox hated the way the MRAP lumbered rather than roared into action, but soon they were thrashing across the forbidding terrain toward the coordinates. Night quickly pushed dusk from its perch and draped a heavy cloak across the country. Two klicks out, Tox pulled to the roadside and glanced into the back. "Rendezvous back here in twenty."

Thor nodded, slid out of the vehicle with his sniper rifle, and jogged into the darkness. He'd recon to verify the GPS location was secure before they made their final approach.

Back in motion, they closed the distance between them and the coordinates. In one klick, they'd go off-road. The lights of the MRAP were a beacon for hillside shooters and RPGs, so they would cut those, too. He glanced at the GPS. "Quarter—"

"Watch out!"

At Ram's shout, Tox jerked his gaze to the road. A shadowy figure leaped into view. He yanked the wheel left to avoid hitting the person. But in the split second after the headlights struck the figure, the face registered.

"Stop stop stop!" Cell shouted from the rear at the same time Tox nailed the brakes.

He threw open the door and pitched himself into the darkness. Tripped but came up running. "Haven!"

"Cole?" Her voice was uncertain, scared.

He raced back the dozen feet to where she stumbled toward him, his adrenaline jacking at the dark stains on her shirt. "Haven! You okay?"

She slammed into his arms, sobbing.

He crushed her against himself, his tactical vest a cruel intrusion on his need to hold her close.

Arms wound tight around him, she shook. "They were dead. They were all dead." The wail that filled the air tore at him. "I was so scared—the birds. The birds were going to eat me."

Her words made no sense. "Who was dead?"

"Cows. All of them. A whole field. They were all around me." She shook her head, the eerie cast of red lights from the MRAP giving her a macabre appearance. She dropped her forehead against his vest. "I prayed. Prayed so hard."

He took her shoulders. Held her at arm's length. "You hurt?"

"N-no." She shuddered. "Just . . . scared. It was awful."

"I've got you now. It's okay."

He hooked the back of her neck and pulled her close again. Tears pricked his eyes as anger rose like a flood within him. Dead cows? What on God's green earth had Alec done? Why? Why take Haven? So many questions, but he swallowed them, his throat tight beneath the raw rage. Too many thoughts assailed him, too much adrenaline and relief, for him to form coherent words. But she was safe again. With him. He kissed the top of her head.

"I think there's a hotel up the road, if you two want to get a room and, ya know, get out of plain sight." Cell was teasing, but the gravity of the situation was not lost on him.

"We need to check it out," Ram said. "The cows."

Tox nodded.

Haven's gaze snapped up. "Go back?"

He stiffened. "You can stay in the MRAP. You don't have to see anything, but we . . ." Curse Alec! "We have to investigate. Do you remember anything?"

Tucked beneath his arm, Haven allowed him to guide her into the MRAP. "No. Not really. Just . . . I woke up because of the vultures and the smell . . . " She accepted Cell's help through the rear door. "I . . . I think I woke up after the explosion—but someone was looming over me." She took a seat, and Tox sat beside her, relegating Ram to driving. "Then I felt a prick at my neck and woke up surrounded by dead cows."

Tox held her hands. Had she noticed they were dirtied with blood? He was relieved when Maangi passed over some wipes.

"That's . . . messed up," Cell muttered.

"Wraith Two to Wraith Actual. I have something."

At Thor's comm, Ram glanced at Tox, then keyed the mic. "Wraith Two, this is Wraith Five. Dead cows?"

"Uh, copy that."

"Send your coordinates, and we'll be en route."

"Roger that," Thor replied.

As they barreled toward the site, Tox focused on cleaning Haven's hands, wiping her face, taking care of her. She sat quietly beneath his ministrations, her eyes red, a knot at her temple. He gritted his teeth.

Tox freed the bite valve of his CamelBak and extended it to her. Eyes widening, she leaned forward and took a long draught. Then another. After a sigh, she did it again. There was a small nick in her cheek. Her nails were ragged.

"This dude needs a special, torturous death," Cell bit out beneath his breath.

"We are of the same mind," Ram said as the vehicle lurched to a stop.

They all were. Tox cupped Haven's face and held it until her eyes met his. They stared at each other for a few seconds, then she trapped his hand between her jaw and shoulder, fighting more tears.

"I'm going to check out the scene," he said.

She nodded, her face a mural of grief and terror.

He hunched forward, planted a kiss—very gently—on the knot, then turned to his comms specialist. "Cell."

"You got it, Sarge," Cell said, shifting into Tox's seat.

When Tox's boots hit the ground, he was assaulted by the stench Haven had spoken of and looked back as Cell settled a wool blanket around her shoulders. She looked battered. Terrified.

Fingers curling into fists, Tox clenched his teeth.

"Griffon vultures," Thor explained as he rejoined them, luring Tox to the front of the vehicle. "At least thirty of them."

The headlamps threw light over the hunched birds pulling meat from the carcasses. Every so often, a bare head would angle up on a long neck and consider them for a second, then return to the picking.

"Livestock?" Ram asked.

"Cows, mostly. A few goats, but they're just bones now."

"What is this?" Tox whispered, his disgust roiling. "Killing livestock. Putting Haven in the middle."

"Some kind of sick sacrifice?"

"I'll give him a sick sacrifice," Tox growled. He'd kill Alec. "Let's get her back."

Without another word, they climbed into the vehicle and logged the coordinates to have SOCOM check out the slaughter during daylight. Tox wrapped Haven in his arms as the vehicle rocked them into silence, giving him time to stew, to plan.

"So, King?" Thor finally said. "I mean, who else, right?"

"There's no one else stupid enough to mess with the sarge's girl," Cell muttered.

"What about that paper?" Ram asked from the front. "The boy's drawing."

In his arms, Haven shifted to look into his eyes, so Tox tugged it out and showed it to her.

She pointed a dirty finger. "That looks like a person." She traced the squiggly circle, then the other line on the top. "Maybe this is a turban?"

"Crown!" Cell said, peering over the top of the paper. "Look." He pointed to the messy rising and falling lines. "Crown. King."

Tox snapped his attention to Ram as tension folded into knots at the base of his neck, pulsing into his head.

"We have to find out about this crown," Ram asserted.

Folding away the drawing, Tox nodded.

Cell looked up. "So we're calling in the hottie?"

VVolt whimpered from the corner and shifted between the guys' knees. There had been costs today, and the Belgian Malinois was a poignant reminder.

213

THY LOVE
OUR JOY
AND SHIELD!

A spark traveled down the hillside, leaping down into the Saracen camp. One small fire against hundreds. Thefarie watched as it was swallowed by the Abuyyid tents. That was the signal. It had taken almost two years to bring this night to bear.

"'Tis strange to trust the Saracens," Ameus muttered.

"Trust?" Thefarie shook his head. "I would not go that far."

Giraude grumbled, "Yet here we are." He motioned to the campground of the enemy. "Staring into the mouth of the lion."

That alone should be proof enough that Thefarie did not believe the assassin would make good on his word. They slunk around the tents and bedrolls of the sleeping camp. Posted sentries, brother-knights, and sergeants waited on the outskirts, ready to draw attention should Thefarie, Ameus, or Giraude be discovered. They were three

Soldiers of Christ against hundreds of pagans. For them, the battle would not end until the crown had been restored. Thefarie's chain mail served as a weighty reminder of the oath he'd taken, the banner under which he operated.

As the brother-knights negotiated the camp with stealth, the Nizari Ismaili would come from the north. They would converge against Saladin. Rashid ad-Din had come for the sultan, Thefarie for the crown. Though he may not trust the Old Man to bring him the diadem, he did trust him to eliminate their common enemy.

Within twenty paces of the sultan's tent, a soldier patrolled right into Giraude. The knight grabbed the Saracen, cupping an iron hand over his mouth, and used his dagger to silence him. It happened in a heartbeat and whirl of black fabric.

Thefarie kept moving. Any moment they could be discovered or an alarm raised. He would not fail this night nor the one true God. Not this time. Scurrying up the path between canvas walls, he approached the great tent.

A shape emerged. Draped in black. Moving like a shadow in the night. A very fast shadow. Darting here. Sprinting there. In one corner. Around another.

Rashid. He did not even look over his shoulder but kept advancing. Unafraid. Confident.

Something nagged at Thefarie as he rushed up to the tent. Though he would not have to encounter the sultan, he anticipated trouble from the guards. He slid along the perimeter, freeing his sword.

A shout went up from within.

Heart thundering, Thefarie stilled.

Something toppled with a loud bang. "Find him! Stop him!"

Dread coiled in Thefarie's veins—the sultan wasn't dead. Betrayed again, he whirled and dove between the tents, seeking shelter behind the corner of another. Why hadn't Rashid killed the sultan?

"He was here! He was here!" Saladin burst into the open, waving something in his hand. "Wake the camp! He was here."

This was Thefarie's chance to retrieve the crown. He drew his dagger from its sheath. Glided again toward the sultan's tent, hefted his blade, and drove it through the canvas, slicing enough to slip inside.

Darkness and a strange oily smell assaulted his senses as he stood on the pelts and hides covering the ground. He scanned the interior. The pallet. The chairs. The table. A large chest sat opposite the pallet. Three strides carried him to it. On one knee, he opened the chest and rifled through the contents. Tunics. Sashes. Scarves. Breeches. But no crown.

Thefarie pivoted and looked around. On a table sat a basket. He hurried to it but found only combs and oils. He dumped the contents on the ground, frustrated. Where was the crown?

"Rashid ad-Din!" Saladin cried outside.

"He tried to kill you?" another Saracen asked.

"No, he left a message!"

A message? And a missing crown. Had the Old Man stolen the crown? Teeth on edge, Thefarie exited the sultan's tent the way he had come and sluiced through the narrow passages of the camp, bent on escaping and finding the traitorous Old Man of the Mountain. As tents spread out and the paths grew wider, Thefarie quickened his pace.

A shout barreled into the night. "Crusaders!"

A man emerged from a tent, right in Thefarie's way. When he saw Thefarie—his gaze falling to the white mantle—his eyes flashed wide. His mouth opened.

Before the man could utter a sound, Thefarie forced him back into the shadows of the tent and silenced him forever. Lowering the felled Saracen to the ground, Thefarie scanned beyond the tent flaps. Chaos reigned. Running. Shouting. Arming themselves.

If he could make it out of the camp, he might have a chance. He would run with all haste to the river. Perhaps borrow a horse. As if in response to his thoughts, a nicker drifted on the urgent winds.

Thefarie reached for the tent flap as a chilling realization hit him. Around the tent, close to this spot, silence had fallen.

He lowered his gaze, listening both in front and behind.

Crunching.

He clenched his fists. Someone must have seen him enter the tent. He firmed his grip on his sword. He could just vanish. He'd not allowed himself that extravagance in a very long time, but neither would he abandon the mission.

Leave the crown.

No. Not until he knew its fate.

With a flourish, Thefarie flung back the flap and ducked through the opening. He straightened, arms at his sides, and faced a dozen Saracens.

One hefted his sword from the scabbard and, with a primal scream, turned it toward Thefarie.

"No! Bring him," a man commanded.

The Saracen shuddered to a stop, the top of the sword glancing off Thefarie's mantle and clinking against his armor.

Annoyed at the cut in his mantle, Thefarie glowered at the man.

"Walk!" another demanded, pointing to the path.

They led him to an open-sided tent where Saladin stood with his generals, talking animatedly. The sultan's gaze rammed into Thefarie's as he bent to enter. At his full height, Thefarie felt canvas graze his head. Four large bowls on pillars roared with flames that provided enough light and warmth for the large gathering place.

Saladin moved around his generals to face him. "You were with him."

Thefarie gave no answer because he still had too many questions. Why had Rashid not assassinated the sultan? Why enter the tent and then leave? He'd carried no box or crate or bag, which meant he couldn't have stolen the crown.

Saladin wasn't wearing it. So where was it?

The sultan, shorter than Thefarie by a hand, advanced but also hesitated. *He is afraid.* "With Rashid ad-Din. You were with him?"

Noise from behind begged Thefarie to look back, but he refused. A moment later, someone was thrust to the ground beside him.

Ameus. Face and mantle bloodied, he spit and pushed to his feet.

"Two. Two Crusaders in my camp." Saladin circled several chairs before resting his hands on the center one. "You want me dead, yes?"

Thefarie squared his shoulders. "I care not whether you live or die, Saladin."

"Then why are you here? Why did you come with the *hashshashin*?"

"We did not come with them," Thefarie countered. "I came for the crown."

Understanding spread over the sultan's face, bringing with it a frown. "You waste your time, *Dawiyya*. You should have left with the Old Man."

"He stole the crown," Thefarie said. "Are you not concerned he will kill you?"

Saladin smiled. "If he wanted me dead, I would be dead." He held out his hands with a shrug. "And no, he did not steal the crown." He lifted a finger in emphasis. "Rashid wanted my attention, and he has it, as do you." He stroked his dark beard for a moment, then narrowed his eyes. "You went to Rashid to form an alliance against me, but I will turn this back on you, *Dawiyya*."

"I made no alliance against you," Thefarie argued. "I seek only the crown."

"He wants your crown?" A general balked, affronted. His face contorted in rage. "Kill him where he stands!"

But Thefarie held the sultan's gaze. Both knew it was the Crown of Souls he sought, not a crown of political power. "You are a wise, shrewd general and a skilled sultan. Your rise to power has been . . . fast. But it should not have been this fast. The crown tears at the fabric of your soul and will consume you," Thefarie warned. "In the end, you will fail. You will fall, Saladin. Surrender the crown to me now, and no more will be said or done."

Smirking, Saladin shook his head. "Said as only the conquered can." He went to a serving table and poured a cup of water. "It was you, was it not?" Cup in hand, he turned. "The one I stole it from all those years ago."

"It does not belong to you. It belongs to the past. If you have it, allow me to—"

"No!" Saladin came forward piously and stood perfectly between the two knights. "It does not belong to you, Christian."

"It is my mission, my purpose, to retrieve it. Whether from you or the Old Man—"

"I have already told you, he does not have the crown."

The cup turned a slow circle on dark fingers. Thefarie's pulse hitched. It was said that if the sultan offered a prisoner a drink or food, he would allow that person to live. But if nothing was offered, the person would be killed. One cup. The sultan held only one cup. But there were two Crusaders before him.

Would he hand the cup to Thefarie or Ameus?

Thefarie could not allow the mission to end in this way. He would not. As Saladin droned on about his purpose and his power, Thefarie eyed the tent. The tethers. If he could but get a sword! His gaze slid to the side.

"Would you have a drink?"

Thefarie returned his attention to the sultan and found the cup inches from his chest. His stomach knotted. Saladin intended to kill Ameus.

His brother-knight shifted.

"Fire! Fire!" a voice outside yelled.

Saladin's gaze shifted beyond Thefarie.

"Sir!" A general burst into the tent. "The camp is ablaze."

Saladin turned toward the threat, his shock evident.

Thefarie lunged to the right. Snatched a sword from a nearby soldier. Sliced through the tent support, the canvas sliding loose and collapsing atop the generals and the sultan.

"Go," Ameus shouted, having come to his feet.

Thefarie dove for the side, then shouldered into one of the large fire vats.

Saladin was there, understanding creeping into his shocked features.

"Where is the crown?" Thefarie demanded over the screams and pillars of smoke rising into the predawn sky.

"It is not here," Saladin said.

Thefarie pushed.

"No, I swear it. The crown is not here."

Thefarie upended the chest-high pillar. Oil rushed out, greedily pursued by flames. All racing straight toward the sultan.

22

Guilt hung like anchors around the necks of every Wraith member as they waited for the debrief. They'd scrubbed and showered after returning to base, then gathered in the conference area. Quiet boomed through the room, each drowning in their thoughts, the oppressive memory of Keogh's fight for his life, Haven and the livestock massacre. Keogh could die. Haven could have died. They all could be shipped home in boxes.

Warm air rushed in, pulling their attention to the door. An officer stood there, looking at them tentatively. When his gaze settled on VVolt at Thor's feet, Tox rose from his chair. "Can I help you?"

"Tech Sergeant Haig. I'm here for VVolt N629."

The Malinois's ears perked and swiveled as his head came up.

"Who says?" Cell groused as he stood, too.

"I have my orders. After the explosion and handler loss, he needs to be evaluated by our staff." Haig unhooked a lead. "VVolt, heel."

Though VVolt lumbered to his feet and obeyed, he had his head down and his tail between his legs.

Tox roughed a hand over his face and turned away as the airman left with the working dog. The futility coursing through his veins made him want to climb the walls or punch someone.

"That's wrong," Cell muttered. "VVolt's one of us."

"Why haven't we heard anything about Keogh?" Thor asked.

Ram, Cell, and Maangi just hung their heads. Instead of sitting and sulking, Tox planted himself against a wall. Haven came to him, and he took her into his arms without a word. She fit squarely against him and somehow it helped to have her close. To know Alec couldn't get to her here.

The door opened again, and Tox fought the urge to ignore whoever had entered. But when Haven straightened, he braved a glance and came off the wall in surprise. "Runt."

The twenty-something kid nodded. "Hey." Scratching his blond hair, he skirted a look around the room.

"What're you doing here?"

"I . . ." He met Tox's gaze, then backstepped. "I'll be right back." Lifting a phone from his pocket, he was dialing as he pulled open the door.

Something about that drew Tox after him. He caught the door. Sensed the others grouping up, too.

"Hey," Runt said, facing away, unaware of Tox behind him. "They don't know." He nodded, then shook his head. "No way, man. This is on you. I'm here—" A swing of his head spoke of his annoyance. "This is wrong. I—"Runt jerked the phone from his ear and looked down at it.

Hands on his belt, Tox shifted forward. "What don't we know?"

Wide blue eyes hit his as Runt spun.

"Yeah, 'fess up," Cell said.

Lowering his gaze, Runt sighed, then pointed to the room. "Let's . . . go . . . in there."

Irritation pushed Tox back a step, but he nodded Runt through the door. Did Runt realize he'd just tried to take control? Tox followed him into the room, reaching for Haven, who gave him a concerned look. More than ever, he wanted her close.

In chairs but not settled, the team turned hesitant gazes toward the asset.

"Listen." Runt spread his arms, palms out. "This sucks. I had no idea when I walked in that—"

"Just tell us," Ram said, his tone curt, his expression more severe than ever before.

"Okay. I hear you." Runt planted his hands on his belt. "There's no easy way to say this. Sergeant Keogh didn't make it. They sent me to fill the hole."

"No freakin' way." Cell hopped to his feet, his expression screwed tight. "We don't need you."

"I get it. I understand—"

"You got nothing, punk," Cell growled. "You don't know the first thing about us or this team. Keogh—"

"Cell." Tox held up a hand, then turned to Runt. "The phone—was that Rodriguez or Iliescu?" He wanted to know who was tightening the noose this time.

"Iliescu."

"So you're CIA," Ram stated.

"No way," Cell snapped.

Thor cursed. "Unbelievable."

"Easy," Tox said, knowing their reactions had more to do with Keogh's death and less—though not much—to do with Runt's addition to the team. "Okay. Keogh . . . that's a blow. Let's take some time to work through it." He glanced at his watch. "We have a conference call with Dr. Cathey in an hour. We'll regroup then."

The movement of the team riffled the air, thickening it with tension. Tox waited, heart heavy over the loss of Keogh. The guys looked ready to combust, so he had to keep it together to keep them together.

He noticed the shoulder bump Cell gave Runt. Thor slid him a seething glare. Ram ignored him. Maangi slapped his shoulder as he passed, the most civil reaction of the bunch.

As the door closed, Runt muttered something.

Tox watched, realizing he was as unhappy as the others. "I imagine this ticks you off, being pulled from years of work in Egypt."

Wary pale blue eyes hit his. "You have no idea."

Tox did. "Back here in forty." Taking Haven's hand, he started for the door.

"That's it?" Runt asked. "No anger? No yelling?"

Guiding Haven out, he said over his shoulder, "You'll either prove yourself or you won't."

* * * *

The team had returned, attitudes and resentment intact. It would take time to work through losing Keogh. But they'd returned. And that said something. So they connected with the professor and got down to business, explaining their situation and Alec's crown.

Tox aimed his attention to the live-feed camera of the computer. "You have any thoughts?"

On the split screen, Dr. Cathey filled the left window. "With the little you've shared, I'm afraid not."

"Tzivia?" Ram asked.

Tox's gaze moved to the right side of the monitor.

Black hair tied behind her head and sticking out in a dozen wild directions, Tzivia shrugged. Her white tank top provided a sharp contrast to her olive skin. She was a beautiful but complicated woman. Too much effort and too many irritations. Though Tox had once dated her, he preferred Haven's simplicity and balance. "I wish there were a clear indication, but there's not."

Tox snatched the drawing from the table. Held it up. "What about this?"

With the cheeky smile she was known for, Tzivia snickered. "Coloring while you're bored?"

"A kid in the city drew this, said the man who came in and put that mark on the wall was wearing this on his head."

"It just looks like scribbling," Dr. Cathey said, glancing around his London office. "Now where are my glasses?"

Cell snorted. "On your head."

Hand to his hair, Dr. Cathey chuckled. "Laugh you may, young man, but someday you'll be doing the same." He slid the glasses on. "Okay, now. Show me that again."

"Why don't we scan it to them?" Ram suggested.

Cell took the paper and started working on that.

"Any word about stolen crowns or strange devices or something?" Maangi asked. "Anything?"

"Not to my knowledge," Dr. Cathey said.

"I've been browsing forums as we've talked," Tzivia said as her eyes ricocheted over a screen, "but I see nothing. There are always looters or thieves stealing from sites, people bragging, but this . . ." She shrugged. "This would be significant. *Everyone* would be talking about it."

"Why?"

"A crown?" She smiled. "If it's ancient, then we would want to know who it belonged to, know its origin and history. We'd want to know where it was found, so we could excavate and discover if its owner had been buried nearby. Some of the most significant finds that unlocked history have been located that way. A crown is more significant than, say, a pottery shard."

"Unless that shard was instrumental in ceremonial—"

"The point is," Tzivia said, interrupting the professor and forging ahead, "a crown is more significant. I could come out there."

Tox and Ram glanced at each other, surprised at her suggestion. Tzivia always wanted to be "in the dirt." And she had been all too ready to leave them after Jebel al-Lawz and the miktereths. Why the sudden change of heart?

"We have no site to excavate," Tox said, trying to let her down subtlely.

"Perhaps," Tzivia said. "But when you find that crown, I want to be there."

Ram cocked his head. Leaned forward, squinting at the screen.

"We're not even sure it *is* a crown," Tox said almost simultaneously with Dr. Cathey.

"I can be there late tonight. I'll have more for you then."

"Hold up," Tox said as Ram punched out of his chair and stalked over to Cell. He whispered something, eliciting a nod from the communications expert. A second later, Ram tugged out his phone and left. What was that about?

Tox frowned and glanced over his shoulder to where Ram had vanished. He wasn't sure which sibling was worse. "Let's wait," Tox said, pulling his focus back to the conference call. "We have no idea where we're headed next—"

"But I should be there, ready for wherever this trail leads." Tzivia waved. "Seriously, no problem. I'll be there. Send me the details."

"Tzivia, wait. I have to get SAARC to clear you and the DoD to authorize your presence on the base." Tox was glad she hadn't hung up as he'd expected her to. "I'll get back to you."

With a loud huff, she rolled her eyes. "Fine." She ended her connection and the screen maximized, throwing Dr. Cathey to full size.

The professor let out a small groan, shaking his graying head. "This . . . this might be bad."

Tox braced himself.

"Best not to speculate, yet . . ." Head down, the professor studied something. He covered his mouth and clucked his tongue. Shook his head again.

"Professor?"

His head jerked up. He peered at the screen as if he'd forgotten they were there. "I have an idea, but I must talk with Tzivia again. *If* she will listen."

"And if she doesn't?" Tox knew the half-Israeli beauty was long on opinions and attitudes but short on good manners.

"She is not the only expert I know. And if this is what I think"—he grunted—"trust me, we will want answers before we go after it. Or it may be the last thing we go after." He removed his glasses. "Pray that this is not what I suspect. Because even Thefarie of Tveria could not recover it, and an entire nation was lost."

23

Nothing could have prepared her for the devastation.

Grief and anger strangled Tzivia as the car pulled up to the chain link fence. She dragged herself from the SUV and stepped into the heat of the day, which paled in comparison to the heat of the anger she felt as she surveyed the destruction. In the spring of 2015, ISIL had blown up this cultural heritage site. Through time it had been known by many names, including Kalhu—or Calah, as the Bible likened it. The centuries-old city had been renamed Nimrud in modern times, after the biblical hunter, Nimrod.

She wished to be a hunter, to find those responsible and dispatch them!

A man strode toward her, his sweat-stained shirt dirtied and his tactical pants dusted from his work. "Horrific, isn't it?" Mehdi Jaro asked with a grim smile as he turned from her and glanced back over the field. "I've worked here for months, and still the tragedy robs me of breath."

Rubble. Nothing but rubble—chunks of rock covered with cuneiform script jutted from piles of dirt that had once been the palace.

227

"Fools," Tzivia hissed, but diverted her attention. "You said you found something big."

"Come." He started back the way he'd come, his steps jagged as he negotiated the debris. "Faeza is anxious to see you!"

It was good, Tzivia thought as she made her way across the rubble, that most of the artifacts had already been removed, or they would have been destroyed and lost forever. Nimrud's Assyrian artifacts were displayed around the world, keeping history alive—despite ISIL's attempts—through the reliefs of Shalmaneser, Ashurnasirpal II, and the legendary winged bulls with human heads—the *lamassu*.

"Why did you drag me out here?" Tzivia asked. Not that she was complaining. Tox didn't want her, so she needed some distraction. Climbing over a knee-high chunk of stone, she saw the carved reliefs in it and stumbled. She paused and knelt, tracing the broken piece of history. Grief wrapped long, barbed claws around Tzivia's heart and constricted.

Replicas could be fashioned from videos, photographs, even the reliefs, so tourists could peek back in time, but there had been something profound about staring at or touching a stone, stele, or artifact that been handled centuries earlier. Tzivia always imagined the hands of time reaching through the artifact and touching her. Ram would taunt her if he knew. So she could not believe in God, but she could believe in some faceless brickmaker or artisan crossing time to touch her?

"Sad, is it not?" Faeza Bendakir trudged toward them, wiping her hands. "But out of the rubble rises glory."

Tzivia frowned, indignant. "Glory? You call this—"

"No. Come see," Faeza said.

She and Faeza had met on their first dig and cemented a friendship amid reliefs, lamassu, inferno-style heat, and passion for the history of this very site.

"There is more to see at the Old Palace and the ziggurat."

"I'm surprised there's still anything here," Tzivia bit out as they entered a small section of the palace.

"If it had not been for the authorities, I'm not sure there would be," Mehdi said. "When the most recent attack happened, much was destroyed. Irreplaceable pieces reduced to dust. Some to rubble that will take years to reassemble, but"—his shoulders bounced as he trudged down some stone steps—"we will rebuild it."

Tzivia wanted to cry. Wanted to rage at someone. "Why am I here, Mehdi?" Her heart skipped a beat as daylight was absorbed by dim mustiness inside the palace. A whisper of unease tickled her nape as she realized tombs of the dead surrounded her. "When I asked after anything unusual, a crown or diadem—"

"Patience, Tzivia. You never were good with that." Mehdi vanished around a corner. Ten years her senior, he'd enjoyed taunting her as much as pushing her to do better. "The attack also opened a new window into the past." He slipped beneath a tent, surprising her as darkness swallowed them. "And down into that past we go."

"He is still good with dramatics, no?" Faeza sighed as she produced a flashlight and rolled her eyes.

"Would it have been so hard for him to tell me what's down here on the phone?" Tzivia turned a dark corner. A light bobbed ahead.

"Yes," Faeza said with a giggle. "That is Mehdi. If he tells you everything, maybe you wouldn't come. Or—"

"You know me better than that." Tzivia paused, breathing out and expelling her frustration over everything she'd seen so far. "He knows that. So what's this really about?"

"He . . . he was afraid the phones might be monitored. He is so paranoid about this dig staying secret." She winked. "And you? You must see to believe."

"I must see to *understand*," she corrected. "Do you know why Mehdi wanted me to come?"

Faeza smiled. "He—*we* want Dr. Cathey's help."

"For what?"

"Getting a grant, money to put up security around this place as we work to see what's here."

Tzivia hesitated. Glanced down the steps again. "He could've told me on the phone."

"Not everything can be understood. Especially this," Faeza said as she guided Tzivia deeper below the ancient city. Her beam of light swept to the ground. "Careful—a step."

Tzivia slowed, surprised. "What is this?"

"A passage. Secret, we believe. There are no sconces or braces for torches—"

"It's quite compact." And was the air thinner? It almost seemed the walls were closing in. Tzivia took a steadying breath, shoving out the memories of the explosion in Jebel al-Lawz that had buried her in rubble. She'd worked excavations for a decade, but since that collapse . . .

Tzivia paused, swaying slightly on her feet. Glanced ahead just as Mehdi's light winked out. She hauled in a breath, disbelieving her eyes. Where had he gone? There weren't any doors.

"More dramatics," Faeza said with a sigh, motioning to the darkness. "The passage narrows until you must squeeze through. I call it the armpit." Her laughter echoed in the tunnel.

So it hadn't been Tzivia's imagination that the walls were closing in. Though she knew that now, each of the twenty paces to the "armpit" made breathing a little more difficult in the ever-tightening space. Anxious for a rush of air and openness, Tzivia sucked in her stomach and courage. Pushed through quickly.

And dropped into darkness.

The ground she'd expected wasn't there, pitching Tzivia forward and down a few inches. She stumbled but caught herself, straining to see.

Mehdi laughed. "Quite a shock, isn't it?"

Light exploded through the room, throwing shadows over a—

Tzivia's breath backed into her throat. She blinked. "A stele." She rushed forward, Faeza right behind her, and stared at the pictorial fragment. It wasn't massive, but at three feet tall and a foot wide, angling upward and narrowing to a point, it was impressive. "It's like the Black Obelisk of Shalmaneser III."

"Complete with five panels on each of the four sides and a cuneiform script that captions each panel," Mehdi agreed. "But this one is red granite, not black."

"Obviously." Tzivia scanned the perimeter of the first panel. Her skills with ancient Akkadian lacked the expertise of Dr. Cathey, but she could probably work out its meaning. "'Four gave' . . ." She hesitated, working through possible meanings.

"'Their souls,'" Mehdi offered.

"Mm, that might work. 'Four gave their souls'"—she moved to the next script—"'to the' . . . something . . . 'and were no more.'"

Mehdi shifted in between her and Faeza to point at a symbol. "This is 'iron of heaven.'"

Tzivia scrunched her nose. "Where do you get that?"

"Over here." He shifted to the side and pointed. "This panel shows something falling from the sky. It calls it the 'iron of heaven.'"

Her pulse sped up. "So the stories are true."

"That a meteor fell from heaven?"

If that much was true, was the rest? Yes, perhaps. "'*And these four gave their souls to the iron of heaven and were no more. Give not your soul to the iron of heaven.*'" With a smile, she turned. Her gaze lit on a winged sun disc, the symbol of the god Ashur. Her fingers danced next to an eight-pointed star, a representation of Ishtar, goddess of fertility, love, sex, and war. "So . . . Neo-Assyrian?"

But then something caught her eye on the panel below it. "This . . ." She squinted closer. "Faeza, bring your torch."

"Older," Mehdi said. "The cuneiform."

Tzivia's heart skipped a beat. "Middle, then?"

Faeza angled the torch so light played with the contours of the script. The beam was harsh, its glow pulling at the back of Tzivia's eyes.

"But this . . ." Her fingertips hovered over a strange depiction. "I've never seen this." Tzivia eased back, trying to get a better overview of the panel. "There are four rulers depicted below this strange marking."

"Push it."

The anticipation and excitement in Mehdi's voice made Tzivia glance at him over her shoulder. "Push?"

Beside her, Faeza smiled as she stood. "It's okay. But you'll want to be up here when you do."

Confused and wary, Tzivia rose. Peered at her friends, then reached for the strange marking. Unease slithered across her nape, sending a shiver down her spine. *Don't be ridiculous, Tzivia.* She pressed two fingers against the symbol.

Cold stone surrendered, sinking flat against the relief with a soft click.

Whoosh! Thump!

Heart in her throat, she whirled. Caught only the plume of dust that erupted at the base of a barrier that had slid into place, effectively sealing them into the tomb. *Not a tomb. Hidden room,* she reminded herself.

"Let the fun begin." Mehdi pointed behind her with a broad smile.

The shadows had lifted their hem and revealed a space equal in size to the one that had just been sealed off on the opposite side. She glanced back, then to the newly opened area.

Though uncertainty wound a tight cord around her throat, Tzivia's insatiable curiosity drew her into the narrow passage. As Mehdi and Faeza walked a few paces ahead, she could not stop imagining a wall slamming between herself and them, entombing her.

"How do you know it won't seal us off?" she asked, her voice echoing against the nearly untouched reliefs lining the passage. Reliefs! She surged forward, compelled by the discovery. Though faded, some of the pigment still offered a hint of the old colors used. "What is this?"

"We only discovered it last week," Mehdi said. "There hasn't been enough time to catalog or even fully explore it, though we've been here nearly every day from sunup until sundown."

"Sometimes later," Faeza said with a smile.

"Also, we've had to hire more security to protect us from ISIL, or they would blow it up."

Shadows lengthened, her friends hurrying on. Tzivia grunted, wanting to linger and study the reliefs. Annoyed that Mehdi wasn't stopping. "Wa—" Awe struck her as she watched his retreating light. If he was brushing past these amazingly preserved reliefs without a blink . . . what was he heading toward? Something more incredible?

Faeza and Mehdi slipped through an opening on the right. Tzivia followed. Carved around the door's edges were more depictions of the meteor that fell, along with— "Nergal," Tzivia breathed, eyeing the many panels of him with various persons, rulers, and priests. "But he was the god of war and pestilence. Sometimes also represented as the sun of noontime."

"And the summer solstice that brings destruction," Faeza reminded her.

"But wait," Mehdi said, his words quiet. "Tzivia, come inside."

She lowered her gaze from the doorframe to her two friends in the many-sided room.

Mehdi's dark eyes bore excitement, but also something else. "Remember that Nergal also presided over the netherworld and stood at the head of the special pantheon assigned to—"

"The government of the dead." Mind buzzing and stomach twisting in dread, Tzivia entered the room, which held nothing but a cage.

"But who?" she asked, circling the cage. "Who did this? Who made those reliefs—"

"We found an inscription on the stele that refers to the 'King of Sumer and Akkad,'" Faeza said.

Tzivia froze. "That could be a number of Assyrian rulers."

"But within these walls, built by Shalmaneser, then rebuilt by Ashurnasirpal?"

With a sigh, Tzivia nodded, again eyeing this cage. Was the air different in here? Plaster and sandstone consumed the walls. The cage was composed of two-inch-thick iron bars that ran from the floor straight up into—and through—the ceiling. "Iron of heaven," she muttered quietly. Circling it, she noted there were no locks. No mechanisms. "How does it open?"

"No idea."

Within it rested an eight-sided pedestal, mirroring the walls of the room itself, inscribed in cuneiform.

"We have no idea what was in there, but it would seem the builders didn't want anyone getting it," Faeza said.

On her tiptoes, Tzivia peered at the top of the pedestal and saw the distinct imprint of whatever had been removed. A nagging hum pulled at her. Maybe it was the thought of being shut into a hidden room within a hidden passage far below the surface. Maybe it had been the narrowing walls. No windows. How were they even getting air down here? *Were* they getting air?

When had she become so pathetic?

Back on track, Tzi. She nodded to the impenetrable cage. "So when

I asked if you knew of something stolen or missing . . . this made you call me." She shrugged and folded her arms. "Well, that and using me to get Dr. Cathey's help."

"You know how hard it is to get grants."

Tzivia reached toward the bars, feeling a distinct thrum bouncing between her palm and the iron.

Mehdi caught her arm. "Careful." He nodded to Faeza. "Show her."

Faeza bent and lifted a handful of dust from the floor. She tossed the grains just outside the cage.

All around the perimeter of the cage, swords sliced from the ceiling and the floor, clamping together. The sound of steel scraping steel buzzed the air as the powerful jaws snapped out of sight just as fast. A split second.

Tzivia hauled in a long breath and held it. If anything or anyone stood too close to the cage, they would be instantly killed. *She* could've been killed. Her head throbbed.

"Pressure plates, is our guess," he said.

"Very sensitive ones," Faeza added. "At least there aren't any flying spears or massive boulders," she said with a nervous laugh.

"How did you know about the trap?" Tzivia asked, pointing at the ceiling and taking a step back at the same time.

"The day it was discovered, we . . . lost a worker," Faeza said. "And we've had a hard time getting anyone to work the site since."

"Not to mention the price we had to pay to keep things quiet. The family—let's just say they won't have to worry about money for a long time."

"Even still," Tzivia whispered, "word will spread." It always did. "No wonder they carved Nergal all over this. It wasn't to invite people in. It was to warn people to stay out."

"No," Mehdi said, ferocity in his expression and word. "Next week, we'll have very good equipment. We'll x-ray the rooms and make sure there are no more traps. Then excavation will resume."

Tzivia's gaze fell to the pedestal again. Then retreated to the space where the jaw-like swords had disappeared. The cage bars. The pedestal. "If something was stolen from here," she said, shaking her head, "how did the thief survive? The jaw-swords and those bars don't look like they'd easily surrender. Are there markings or depictions of a crown anywhere?"

That was an absurd question—there were many rulers depicted here and in the forechamber with Nergal and other deities.

"Beyond the four rulers, we've found nothing else. But something *was* taken." Mehdi bobbed his head and circled the cage. "And recently."

Tzivia nodded, eyeing the pedestal and the mark in the dust left by whatever had once sat there. Circular. Perhaps big enough for a crown. Perhaps not.

She shrugged. Maybe it was enough proof. But probably not. Not enough to tell Tox and Ram she knew where the crown had come from. Or its meaning or origin.

"And this." Mehdi lifted a coin. "Not exactly Middle Assyrian."

Tzivia rubbed her forehead as she studied the silver coin with a crown-like carving in it. Her stomach churned. Head ached. "My head . . ."

"Oh, that's the iron, we think." Faeza pointed to the bars. "They're humming or something. You get used to it eventually."

"We've noticed the vibration but can't guess its source. Another reason we need Dr. Cathey's help and backing—to sneak in experts."

"You're not subtle at all," Tzivia laughed.

"Can't afford to be right now."

Vibrating iron. Strange. But that seemed to go with the territory. If that vibration was bothering her head from several feet away and the crown had been made from the same material, what would it do to the wearer?

She eyed the reliefs again, and suddenly the four kings took on new life beneath Nergal. Maybe Mehdi had been onto something about the government of the dead.

That rattle in the air made it hard to think straight. "So . . . in order to get whatever was in there, they had to know the secrets of this chamber."

"Yes, but I would suggest that they not only knew the secrets, they knew much more. Who the artifact belonged to. And why—I mean, you don't dig for an artifact and so specifically target it unless you know . . . *something* about its purpose."

"Purpose."

Mehdi nodded.

"It's just a crown. Its purpose is—"

"You know exactly what I mean." His eyebrows rose as he looked at the ceiling. "Legends abound—"

"Legends are simply historical facts blown out of proportion."

"Like this cage?" Mehdi said, nodding to it.

Tzivia swallowed.

"Whatever this artifact—or crown, if it is that—is supposed to do, someone went through a lot of trouble to get it." Mehdi sighed. "I would be worried."

24

With the tail of her shirt, Haven wiped the sweat from her face after an early-morning run, then stretched out her legs and arms. Cole had always been intense, but watching him practice kali with a pathetic tree that swayed against his violent strikes . . . That relentless determination to nail every strike, every move, was the same one that made him such a great soldier. He said it relaxed him, but she couldn't help but wonder if it also fed something inside him. A need to keep moving. A need to attack what he couldn't put his hands on—like Alec King.

At least Cole was channeling his anger productively.

"Want a go?" Cole twirled the right stick then clacked them together.

It took a second for Haven to realize he was speaking to her. She started. "Me?"

He grinned and tossed the stick to her.

She caught it and frowned. "Seriously?"

With a step back, he motioned her closer. "Chiji's a better teacher, but I'm not bad."

"Okay," she said hesitantly.

As she drew closer, he planted a hand on her hip and the other

237

stick in her left hand, positioning her. "I want you to be able to defend yourself better." He cupped her wrists, rotating them in and out. "Just a fluid extension of your arms, okay?" His breath dashed across her cheek, a bit exerted from his workout, and warm. "First with your right. Strike high—as to the head." He aimed upward.

She lifted the kali and tapped the tree.

"Now the left." Back and forth until he had her feet moving in a rhythmic motion. "Now low," he said. "Like so." He demonstrated, striking low on both sides. She did that several times, moving quicker with each strike, falling into the motion easily.

"Now high-low-high."

High on the right side. Swing the arm back to the left side and go low on the tree. Then high on the right again.

The new drill made her stumble the first few times, unsure where to strike when, but within a few minutes, they were moving just as seamlessly as they had with the single moves.

It was a thirty-minute workout that had her shoulders and sides aching, but there was something strangely satisfying about the motion, the clacking of sticks. She understood.

"Sarge, Command radioed," Maangi announced from the door to the building. "They're here."

Arms folded, Cole turned. "They?"

"Apparently the professor's waiting at the gate, too."

"On my way," Cole said, grabbing a rag and starting for the door. "Oh. Hey."

Maangi hesitated.

"Anyone contact Keogh's family yet?"

Maangi shrugged—not in a lazy way, but in a weighted, burdened way. "Not that I've heard."

Haven hustled up to Cole. "I doubt Tzivia will like that the professor is here."

"Why's that?" Cole asked as they stepped inside.

"They had a falling out."

He frowned. "How do you know that?"

Haven lifted a shoulder. "She and I talk. On occasion."

"Since when?"

"Since Jebel al-Lawz." Haven wasn't offended by Tzivia or her acerbic nature, nor did the fact Cole and the Israeli beauty had dated make her feel threatened . . . much. Haven had nothing to hide or fear. But Tzivia had been like a moth to the flame, at first displaying open antagonism to Haven and her faith. What had started as a mission to prove Haven wrong had turned into a strange sort of friendship. "Since you and I."

Uncertainty smeared across Cole's sweaty face.

"Does that bother you?" It did, she could see.

"I'm not sure. It's . . . weird."

"Why? Because you dated her?"

"*One* date."

"Then you pushed her away."

His cheek muscle twitched.

"Like me."

Cole spun, hands slipping to her waist easily, like second nature. "No." His blue eyes bored into her soul. "Not like you. Nothing like you."

Okay, she liked those words.

Determination sparked in his blue eyes. "Leave the past where it belongs." He pressed in. "And I'm here with *you*."

"But you *didn't* want me here."

His eyes slid shut. "You're going to hold that against me forever, aren't you?"

"Not *forever* . . ."

"I wanted you safe. That will always be priority one to me." He kissed her before she could say anything else. It was probably to silence her protests. For now, she'd let him get away with that.

"Well, don't you two look cozy."

* * * *

Speak of the devil. Tzi was intelligent and beautiful—like Haven—but she wasn't the grounding wire for his toxic currents. Only Haven could be that. Tox might mangle words with Haven, but he wasn't drawn to Tzivia, and he hated Haven comparing their experiences.

He turned toward the taunting voice. "Tzivia." His gaze slid to

Dr. Cathey. Weren't they supposed to be waiting at the gate with security? "How'd you get in?"

Thor strode up behind the newcomers. "I was at general facilities Skyping with my wife when I saw them. Brought them over."

Tox nodded, noticing Dr. Cathey's large black case. Something in his gut clenched. And at the back of his mind, he *knew* things were about to get hairy. "Well, let's get the team together."

When he stepped into the briefing room, he hesitated at the sight of the person already sitting at the table. Runt was nursing a soda and nodded. Tox lifted his phone, wondering why there'd been no official change of status on Keogh yet from Command.

"Tox." Tzivia closed the gap between them. She licked her lips and glanced around. "My brother."

Why was she nervous about Ram?

"Is he . . . here?"

"Where else would he be?"

"I . . . How is he?"

"He's Ram." He shrugged and shook his head. "What's with the questions?"

She swallowed. Faked a smile. "Nothing."

"Liar."

She punched him lightly in the shoulder and took a seat at the table. Tox noticed Haven standing in the doorway. She'd turned away before he could catch her expression, but she knew that there was nothing to worry about with him and Tzivia. Right? He stepped back into the hall, rounded the corner, and pushed into the bunkroom. "All hands in the conference room. Let's go!"

Cell set down the weights he was using and wiped himself off with a rag. Maangi started for the door, tapping his thigh.

"Where's Ram?" Tox asked.

"Haven't seen him."

"Same." Wallace had a towel around his waist, apparently having just returned from the showers. "Be there in five."

Ten minutes later, they were all gathered except Ram. Where had he gone? Tox pulled out his phone and dialed, but the call went to voicemail. For some reason, his gaze flicked to Tzivia, who sat at the table, looking guiltier than sin. Her weird behavior a few minutes ago nagged at him.

What was going on?

He picked up the landline phone to the base and checked with Command, Communications, and every other place he could think of to find Ram. Nothing. He eased up next to Tzivia and leaned down. "Something you want to fill me in on?"

Her expressive eyes hit his.

"Why is Ram AWOL?"

"Why isn't *he* AWOL?" Cell said, nodding to Runt.

Thor high-fived him.

Runt smirked but said nothing.

"I just got here," Tzivia said. "How would I know why my brother's gone?"

"If I find out you two are screwing us . . ." Sensing Haven's attention on him, Tox moved to her side and addressed the room. "Okay, let's get started. We're here to bounce around ideas in the hope of narrowing down possibilities." He folded his arms over his chest and tucked his hands in his armpits. "Cell, play the video for the professor."

"Wait," Cell said. "I want to know the runt's real name."

The crack of silence spread wider with every second.

Thor and Maangi eyed Tox, who pushed his gaze to the floor. No surprise—they deserved to know who they were working with. But Cell's demand was belligerent. Slowly, he slid his focus to the Wraith newcomer.

Runt shrugged. "I'll give it, but it's clear you won't use it."

"Why's that?" Cell groused.

"Because of that." Runt pointed at Cell. "That attitude. You don't care about me. You just want attention drawn to me, to point out I'm the new guy." He stood. "Look, I'm here to help. I have expertise, and they felt it would be of use to you. Okay?" He met Tox's gaze.

There was a plea in that expression, one to back him up. Tell the team that Runt didn't stand alone. But the team had lost a lot. Keogh wasn't just a warm body, which was what Runt was now. "Your name," was all Tox could manage.

Runt snorted. "Chief Petty Officer Leif Metcalfe."

"Frogman?" Maangi asked.

Runt's blue eyes considered their medic, and he gave a firm nod.

"A frogman?" Thor barked a laugh at the nickname for Navy SEALS. "Brilliant." He leaned forward, roughing his hands together.

"You wanted his name," Tox said. "Now let's get down to business. Cell—the video."

They spent the next thirty minutes reviewing the footage from Egypt and Iraq, then going over enhanced images provided by Cell, the DoD, CIA, and SAARC.

"So, Dr. Cathey," Tox said, eyeing the man who held more experience and degrees than everyone else in the room combined, "right now, we just need ideas. If you can help us narrow it down to a few, we can—"

"There is no narrowing, Sergeant Russell."

Tox drew back a chair and sat. Somehow, he knew this had to be taken sitting down. Maybe it was the sick feeling in his gut. Maybe it was the dread beading sweat on his brow. Or just the cruel scythe of experience slicing away hope for a normal mission.

"But I'll let Tzivia start."

Tzivia shifted forward. "Yesterday, I visited an old Assyrian site once called Calah. The site leader discovered a chamber containing a strange pedestal, which had at one time—recently—held an artifact. There was no indication in the room or passage of what had gone missing. However, the reliefs suggest that whatever it was had brought four rulers to their deaths."

"You think it was this crown Alec's using?" Tox asked.

"There is no proof. However," she paused, "it's possible."

Dr. Cathey splayed some papers across the table. "As Tzivia and I mentioned when we teleconferenced, there are no reports of a stolen crown or other ornamental headdress in our field." He heaved a breath and bounced his head back and forth. "To our knowledge. But what she learned at the site gives us considerable pause."

"Your knowledge?" Wallace said. "But you're the foremost expert in this field."

"Perhaps. And because of that, we have access to most of the antiq-

uities world, as well as some underground and disreputable sources."
Tzivia folded her hands together. "But if something or someone wants
a truth concealed, it can be hidden."

Much like whatever Tzivia withheld from Tox about her brother.

"Yes. True." Dr. Cathey shrugged. "So, to be frank, I have nothing
on a stolen ornamental piece."

Frustration snaked around Tox. Failed missions in Egypt and here.
Keogh dead. A newb on the team, though Tox had a feeling Runt
had a truckload of experience. And Wraith had what? Challenge
coins. Body counts rising. He considered the two archaeologists and
remembered that the professor tended to be exact in what he said
and did. "So what *do* you have?"

Dr. Cathey smiled in a way that said the contents of the box might
as well be what Santa carried from the North Pole. "I'm so glad you
asked, Sergeant Russell. Because after close and careful examination
of the satellite image from Egypt—"

"Wait," Cell said, frowning and shaking his head. "That image was
grainy, and you saw it like two seconds ago. I cleaned it up, but—"

"Yes. You did a wonderful job, cleaned it up just enough for me
to be fairly certain of my theory—"

"And that's all it can be at this point," Tzivia interjected. "At least
until we gather more facts or retrieve the artifact itself."

Tzivia and the professor could debate themselves into the afterlife,
and probably would, left to their own devices. "Understood." Tox
nodded to the professor. "Go on."

"As you have probably guessed, we are almost certainly dealing
with another artifact. From the situation, from the site Tzivia visited,
from the drawing made by the village boy, and from the story you
relayed of Mr. King, the moral decay that you have witnessed and
shared with us—"

"Moral decay?" Tox tensed.

"You said Mr. King has shifted from revenge to vigilantism." He
peered over the rim of his glasses, his gray eyes probing. "Yes?"

Tox didn't like that the professor was reading into the situation.
But neither could he argue. He gave a curt nod.

"So, from the image and the instances you have related," Dr. Cathey continued, "it is possible that we might be dealing with what is known as the Crown of Souls."

"Okay, that name alone gives me the creeps," Cell muttered.

"Everything gives you the creeps," Maangi taunted.

Tox held up a hand, staying the banter. "You came to that conclusion fast, professor. Shouldn't you reserve judgment until we can find it or get a better picture of this thing?"

"No!"

The finality of the answer silenced Tox. He stared, noting the additional gray in the older man's brown hair and beard. Age lines might've carved a map on his face, but a youthful vigor lurked in his eyes, born from his passion for antiquities.

"With the markers, the results, what Tzivia found at Calah, I am convinced." Hesitation hung with apology and grief. Dr. Cathey gave a sad shake of his head. "It can be only one piece."

Man, he was going to hate this, wasn't he? Was he ready to hear this? Were any of them? Leaning back, Tox rested his arms on his chair, grateful as Haven leaned closer, their arms touching. Reassuring. "We're listening."

"The site Tzivia's colleague summoned her to is Nimrud."

"Whoa!" Cell raised a hand, glancing at the table. "Nimrud—as in Nimrod? From the Bible?"

"The ancients called it Kalhu. The Bible and others referred to it as Calah or Caleh. The site was renamed in modern times to Nimrud." Flint struck Tzivia's brown eyes.

Dr. Cathey lifted a digital tablet and scrolled. "Ah, here. '*He was a mighty hunter before the* Lord: *wherefore it is said, Even as Nimrod the mighty hunter before the* Lord.' Genesis 10:9."

"But let's be clear," Tzivia said, her lips tight, "there is much debate among scholars about who Nimrod was in reality. Some say he was Sargon. Some say he was a giant. Others suggest Tukulti-Ninurta I."

"True," Dr. Cathey agreed. He lifted a finger. "But relevant nonetheless."

"Why?" Tox asked, wishing Ram were here to add his two cents.

"Because it is purported that Nimrod built Calah—that is, Kalhu—and many facts place him at this time. He has been listed as the first king of Babylon, Akkad, and Erech, said to have dug canals. The Bible mentions this as well in Genesis 10. According to Jewish tradition, Nimrod inherited garments from his ancestor, Adam, which made him invincible."

"Whoa whoa whoa," Cell cried. "Adam? As in fig leaves and 'it's her fault' Adam?"

Haven leaned forward. "There isn't much in the Bible about Nimrod, just a few scant pieces, right?"

"True," Dr. Cathey said with a smile. "We are told in Genesis and Chronicles that Nimrod was the great-grandson of Noah and a mighty man. But the invincibility, and perhaps this crown—if we can prove it—might explain how he managed to rise to such wealth and power. That and the vengeance he sought against God for destroying his forefathers—"

"There are a lot of legends about him," Tzivia huffed. "Including that he was a giant. That he was ambushed by Esau and beheaded. That he built the tower of Babel. That his twin sons birthed the Huns and Hungarians. One even includes a parallel to Shadrach, Meshach, and Abednego with a fiery furnace!"

Something had lit Tzivia's fuse. Before the whole thing blew up in his face, Tox knew to rein it in. "Doc?" He loved history more than the next person, but time was a vicious enemy. "The crown?"

"Oh. Yes. Sorry." Being the professor that he was, he handed Cell a laminated image and asked him to pass it around. "The Crown of Souls dates back to the Bronze Age. There is a story that says iron fell from the heavens—a meteor, perhaps—and was found to be very powerful."

"The site I visited," Tzivia said, "has a relief that depicts that. It shows something falling, but it's impossible to make out what it is."

"I cannot wait to see it in person." Dr. Cathey nodded, anticipation making him antsy, but he shot Tox a quick, nervous glance and refocused. "The Assyrians believed this iron captured and carried off the souls of their enemies. Some say it was actually a crown, or that a crown was made of this iron. It was highly prized, but there is nothing left of it, except perhaps the crown."

"A meteor," Tox said, tapping the table. "Carrying off the souls—"

"That may not be true," Tzivia said.

Of course she would argue. "What? Carrying off the souls?"

"That there is nothing left." She chewed her lower lip. "At this site I visited, there's a cage made of iron. It completely encases the empty pedestal I mentioned. But there was . . . The place thrummed. Gave me a headache."

"I must see this," Dr. Cathey declared.

"It sounds pretty incredible," Haven agreed.

"But seriously?" Tox said, twisting his mouth to the side. "Meteoric iron? Carrying off souls . . . ?"

"You have to understand the culture," Tzivia said, her tone impatient and borderline patronizing, but whether that was aimed at the professor or Tox, he wasn't sure. "The Assyrian culture was deeply rooted in worship and service of their gods. Middle Assyrians were polytheistic, believing in and worshiping over two thousand gods, including Anu, Enki, Enlil, Ashur, Shamash, Shulmanu, and Nergal."

"Two thousand gods to appease?" With a snort, Cell shook his head. "I can't even keep one happy, so I wouldn't have a prayer in that place."

"So," Tzivia continued, ignoring the sarcastic comment, "in light of their culture, believing a meteor was sent from Nergal—there was an entire relief dedicated to him at this site—to carry off the souls of his enemies is a legitimate belief for the people who believed Nergal oversaw the dead. But the iron," she said with a slight lift of her chin, "scientists theorize—"

"Yet have no proof," Dr. Cathey interrupted, stabbing a finger in the air.

"It is entirely reasonable," Tzivia shot back, glaring at Dr. Cathey.

"Here they go again," Cell muttered.

"Reasonable!" he scoffed.

"Just because it does not fit with your theories—"

"Fit with mine? You are the one who must dig for excuses."

"It's science! Not excuses."

"Are y'all going to have a cat fight?" Cell asked, reaching toward his back pocket, "'cause if so, I want to get my phone out to You-Tube it."

"You and me both," Runt added.

Cell shot him a glare.

Steepling his hands did nothing to help Tox harness his own frustration. He scratched his forehead, felt Haven's soft touch. Secretly wished Chiji was there for sage advice and resented that he wasn't. He grunted when the bickering didn't stop. "Tzivia!" he snapped, silencing the two archaeologists but hating the way Haven flinched at his remonstration. "Tell us what you were going to say."

Dr. Cathey clicked his tongue. "She wants to rationalize how the crown can destroy the moral judgment of its user. That—"

"Destroy?" This time Thor snorted. "You're kidding, right?"

"Okay," Tox said, holding up a hand. Their reticence and speculative responses were expected. As Chiji had told him before, Westerners had become very skilled at rationalizing everything or trying to stuff the supernatural into the box of their own understanding, much like Tzivia and her science. "I need to hear what she has to say." He skated a look around the room. "We all do. What happens from this point forward is based off intel and information gleaned."

But the phrase gonged in Tox's head—*destroy moral judgment*. Alec's moral judgment. It made sense. Was the destruction permanent? Could it be fixed?

He had to believe it could.

But first they had to know how. "How does this thing . . . ?" He couldn't even say it out loud, so he motioned with his hands.

Tzivia heaved a breath, skidded a look to the professor, then back to Tox. "Like I said, when I was there, I could sense a vibration from the iron. And scientists have long theorized that the Crown of Souls emitted a . . . frequency."

"That is true," Dr. Cathey agreed. "There are multiple reports of people hearing what they thought were ghosts in areas where the crown was worn or used."

"What?!" Cell slapped his pen down. "That's gotta be it." His gaze glinted with determination. "We got those frequencies—the ghost skips."

"The what?" Runt asked.

Maangi gave him a quick recap of what had been happening as

Tox absorbed the news about the iron and its "power." Wrestled to accept it.

"Right, Sarge?" Cell wagged his finger at the pages in front of the doctor. "So what happens—I mean, how does it destroy the moral judgment?" By his slightly narrowed eyes, he was working through the technical aspects, his intelligence unfair and lightning fast. "If it emits a frequency, how does the crown target the part of the brain that sorts right and wrong?"

Tzivia's eyes were leaden. "I don't have the answer to that because we don't have the crown. And this is all supposition based on mythical times and legends bloated with nonsense."

"Well, King has the crown," Thor said. "So get King, get the crown. Right, Sarge?"

"Does the frequency affect those within close proximity but not wearing the crown?" Maangi asked.

Tox clenched his jaw. He hated this. Hated where this was going. The implications . . . What would they face going after this crown? It was one thing to track Alec and bring him back. It was another to be on the prowl for an artifact that destroyed moral judgment. The ramifications grew with each second.

Ultimately, Tox cared about one thing. "How do we stop it and save Alec?"

"Because that's what you do, isn't it, Tox? You save people." Acid scraped against Tzivia's words, lingering in the air with a hidden message.

"Sorry?" What did that mean?

"Understand that powerful artifacts like this are not talked about openly," Dr. Cathey said. "You recall, yes, your experience with the miktereths?"

"My chest recalls quite well, thank you very much," Cell said, a hand on his chest where he'd taken one of the AFO's arrows.

Dr. Cathey stroked his beard. "I fear you may walk into more of the danger you faced in Israel with the conspiracy of silence about the Aleppo Codex. The crown," he said, holding up a finger, "whether supernaturally or scientifically, destroys the wearer from within. They lose the ability to tell right from wrong. So there will come a time, if it has not come already, when your friend will no longer be your friend. You will be enemies."

As anger writhed through him, Tox fisted his hand. Why? Why another artifact? Why intersect Tox's life with these deadly pieces of history? He shifted forward, disturbed. Agitated. Ready to push this guilt, this frustration back on Dr. Cathey. "You didn't answer my question." He rubbed his knuckles. "How do we save Alec?"

Cell hesitated, a pen in the air. "You mean *stop* him."

"The two are not mutually exclusive," Tox said evenly. Then came to his feet. "What I want everyone in this room to realize is that Alec was one of us. He's a brother-in-arms. He did what we do."

"And then he went off the rails, drove right off the sanity reservation," Cell snapped back.

"And we need to bring him back." Tox pinned Dr. Cathey with a long, serious look. "With the miktereths, you burned them. With the mace, we returned it to the cradle. How do we stop the crown?"

Sadness wrapped a dark sheath around Dr. Cathey's eyes. "Unfortunately," he said, his shoulders sagging, "there is very little in the annals of history about the crown. Even in my own research, I have found little. I have no answers on how to stop it—or even if it can be stopped."

"That is true," Tzivia said. "Considering what the crown is capable of, it's surprising there is so little written or discovered or available—but that room I discovered may have more information about it. Mehdi will let me back in, I'm sure."

Palming the table, Tox eyed them. "So that's all you know about the crown?"

"Not exactly," Dr. Cathey said. "It's said Saladin had it at one time. But that is when it vanished."

"A disputed report," Tzivia said.

"Saladin?" As a history buff, Tox knew of the incredible warlord who unified the Shiite and Sunnis in a massive confrontation against the Templars. No way Tox would put too much thought to the Crusaders. "So if there's a way to stop it," he mumbled, "that's what we need. That's our mission—to locate that way."

"But how?" Tzivia brushed her dark hair from her face. "Even if the site I visited held the crown, it was clear they didn't know how to stop it, only how to stop people from using it."

"What do you mean?" Tox frowned.

"They enclosed it in an iron cage and set traps around it—massive swords slicing together like steel teeth if you approached it. Someone clearly removed the crown, but we have no idea how."

"So you're saying, what? We're spit out of luck?" Cell asked, agitated.

"We're just chasing our butts?" Thor joined in with his frustration.

"No," Dr. Cathey said softly. "The answers exist."

"Tell us," Cell said, "and we're all over this like butter on a biscuit!"

Hands on his tactical belt, Tox straightened. "So where? What do we do?"

Dr. Cathey smiled, as if he'd been waiting for Tox to speak up, to ask. "To get the answers to stop the crown and save your friend, you must find the Keeper of the Codices."

This had to be a joke. Tox considered the professor, searched his eyes for confusion or wild chaos, but found instead only sincere belief.

"You serious, dude?" Cell snickered. "That's really a person, the Keeper of the Codices? Sounds like something out of a comic book."

"Understand," Dr. Cathey said, with a definitive confidence that Tox envied, "that each time your friend uses the crown, his thirst for its power will grow until he will no longer be able to separate himself from it. He will be lost and notoriously wicked, just like Nimrod."

"This sounds like something from those movies about that ring." Cell grunted.

"Do we have a lake of fire to throw it into?" Runt added.

"Are we going to Nimrod, then?" Cell asked.

"Nimrud," Tzivia corrected.

"No, not till we find this Keeper," Tox said. "We need more on this crown before we step into a tomb."

"It's not a tomb. It's a . . . they caged the crown." Tzivia shrugged. "Okay, it's a tomb."

"The crown was in existence long before any fiction." Severity drew Dr. Cathey's brows together. "It will destroy every sinew of goodness and morality within. If you fail to stop your friend, then as it did with Nimrod's enemies, the crown will carry off his soul."

25

Was this karma?

Tzivia wasn't sure if she believed in it or not, but it seemed all the wrong she'd done, the unflinching, acerbic methods employed to seize success, might be coming back to bite her. She would've used words like *driven, determined, focused*. But she'd heard the whispered *hard-nose* and the colorful b-word.

Tox bent over the conference room table, staring at documents, images, and maps. He straightened, rubbing his stubbled jaw. He stood a well-muscled six two. But it was those blue eyes. They'd always been able to home in on her heart. Much like her brother. Too much.

Tzivia braced herself and stepped through the door.

His gaze hit her, and a frown tugged at his handsome features. "Something wrong?"

With a sigh, she handed over the file she'd brought. "After visiting Nimrud, I dug up everything I could about the crown and got Mehdi to send me some articles, images of reliefs—anything he could get his hands on."

Tox took the file, and Tzivia hoped she might get out of here with her secrets intact.

251

"I think Dr. Cathey might be right this time. There's something"—the word *supernatural* tasted like chlorine she couldn't spit out—"unusual about it. That cage at the site? It was unlike anything I've ever seen in a Middle Assyrian dig. And the humming iron?"

Surprise wove through Tox's irises. "Earlier you said there might be a scientific explanation for that."

"And as you can also probably guess, since the crown hasn't been seen in over two thousand years, the base metals are unproven and haven't been studied. So theories abound. That's it."

Tox scowled.

"What?"

"That sounds entirely too much like you agreeing with the professor."

"So?"

"What happened to your vitriolic responses to his supernatural theories? To your rage when he brings up God or the divine?"

"Sometimes the simplest answer is correct."

He narrowed his eyes, and her stomach squirmed. "Since when have you been a fan of Occam's razor?"

Tzivia laughed off her nervousness.

Tox set the file aside and shifted so his leg was hiked up on the table, his knee pointing toward her. He leaned forward. "Tzi, what's going on?"

Her heart thudded. "What do you mean?" She should've known better than to think she could pull wool over Tox Russell's eyes. "I just wanted to bring you some articles on your crown."

He folded his arms and straightened, feet spread shoulder-width apart. He wasn't moving until she told him. "Where's Ram? What's going on?"

Light-headed that he'd so quickly put that connection together, Tzivia brushed her temple. He wouldn't lay off till she gave him something. She had to think fast and clear. "I believe he's going after a man named Omar Kastan."

A frown twitched his mouth and eyes. "Who's that?"

"A Mossad agent."

The frown deepened. "But Ram . . ." Tox scratched the side of his face. "Look, I can't pretend to understand the intricacies of your brother's connections to the Mossad, but—"

"I'm dating him. Omar." More like using him. For a legitimate purpose, of course. Though that didn't assuage her guilt or stem her growing feelings.

Tox stilled. Considered her long and hard. Gave a curt nod. Somehow, he'd detected the sliver of deception sliding beneath her words. Her actions.

"Look, I'm just telling you this because I think it's distracting him," she said.

"Distracting him from what?"

"From this." She swept a hand over the table.

Annoyance tugged at his features, warning her she hadn't adequately connected the dots for him. "No—"

"If he were here," she said, feeling as if she'd stepped into quicksand, "he'd mention the most likely connection for the Keeper of the Codices—what a ridiculous title. Can you believe people actually still use that title in modern times? Keeper of Records, Keeper of Art. London even has a Keeper of the Queen's Swans." She shrugged. "I guess it's no worse than zookeeper or storekeeper."

Stilled, Tox stared at her through his dark brows. "What connection?"

"Think about it—who did Cathey say was the last person to have seen or owned the crown?"

"Saladin."

Tzivia smiled, having hooked him. "And Saladin fought . . . ?"

"The Crusaders."

"Come on, Tox. You're not this dense." Mockery had always ensnared the hard-hitting soldier. "Who have we met in the last year with more information on the Poor Fellow-Soldiers of Christ than anyone or any other library?"

With a deflated sigh, Tox lowered his gaze.

"But you already knew."

He roughed both hands over his face. "There has to be another way." His expression was almost tortured.

"He's not that bad, is he? He helped with Spain and—"

"He *didn't* help," Tox growled. "He led us around like dogs on leashes. And he enjoyed it."

"You're just upset because he freaked you out with that hallucination."

He ran a hand down the back of his neck. "Something's not right about Ti Tzaddik."

"But he has the writings of Thefarie."

"Which is no guarantee they include anything about the Crown of Souls, or even that they're real. He could be making them up."

Tzivia laughed, relieved to have Tox focused on someone other than herself or Ram. "That's stretching. Even for you." She flicked a hand dismissively. "But chances are high those writings contain some mention of the crown."

"Remember," Tox countered, "there wasn't just one crusade. There were many, depending on which view you take in categorizing them. But they span hundreds of years. There's no proof Thefarie was anywhere near Saladin."

"Maybe. Maybe not. We'd have to talk to—"

"Don't *have* to."

"We should." Tzivia pushed off the table and stood facing Tox. "Are you really going to wuss out over a man who appeared in your dreams, dancing in fire?"

He cut her a searing look.

She grinned. "The Tox I knew wouldn't shrink from an enemy."

"I don't shrink," he bit out.

"Then start with Ti Tzaddik."

* * * *

"So, no word on Alec?"

Special Agent Wallace shook his head. "SAARC hasn't been able to track him down, and he hasn't left any more love notes for you."

Tox ground his teeth at the well-placed words.

Cell grunted. "I'll show him my love of weapons, if I see him anytime soon."

"Almstedt asked if you'd heard from King recently," Wallace said.

There was an undercurrent in that question, an implication that Tox might be holding back information. "If I had, she'd know."

"That's what Kasey told her." Wallace's tone made Tox hesitate. Why wouldn't he give up on her nickname? Was it his way of hanging on to the almost-relationship he'd had with Haven?

But there was more in that statement that Tox didn't really want to entertain or explore: Haven was reporting on him to SAARC.

The door flapped open, and with the gust of hot air came Ram.

"Where have you been?" Tox asked. "I've—"

"Making calls," Ram said. "Finding answers."

Tox felt his frustration rise. "What'd you find?"

"Not exactly found, but close," Ram said. "We have to go see Ti Tzaddik."

"I know."

Ram paused. "How?"

"If you'd been at the briefing, you'd know the answer."

Anger glinted in Ram's eyes.

"Tzivia and I had a talk."

That rock-hard façade shifted. Ram looked away. "Tzaddik was hard to find when we met him in Syria six months ago. But with the Russian attacks and attempts by ISIL to destroy Aleppo, it's become next to impossible."

"Next to. But not completely, right?"

Ram sighed.

"Hey." Tox shrugged. "I need that tiny distance between the two, or we're screwed."

Ram shifted toward Cell, but his gaze was on his phone. "Sending this to you. Can you put it on the wall?"

"Roger that," Cell said, sliding behind a laptop at the head of the table. "Got it," he mumbled, fingers pecking the keyboard. "And there we go."

An image of rubble splayed across the wall. White plaster and gray cement heaped amid splotches of green.

"That's what's left of Tzaddik's home," Ram said.

Thor let out a low whistle.

Tox scratched his jaw. "Is he . . . ?" Interesting that the radius of damage was focused mostly around Tzaddik's home. A house or two on each side bore minor damage. A few cracks and some corners busted up. Otherwise intact.

"Wait," Cell said, pointing to the image, "so did *he* get targeted?"

"No proof, but most agree the hit was strategic. But it's not uncommon for terrorists to be inept in working with explosives," Ram said. "They're exuberant, inexperienced, and often lack the necessary knowledge. Many wrong buildings have been blown before. But as you can see, the other houses aren't destroyed. Pretty convenient. So Tzaddik is being cautious, as you can imagine."

"Why can we imagine?" Thor asked.

"Because," Tox said, "ISIL is targeting historical sites and artifacts, trying to wipe anything other than their radicalized form of religion from the face of the earth."

"With Tzaddik's collection, he's not taking chances," Ram added.

"So he's hiding?" Cell asked, tapping a pencil against his lower lip.

"He is. But I've located a last-known."

"There are too many of us to go together," Tox said.

"SAARC won't authorize splitting up," Wallace said, his eyes dark.

"They will if they want this solved," Ram countered. "We go in with a half dozen men, and we might as well paint a target on Tzaddik's head. He has too much to protect to let that happen, and we need what he has."

"Then we break up," Maangi suggested. "Two- or three-man teams."

"You're missing the point," Ram said, his expression and tone unaffected.

Tox looked at his friend. "You talked to him."

Hesitation guarded Ram's hazel eyes. "Not directly."

"What'd he say—*indirectly*?"

Jaw muscle twitching, Ram said, "Only you and Cortes."

Tox turned away at the same time Wallace barked, "No way!"

Ram's gaze morphed into granite. Hard, cold. "SAARC will have its hands in the pot, and by association, you will too, along with DoD. That means our terms will be met. So will his."

"It's too dangerous to send Kasey in with just him."

"Doesn't the lady have a say?" Thor asked.

"I agree with Wallace this time," Tox said, hating himself for it. "It's too dangerous, especially in light of the costs and threats. Alec would have easy access to her. If something happened to me, she'd be there alone." He shook his head, fear and dread boiling in his gut.

"I may not have Krav Maga skills like Tzivia," Haven said softly, "but I can hold my own."

Not realizing she'd come in, Tox pulled up straight. He hadn't meant for her to hear that, nor to hear his terseness.

"I want to go," she announced as she moved to the other side of the table and held on to a chair. Like a barrier. "I'll do what needs to be done to stop Alec King." She shrugged. "Besides, Mr. Tzaddik likes me."

"That's true," Ram agreed.

"And her voice," Cell added. "He liked her voice."

"Tox?" Ram asked.

He eyed Haven again. Waited for her to look at him. When her green eyes rose hesitantly to his but bounced away, he moved closer.

"Regardless of what he might think," Haven said to Ram, "it's imperative I go. You said Tzaddik wanted me there, right?"

Ram hesitated, eyeing Tox, as if afraid he'd step on a pressure plate.

Her eyes, lit with anger and determination, struck his. "If you want to finish this mission, then I have to go."

A challenge. A harsh one. What was wrong?

"Sarge," Cell called loudly, drawing Tox around. "Incoming from General Rod."

"On the wall." Tox checked Haven one more time before focusing on the feed. "Sir."

"Sergeant, we've got a jet prepping to get you to Israel."

Israel. "Yessir."

Ram had apparently gone to the general with information before he'd shared it with Tox. Not cool. But his biggest concern was the location itself: Israel.

Ram's territory. Where his connections were strong. And the Mossad even stronger. The question of Ram's loyalty came screaming back.

"Since we have no idea what intel you'll get from Tzaddik or when King will next strike, we're sending the team with you. They'll stay on the plane while you, Cortes, and Khalon track down Tzaddik."

Ram on the ground, too. Interesting. "Understood, sir."

"Wheels up in thirty."

When the feed ended, Tox faced his team. "You heard the general. Grab your gear and meet on the tarmac."

As the team pushed out of their seats and headed out, Tox started for Haven. But she wasn't in her last position. He scanned the room and spied her slipping out ahead of the others. He started after her.

"Sarge?" Cell called.

"Hang on," Tox threw over his shoulder, hustling. He pushed the door open and looked down the hall to the main entrance. No Haven. He spun to the left. Dark, empty. She must have made it outside already. He jogged to the end of the hall and stepped into the night.

A sedan, a truck, and an MRAP littered the open area. Four Marines emerged from the USO building, rowdy and laughing. The dining hall was locked up for the night. Where had she gone?

His phone belted out a song. He tugged it from his pocket and glanced at the screen. No identification. But then, he was used to that with his field of work. He answered. "Russell."

"Do you have an answer for me?"

Ice snapped through Tox's veins. "Alec."

26

"I think I've been more than fair—"

"Fair? *Fair?!* You snatched Haven and—"

"She was unharmed."

"If you try that again or harm her, I will kill you. We clear?"

"I've given you time to make a decision," Alec said, annoyance clamoring through the line. "What happened with your girlfriend is symbolic of what has happened to me, to so many across the world. We have been left powerless when those we care about are harmed. I hear you lost the dog handler."

Tox pinched his lips together. "You're sick, Alec."

"You have a decision to make."

"And threatening Haven is not the way to get me on your side."

"Side?" Alec laughed. "Tox, this isn't about sides. It's about answering a call. One you were designed for from the time you were a boy. Remember the story you once told me, the one your mother shared about you low-crawling up a hill with a toy rifle over your arms."

Tox bit back a retort.

"It was in your blood, your mother said. Why?" Alec hissed. "Why do you think that's the case?"

259

Arguing calls and purposes was an exercise in futility. "I can't leave my team. Or our mission," Tox said, noting Ram coming out of the building. He pointed to his phone. "I won't abandon my men, Alec. Even you wouldn't do that."

Ram immediately yanked out his phone and dialed, talking quietly and surreptitiously. He waved his hand in circles, indicating to keep Alec talking.

"No, I wouldn't—*didn't*. And each of their deaths is burned into a memory fragment that haunts every waking breath." Silence pummeled the connection. "Is that what it will take, Tox? Will it take the loss of every person on your team for you to see the light?"

Dread turned to anger. "Are you threatening my men?" His breathing went ragged. "Because you know that I don't take threats lightly."

"I thought by now you'd have seen the obvious."

Tox took a slow, measuring breath to calm down. "What's that?"

"That you are made for this, Tox. You're a leader. You're a soldier— a warrior," Alec growled. "We both are. Called and gifted by God to deal with ugly, horrendous evils that others can't face. To do violence on behalf of the innocent."

"Called to *answer* it, Alec," Tox said, hand on his belt as if trying to brace himself. "Not become it."

"You mentioned that before. Is that what you think?" Amusement and mockery bled through the connection. "That I've become evil?"

Ram motioned that the team was close to tracing the call.

"'Whoever fights monsters should see to it that in the process he does not become a monster,'" Tox said.

"'And if you gaze long enough into an abyss, the abyss will gaze back into you.'" Alec finished the Nietzsche quote with a long, satisfied chuckle. "Oh, this is rich, Tox. Quoting a philologist who collapsed and lost his mental faculties at fifty-five?"

Tox rubbed his forehead.

"Honestly, are those the depths you plumb? What did Nietzsche know of war? Of combat? Is that why I must lead you out of the darkness and into the light? Help you see that you were made for this? *Made* for it."

"Maybe you have more in common with Nietzsche than you real-

260

ize, Alec." The gaping silence fueled Tox. "Dismembering people? Slaughtering cows? That sounds like someone who has lost his faculties." He sighed. "Come in, Alec. I'll help you. I'll make sure you get what you need."

"I'm disappointed, Tox."

"Alec—"

"But I'm gracious. Your attention is divided, so you have twenty-four hours to give me your answer."

With a thumbs-up and a circular motion with his finger, Ram indicated they were nearly there.

"Or what?" Tox asked.

"Or the gloves come off. Next time, you won't find her wandering a dark, dusty road. You'll find her dead."

The call ended.

"Augh!" Tox punched the air. Wished it was Alec. He fought the urge to throw his phone against the wall. "Son of a . . . biscuit!" Stealing Cell's phrase didn't help. He pressed his hand against his forehead.

"His location bounced all over the place," Ram muttered, shaking his head. "What'd he say?"

"Gave me twenty-four hours to join him or the gloves come off. Said Haven wouldn't be found alive next time."

"Send her home?"

Breathing grew hard. They could send her back. He didn't want to have to worry about her while trying to bring Alec down. But then she'd be away from him. Unguarded. "No. She stays with me—or you. At all times."

Ram gave a curt nod. "Agreed. If I could put a leash on Tzivia, I'd keep her close, too. I don't trust King to leave our loved ones alone."

This time Tox snapped a nod. "Speaking of Tzi—what's with her and this boyfriend?"

Fury glinted in Ram's gaze. "Boyfriend."

"The Omar guy."

"Is that what she called him—*boyfriend*?" It wasn't a question. More of a statement filled with challenge. And anger. A truckload of it.

"What's going on with you two? Where have you been—and don't tell me you were working this mission."

Ram adjusted his beanie, his gaze drifting away. "If I could tell, I would."

"That's bull!"

"It's the truth."

"You boys are so cute when you argue," Tzivia said as she walked up to them, her voice coy.

That ticked Tox off even more. "Leave it, Tzi."

"Touchy." She lifted her chin, defiance glinting in her eyes. "I need to go into Jerusalem. A friend has possible information on a missing artifact."

"You go with us until we find out where to meet Tzaddik," Ram said.

Tzivia popped a seething salute.

"Sarge!" Cell shouted across the gravel parking lot. "Plane's ready."

* * * *

— DAY 26 —
JERUSALEM, ISRAEL

"Visiting Jerusalem twice in one year," Haven muttered to herself as she strode down the cobbled path between two rows of shops.

Cole glanced at her but kept moving. The open-air shopping center bustled with customers and modernity. A strange but neat difference from when they visited the Old City six months ago. There was still plenty here to remind Haven that she wasn't in America, like some women wearing hijabs, the Muslim muezzins, or the very frequent sight of haredim. And the Hebrew lettering that seemed inspired by the finger of God.

"Chiji will be mad he's missing this," Cole muttered.

"It's strange not having him here with you."

"No kidding. I feel like a lost kid." But he plowed on. Past clothing stores, jewelry shops, and a coffee shop flanking the cobbled walk. Sunlight streamed down and emphasized Cole's broad shoulders as he walked a few paces ahead with Ram and Tzivia, who seemed tense.

More than her usual tough-girl persona. When Haven thought about it, Tzivia hadn't been herself since she'd rejoined the team yesterday. She seemed on edge, frustrated. Annoyed. There'd been a terse exchange with Cole before they boarded the jet and headed here. Though she'd wondered at first if Tzivia was simply angry with Cole for dating Haven, she sensed there was more to this. Something was going on with Tzivia. Something deep, dark.

Cole and Tzivia angled toward one another, talking quietly. Haven fought that jealous surge again. What were they whispering about? They stopped, and Haven's heart caught. Cole might be facing Tzivia, but his gaze was on Haven. Curse him for making her heart skip a beat. She was annoyed with him for once more deciding what she would and wouldn't do. All in the name of safety, of course. But she'd like to be consulted, reasoned with. Rather than dictated to and about.

His blue eyes radiated intensity. "We're here."

To her right the Aroma Café wafted the scent of coffee beans through the hot afternoon. Clearly a popular spot, the café spilled customers out onto the open walkway.

"Go inside," Ram said and handed Haven a piece of paper. "Order this drink."

"Me?"

Ram gave her a small smile. "You'll be fine. I'll be back."

Nerves thrummed as Haven glanced at the detailed description, then to Ram's retreating back. How did they know to do this? What would happen when she placed the order?

Cole caught her arm. "C'mon." He guided her past a half dozen people lingering outside. His hand stayed at the small of her back as they waited in line. "You okay?"

When she looked up at him, she was surprised to find his gaze skimming not the café and exits, but her face. "Sure." No, she had to be honest with him. "Actually—"

"Can I help you?" the cashier asked.

Haven straightened. "Yes. I'd like an iced cappuccino, please." A small twitch of Cole's hand at her back reminded her. "Oh, with chocolate."

The twentysomething nodded and gave her the total. After paying, Haven moved to the other end of the counter and waited near the serving bar for her drink. Cole ordered a bottled water and joined her, but even as he did, she noticed his gaze skidding across faces and out through the glass walls.

They'd gone over this on the plane. Although she'd heard them say a thousand times that nobody knew whether Tzaddik would show up, Haven couldn't help searching the café and the people walking the mall outside, too.

She swept the sidewalk and tables with her gaze. Where had Tzivia gone? But even as her hand went to Cole's arm, she spotted Tzivia slipping into a store. What was she doing?

"Iced cappuccino and bottled water." The person behind the counter slid a cup across the slick surface. The creamy iced drink stirred a sudden thirst in Haven. Water in hand, Cole started for the exit and pushed it open, sliding up against her as he did. It wasn't a romantic thing. He was pressing ahead, scouting for trouble.

Maybe that *was* romantic. He was protecting her. And he always would.

Haven glanced at the shop across the wide sidewalk. Through the etched glass and beyond the racks of clothes, she spotted Tzivia talking with a man. "Cole," she said softly as they eased into chairs at a table.

"I see them."

"Who is he?"

"I'm going to guess Omar Kastan."

"What is she—"

"No idea."

"Should we do something?" She lifted her drink and caught the straw with her fingers. It wouldn't move. She tugged, and the lid came loose. Setting down the drink, she realized the problem—there were two lids. "Guess they stuck together."

When she removed the extra one, Haven froze, her gaze on the black lettering scrawled beneath the top lid. No, not lettering—numbers. "Cole."

The terseness of her tone jerked his attention to her, and she showed him the lid. He took it. Then set it down and dropped back against his chair, lifting his water. "Drink your cappuccino."

"But—"

"Eyes."

It took her a minute to realize his hidden message: They were being watched.

* * * *

Tox pulled out his phone and used it, as much to blend in as to get in contact with the team. The numbers on the lid of Haven's cup were most likely coordinates. But with so many people, possibly even Alec, after Tzaddik, he knew they had eyes watching. Leading the enemy to the only person who could help them wasn't cool.

He sent a secure text to Cell: *Hack cameras in clothing shop?*

Within seconds came a response: *On it.*

To his surprise, Haven's phone rang. Who would call her here? He guessed having a brother-in-law who was the president and working for SAARC meant she needed a phone that worked in other countries. She pulled it out and glanced at the screen. Her face fell.

His heart staggered, thinking it was Alec. "What?"

Her green eyes came to his as she showed him the caller ID: Charlotte Russell. "It's your mom."

Crazy how those three little words packed such a big punch. He hadn't talked to his mother since his "death" almost five years ago. Hadn't seen her. Hadn't heard her voice. "Answer it."

Haven's eyes widened. "What?"

"Keep it short." He indicated her phone. "Put her on speaker."

Understanding smoothed the concerned knots in her delicate brow. "You sure?" She had been filling him in on his mom for the last six months and unwittingly stirred a bone-deep ache within him to see her.

His pulse rapid-fired, but he nodded.

Haven wet her lips, then answered, selecting the speakerphone feature. "Hi, Charlotte. How are you?"

"Wonderful, dear. And you?"

Her voice was beautiful, vibrant. Though his mother was from

Vermont, she had aced southern congeniality. It rang through her voice.

"I'm good," Haven said, green eyes monitoring him. "Sorry for the noise, but I'm on a business trip."

Tox nodded. Good deception.

"Oh, well, I don't want to bother you—"

"No bother. What can I do for you?"

"I wanted to set up a meeting with you about Endeavor." Charlotte gave a snicker. "I must say, it's turning into quite the event. Everyone's very excited, but I admit I'm coming to you a little behind. Can we get together over lunch sometime? I just love having you around, and your attention to detail and decisiveness is so refreshing."

Haven's smile was genuine. As she beamed, her gaze on the phone, Tox suddenly realized how much she was like his mother. Her manners. Her wit. Charm. Beauty.

And they both had his number. Knew how to pull him up by the scruff of his neck.

"I . . . I'd love that. I'm not sure when I'll be back, though."

"Oh, that's okay. We can videoconference."

"Whatever you need, Charlotte. I'm glad to help."

"Oh, you are an angel. Do you have any idea who you'll bring?"

Haven blinked. "Bring?"

"I want to meet that special man you spoke of when you were here last."

Tox bounced her a surprised look, watching the crimson fill her cheeks, matching those rosy lips.

"Oh, Charlotte," Haven said, her voice breathy. "You're too much."

"Bring him! It'll be perfect."

Haven shrugged at him. "I . . . I'll have enough work and worry just helping you coordinate."

"Well, shoot," his mom said. "If this had happened years ago, you could have gone with Cole." Her laugh was soft, hollow.

The grief was so palpable it reached through the phone and smacked Tox in the face. He sat there, like the seven-year-old boy reprimanded for breaking a vase. Or the twelve-year-old caught messing with his father's hunting rifles.

"You know I would've wanted nothing else," Haven said with a lilting laugh. Apparently, it was no secret in their family that Haven had liked him.

Why had he been the only one blind?

"I know, dear. I know. If only things had gone differently."

"Well, I need to get going, Charlotte. Let me know when you want to talk."

"All right, dear. Be safe. Godspeed."

"Bye, Charlotte."

"Love you."

The words were so familiar. So sweet. So drawn from the past.

"You okay?" Haven asked.

"I hate that she thinks I'm dead."

Her small hand wrapped around his fist. "You and me both. And I will never stop working on Galen, and anyone else, to let her know the truth."

He stood and held out a hand to her. They fell into step together. He deliberately walked past the shop where Tzivia was talking to the mystery man and made eye contact with her. "You can't take me, so who *are* you going to take to the Endeavor event?"

Haven's eyes lit up as they climbed the steps up to the footpath that crossed the busy streets below. "Me, myself, and I." She lifted her chin. "Unless you come."

"Yeah, that'd go over real well—give her a heart attack."

She shrugged. "I could suggest we make it a masquerade party."

They strolled out of the Mamilla Mall and up the steps to the footpath that crossed over Omar Ben el-Hatab Street and delivered them to the Tower of David.

"Those don't really work. You know that, right?" He directed her up through the Jaffa Gate.

They eyed the great stone structure that had been erected in the time of the Crusades with the belief that this site was where David had built his palace.

"This is really unfair, seeing all these great sites but with the threat of death hanging over us," she said.

"Unfair?"

"Well, yes. I mean, this should be . . ." She shook her head and again went crimson.

Tox stopped and faced her. Though he knew what she was thinking, he wanted to hear her say it. "What?"

"I wish we were here on a vacation. Together. No threats. No danger." She sighed. "No Tzivia."

"You still think I like her?"

Another sigh. "No, but I think she's quite fond of you."

"She has a boyfriend. Anything she saw in me is gone. And vice versa." He shifted to look at her. "Tell me you know that."

"I do." She squinted one eye closed, the sun glinting off her irises. "But I still like hearing it. And hearing that despite her being a total bombshell . . ."

She didn't finish that thought, and he could guess why. What she wanted to hear. Tox just wasn't sure he was *there* yet. He pivoted, slid his hand around Haven's neck, and tugged her closer. "I know how you feel. Thinking about you taking some other guy to that event . . ." He shook a joking fist.

Haven laughed. "So you'd be upset if I took Levi?"

"No," he said, clenching his teeth. "I'd be ticked."

She raised an eyebrow and smirked. "Good." Amusement shone in her eyes and with it, pleasure.

"So you won't take him?"

She laughed. Then turned and started walking along the curving, sloping road.

"Wait. Are you serious? You'd take him? Tell me you wouldn't." Tox flared his nostrils and caught up with her in two long strides.

She glanced around them. "Do you know where we're going? Or are we just walking?"

"You said you wanted to do something romantic."

"Oh, like arguing?"

"Now you're avoiding my question."

"So are you."

"Promise you won't take him."

Jaw jutted, she looked at him. "Why? He's a friend."

"He's a guy. Who has given you looks I don't like. And you dated him."

"So?"

"He has ideas. Memories. And he's a *guy*."

"You're a guy."

"But you're dating *me*."

"Took you long enough," a foreign voice intruded.

Tox pivoted.

In the shadows of a climbing, flowering vine stood Ti Tzaddik.

27

— DAY 26 —

JERUSALEM, ISRAEL

It shouldn't have come as a surprise that Ti Tzaddik had located a building over a tunnel system. Nor should it affect Tox that he was now leading them through that maze beneath the city.

Time held no power over this man, it seemed. And Tox getting impatient would only extend their wait and time wasted.

So he followed. Just as six months ago they had followed an ultra-Orthodox Jew through another system to a secret repository of scrolls, books, and documents. And with ISIL intent on rewriting history in their favor and wiping out anything that didn't promote their religion, Tox understood Tzaddik's extreme measure.

"We saw pictures of your home," Haven said as they walked, bent, through the cramped passage. "Were you there when it happened?"

Shoulders hunched, brown hair and beard neatly trimmed, Tzaddik nodded. "Down in the library poring over writings. But I survived—as you can tell." His chuckle drifted back to Tox, rankling him. "I had help getting my collection out safely and transporting it here. Very tricky, that. But we accomplished it."

They climbed a short flight of stone and dirt steps into a small foyer, where Tzaddik let them into a large room without windows.

A rug sprawled over the stone floor and reached toward ceiling-high shelves built into the wall and made of the same stone as the floor. Scrolls and bound tomes filled it to capacity.

"Come in, come in." He motioned them inside and shut the door behind them. "So, what can I do for you?" He waved to the chairs around a long, wooden table.

"We have to find the Keeper of the Codices," Tox said.

"Mm," Tzaddik said with a nod. His large frame filled the room. Impressively tall, yet . . . not. He squared his shoulders. Chin set straight. "Yes, the Keeper."

Tox hated this. Hated that he even had to engage this man again. Hated that they were dependent on his collection for answers from antiquity. "Dr. Cathey—"

"Mm-hm!" Tzaddik pointed. "Good man, that one. His work with the miktereths is all over Israel and the historical societies. Not a day goes by that—"

"He said that to get answers to our mission, we had to talk to the Keeper." Tox bit back his frustration. Well, some had leaked out in his rude interruption. "Considering your collection"—he nodded to the wall stuffed with documents—"we thought you might know who the Keeper is or where we could find him."

"Of course." Tzaddik situated himself in the armchair that had been in his Aleppo home. He rested his feet on a small leather stool. "What do you want to know?"

Was he serious? Tox and Haven shared a look, then he leaned forward. "We need to know where to find the Keeper." Hadn't he just said that?

"That's easy," Tzaddik said, lifting his hands in a lazy shrug.

They waited.

"Well?" Tox asked.

Tzaddik's eyes widened a little. "I thought it was clear—*I* am the Keeper."

Rubbing both hands over his face, then up over his head and down the back of his neck did nothing to release the tension in Tox's shoulders. Life was sliding down a never-ending chasm of frustration and danger. "Why am I not surprised?"

"Because you know my arsenal," Tzaddik said, waving behind him toward the shelving. "What are you looking for, friends?"

"Why does it have to be you?" Tox muttered and closed his eyes. Their paths kept crossing, and it no longer felt like a coincidence.

"What does it matter who it is, as long you find answers?" Tzaddik, didn't seem a day over fifty-five, yet he had the wisdom of the ages wreathed beneath that silver-streaked brown hair. And those eyes were old enough to have seen far too much yet still be amused by the simplest of things.

"So, *Keeper*," Tox said, redirecting the conversation, "what Codices refer to the Crown of Souls?"

Tzaddik rose from his chair, his large frame casting shadows over the room, nearly blotting out the candles.

But there weren't any candles. Only lamps.

And Tzaddik never left the chair.

Something went crazy in Tox's mind, shoving him back to the explosion in Kafr al-Ayn four years ago that buried him beneath rubble, only to find a fiery variant of Tzaddik standing over him.

Pulling me to safety.

No. Tox looked down. No, *the team* had pulled him to safety.

"So." That single word slammed like an anvil against the quiet room. "It has resurfaced." Ti's expression grew dark, brooding. His gaze a thousand miles—or centuries—away. "How have you come to know about the Crown of Souls?"

"We haven't." Tox was surprised at the defensiveness roiling through him.

An assessing gaze swept over him. "Ms. Cortes," Tzaddik said, "why don't *you* tell me why you've come to me about this"—a sneer crept along his lips—"artifact." His smile was forced. "I like the sound of your voice."

Haven glanced at Tox, as if asking permission, but then started talking without waiting for a response. "A man has been killing people. At first, it seemed to be only for revenge, but things have worsened. There is footage of this man wearing something like a crown when he carries out these executions. Dr. Cathey believes this man's moral judgment is declining—"

"Decaying," Tox corrected.

"Decaying," Haven repeated with a nod. "He suggested we talk to you."

Flicking his fingers slightly, Tox gave her a nod. Enough information.

"But that's not all, am I correct?" His brown eyes bored into Tox. "How are you connected to this, Russell?"

Something about the way Tzaddik said his name bugged him. He'd almost mangled it. Made it into another name. Why that even mattered, Tox didn't know. Maybe it just irritated him. Then again, everything about this man irritated him.

"So you are connected to this," Tzaddik persisted.

Tox clenched his teeth. "The man possibly in possession of the crown is a soldier I know."

"Just a soldier?"

Teeth grinding, Tox resented the prying but also knew Tzaddik would have his answer one way or another. "We were . . . friends."

"Ah. Better. And as I suspected." Tzaddik sat back again, touching his chin. "What makes you think it's the Crown of Souls?"

"At this point, guesswork," Tox said. "Dr. Cathey suggested it. Tzivia found a site containing reliefs that pointed to a crown, to four rulers lost to the effects of the crown."

Tzaddik did come out of his chair this time, gripping the arms. His expression was more alive than Tox had ever seen it. "She *found* it?"

What was that about? Tox eased away, uncertain he should give Tzaddik any more intel.

"Please, guardian," Tzaddik said, settling on the chair cushion with a dismissive wave, "I have more information than you could imagine."

"But you didn't know about the site, that Tzivia found it." Tox realized he had a bargaining chip. For the fist time in his dealings with this man, he might have the upper hand. "Show us what you have on the Crown of Souls, and Tzivia will take you to the site."

Tzaddik scoffed. "Agreed."

"Why did you scoff?" Haven asked.

"Because what I have is little more than a riddle within a riddle."

He circled his hand. "Within a riddle. It's maddening. It is of little use to most."

Tox rose to his feet.

"But with the site, you may be armed better than anyone else in the history of the crown's existence." Tzaddik turned to the shelves, dug through a pile near the top, and drew out three scrolls and a leather-bound book. He delivered them to the table. "I will show you."

Tox joined him, bending closer.

"I've read this story many times—a favorite, you might say." Tzaddik opened the book. "It would seem that our old friend Thefarie had long been searching for the key to the crown, the way to stop it. His journey and efforts met with utter failure and greatly discouraged him. Haunted him."

"He never stopped it?" Haven asked.

"No, but he also never stopped looking," Tzaddik said. The coarse crinkle of turning parchment rattled through the musty room as he sought the right reference. "You see, Thefarie pursued the crown from a brother-knight Gregorio and then into the hands of Saladin, who enjoyed an unusual and meteoric success from the lowest of ranks."

"Saladin." Tox's interest was piqued. "Are you saying he wore the crown?"

"Look at his success and power."

"Just because a soldier has success doesn't mean he's cheating."

"That is true," Tzaddik said. "But in his writings, Thefarie records the journey he and his brother-knights took to track the crown. In the end, it was lost to history."

"What happened? Did he have an idea?"

"Here," Tzaddik pointed to the text. "From Thefarie's journal. 'My brother-knights and I, in the name of our Lord Jesus, pursued this crown of wickedness unleashed in this most unholy battle. Though our eyes but once beheld the crown, 'tis not a sight we can forget, having witnessed Saladin, the great Saracen, cut down one brother-knight after another, Christian after Christian in the Holy City, wearing that abomination. I, Thefarie of Tveria, saw the wildness in his eyes, the fury of his movements, and can only describe it as evil. As is my duty,

274

I provided the Saracen with fair warning that I would return that piece to its unholy origins. From that day forth, the crown was never publicly seen by myself or my brother-knights. . . .'"

Motioning at the book, Tzaddik sighed. "He goes on at length about the ravages of the lands during Saladin's time, how the sultan grew in power and stature." Tzaddik's gaze once more traveled through the years to that distant moment. "If you have time, I would recommend the reading. It's . . . enlightening."

"I'm afraid our time is short," Tox said. Though he would readily read more of Thefarie's trials. By all historical accounts, Saladin seemed as vigilant and cunning as any Western war hero. "I just need to know how to stop it."

"Therein lies the problem," Tzaddik muttered, going to the shelves again. He dug into the scrolls, carefully moving them aside as he lifted another tome and carried it back to them. "Even Thefarie could not resolve how to stop this crown."

"Because he couldn't locate it?"

"Well, that is true." He slid a journal across to Tox. "Here Thefarie tells how, when he finally fought his way into Saladin's camp, the Saracen vowed the crown would never again be found. He refused to give it to Thefarie for destruction, possibly fearing the Crusaders would use it against his people. Here"—Tzaddik pointed to the rhythmic scrawl—"he said the Saracen remained true to his word, even to the date of the journal, which was at least ten years after Saladin's death."

Tox rubbed his face. "Thefarie might not have found it, but Alec did."

"Did he?" Tzaddik arched an eyebrow.

"He's using a crown that matches the . . . influence of the Crown of Souls." Tox shook his head. "I have to stop him, but to do that, if I understand correctly, I have to stop the crown. Destroy it or something."

"I find it strange that a knight who searched for decades could not recover the crown, but your friend, this soldier"—Tzaddik made a *pfft* noise—"finds it. All by himself?"

Tox realized they'd been assuming *Alec* had found the crown. Was it possible someone else had?

Tzaddik flipped a few pages of the journal and tapped it. "There. That is what you need." He reached out and took Haven's hand, drawing her closer. "Let the one with an angel's voice read it."

Easing in beside him, Haven took a chair and drew the book nearer. She wet her lips and began reading in a halting cadence, translating the Latin as she went.

"I, Thefarie of Tveria, a Knight of the Poor Fellow-Soldiers of Christ, have given my very best effort to stem the long, devastating campaign of the crown of lordship over the souls of men. Despite this rigorous and unrelenting effort on my part and that of my brother-knights, we have failed. The legacy of the crown has exerted its power since the time of Tukulti-Ninurta I and possibly his father before him. In our hunt to stop the desecration, I have gathered knowledge from the four corners of the earth. It is my belief that there is a recipe for the ruination of the Crown of Souls, a method not only to limit its destruction against the heart and mind of its wearers, but to destroy and banish from this earth the crown itself. Despite my failure in locating this wicked tool, I know it will not remain hidden forever. So I pen this letter to the guardian chosen by Our Lord Jesus and charged with its destruction.

"First, I must explain the legacy of this device. When a great storm sent a meteor from the heavens, it was found to contain a powerful form of iron. In my search, I have found one Assyrian king who says a crown fell from heaven. However, it seems the great kings of the past too late recognized its destructive effects, not only to the enemies of its wearer, but to the wearer himself. Cursed with madness and a reprehensible lust for power, the rulers were shut away from the people to preserve their legacy—and to prevent their vicious attempts to recover the crown. Wise priests of the time managed to secret the crown away, dismantling it and its legacies. It vanished from time and history until I discovered its reappearance.

"To my great sorrow, one of my own brother-knights

attempted to harness its power—and died. It then was delivered to the upcoming Saracen sultan, Saladin. Despite what the annals of time may record, the future reader of this account cannot deny the plausibility of my assertion. As history will surely attest, I have never met so fierce and determined a warrior as Saladin. He is so elegant in his strategies and his determination to see his purpose—the conquest of the Levant and Our Lord Jesus Christ's Holy City—fulfilled.

"When I had at last confronted Saladin and made a demand of him, out of honor, out of fear for humanity, to return the crown so that it might be destroyed, he refused. Neither trust nor allegiance existed between us. I have it on his word that the crown is buried, its power and its destruction to never again find man's hands. Though I doubt not his sincerity, I also doubt not the determination and lust of mankind for power and greed. It is a perverted and demented power that must be contained. As such, my search to destroy the crown will never end until it is destroyed or until I draw my last breath.

"It was told to me by an aged priest that for the crown to be resolved and neutralized, each legacy must be returned to it. Until then, the brokenness of the crown will consume its wearer, until all that remains is withered skin and bones. Once the legacies have been rejoined, its power will return to the heavens from which they were thrown.

"Yet as of this writing, I have not met with success. However, it is my eternal hope that one will come after me, find the legacies, and force the crown to relinquish its hold on man once and for all.

"To you, faithful guardian, I task what I have failed to accomplish. I have spent four and twenty years hunting these elements in my pursuit to destroy the power of the crown, to free humanity of its destruction. Our mighty God and our Lord Jesus Christ will aid you, just as They directed my paths. And so I pass on the knowledge I have gained, but carefully to protect the work and prevent discovery of the crown by those of disrepute.

277

The seal of Shalmaneser ruled Tukulti-Ninurta
At his city where queens are buried, in great relief
Draped in black at the feet of Ashur
For Shamash in amulet of red grows angry
Lapis lazuli cuffed me in failure and shame

"Find the five legacies, guardian. Remove the burden of madness and thirst for this power from all your kind. Locate them and return the crown to its crypt beneath the dust, where it may be destroyed for eternity. Succeed where I have failed."

Tox was more unsettled now than when they'd first arrived. "This reads like something from a fairy tale, finding a crown with power and destroying it to free people." He shook his head.

With a broad smile, Tzaddik thrust a finger into the air. "Yes, indeed—and fairy tales have happy endings, so perhaps this mission of yours will as well."

Tox wanted to snap back that his mission was to find Alec. But in the split second that thought shot through his skull, he saw a very ugly scenario playing out, one where Alec wouldn't listen. As he hadn't on the phone. As he hadn't in the restaurant. Which left one resolution—bringing down Alec. What would happen if they didn't succeed?

That question left Tox feeling like he'd stepped out of water, weighting his clothes and limbs.

Tzaddik lifted an eyebrow. "You see it now, yes?" There was a sadness in his eyes that seemed to plug right into the core of what ate at Tox. Between them resonated an understanding. "Finding this friend-soldier isn't the whole of your problem. You could find him, but if you do not stop him, stop the Crown of Souls, the entire world could pay."

Having his mind read sent shards of panic through Tox. He slammed his fists on the table. "*How?*" He ignored the soft plea of Haven's voice calling his name, and homed in on the Keeper. "*How* do we do that?"

"Is all the work to be done for you? Do you think Thefarie had someone handing him journals to cheat from?"

"Cheat?"

Tzaddik smiled, apparently having a good laugh at Tox's expense.

They had to get out of here. But first— "Can I take pictures of the pages?" Tox asked, pulling out his phone.

"Please—help yourself." Tzaddik shifted his attention. "Do you understand the riddles, Ms. Cortes?"

* * *

"Well, I love puzzles, but I'm not sure . . ." Haven leaned over the book as Cole turned a page. She trailed her finger over the part of Thefarie's letter Mr. Tzaddik had referenced, while Cole continued taking pictures. "Okay, here. Five legacies. '*The seal of Shalmaneser ruled Tukulti-Ninurta at his city—*'"

"Back up," Mr. Tzaddik said. "I broke the lines intentionally. So the first one is the seal of Shalmaneser."

Haven frowned. "*You* broke the lines?"

He wagged his hand dismissively. "I meant in copying the lines. Obviously it was Thefarie's letter."

"Okay, so the seal of Shalmaneser ruled Tukulti-Ninurta." Tucking back her hair, she peered up at Cole. "So we're looking for a seal?"

Cole's expression flickered. "The ring of a king held a seal. It was a sign of his authority—a ring could be the seal of a king."

"Mm," Mr. Tzaddik murmured, steepling his fingers in front of his mouth and tipping his head back as he looked down his nose. "Very good."

Head tipping and looking down the nose were signs of superiority. Steepling his fingers in front of his mouth meant he held back information, again from a position of superiority.

"So we're after a ring?" Haven wrote that down in her journal.

"Very possibly," Mr. Tzaddik said. "Now, the next one?"

She scanned to find her place in the letter again. "Next is '*At his city where queens are buried, in great relief.*'" She lifted her head. "Does 'his' refer to Shalmaneser or Tukulti-Ninurta?"

"It would most likely refer to Tukulti-Ninurta, who was said to be Nimrod, since he wore the seal of Shalmaneser. In fact . . ." Mr.

Tzaddik nodded as he pushed himself out of his padded chair. He strode over to the shelves and removed a book, flipping through the pages.

"So, Nimrod's city is . . ."

"Shalmaneser built Ashur." Mr. Tzaddik's distant voice reached them as he rifled through his collection. "But Nimrod built Calah."

"Neither of which exist anymore, right?" Cole asked.

"Yes, but Tzivia—"

With a sharp shake of his head, Cole silenced her. Gaze still on hers, he angled his head toward the rear, where Tzaddik was returning. "So how do we find something in a city that doesn't exist? And what are you looking for?"

Mr. Tzaddik again flicked his hand dismissively. "Keep reading."

"It'd help if—never mind." Huffing, Cole shook his head and turned to her. "Let's get this over with."

The thing with these two, she realized, was that when they occupied the same room, there was entirely too much testosterone. Mr. Tzaddik might be older and give off the air of an old man, but he was in good shape. And there was a lightning-quick mind beneath the sun-carved lines of his face, sharp with strategy and intelligence. And in every respect, Cole was the same. Except younger. And more handsome. Even now, those blue eyes were darting over Thefarie's writings, searching for the solution. Anxious for it. Begging for it.

She pushed her attention back to the wording. "A relief . . ."

"A bas-relief or similar?" Cole offered.

"Oh." Haven nodded. "Yes . . . yes! Is he saying to find a relief in the city where queens are buried?"

Mr. Tzaddik held up a hand. "Not just any city where queens are buried. The Assyrian kings were often buried at Ashur, but wives— *queens*—were buried at Kalhu—Nimrud."

Haven felt a shot of heat rush through her, remembering Tzivia had just been there. The relief . . . she'd seen a relief. She implored Cole with her gaze, but he shook his head again.

He tapped the journal, his brow twitching as if telling her to hurry. "*Tempus fugit*," he muttered.

Irritation kneaded her. "Do you know Latin?" She turned the book toward him with more defiance than she probably should have allowed. Cole no more spoke Latin than she spoke Arabic.

Annoyance and regret rolled through his face. Palms toward her in surrender, he inched away. "Fair enough."

She pulled the tome back toward her. "This isn't the time to hurry. We hurry and mess up, it could have devastating consequences."

"Wisdom has spoken," Mr. Tzaddik said, face still pressed to another book.

Cole licked his lips. Pointed to the book. Probably ready to be done with this place and this man. "Third clue?"

With a deep inhale, she let out her breath through puffed cheeks. "Okay, third—uh . . . '*Draped in black at the feet of Ashur.*'" Hands on her hips, Haven stretched her back. "Yes, that's very helpful. My brain can come up with a dozen different solutions to that clue—feet of Ashur could be the foundation of the city, or it could be the foundation of a gate or a statue. So is Ashur a city, a gate, a statue, or a god in this case?"

"Indeed," Mr. Tzaddik said, returning with another book. "And the fourth?"

Haven returned to the parchment. "'*For Shamash in amulet of red grows angry.*'"

"Well, at least this mentions something tangible—an amulet," Cole grumbled.

She sighed. "Ashur, Kalhu, an amulet . . . These are really vague clues. Wait." She slid her gaze over the notes and text again. "That's . . . that's only four legacies. But Thefarie said to find *five*."

"Indeed. And yes, they appear to be vague," Mr. Tzaddik agreed. "But continue."

Irritation scraped along the edges of her frayed nerves and she could tell Cole wasn't doing any better. He looked tired. Frustrated.

"I came here hoping you had answers, and now we have"—he swept his hand over the book—"riddles. Do you understand what Alec's doing? What we're trying to do?"

"I do, but I don't think you do," Mr. Tzaddik said. "Alec is only doing what that crown allows him to do. You! You're doing . . . what?"

Cole flashed his arms out in a wide arc. "Searching for answers!"

"Are you? Or are you running from them?"

Oh. Ouch. The impact of those words shone on Cole's face as he rubbed his fingers over his brow. "Look, I get it." He motioned to the room. "You want to be a sage or some ancient philosopher, but we have zero time for lectures or guesswork." A storm moved through his features. "How are we supposed to know one amulet from another? Where to look in a city-turned-archaeological-site that now lies in ruins?"

"What you must remember," Mr. Tzaddik said, brushing past Haven and splaying out a parchment, "is that Thefarie's entire purpose in his last years was to destroy that crown. He failed. So writing what he knew of how to destroy it, what it would take—he could not openly lay that out, should it fall into the wrong hands. Yet he needed to be sure there was enough for the next guardian."

"You keep saying that word," Cole said.

"Guardian. Yes." Mr. Tzaddik smiled. "I became fond of it after cataloging the writings." He shrugged. "It seemed a good fit. After all, you are tasked with these artifacts just as Thefarie was, and as others between you and him have been throughout time."

Cole turned from the table, then spun back. "Fine. Whatever. Just—tell us what we need to know, so we can do this and stop Alec." He swallowed.

Haven's stomach cinched at Cole's unconscious reaction—swallowing—which told her that he didn't believe he could stop Alec. Or . . . did he think he'd have to do more than stop him?

Something glinted in Mr. Tzaddik's brown eyes. "You know he has gone too far. He has too long worn the crown."

Anger stabbed through Cole's expression. "Just tell us."

Eyebrows pinched together in sorrow, Mr. Tzaddik inclined his head. "I will share what I know. But—"

"We're ready. Go." Cole's jaw muscle popped. He tapped the parchment Mr. Tzaddik held. "What's in there?"

Slowly, Mr. Tzaddik looked down. Stared at the scroll. "To understand how to stop the crown, we must understand its origins, yes?"

"So, a history lesson." Anger roiled through Cole's words. "Again. When I just told you we're out of time."

Haven frowned at Cole, then shifted between the two men. "Please. We'll listen. Go on."

After a sigh, Mr. Tzaddik relented. "This scroll contains extracts about Adad-Narari I, Shalmaneser I, and Tukulti-Ninurta I. Adad-Narari was responsible for many great victories in battle, uniting most of ancient Mesopotamia. Warrior blood ran through his veins and that of his son—Shalmaneser—and of his grandson, Tukulti-Ninurta. These kings were ferocious warriors. Fighters. They conquered the lands around them in the name of their gods, Ashur and Shamash."

When Cole groaned, Mr. Tzaddik lifted a hand. "Someday I hope you will trust that I have a purpose when I bring up topics you do not readily understand, Mr. Russell."

"Someday I hope you will be quick with information instead of taking us a mile around the topic to get there."

"You know," Mr. Tzaddik said with pinched lips and resignation in his tone, "Thefarie had a brother-knight, his closest friend, whom he traveled with who was much like you."

"Quick and ready to do battle?"

"Impatient and easily angered."

"Not angered," Cole corrected. "Just ready to do violence on behalf of the innocent."

"As was Giraude."

These two were like children! Haven heaved a breath and stepped forward, but Mr. Tzaddik stilled her. "Your complaints are heard, Ms. Cortes."

Complaints she hadn't voiced, yet he somehow still heard. How was that possible?

His somber gaze drifted to the scroll in his hands. "Tukulti-Ninurta I is believed to be Nimrod."

Cole leveled his gaze at Mr. Tzaddik. "We know."

Mr. Tzaddik ignored him. "There is an Arabic work known as the Kitab al-Magall, or the Book of Rolls," he explained slowly, his tone frayed with irritation still, "that says Nimrod 'saw in the sky a piece of black cloth and a crown.' He said the crown came down to him from heaven."

Cole shifted.

"You have heard this, then?" Mr. Tzaddik inclined his head. "It is said that Tukulti-Ninurta called for Sasan the weaver to have the sheet adhered to the crown. Later, he embedded jewels in the crown."

Cole leaned in, his brow a knot of ferocity. "So you're saying it's the same crown?"

"I'm saying Tukulti-Ninurta had an unusually effective battle campaign, uniting a disjointed region that suffered much infighting." Mr. Tzaddik's lips were tight, his posture stiff. "But if you are looking for definitive proof, there is none. Do you trust me to help, or would you like to explore my library on your own?"

Which would take months, if not years, to find the answers. They needed Mr. Tzaddik's guidance, even if Cole was too bullheaded right now to see that.

"We trust your word." Haven ignored Cole, who shifted, shaking his head, and did her best to lure the historian's attention back to the documents. "We do. Or we would not be here, seeking your counsel."

"*You* seek counsel." Mr. Tzaddik wagged a finger at Cole. "He seeks quick, unrealistic answers."

"We came to you for help!" Cole protested.

"That's what I'm doing!"

"You're playing games."

"I'm helping you understand!"

"What I want—"

"Get me some water!" Haven had to shout over their rising voices to be heard. When Cole's gaze flashed to her, Haven almost regretted her firm words. But the two men were accelerants, fanning the flames of anger and unproductivity in each other. "Please, Cole." She nodded through the doorway to the small kitchenette. "A glass of water. From the tap."

AND IF WE FALTER, LET THY POWER

The main port of the eastern Mediterranean, Acre was populated by over twenty thousand people. Thefarie rode into the city with his brother-knights, Giraude and Ameus. It had been eight years since the brother-knights began their pursuit of the crown, yet they kept their spines straight as they trotted through the wealthy Jerusalem kingdom, tunics glaringly white in the afternoon sun, which thrust itself against their mail and sparked in their eyes.

"Tveria is not far," Giraude muttered.

A mother rushed her two young ones out of their path. "Far enough," Thefarie said. "We meet the summons, then return. Saladin—"

"Will be waiting. That Saracen is always waiting," Ameus finished with a sigh. "What I wouldn't pay to see my sister and her children."

"Why have you not taken a wife?"

285

"He's too gray," Giraude taunted.

"Aye, and how have I angered the Lord that he would give me gray hair and keep you rogues in health and vigor?"

"Blessed favor," Thefarie returned. As they approached the gate of the fortress, he wondered for the thousandth time why they had been summoned to the Templar outpost. The journey had taken them more than a day and given them plenty of time to consider their sins and the penances demanded by Rome.

Once through the gate, they made their way to the chapel. There a brother-knight greeted them. "Come this way," he said without further introduction or welcome. He led them down a flight of steps and into a tunnel system.

Quiet draped Thefarie and his brother-knights as they trod the torch-lit passages beneath the city. Dampness pressed against his joints, an indication of the seawater lapping the other side of the stones.

"Where are we going, brother?" Thefarie inquired, hearing the bells of Matins above. All knights were required to partake in prayers at chapel. Why force them to break the rules?

But the brother-knight neither stopped nor replied. They rounded a corner into the refectory, and though they expected no one to occupy it at this hour, a contingent of twenty brother-knights arced around one individual.

Thefarie's heart gave a start at the sight of the white mantle and cloak bearing a black cross. The brother-knight who'd led them swept aside and left Thefarie bare. He hesitated for only a moment, the space of the few heartbeats that it took for his mind to register what was expected. He crossed the ten paces and knelt before none other than Grand Master St. Amand.

"Leave us," intoned the Grand Master. The gathered knights, including Giraude and Ameus, filtered out of the room. "Stand."

Thefarie rose, acutely aware of how every sound echoed off the arched ceilings and cobbles.

St. Amand's steely gaze probed Thefarie. "You take your position with levity, Sir Thefarie?"

"Absolutely not, Grand Master."

St. Amand grunted. Hands behind his back, he paced. "Then

explain why you failed so miserably in retrieving that accursed Crown of Souls."

Thefarie stiffened. Few knew of his purpose in this region, though his name was known and his diligence revered. Until now.

"That single piece of iron has cost far too much over entirely too many years. I was told you could be trusted," the Grand Master chastised. "I was told if anyone could capture it and end the tyranny of its existence, it would be Thefarie of Tveria."

Shamed, Thefarie lowered his gaze to the cobbles, though he never once lost sight in his periphery of the Grand Master's movement.

"Your weakness, your failings, have a significant price—the rise of this great darkness known as Salah ad-Din!" The Grand Master's remonstration was not wholly accurate. Saladin was a shrewd, brilliant warrior. The Saracen's power, influence, and notoriety were only assisted by the crown, not wholly accomplished by it.

Yet therein lay the truth. It *had* helped him. Because Thefarie *had* failed.

"What is my penance?" Would he be removed from the field? Would he be—

"Think you penance is due?"

"Aye," Thefarie confessed. "Despite my every effort, this crown has eluded me. The years have grown long, the nights hard in my pursuit."

"So you have not given up?"

"Given up?" Thefarie swallowed. "Nay. Not for a beat of my heart. The crown is a cruel taskmaster, turning friend to foe. Decaying the soul of its wearer. I want nothing more than to send it to its grave!"

The Grand Master gave another grunt, wandering once more around the cavernous space, deafening silence permeating the room. "You certainly have the passion and fervor to stop it."

"I do," Thefarie agreed.

The Grand Master stopped. Looking over his shoulder, his thick, gray beard brushed his cloak. "Then do it. Stop this crown. Find it. Destroy it." Fierce eyes locked on Thefarie's as the Grand Master turned and stalked closer. "Or I will have you stripped, punished, and sent back to Tveria and your wife in shame!"

28

A war raged within Cole as he locked gazes with Haven. He was used to giving orders, not taking them. He was probably angry that she'd snapped at him. She wasn't happy with herself for it, either, but enough had been enough. When his attention diverted to the book and scroll, she saw his hesitation, his fear of missing something. Or maybe he was worried she'd withhold information. The thought hurt, but she gave him a small nod, urging him to leave.

There was nothing in his expression as he pivoted and strode into the other room.

"Think not for an instant, Ms. Cortes, that you are anything but infinitely important in his life."

Haven started. "Sorry?"

"I've known many warriors in my lifetime, and few have had the level-headedness of a woman like you at his side. He respects you. Cares for you."

Ignoring the heat climbing into her face, Haven wasn't sure whether to smile or argue. "Thank you, but—"

"He cares for you deeply."

She looked into the kitchen, where Cole stood with his back to her, palms on the edge of the counter. The war within him tore her up as much as it did him. She hated it. Hated that he thought so poorly of himself. "Why would you say that?"

"Because he listened to you. When everything in him told him to fight, he listened." Mr. Tzaddik's kind brown eyes met hers. "Loving a warrior is not easy. I pray our Lord Jesus will strengthen you for the journey."

Stunned at both his declaration and admonishment, she watched Mr. Tzaddik turn to the scroll and run his large hand along the script. She stole a minute to peer again at Cole. This time, his blue eyes bored into her. Not in anger, but watching.

No. Waiting.

Waiting for what? Permission to return? She nearly laughed at the idea. Or was it to get himself under control? Then again, wasn't Cole always in control? He held it in an iron fist.

"Do not let your confidence or love be easily removed or frightened by the rage of a warrior."

"Oh, I'm not that easily put off," she said, then glanced down, her guilty conscience forbidding her from meeting Cole's gaze. Time to shift the conversation. The book. The map. Her notes. "Okay, so what else is in there about Nimrod or the others?"

"Thefarie wrote little about Tukulti-Ninurta, save the power he gained and that the madness of his egotism passed to his son, who seized the throne and locked his father away in his palace, then later killed him. Thefarie suggested the madness of Tukulti-Ninurta as the reason his son betrayed him."

"Madness," Haven whispered, avoiding Cole and the way he stiffened.

"I believe, though there is no mention of a unique crown before Tukulti-Ninurta, the power of the crown began with Adad-Nirari. His reign is marked by three elements, which have in all cases shown themselves to be true to the wearer of the crown. First is a seeming inability to be stopped. Second, a notable arrogance asserts itself, and last, the descent into madness. All three—Adad-Narari I, Shalmaneser I, and Tukulti-Ninurta I—show these traits, though arguably the madness could, by some, be reasoned as the ethos of passionate warriors. They were victorious in battle, building the Assyrian empire into an unstoppable force."

"And the madness?" Haven's stomach tied itself in a knot at learning what might happen to Cole's friend. Though Alec was killing people, to Cole he was still a friend in need of help.

"As one can imagine, madness is not easily defined," Mr. Tzaddik said. "But driven by the crown, these three did not stop in their pursuit of more power. Many rulers after them might have worn the crown before it vanished and reappeared in the possession of Saladin. If we wanted to follow the trail of vicious campaigns—"

"Which we don't want," Haven asserted. "So the city where queens are buried is Nimrud." Her heart thumped each time she thought of it—Tzivia had to have found the right place. "So one of the reliefs in Nimrud is the key?"

Mr. Tzaddik's eyes gleamed with some hidden insight that left Haven's stomach feeling a little queasy. Somehow, this was about to get weird.

She squinted. "Am I missing something? Because this still feels really vague. What does he mean by legacies, and what is the fifth one? How are we supposed to narrow down the location—searching an entire city for a relief? And a seal—a ring? Where? How do we find that?" But then she remembered. "You mentioned jewels earlier, that"—she glanced at her log book—"Tukulti-Ninurta had jewels embedded into the crown."

More amusement trickled through Mr. Tzaddik's expression, but he still didn't answer.

"Could the jewels be the legacies?"

His gaze twitched from her to the kitchen doorway, where Cole stood with a glass of water, his expression washed of anger. "You have a very beautiful, intelligent woman with you, Mr. Russell."

"At least we can agree on that." Cole planted a hand on his belt. "So. The legacies are jewels."

* * * *

"Why does he do it?"

Hands evenly placed—one on the large tome and the other holding a pen over the paper she'd been taking notes on—Haven looked up. Her gaze bounced to Tzaddik in the kitchen. "I don't think he—"

"No." Tox's heart slammed against his ribs. "God."

Her eyes widened a little, but then she marked the page and set down the pen. "You said that like a question, but I heard more of an angry statement."

He snorted and gave a nod. He should've known she'd read him. "I *am* angry. We're sitting here—again—hunting down an artifact that has reached out of the past and punched us in the gut."

"Punched you how?"

Tox studied her for a second, noting that she'd said *you*, not *us* in that question. Then it was just him? Was he the only one seeing the parallels again? "This stuff"—he indicated the piles of papers on the table before confirming Tzaddik was still busy preparing sandwiches in the kitchen—"this *crown* destroyed kings. And now it's . . . affecting Alec. Alec *King*. Tell me that's not some cheesy irony."

"But that's Alec, not you." The knot of confusion hanging over her beautiful green eyes wasn't born of real confusion—she understood this situation. Perfectly. Better than he did, apparently. She knew what she was saying. What he was saying.

He also read her implication. "Dr. Cathey said Alec was suffering moral decay. Like something in him was rotting."

"There *is* something rotting in him."

The invisible tether between them turned into a rappelling hook, its sharp barbs digging into his heart. Her words were true, which meant . . . "Then there's something rotting in me, too. Alec and I are made from the same cloth."

"You were," she said, her voice soft. "But not anymore." She placed her hand over his. "And he's not just letting it rot him—he's feeding that demon."

But weren't they all? Wasn't that why he was still chasing terrorists? Because he was good at it. And wanted to be better, more effective.

"Cole, I love you too much to let you keep thinking you're like Alec. You're not. You're good. You pursue justice. You're not a monster who kills innocent people. You aren't driven by anger—"

"But I am!" The growl that leapt out startled him, but he wasn't backing down. "I'm angry that innocents are hurt. I'm angry I was told to stand down in that village and Gabir Karim got away. I was

292

ticked when that same piece of crap then killed good soldiers. I"—he slapped his chest hard—"could've stopped that."

"But you were ordered to stand down. And you obeyed." She squeezed his hand.

"Yes, and now McKenna is dead and those villagers and—"

"Cole." Her tone wasn't remonstrative, but she was firm, calm. "Do you see what happened in the words you just spoke? The villain changed." She leaned in, a grieved smile on her soft lips. "The villain you chased changed from Karim to Alec."

Metal scraped against cement as Tox punched to his feet, knocking back his chair. Her hand fell away, and at her shocked expression, ice blasted through his veins. "I need air."

As he marched through to the main room, ignoring Tzaddik, he couldn't shake Haven's words. She'd made Alec a villain. Then wasn't he one, too?

"You're not a monster who kills innocent people."

But he was. He was that monster.

If a monster was someone who killed innocent people—as Alec had—then so was Tox. Haven just didn't know. She didn't know about al-Homsi. About the fallout. About the collateral damage.

He plunged down the narrow passage, back up the stairs, and out into the open, hot air. It was arid and dry, but he welcomed it. Anything other than being trapped down there.

Who was he kidding? He was trapped by his own guilt. He'd never get away from it. If Alec should die, then he should die. Staring up at the sky, he ran a hand over his mouth, feeling the coarse stubble on his jaw.

"Cole?"

Eyes clenched at her intrusion, he breathed out heavily. "Haven, please. I just need room."

"No."

He spun to her. "Excuse me?"

"No." She shrugged and pursed her lips, unrepentant. "I won't. I won't excuse this, and I won't walk away from it or you. Not anymore. I know you believe you're the same as Alec, but you're not."

He scoffed. "You—"

"Alec isn't worried. He isn't bothered by his actions or who he hurts." She came closer, her long blond hair curling around her neck and shoulder. "And worst of all, he is content with his actions. You?" She smiled around an airy laugh. "You're running from yourself. From anyone who sees good in you. Because you're struggling with it, with the belief that you're the same, that you've done bad things. That guilt, that shame? *That* should be your compass, Cole. But I don't need a compass to know you're not the same as Alec. And I wish my belief in you was enough to convince you. The actions of man speak to what's in his heart." She pressed a hand to his chest, right over the four-valved organ pumping blood through his veins. And it seemed in a hurry right now. "Read what's there, Cole."

Breathing was hard. A struggle as he stared into her rich, green eyes. She made sense. Haven always made sense. But . . . let himself off the hook? Give himself a pass for all this?

Too easy. He hadn't earned that.

"Why are you chasing Alec?"

A piece of that guilt and shame she'd mentioned a second ago twitched beneath her question. "To stop him." Safe answer.

"Exactly." Her head cocked a bit. "You *know* he needs to be stopped because what he's doing is wrong." She smiled, tender, soft. Sweet. "He doesn't see it as wrong. He doesn't believe he has to be stopped. He's doing *more*, and it's still not enough. It'll never be enough for him. For you—it's already more than enough. It's *too* much."

Man, he wanted to believe that. Wanted to let those words in, let them be a Band-Aid to the gaping wound in his soul. But there were things . . .

"Haven." He wanted to come clean. Grasp the olive branch she'd offered. But it scared him, what she'd do or say once she knew the full truth. Scared him that he might lose her. That she'd no longer see him as the hero who made her knees weak. Maybe it was better she knew now. "You don't know—"

"I *do* know. I know you."

"*I love you too much* . . ." His heart misfired. Slung him backward to five minutes ago when she'd said that. Why had it taken him so long to *hear* those words? Had she really said it? She loved him. She loved him?

He wanted that. Wanted her, her love. But it seemed an obstacle course loomed between him and that love. A gauntlet of self-hatred. Murky miles of guilt, and shame that had him burning in a lake of fire. But she . . . she was cool ocean water—clear, calm—that he wanted to immerse himself in.

In contrast to the violence of his career, she was soft. Innocent. He ran his knuckles along her cheek and down her jaw, relishing the way she responded.

Could he? Could he let it go and seize this chance?

A tentative smile curved her lips as he slipped his hand beneath her thick hair and thumbed her jawline. Color filled her cheeks.

Half his brain told him to back off, but a roar filled him with hunger. He saw the hitch in her breath. Her soft lips parted.

Tox homed in. Captured them. She stumbled back a little, and he gave chase, though it was just an inch. Her lips were sweet. Her response sweeter, igniting a response in him. A desperation. For her. For her goodness.

When she gripped his sides, Tox deepened the kiss. She was perfect and beautiful. He couldn't get enough. He trailed a kiss along her jaw. She shivered, her body arching toward him. He teased the spot behind her ear.

God, help me! I love her.

Surrendering, Tox buried his face in her neck. Held her. Breathed her in. As if her goodness could somehow infuse him. Wash away the taunting darkness.

She stiffened in his arms. "Do you see it?"

Her scent—a bit floral and soapy—saturated his senses. He didn't want to break apart, certain that in the absence of her touch, the void in him would grow.

She cupped his biceps. "Cole."

Her tone was icy. Frightened.

He lifted his head from her silky hair and saw it—the fear in her eyes, which weren't looking at him but down the street.

Instincts flared. Shielding her, he glanced in that direction.

Painted on the side of a small shop—Alec's symbol.

29

Responsibility had a weight to it. Approximately 6.2 pounds, to be exact.

Alec King sat on a high-backed chair in the library. He stared across the room to the lone window, which threw beams of light like fiery daggers. The history of the world was tucked neatly between the spines and covers of leather-bound books that shielded the walls and his mind from futility and uselessness.

He had taken on the mantle of leadership in the crusade against injustice. After years of watching evil go unchecked. Of watching politicians wipe each other's backsides with the lives of the innocent. He had stepped too late into the role to protect his wife and daughter, but he would not allow the ambivalent to cause more harm.

He would make those with too much power and those too blinded by their own comfort to feel with an aching fury the cost of looking the other way.

"What next?" he asked, reaching back through time to the power that had imbued the crown.

A peripheral awareness of those guarding him and this room

flickered in and out as he allowed his gaze to find the bank of monitors lining the wall. News and talk shows. Flooding his senses with injustices, wrongs, murders, kidnappings.

"Who is next?"

The crown would show him. Tell him where to focus his skills and men.

A small shape drifted through the shadows and glittered in the sunlight of the tall window. "Daddy!"

Rushing to his feet, Alec smiled, laughter building in his chest. He bent to receive his little girl in his arms. "Marissa!"

She leapt toward him with an airy *whoosh*.

Alec blinked. Felt air against his face but not the weight of his seven-year-old daughter against his chest. He stared at the half-shadowed spot where she'd last been.

It stood empty.

He scanned the room. Dusty. Musty. No laughter.

"Where did you go?" he called. She'd always loved games.

"Sir?"

Alec swallowed, suddenly remembering—*how could I have forgotten?* Marissa had died. Years ago. At the hands of Gabir Karim's associates, he was sure of it.

Jason Bollinger stood in the middle of the library with his weapon holstered at his shoulder. "Did you need me to get something for you or *your guest?*"

"Guest." But even as he spoke the word and felt Bollinger's insinuation that he'd forgotten something, Alec was turning to where he knew a man sat in a wingback chair.

Though no smile lay on his lips, the man hid one in his dark eyes. Mocking eyes. "Has it spoken to you, Alec?"

Again, Alec looked to the sunny spot that was now dark. He felt the weight upon his head. The crown. Felt the heat of it, the certainty that existed when he wore it. The power. He needed both its certainty and its power.

How could he have forgotten his own daughter's death?

"Leave us."

Bollinger retreated up a step before pivoting and stalking out.

Alec gathered the frayed remnants of his thoughts and turned to his high-backed chair. To the man. "Why are you here?"

"You've been using the crown too much, Alec."

"I'm making a difference," he muttered as he eased himself into his chair. "Besides, it fits me like a glove." He shifted his attention to the monitors. "Now, I have work—"

"Tox Russell is not going to join you."

"I can convince him. He just needs motivation."

"He's contacted a source who can tell him how to destroy the crown."

Stunned, Alec stared at the man. Then a swift rage tore through him. "How can you know this? Tox would never do that! He understands the importance that violence of action plays. He's a warrior like me. He—"

"Look at your monitors, Alec."

He complied. Tensed as every screen went blank and then flashed with images of Tox and that woman seated outside a café. They got up and started walking, and the footage skipped ahead to the moment when an older man approached them.

"That is Ti Tzaddik, a foremost expert on ancient artifacts."

Anger thundered through him. "What do I do?"

"You already have men tracking Tox, yes?"

"Of course."

"We think Tox needs that motivation you mentioned—"

"Yes."

"—to understand the injustice of those he cares about being harmed."

"Yesss."

* * * *

Defeat crowded Tzaddik's features when Tox told him about Alec's symbol. He sighed. "We are discovered."

"Yes," Tox said. "Pack up—"

"No."

Tox stilled. "I don't think you understand—"

"It is you who does not understand. I have many enemies, but these are not mine. They are yours."

Tox's phone rang. He lifted it to his ear. "Russell."

"It seems you have failed to understand my offer."

"Alec." He flicked a look in Haven's direction.

"And it seems you need to experience what it's like to have someone under your charge killed before your eyes."

"That happened in the village where you planted IEDs. Remember? You killed Keogh."

"Look out the window."

Panic trapped the air in his throat. He let it out and rushed to the glass, his mind scrambling to catch up with the fact that Alec knew where he was. Which meant Alec probably knew what he was doing—trying to find a way to stop the crown.

Tox reached for the lace curtains covering the window.

"Honestly, I'm disappointed we must do this, but then, I know he's not truly yours. Had I more time to make this point, we would have picked someone closer to you. Perhaps that Israeli. Or the god of thunder."

Crap. Alec knew the men on his team. So if he hadn't grabbed Ram or Thor, who . . . ? Tox's hand trembled as he tugged aside the curtain. The bright afternoon speared him with a glare, but he stared out, waiting for his eyes to adjust.

The sidewalk was clear. So were the cars.

Behind him, Haven gasped at the same time Tox saw him.

In the middle of the road, hands behind his back, knelt Levi Wallace.

"I believe your men call him Superman—"

"Don't do this."

"—but I seriously doubt he's invincible."

"Alec, stop!"

"Shall we test that?"

"No!"

"Oh, I think we should. We must. You have to see the higher path. And that understanding only comes with pain."

Tox pointed at Haven. "Stay!" He sprinted for the door and burst out into the afternoon, heat blazing through his chest. He threw himself between two parked cars. Broke into the street.

Wallace snapped up his gaze. His eyes went wild, panicked. He frantically shook his head, unable to speak through the tape across his mouth.

Wary at the obvious setup, Tox couldn't fathom why Alec would leave Wallace in the middle of a quiet street. He glanced around, searching for snipers. Shooters behind trees. But saw nothing.

Still Wallace shook his head, hard. Sweat poured down his temples. He was pleading frantically for Tox not to come. He glanced at his own chest, then again. Several times.

Tox stopped, realization flooding him. Noting the too-thick chest. The bulges. He went to a knee. Pressed a fist to his mouth.

They'd put a suicide vest on Levi.

Shoulders slumping, Wallace lowered his head. Defeated. He'd given up.

Haven's whimpers drenched the air and Tox's nerves. He rose to his feet and turned.

"Haven." He waited until her eyes met his. "Go inside. Call Ram. Tell him what's happening. Then SAARC. I need a relay or something to walk me through this."

She stared at him, a thousand questions and fears swimming in her eyes, then finally moved back into the house.

Tox faced Wallace. Surely whoever had outfitted him had a way to blow him to pieces. If Tox crossed the twenty paces to him, would they remotely detonate it? "Wallace."

The special agent's shiny black head came up.

"Is it radio command?"

Hesitantly, Wallace shook his head and half shrugged. So probably not, though he couldn't be sure. Nobody could. But Tox wouldn't leave him out here to die. He had to try. He started forward.

Wallace again wagged his head hard.

Five paces in, and nothing had happened. He had to wager that Alec wouldn't kill him, too. There was a point to this—hurt Tox. Not kill Tox. At least, he hoped that was the goal, because it bought options, time.

He walked a wide arc around Levi, eyeing the scene. They'd bound his wrists to his ankles with cuffs so he couldn't remove the vest or run. The FBI-issue jacket concealed the obvious payload beneath.

Another five paces, and Tox felt someone join him. "We need to get that jacket off to see the device." Tzaddik.

"You have experience with suicide vests?"

"About as much as you."

Snorting, Tox unsheathed his KA-BAR and closed the gap. He was still alive, but he couldn't breathe any easier. He crouched before Wallace and peeled the tape from his mouth.

The FBI agent gulped air. "I'm sorry."

"Yeah, you and me both." Tox eyed the bulk under the jacket. "I'll kill you later for this." He jutted his jaw toward the bomb. "The jacket. They put it on you after?"

Wallace nodded. "They wanted me to look normal."

"They should've given up while they were ahead," Tox teased. "I'm going to ease the jacket away so we can see the device."

"Don't." Wallace's blue eyes sparked with panic and worry.

"I'm not—"

"She needs you."

Tox swallowed.

"She'd never forgive me if something happened to you."

"If you believe that about her, you don't know her. She's better than both of us." Tox scanned what little he could see of the device. "Now hold still."

Tox carefully unfastened each of the snaps holding the front of the jacket closed. Using the tip of his knife, he lifted the fabric away from the vest. Made sure there were no wires or tabs attached to the lining that would set it off.

"Looks clear," Tzaddik said, eyeing the back.

"Let's cut it away." Tox gently sawed the material, going straight down Levi's back, then drew the two pieces apart and down, leaving the arms intact. The halves bunched around Wallace's forearms, but the less they messed with, the better.

Or so he thought. When he saw wires threaded around the agent's sides, no doubt leading to a deadman's switch, Tox glanced at Wallace's hand. He grunted at the button beneath the agent's thumb. "You could've warned me," Tox gritted out.

"Unrealistic hope that you'd figure a way out," Wallace mumbled.

Tox pressed a fist to his mouth. They'd never get this off him.

"See? You can't remove it. They told me as much," Levi mumbled. "Just go. Get clear—"

"We could break your wrists."

Mouth snapped shut, Wallace eyed him.

"Kidding. Mostly." Tox thrust his chin at him. "Lean forward. Stay still and keep quiet." He traced the wires, packs of C-4, and the power source. Could he just remove the batteries?

"Maybe we can lift it over his head," Tzaddik suggested.

"Side wires," Tox countered, pointing his knife to the wires along Wallace's ribs.

"What if I can get his hands free?" Tzaddik moved behind, peering at Tox over the agent's shoulder. "Will that work?"

Tox swallowed. He wasn't an explosive ordnance disposal tech, but it seemed . . . "Maybe." He swiped his knuckle along the edge of his jaw. "Unless there's some sensor that trips it."

"Not worth it," Wallace said. "I don't want—"

"Shut up," Tox bit out, then regretted his harshness. He met Levi's gaze evenly. "Just . . . let us figure it out." He pried free of the agent's probing gaze and again studied the bomb.

A buzzing made his pulse spasm. Phone. *Just my phone.* Alec must have hung up after Tox sprinted out of the house. Now another call was coming through—his team.

He answered. "Help me out."

"Uh, yeah," Cell said, "I don't know much about bombs, but DoD is getting someone there, and just FYI: they're saying SOP for radio command vests like that is to cut all wireless in the area, so we might lose contact. Also, we . . . we received a message from King."

Tox stilled.

"He's giving you two minutes to say good-bye."

"He's watching."

"That'd be my guess."

"Get me Rodriguez."

"No time for that," Tzaddik said, his voice ominous. "Look."

Tox shifted around and peered at Levi's shoulder. One of the C-4 bricks had a small digital timer. It read *0:45*.

Forty-five seconds! A curse shot from Tox's mouth.

"I'll break the bonds," Tzaddik said.

"How do you plan to break carbon steel?"

"They're rope cords. Get ready to draw it over his head."

Rope? Tox would have sworn he'd seen metal. But he'd take that mistake to even out the odds a little. "Need a knife?"

"I'm good," Tzaddik said.

"Wait," Wallace said, his breathing shallow. "What if lifting it—"

"In forty seconds it won't matter." Cold, hard truth. Palms slick, Tox positioned himself. Crouched, hands gripping the shoulders of the vest. Muscles tensed, ready to spring into action. "Arms up. Dive backward," he instructed.

Hair matted to his forehead, Wallace nodded.

Running feet caught Tox's attention. He glanced toward the sidewalk and spotted Ram. Hands on his head, expression strained, he hovered.

"Almost . . ." Tzaddik gritted his teeth. Strained. His face went red. Veins popped at his temples.

Beep.

Beepbeep.

Beepbeepbeepbeepbeepbeepbeep.

Tox's pulse rapid-fired at the accelerating noise.

Wallace sucked in a breath. Glanced down to where Tzaddik worked on the restraints.

"Go!" Tzaddik finally announced.

Wallace's arms vaulted up.

Tox hauled the vest to the sky. Twisted himself around and lunged from the two men. With a step and every ounce of strength he could muster, he pitched the vest away from them.

In that instant, his vision went double. He saw two sets of arms throwing the vest.

Bright white exploded.

A powerful fist pounded Tox into the ground.

30

Emergency vehicles crowded the street, along with EOD vans and forensics teams. Tox stood next to the gurney where technicians were running IV lines and applying salves to Wallace's burns. He had more than Tox, but way fewer than they both should have, considering the vest had detonated in the air.

In a cooperative effort between the Israeli and American governments, names and identities were being kept out of the news. This would be recorded as just another radicalized incident in Israel. The EMTs loaded Wallace into the back of a nondescript van and drove off.

"You okay?" Ram asked.

"I'll live." He had burns, but that was the worst of it. Well, except the discrepancies his mind warred with.

"I don't know whether to punch you for messing with that vest or say good job," Ram muttered.

"I wasn't going to let them turn him into ground meat in the middle of the street." Tox saw Haven and Tzaddik talking with the responders.

"I know. And apparently King knew that, too."

Roughing a hand over his face, Tox fought his weariness. His frustration. The vest. The hands . . .

304

Ram indicated a man who had joined them. "This is Anthony Dobbs. He's an EOD tech. Has a few questions for you."

Tox shook the tech's hand. "What can I do for you?"

"You have EOD experience?"

"Limited."

Dobbs nodded, stretched his jaw. "Can you explain how you got the vest off?"

"We broke the wrist bonds, then lifted it over his head."

"Lifted it over his head." Dobbs's eyes carried a message. A disconcerting one.

"That a problem?"

Dobbs nodded again. "Yeah."

"Why?"

"We canvassed the scene. The remnants we found show an improvised tilt switch/trembler switch that would initiate in the case of movement."

"And that's . . . bad."

"It means you should've been all over the street as soon as you touched the vest."

"Maybe you're reading it wrong."

Dobbs snorted. "We do this on a daily basis. How often do you?"

Tox's gut churned. "Excuse me." He walked into Tzaddik's house and strode down the short hall to the bathroom. He tucked himself into the bathroom and locked the door behind him. Just to get away. Get some space. Slumping against the door, he gripped his knees.

Was he losing his mind?

Two hands. He'd seen two right hands throwing that vest. His hand and . . .

Had to have been the heat. The wake from the explosion blurring his vision. Right?

Sure. That was what he kept telling himself about the tunnel collapse and the fiery image of Tzaddik that had visited him, too. A trembler switch. Couldn't be. The EOD tech had to be wrong. Maybe there was a glitch in the wiring? The batteries? Were there even batteries?

Feeling that heat. Knowing the vest had been remotely activated. Knowing the explosion was happening right in his face.

Yet . . . He glanced in the mirror on the opposite wall. No burns there.

He snorted. Who cared about burns? He was alive when he shouldn't be. There were no answers. No explanations. It just was. He just was . . . still here, still confused.

Pushing off the wall, he glanced in the mirror one more time. Then splashed water on his face, toweled off, and opened the door.

Ram waited there, arms folded, confrontation in his hazel eyes. "What happened out there?"

"Come again?"

"I see it all over your face—something's bothering you."

"Alec tried to kill Wallace." He didn't want a lecture or conversation now.

"Dobbs say the bonds are missing."

Tox blinked. "The bonds?"

"You said Wallace had his hands bound to his ankles, and there's proof on his wrists and ankles—scrapes and chafing—but the evidence team didn't find the bonds."

With a slow shrug, Tox shook his head. "I have no idea. When the bomb detonated, it slammed me to the ground. I was out cold and came to with Haven standing over me." He rubbed his jaw, thinking about the glint he'd seen when he'd first inspected Wallace's situation. The glint of metal. "Tzaddik said the bonds were rope." That made more sense, right?

"You think they burned up?"

Tox shrugged.

"How'd you come out with such a minor injury?" Ram pointed to the bandage on Tox's forearm.

Leaning against the doorjamb, Tox sighed. "I don't know, man. It's messed up." He sighed and ran a hand over his head and neck, unable to sort through the confusion. "What about you? Why are you here? I thought you were heading back to the plane after we connected with Tzaddik."

Ram deflated. "I'm doing damage control."

"Because of the bomb?" But that wouldn't explain why Ram had been close enough to get on-site before the detonation. "Tzivia." It was the only other option that made sense.

Ram's nod was almost nonexistent.

"Her boyfriend?"

"Omar is an intelligence director."

"So she's using this guy?"

Ram sighed. "I don't know." Frustration and exhaustion pressed in on his answer.

"Why isn't she going through Iliescu or Almstedt?"

"Because it has nothing to do with you or the crown." Ram shook his head. "She's using Omar to get answers about our father, and it's put both of us in a lot of trouble and a lot of danger."

"Your father? I thought he was dead."

"He is. But"—Ram gave a cockeyed nod—"the circumstances were . . . suspicious. I've been quietly looking for answers, but it wasn't fast enough for her. The Mossad is aware of what she's doing, and they aren't happy. Omar is suspended. And . . ."

Tox's gut twisted. "What?"

"Tzivia is missing."

"They got to her?"

"I . . ." Another shake of the head. "I think she's gone into hiding, which is the smartest thing she's done in a few weeks. The last anyone saw of her was that meeting she had with Omar in the clothing shop you had Cell tap into."

"Maybe Omar helped her vanish."

Ram pinched his lips. "Not likely."

"That's why you were close by—looking for her."

"Trying. I have to play two hands. The Mossad knows I want her found, but they also know my loyalty to them is absolute."

Tox squinted. "Is it?" Would he have to worry about his friend choosing between Israeli and American interests?

But Ram didn't answer. Didn't allay the fears grinding through Tox's mind like a slipped gear. "Israel wants the crown stopped, too."

"That's not an answer to my question."

"But it is an answer to our immediate situation." Ram shifted and took the conversation with him. "Get what you needed from Tzaddik?"

Tox didn't like the way this was being turned. "Maybe. A lot of riddles. Confusion. But he says we have what we need."

"Then let's get back to the professor and run it past him."

Tox was more than ready to get out from under Tzaddik's mystery-upon-mystery methods. "Agreed."

Ram headed to the front room, and Tox pulled the bathroom door to. As he turned, he noticed the door across the hall hung open an inch. There, on the bed inside, lay a small jumble of metal.

Tox froze, his gaze locked on the item. He slipped into the room and crossed to the bed. Cold metal rings connected by a short chain teased his fingertips and mind.

Handcuffs.

The ones that secured Levi's hands. Not rope. Carbon steel.

The ones the evidence response team couldn't find.

They were here. On Tzaddik's bed. Broken. The metal strained apart.

* * * *

— DAY 26 —
SAARC JET

"Tzivia's missing?" Dr. Cathey peered over his rimless glasses, stroking his beard.

Haven coiled in on herself, thinking about the Israeli beauty. There was so much going on in her, so much animosity, so much turmoil.

"She's protecting her whereabouts," Ram corrected. "I don't believe she's in immediate danger, but she is aware of the threat, the trouble she's brought on herself."

"By looking for your father?" Cell asked, his wrinkled brows climbing his forehead.

"Our father is dead." Ram's voice was flat, emotionless. Like his expression.

Which made Haven wonder what he was hiding. She wished this conversation was being recorded, so she could play it back later. Something had been off with Ram and Tzivia since the team started trying to stop Alec King.

"Sorry," Cole said, holding up a hand, "but we need to get back on track."

"The crown," Thor said. "And putting a massive hole in the back of Alec King's head."

"Hooah," Cell muttered, but they all saw the glower from Cole. "I mean, I get it—you were his friend, but you have to admit, Sarge, that this guy has to be taken down."

"If by 'taken down' you mean 'stopped,' then I agree."

"'Stopped.'" Cell tucked his chin, peering through his muddy brown eyebrows. "You seriously think *stopping* him will work? I can't see this guy giving up just because we slap cuffs on him."

Cole flinched. He hadn't been the same after returning from Tzaddik's. Something there had changed him. Though he'd kissed her like there was no tomorrow at one point, he'd been withdrawn and contemplative ever since. Maybe even angrier, which she hadn't thought possible.

What was going on?

"The crown," Cole repeated. "Haven took some good notes, and I snapped photos of Thefarie's journals." He glanced at Dr. Cathey. "You get those?"

"Yes, and I've studied them while we waited for your return." The professor drew off his glasses and pointed them toward the wall. "Had you but a longer flight, I might have more material. As it is, I found"—he waved a paper, donned his glasses, and started reading—"that Shalmaneser II, a descendant of Shalmaneser I and Tukulti-Ninurta I, has a monolith inscription of Column I that states in one translation: '. . . *when Assur the great lord in the determination of his [heart] had turned upon his illustrious eyes, and had called me to the government of Assyria; had given me to hold the mighty weapon which overthrows the rebellious; had [invested] me with the [sacred] crown; the lordship over all lands.*'" The professor smiled at them. "There—'*the crown*,' which gave '*lordship over all lands.*'"

"But don't all crowns mean lordship over the lands?" Cell asked. "Like, the Queen of England wears the crown that names her queen."

"Perhaps," Dr. Cathey said, "but the Assyrians wrote using words that imbued life-giving properties to this crown."

"What?" Cell asked.

"There is an inscription that says crowns gave witness—literally, not figuratively," Dr. Cathey said, shaking his finger. "The crown literally gave witness in trials and made decisions. It's unique terminology that personifies this crown unlike any inscription before."

"So, you're saying," Cole said, rubbing his jaw again, "that Shalmaneser believed one of their two thousand gods gave him the crown that made him ruler over all the lands?"

"I am. And who is to say this is not the very same Crown of Souls that his forebears had, that Tukulti-Ninurta"—he motioned to Haven's journals—"or Nimrod, believed came down from heaven?"

"How do we stop it?" Cole sighed. "That seems to be the part nobody really wants to define."

"Perhaps because a definitive solution is not entirely possible."

The frown Cole gave the professor mirrored the one the rest of the team wore. "How is it possible not to have a solution if we have to stop it?"

"Because it has not been previously stopped, nobody can define the method to . . . neutralizing its effects." The professor seemed a little too pleased with himself for that explanation. "In the notes, it says that Thefarie identified four of the five legacies."

"What legacies?" Cell asked.

"The jewels," Haven said. "And the fifth is unknown to us, maybe even to Thefarie, since he didn't mention it."

"Do we know what type of jewels they are and what they look like?" Thor asked from where he sat next to Haven.

"We do—well, we have clues." Dr. Cathey pointed to the wall again. "I've put together a chart, using Haven's notes, Mr. Russell's photos, and my research. It is my belief that not only must we take into account Thefarie's narrative of what he claims to know, but also the character of this Crusader-knight and his mission—to protect mankind. I suspect the narrative not only tells us where to look but what to look for. First line of his script: '*The seal of Shalmaneser ruled Tukulti-Ninurta.*'"

"Weren't signet rings that held the seal made of gold?" Cole shrugged. "There's no jewel in that."

"Yes, and that may prove to be a problem. I have no solution for that one yet, but I will continue my search." Dr. Cathey bobbed his head toward the wall again. "But next it said, 'At his city where queens are buried, in great relief.'"

"Right," Haven interjected.

"Nimrud—ancient Kalhu—is where the queens were buried."

"Mr. Tzaddik thought a relief might reveal what the riddle meant."

"Indeed," Dr. Cathey said.

"So we go to Nimrud and walk around reading all the reliefs?" Maangi asked, his annoyance strong.

"We will need to visit both sites—"

"Wait." Tox frowned. "Both?"

"Yes, Nimrud is only connected to the queens. We must also visit the site of the kings to solve these riddles. Within the two, we can narrow down where to look, because every relief and depiction is meticulously catalogued. And I've drawn a few to consider—I have an idea about where to look at Ashur." He clicked a button and flicked through three images. "It makes sense to visit that first, since it is closer and might be quicker. Then on to Kalhu."

"Ancient Ashur?"

Dr. Cathey nodded. "Modern day Qal'at Sherqat."

31

The sands of time carved cruel lines through the desert, mocking the efforts of man to establish its mark on the world. Strong and obstinate, Tabira Gate—three arches set one behind the other—remained upright, defying the elements and time. Refusing to collapse beneath the weight of history.

Tox crouched as the Black Hawk lifted off, rotors slapping grains of sand at the team it had deposited. Bracing himself against the gusts, he stared at the gate. Couldn't help but think how much Tzivia would enjoy this view and opportunity.

But that was what she got for hiding. He'd sent her a message before heading out, pleading with her to contact them. They desperately needed her help. She couldn't have picked a worse time to try to hunt down information about her father.

"Incredible, is it not?" Dr. Cathey's voice boomed once the helo noise faded. "Look at it! So glorious against a rugged terrain. Defiant to the end, the Assyrians."

Defiant. A lot like someone else Tox knew. Squinting, he scanned the area. Had Alec been here? His nerves thrummed. He wouldn't put it past him. Alec had been at least two steps ahead of them constantly.

"Their religious capital survived those who built it and those who

312

expanded it," Dr. Cathey went on. "Here, kings were crowned, and here, they were laid to rest with the land."

"Dude, we aren't digging up bodies, right?" Cell rolled his shoulders. "I just want to find one of those gems and get out of here."

A check for radio frequency broadcasts could tell them if Alec had been here. Haven was smiling and talking with Maangi, who pointed to something in the distance. Protectiveness shot through Tox, remembering how Alec had hit Wallace and Keogh. "Cell." Tox jerked toward the communications specialist. "Get your equipment set up. Search for the ghost skip."

"Copy that. Leavin' y'all to the grave-digging," Cell muttered, dragging the big black case that contained his special equipment. He trudged along the stony hill that traced the Tigris River. "Come on, Runt. You can be my beast of burden."

"You do realize I outrank you," Runt said.

Cell laughed and merely indicated the equipment for Runt to pick up.

Runt glanced at Tox.

He had a lot more experience, Tox knew, but he also had an expectation, an arrogance, that he should be able to step into a position equal to that held by Ram. So Tox gave him a nod, telling Runt to go with Cell. It would do him good to get his bearings with the team.

"There, the Tabira Gate," Dr. Cathey said, pointing.

Tox followed the professor's leading. The three arches stood in the middle of nowhere, exhibiting that defiance the professor had mentioned. It was hard to imagine a thriving trade culture here when most of it was barren or rocky. But the professor had shown them satellite imaging that revealed a ghosted grid of civilization. Tox still couldn't get the image out of his head, as if the past lingered in the dust. Ghost skips. Ghost cities.

Too many ghosts.

He shifted his gaze to where the old palace and ziggurat protruded from the desert-like terrain.

"We're in Iraq."

Tox glanced at the professor. Was there a point? Of course they were in Iraq.

"In the al-Sherqat district."

"I would guess that's why they call it Qal'at Sherqat."

"Right," the professor agreed with an ardent nod. "But did you know it's a small panhandle of the Salah ad-Din Governorate?"

His ears weren't playing tricks. "Saladin?"

"No, but that is where the name came from," Dr. Cathey said with a smile.

"More history for the history buff," Haven quipped as she joined them.

Saladin. Hearing that name from Tzaddik was bad enough. Tox swallowed, once more taking in the area. He wanted to get in and get out. Fast. "What do we need to find here?"

"And *how* are we going to find it?" Maangi asked, his gaze distant as he took in the site. "Look at this place—most of it buried, destroyed, or unknown."

"This way." Dr. Cathey hustled down an incline, then hurried on a course parallel to the Tigris. Spreading his arms to the side, he was more exuberant than Tox had seen him in a while. "To your left was the house of the incantation priest."

"I'll incant something if we run up against any radicals," Thor promised.

"Over there is the temple of Sin and Shamash."

Thor scowled. "A temple for sin? Sign me up!"

"Sin, the moon god," Dr. Cathey clarified. "Later, a temple to the goddess Ishtar was built, but Ashur dates back to the third millennium BC. Long before the Assyrians showed up, this site was populated by the Sumerians. Because of its location along the Tigris, Ashur was a thriving trade city."

"Now it's a heap of rubble targeted by ISIL," Maangi mumbled.

"Where are we headed, professor?" Ram asked.

"There," Dr. Cathey said, huffing. "The ziggurat."

Tox hesitated for only a fraction of a second, looking at the structure that seemed more like a mud mound than a ziggurat. "We allowed in there?"

"Sure, assuming we get there before the army."

"The army?" Thor's voice pitched high.

"Indeed. Security has been heightened since the attacks by ISIL. Or we could have a confrontation with the antiquity authorities," Cathey said with a shrug. "But we should be gone before they're aware of our presence."

Should be. Tox gritted his teeth that Almstedt had signed off on this little excursion, knowing the risks to the team. Then again, their job came with risks.

It took twenty minutes to hoof it to the ziggurat. They entered a portal of carefully laid brickwork that formed a tunnel.

Tunnels. Why did it have to be tunnels? Painful memories of being buried alive in Kafr al-Ayn rushed back at him.

The path sloped down, taking them out of the Iraqi heat and into the musty, cooler underground.

Underground. Of course.

"Chicken?"

Tox arched an eyebrow as Ram took up position at the lip of the entrance with Thor, their weapons and minds ready for trouble. Tox guided Haven down the path with the others.

"You think there are reliefs down here?" Tox asked.

"Down here?" Dr. Cathey glanced back, surprise in his aged features. "Oh, not down here."

Tox slowed. "Then why—"

A figure stepped from the shadows.

Tox snapped up his weapon, cheek to the stock. "Hands!"

"No no no," Dr. Cathey shouted.

"Easy, Hot Shot." The voice was feminine, coarse.

Tox turned on his shoulder-mounted SureFire light. "Tzi." A man stood with her. He looked ready to wet himself.

"He's with me. Javier Espinoza, meet fierce special operators with guns," Tzivia said in a droll voice. "Guys, relax. He's the one who got us in. He'll pace us—he's a bit obsessive about overseeing this little venture."

Tox shouldered past the guy to Tzivia. "What are you doing here?"

Her eyes sparked. "I thought it was obvious—hunting your mysterious artifact." She winked and turned to the others. "C'mon. Wait 'til you get a load of this. It's beyond imagining!"

"We must hurry. If they find I've brought you in . . ." Espinoza rushed to the side, disappearing into darkness. Dr. Cathey and Tzivia went right behind him.

"Uh . . ." Maangi glanced over his shoulder at Tox.

He didn't like this. They had no idea who this man was, and they weren't exactly here on legal terms. And Tzivia had serious heat coming after her. If the Iraqi government found out, he might get buried alive . . . again.

Tox grabbed Haven's hand and planted it on his side. "Drag strap," he instructed and felt her fingers coil around the band at his ribs. Moving forward, he inched toward the ebony void in the wall the archaeologists had slipped through. Aimed his SureFire at it. A small opening gaped back. He shifted sideways and squeezed through, Haven still holding tight.

It was a classic compression-release tactic, the narrow space opening up into a large room. On the far side, two enormous winged bulls stood facing the entrance. Standing guard. The space between them receded, creating a small alcove. Strange that the bulls weren't rear to rear, but facing the middle of the room. The wall behind them bore an intricate tile mosaic. Running along all four walls, reliefs rose to nearly shoulder height. Beneath the ceiling and spanning the perimeter of the room were three rows of alternating dark and light blue tiles, inlaid above and below a row of black circular pieces. Stunning. It reminded him of the images he'd seen of the reconstructed Ishtar Gate from ancient Babylon.

Haven let go of him and turned a circle, taking in the marvels. "This is incredible!"

"Whoa," Maangi said as he and Thor entered.

Tzivia, Dr. Cathey, and their guide were bent over a small section in the corner, talking and pointing to what looked like stick figures pressed into the wall.

"Got something?" Thor asked, crossing the space as he, too, took in the smear of desert-colored antiquity.

"I believe so," Dr. Cathey said, jotting in his notebook. "There was indeed a ring—representative of the seal as Mr. Russell suggested. This is why I said we must come here. To look at the exact cuneiform to be sure of the meaning. It says here a jasper ring was given to Shalmaneser as a gift for his inauguration."

"Okay. Great. It's mentioned." Tox nodded. Glanced around at the men. "But *where* is the ring?"

"Right. We need the legacy itself," Haven said.

"I . . . I have no idea." Dr. Cathey looked up. "It's depicted here, but where it went, one cannot guess."

"Then this site is a fail, too?" Irritation scraped away the thin layer of hope coating Tox's thoughts.

"You call *this* a fail?" Tzivia spun. "It's not like in the movies. Archaeology takes time, Tox. We can't just randomly find a script then—ta-da!—we magically discover the hiding place or location of the artifact referenced."

"Worked for Indiana Jones," Thor muttered.

Tox eyed the text. Scanned the room. Noted Haven. "How long?"

Irritation bled from Tzivia. "As long as it takes."

Getting mad wouldn't help. And there was no point. Anger didn't net results. It just meant more frustration. They needed a game plan. If they got organized, they could get out quicker. "How do we help?"

"Unless you can read ancient Akkadian or Sumerian or Assyrian . . ."

"I took two semesters of Spanish," Thor offered.

"French, Spanish, and German," Maangi said.

"Overachiever," Thor threw back.

"It's called intelligence."

"Keep telling yourself that." Thor shook his head.

Tox noticed Haven had stopped moving. She stared at the giant winged bulls with human heads. He made his way over. "You okay?"

She nodded but didn't say anything. Didn't move.

Tzivia called from the corner, "They're lamassu, protective celestial beings placed at the entrance to palaces."

Moving closer, Haven studied the lamassu on the left, which stood at least ten feet tall at the shoulder.

Tox could appreciate history. Art, not so much. Time was ticking. "Cell," he said into his comms, "report."

"Here, Sarge. Set up, but we have zero RFB."

"Zero?" Tox frowned. "You sure?"

"One hundred percent. No ghost skip."

"So . . . he was here so long ago, we lost the signal?"

"Or he hasn't been here," Cell said.

Tox's pulse caught. Alec hadn't been here. Which meant he most likely didn't have the gem. Assuming it was here. "We're ahead of him?"

"For once. Maybe. Dunno. I want to check something else just to be sure."

"Copy that. Keep me informed."

"Roger."

Haven was still inspecting the lamassu.

Now his curiosity was piqued, too. "What's up?" He moved to her side, looking up at the statue, but then noticed her gaze had traveled along the top of the ceiling and around the wall to where the second one stood.

"She said entrance," Haven muttered, stepping back again. She twitched. "It's a door!"

Tox stilled. "What?"

Haven pointed to the wall. "Tzivia said the lamassu are placed at entrances, so that would make this a door, right?"

"But it's a wall."

She pointed to the other side of the room. "That's the exit . . . so"—she turned back to the lamassu—"that's a door."

Intrigued by the logic, Tox shrugged. "Could be."

"Oh, very good." Tzivia was suddenly beside them, peering into the space between the winged bulls. Tentative steps carried her to the mosaic. She ran a hand along the tile. She tapped. Tapped again. Along the perimeter, the sound went from hollow to solid. "She's right."

Haven's eyes brightened, coloring her cheeks in an excited flush. "There's a door?"

Finally. Progress. "How do we open it?"

"Aren't we getting off track?" Maangi asked. "We're looking for an artifact, right? A seal—a ring. Remember?"

"Perhaps," Dr. Cathey said. "It could be nothing, a diversion or an antechamber."

"I doubt it." Tzivia backstepped. Pointed to the ledge that circled the ceiling, hanging above the lamassu and mosaic. "Look." A symbol stretched over the new door. Large. Gaping. Winged.

"A man in a skirt," Thor grumbled. "Just gets better and better."

"Shut it," Maangi hissed. "Traditional Maori garb includes a knee-length kilt."

"Even better," Thor laughed. "When do we get to see you in yours?"

Tzivia glowered. "That's Ashur."

Draped in black at the feet of Ashur. The words from the letter spirited through Tox's mind as he glanced at the door. Then back to the symbol. Game changer. "Whatever we need might be beyond that mosaic."

"C-4 it?" Thor snickered.

Tzivia spun, fire in her eyes.

"Easy," Tox said, giving Thorsen a warning look before redirecting his efforts toward the archaeologist. "How do we get it open?"

"*Without* damaging it?" Tzivia shrugged, then deflated, her anger leeching out. "Haven't a clue."

The next forty minutes were spent exploring areas around the mosaic to find a hidden catch, trigger, or locking mechanism. Something. Anything to open the door Haven had found. Tzivia slapped the wall in frustration, sweat dripping from her temples. Dr. Cathey slumped against the ground and shook his head. Frustration ran its course, and Tox paced a slow circle, eyeing the tile work on the floors and ceilings, as well as the reliefs.

"Cole," Haven said, her voice hesitant.

He glanced over his shoulder.

She stood staring up at the symbol of Ashur, then turned to him. Mischief thrummed through her green eyes. "Give me a lift?"

"What?"

Tzivia looked up. "Yes! I think she's right. But she's not tall enough. Tox, Thor. Between the two of you . . ."

"I could help," Ram offered.

"Too short," Tzivia said, steering the two tallest of the team toward Haven's position. "Tox, climb up on him."

"You gotta be kidding me," Thor grumbled as he stomped over to where Tox stood below the ledge. With a sigh, he threaded his fingers. "This gives new meaning to letting you walk all over me."

"And you love it." Tox stepped into the makeshift stirrup, planted a hand on Thor's shoulder, then hiked up—at the same time Thor hoisted him. Tox used the wall to balance as he climbed onto Thor's shoulders. The other man was strong and steady.

"What am I doing?" Tox reached high to trace the tiles.

"The black ones," Haven said.

He peered up, all too aware that one wrong move would make for an interesting trip down, and strained his fingers toward the line of round, black tiles. "They're flat."

"You're not under his feet."

"No," Thor said, "I'm under his."

"Not yours, Ashur's," Tzivia said. "Thor, shift right an inch."

"You got—"

"Just do it!"

With a huff, the big guy complied.

The world canted beneath Tox's feet. He threw his arms out to steady himself, then grabbed the ledge. "Easy!"

"Sorry."

Fingers trailing over the tiles again, Tox craned his neck for a better view. Lined up the relief of Ashur with the black tiles. Smooth. Smooth. Sm—round! He pressed it.

Shunck!

Something spat at him. Involuntarily, he jerked back, instinct protecting his eyes. At the same time he swiped at whatever had hit his face, too late realizing his mistake. He toppled backward off Thor's shoulders. Landed on the ground with a thud. Air punched from his lungs.

"Tox!"

Arching his back, he writhed for air. Groaned at the pain pummeling his spine. But he smiled through the grimace.

Ram was there with Haven. "Tox!"

Though pain had control of his back and lungs, exultation seized him at the small piece he held. He grinned and showed Haven his palm.

She gasped. "Onyx!"

The third of the five legacies. The lamassu chamber had nearly tripped them up, but Haven figured it out. It made him proud of her. Again.

Now they had one of the legacies. Hope that they could neutralize that crown burned like embers within him. He just prayed Alec never caught on to what they were doing. They didn't need a race against him as well as time.

"Sarge," Cell growled through the comms. "We got tr—"

Shots peppered the connection.

"Go go go," Ram shouted, and the team was in motion. They funneled through the chamber exit then filled the passage, shoulders bouncing against thousand-year-old earth as they hurried.

Shots echoed down the passage, followed by return fire.

Ambushed. Tox got to his feet and pointed at Haven and Tzivia. "Stay here with the professor. Protect this." He tossed the gem to Haven and pivoted to the door. "Cell, what's your location?" He jogged, feeling the press of time and space as he pushed through the narrow tunnel, seeing the flicker of light from the team fifty feet ahead.

"Wraith Two, what's your situation?" he asked, unable to see well enough.

"Two tangos engaged." *Crack! Crack!* "One down."

"I'm a klick north of the drop-off," Cell shouted, shots nearly drowning his voice.

"How many?" Half bent, Tox sprinted through the passage as much as he could.

"Too many—they're *shooting* at me!"

Tox rounded a corner and light bloomed through the tunnel. Whatever the team faced, they'd cleared. He sprinted, finally seeing a body at the bottom of the steps. Not wanting to get shot in the back, Tox verified the target was dead, then hiked up the stairs. Shoulder against the opening of the tunnel, he peered out. Spotted the team hunched by a row of SUVs. He sprinted to their position.

"Runt, report," Tox subvocalized once he was behind cover with the others.

Ram's gaze flicked toward him with concern.

"Runt, this is Wraith Actual. Give me a sitrep." Tox shook his head. No response. Had Runt bitten one already?

Weapons fire cracked the air.

Tox stilled. Motioned the team back toward the other side of the vehicles. Gave signals to head north, use the ruins for cover. Thor and Maangi slithered around out of sight. Ram turned—but then jerked back. Eyes wide.

Tox felt the shadow as it fell over his shoulder. He spun and found a man coming up on him, backlit by the setting sun. The shape told Tox he had an M4. Coming fast.

Glock 22 in hand, Tox raised it but knew he was too late. Knew he was dead meat. But he wasn't going down unarmed or without a fight.

Even as the man said, "He knew you'd be here," Tox dove into him. Heard the meaty grunt of impact. Heard a silenced weapon. Then he hit the ground. Bounced with the guy under him. Tox lifted his gun to the man's face.

Unbelievably, the tango wasn't moving.

Tox pushed away from him. Straightened, staring in disbelief at the blood spreading over the man's chest.

"Sorry I didn't respond," Runt said in his twangy drawl. "Didn't want him to hear me coming."

32

"How did King know where we were?" someone asked.

"It made sense," Thor said. "If he knew we were looking for the legacies, he probably has access to the same kind of intelligence and experts as we do."

"Access to Ti Tzaddik?" Ram scoffed.

"Too easy," Tox said. "He shouldn't be this on top of things. We stepped into his game, then shifted directions."

"He should be scrambling to catch up," Runt suggested.

"So he's got resources," Ram said.

"Yeah, like whoever gave him that crown," Cell growled, "because I'm not buying that a guy this whacked found it on his own."

"So who's the benefactor?" Ram asked.

"Another question we don't have the answer to," Tox muttered.

"That ticked me off, him finding us here," Cell said. "It's one thing to be where ancient people buried their dead, but to become one of them—that's another story."

"At least your burial would've been cheap," Maangi said.

"Yeah, we could just drop him in one of those canals," Runt muttered.

"What canals?" Cell asked.

"There were ruts all around that place," Runt said. "Didn't you see them? They probably piped in water from the Tigris." He pointed to Dr. Cathey. "Didn't you say one of those kings built canals?"

Dr. Cathey's eyebrows rose. "You paid attention."

"I never forget," Runt said.

"So we're headed to Nimrud now?" Maangi said. "Why?"

Bent forward, Tox rested his elbows on the table, the roar of the jet engines numbing his arms and legs, and studied the proposed next step in the mission.

Tzivia guzzled water, swallowed, then set down the bottle, clearly agitated. "The queens were buried there. Next legacy. Or did you already solve everything with the onyx?" Her seething sarcasm was as toxic as his nickname. She stood and left the conference room.

Tox followed her out, touching Haven's shoulder to reassure her things were fine, and caught up with Tzivia at the galley bulkhead. "Why'd you run?" he asked quietly.

She came around with a fist, but then deflated against the counter. Shook her head. "I had to."

"You did something you shouldn't have done?"

"Worse," she said, fidgeting. "I hurt someone. Used him."

"Omar."

She swallowed and looked away. "I thought I could do it. You know— be a spy. Use him to get what I wanted." She wet her lips. "And what's worse is that he knew—*knew* I was using him. . . ." Her voice had gone from defiance to a raw ache. "I never meant for him to get hurt."

"You mean, you never meant for him to get hurt *by someone else*."

She stared at him, her chest rising and falling unevenly.

"Because using a guy, even though we're guys—it still hurts. Ticks us off."

Lips tight, Tzivia said nothing. The whites of her eyes were scratched red. "He's Mossad. He knew who I was."

"Which should have made things easy. Right?" He cocked his head. And took stock of the fact that Tzivia Khalon actually looked penitent. If he didn't know better, he'd think she might cry. "What, did you fall in love?"

Tzivia shot to her feet. "No." She put her hands on her hips, then turned away, shoving long bangs off her face. "He fell for me. Lied to protect me. They caught up with us, but he sacrificed himself for me."

"What do you care?" Tox leaned back and held out his hands. "You were using him."

"He lost everything. His job. They closed his bank accounts. Car repossessed. He went to *jail*."

"So?"

She flung a glower over her shoulder. "I just wanted answers."

"And a little sex?"

Pain twisted her features. "It wasn't . . . I didn't . . . I didn't know what I wanted." Swallowing, she looked toward the conference room.

"And you do now?"

Her eyes were large and round, pooling with tears. "He'll kill me if he finds me."

"You played with fire and now you're afraid of getting burned?"

"What do you want from me, Tox?" she yelled, her face crimson.

"Nothing, Tzivia." He started past her.

She screwed up her face, whipping away from him, tears streaking down her cheeks.

"That's not true," he admitted, glancing back. "I want to see you happy."

"I was happy," she whispered around a trembling chin and slowly brought those round eyes to him. "Once."

He shook his head. "No, I was a challenge. I would've bored you, unwilling to play your game. But this? Going after an experienced operative? Even you know better."

"I just wanted answers about my dad."

"What answers?"

She ducked, drawing in several hard, long breaths before she gave a quick shake of her head. "I can't."

He touched her shoulder, a small sign that he wasn't mad. "Then neither can I." He slid around her and moved toward the galley. "SAARC and DoD are conferencing in ten." From the small fridge, he grabbed a bottle of orange juice. Then snagged a protein bar from the counter. When he turned, Tzivia was still there. He wished he didn't have a soft spot for her, for those wide eyes of hers.

It wasn't *that* type of soft spot. Haven had cured him of any foolish weakness. Tzivia was like a kid sister he'd do just about anything for.

"Do you even care?" she asked.

"Don't do that," Tox said, pointing at her. "I'm not an enemy. You know I do. But if you don't want to talk—"

"Omar said my dad's not dead."

Tox stilled, disbelief pushing him back against the counter. "What?"

She shrugged, hugging herself. "Right?"

"Does Ram—"

"No." She swiped a finger beneath her eyes again. "And he can't know. I . . . I'm not even sure Omar was telling the truth."

"You think he was working you?"

"I *know* he was. It was kind of our thing," she said with a snort. "But I don't know if he was lying about that. Within hours of him telling me, he was arrested. Coincidence?" She hunched her shoulders.

Understanding dawned. Tox snorted. "That's why you showed up at the dig. Protection." He folded his arms. "You want SAARC to protect you now." The guilt he'd felt transferred to her with a jolt of turbulence.

She slumped into a galley chair and pulled her legs up, propping her shins against the table.

"You have to come clean with them."

"No!"

Tox leaned down. "You come clean so they have everything they need to protect you." He felt an old flash of anger. "Do it, or I will—and I'll start with Ram."

"You wouldn't."

"In a New York second." He eased into her personal space. "Your little quest already ruined one man's life. I'm not going to let you infect my team."

"Tox!" Cell called from the far end of the gangway. "SAARC's live!"

With a nod to Tzivia, he strode down the plane, knowing this wasn't something anyone could fix for her. She had the power, but it seemed she still needed the wherewithal to do the right thing.

He entered the command center and immediately locked onto Haven. He moved to her side. The wall screen had filled with three faces: Almstedt, Rodriguez, and Iliescu.

"What's the latest on Wallace?" Tox asked, sliding into a chair beside Haven, glad to be next to her. Glad that he was dating *her*. She might not be as hard-hitting as Tzivia, but she had a depth of sincerity and gentleness that he appreciated. Needed. She cared about people. In the war of life, she was the medic and he the guy on the front lines fighting.

She slid him a grateful smile, apparently appreciating that he'd asked about Levi. He might not like that she'd dated the guy once, but he didn't want him dead. Most of the time.

"Recovering. Amazingly, most of the burns were minor. The ones to his left shoulder and pectoral were second degree but are already healing well. They've considered a skin graft, but the doctors don't think it'll be necessary."

"Good to hear," Tox said.

"Have you found out anything about the onyx we found?" Ram asked, adjusting his ever-present beanie.

"Well, we only have images, but it definitely appears to date back to the Middle-Assyrian period," Almstedt explained. "We've done some research on the other gems you might be looking for. With Dr. Cathey's help, we've come up with some suggestions."

"Let's hear them," Tox said, aware that Tzivia still hadn't shown up.

"We believe he's right that the seal of Shalmaneser is a ring. A jasper one. We've located one that has a bit of a history to its travels."

"Travels?"

"I've had to pull a lot of political strings," Iliescu said. "But we're sending a plane to retrieve Dr. Cathey and take him to Berlin."

"Berlin?" Dr. Cathey sat a little straighter in his chair, his eyes brightening. "The Vorderasiatisches Museum."

"Yes. Seems they have a scarab ring of jasper that was given to"— Iliescu glanced down at his notes—"Ramesses II and kept in Egypt until it somehow made its way to the museum."

"Wait," Tox said, amused, "Ramesses the pharaoh?"

Dr. Cathey stroked his beard. "Interesting."

"Rad," Runt said, grinning. "Back to home territory for me."

"Home territory?" Tox said, sitting forward.

Runt shrugged. "Egypt. I've spent the last two years reading up on all their history and politics. Ramesses II"—hesitation caught him, and he looked at the screen—"wasn't he the pharaoh who entered into a peace treaty with the Hittites?"

"He is," Dr. Cathey said, not giving SAARC or CIA time to answer. "So it makes sense that Hattusili, who was probably Nimrod's grandson and the Hittite king at the time, might have stolen the gem from the Crown of Souls and delivered it to Ramesses as part of the treaty."

"Did the pharaoh know the power of that gem?" Maangi asked.

"The gems don't have power." Tzivia had finally joined them. "They just belong to the crown."

"Which has power." Maangi nodded around the room, looking for agreement from the team.

"No, it emits a frequency—" Tzivia huffed and rolled her eyes. "I thought you people had this figured out. Aren't you chasing radio signals all over the place? And to answer your question, Maangi, yes, it's entirely likely that Ramesses knew the significance of the jasper stone."

"Okay, good." Tox tapped the table. "We have the onyx, and Dr. Cathey will get the jasper. Two of five gems. What's next?"

"Nimrud," Tzivia said. "Where the queens are buried. My friends just discovered that underground chamber I told you about. We need to get in there and find something related to the crown or gems."

"Remember," Dr. Cathey said with a nod, "that most ancient gems were not the gems we value today. There was the lapis lazuli, the carnelian, the opal, the onyx, tiger's eye . . ."

"Noted. Nimrud, and what else?" Tox asked.

"The other clue references Shamash and an amulet of red," Haven said.

"Most likely carnelian," Tzivia suggested. "Shamash is the sun god. We should watch in Nimrud for that as well."

"And lapis lazuli is mentioned at the end of Thefarie's letter," Tox said.

"It is," Dr. Cathey agreed, "but remember what that line said?"

"Uhh . . . something about his failure."

"'*Lapis Lazuli cuffed me in failure and shame.*'" Dr. Cathey considered the line. "Which does us no good."

"Except to tell us which gem he could not find."

"Indeed—a crusader known for stopping many terrible disasters and madmen, and that he could not find a gem only makes you shrug?"

"Can't change or help his failure," Tox said.

"So, Nimrud," Ram repeated. "At least we know that much."

"Anything new with King?"

Tox peered up at the screen, where Rodriguez stared back, the alignment of camera angles off. And he was glad.

"Besides trying to blow up Wallace in Israel?" Cell grunted.

"Or killing Keogh in that village."

"Yeah," Tox said, leaning forward. "Speaking of—how'd he find me in Israel?"

"We've been working on that," Iliescu said. "Running tracers on imaging and feeds. We aren't finding any piggybacking of our lines or tracking. Best guess is he had you tailed."

"Tailed." That ticked Tox off.

"And we didn't see him? *Psht.*" Cell shook his head, rocking in his chair. "Not buying that. I'm running software all the time and randomizing our movements. No way. He had to have something sophisticated to know where the sarge was."

"What about Wallace?" Thor pushed back in his chair, tilting it on its rear legs. "He was tailing Tox—right? That's how he got nabbed by King. What's that about? Almstedt, why were you having him do that?"

"That was not my call," Almstedt said, her voice defensive. "His orders are the same as yours when you're on mission."

"So he went rogue," Cell said.

Lowering her head, Haven shifted in her seat next to Tox. "Why would he do that?"

"Hold up," Tox said. "Let's dial this back. When Wallace can answer for himself, he will. For now, just confirm we're all on the same page. Same mission. No back-office deals or maneuvering. Right?"

A universal *yes* rang out.

"That's all we need right now. Our mission is Alec. We aren't letting him get in our heads and divide us. Now"—he stood, tugged Tzivia aside, then motioned the others out of the room before he looked at the camera, feigning peering into the eyes of his superiors—"someone has something to say."

Tox noticed Haven lingering just inside the door. He slipped a hand to the small of her back and nudged her out, glancing back at Tzivia, whose face had gone pale. He gave her a nod.

"What was that about?" Ram asked as soon as Tox closed the door behind him.

"Tzi needs to come clean with them about her reasons for being here."

Ram's eyes went hard. "She's still hiding."

Tox squeezed past his friend and caught up with Haven, who'd hung back. "Not my story to tell."

* * * *

With most of the team grabbing rack time, Tox sat in the plane's conference room, going over details. Trying to assemble some sort of method to this madness. He scanned the paperwork sprawled over the table. He scratched his jaw, wishing for inspiration. For truth. Cathey would hopefully locate the jasper ring, and then they had to find something with a lapis lazuli. But what would they find among the dead queens? He had to admit, he was anxious to see that iron cage Tzivia talked about. Get near it, feel the thrumming. It sounded too fantastical to be true.

And that was the small stuff bothering him. The story of the crown's power over Nimrod worried him. He pored over the articles on Nimrod, but things still didn't bode well. Nimrod had set himself against God. He was vicious and notoriously powerful.

Much like Alec.

Maybe having a friend come alongside him would help Alec find the right path. Was it possible Tox had been wrong? That he *should* work with Alec?

What would it hurt?

Laughter spiraled through the plane, drawing Tox's attention. That was Haven. He glanced at the papers before him. Her laugh and his line of questioning collided. What would it hurt? Everything he had with Haven, that was what, because it would hurt her.

He shuffled the mess into a stack and made his way down the gangway. Not finding her, he then hit the bunkroom. A small light glowed from the lower left bunk.

The weird LED hue drew ominous lines across the professor's face.

"Lookin' a little pale there, Dr. C. You okay?"

Dr. Cathey glanced over his rimless glasses and gave a grim smile. "Not in a long time, Mr. Russell."

"Just Tox. You can loosen up around us, unwind."

"I'm afraid if I do that," Cathey said, eyeing his notes with a sigh, "we may lose this battle."

"Battle?"

"The battle for souls, Mr. Russell."

Chiji had long said that Tox had been chosen to fight these battles by the Lord. And since they'd handled two artifacts already—the Mace of Death and the Aleppo Codex—it was plausible, right, that they'd figure this out before Alec?

"A battle for more than Alec."

"I'm afraid so."

"How? Alec's wearing the crown. *His* soul is at stake."

"Yes, but the risk will exist to any who encounter the crown, and to the victims of its wielder. Making the wrong choice here could cost you much, perhaps even your soul."

The words annoyed Tox, though he wasn't sure why. He folded his six-two frame onto the edge of the bunk, feeling the weight of that possibility. He thought of his own documents. "You have all the research—"

"Not all."

"Well, most." He forced his gaze to the professor, desperate for inspiration. Anything to tell him he was on the right track. That he wasn't losing it. Or losing himself. "Can I save him?"

"*Save* him?" Surprise riddled Dr. Cathey's expression.

"Stop him." Tox shook his head. "End this."

Sadness rippled through the professor's gray eyes, and he slowly tugged off his glasses. "Where is your friend, the Nigerian?"

Tox gritted his teeth. "Dealing with family business."

Quiet settled between them as the older man squinted at Tox. "And you feel lost without him."

"Lost?"

"I believe your Nigerian friend has told you before that you were chosen."

Tox snorted. "If I could do everything Chiji believed I could, I'd be invincible."

"I think he simply sees in you the fighter honed through the years— and I do not only mean your physical abilities."

Tox nodded again, then stood. "You should rest. Once we land, you'll be going nonstop for the next thirty hours or so. Good night."

He strode out, feeling no closer to finding an answer or solution. When the last bell of the fight rang, would Tox do what it took to end it? Could he pull the proverbial trigger? The question haunted him as he trudged to his bunk.

Chosen.

Chiji had said that many times. But in this case, chosen to do what? Which was the stronger course?

On his tablet, he considered the last military personnel photo of Alec. When they'd served together, the guys had teased Alec relentlessly about looking like a Nazi with his blond hair and blue eyes. His hard-core personality made things worse.

Seven years ago, that taunt was funny. Now it was haunting.

Tox pushed back against the hull of the plane and propped one foot on the edge of his bunk. The other leg he stretched out and let himself think. Be quiet. Sort through things. Dr. Cathey would head to Berlin with Thor. Tox would take the rest of the team to Kalhu.

Part of him wanted out. To end this mission now. No more lives should be risked. No more danger to the team or Haven. Was it better to make a sacrifice, offer to help Alec, and get on top of this thing from the inside? He tugged out his phone and thumbed to his Contacts. Alec's, to be precise.

Tox pinched the bridge of his nose and clenched his eyes shut. *I cannot believe I'm thinking about this.*

"Have you accepted the truth?" A soft voice pried him from his thoughts as the mattress sank beneath Haven's weight.

Tox smiled down at her, glad for her presence. "What truth?"

"That you're not him." Her green eyes were soft beneath the ambient light of the plane.

"I know I'm not him."

"But you want to save him."

"Of course I do," Tox snapped. "And I would hope every man on this plane would do the same for me if I got misguided. If I ended up like him."

She sidestepped his terse tone. "Cole, he is not misguided or confused."

"No, he's *affected*. Somehow, this crown"—he dragged the image of the gold-plated crown from the file—"has done a number on his brain."

Something rippled through her brow as she rolled her head to the side. "You can't believe that."

"I can. I do."

"Choice, Cole." She touched his hand, a move that shot a spark to his heart. "He had a *choice*. To put on that crown. To listen to it. There is no evil known to man which our Lord has not known. Maybe it takes a different form or wears a different mask, but it is the same, and we, each of us, must choose what we do when it invites us into its snare."

Invites us into its snare. Withdrawing his hand, Tox broke her gaze, but not before he saw her expression fall.

She stood up and faced him. "You're . . ." Though there were more shadows than light, he saw the color leave her face. "Tell me you're not thinking of joining him. The man who shot you, killed others in the name of vengeance."

The way she said that, her tone, the panic in it, hit Tox in the gut. It sounded pretty ridiculous coming from her.

He slid to the edge of the mattress and reached for her.

Haven stepped away. "You're kidding me, right?"

"Haven—"

"No. Say it right now, Cole." Her eyes watered, chin dimpling beneath roiling panic. "Say you're going to take the high road, rise above this, above him—"

"Haven, if I help him to see this is wrong—"

"He doesn't *want* to see it's wrong!" The crackling, angry words freed a tear. "He wants you to kill people with him."

He hung his head. Closed his eyes. It was futile and stupid, he knew. But . . . "I have to do something. There has to be a way to save him."

"Why are you so hung up on this?"

"On saving him?" He stood. Took her hand but couldn't quite meet her gaze. "Because I know what it's like to be saved." Now he did look at her. "You believe in me so resolutely"—he traced the line of her jaw—"though I have no idea why."

She breathed around a smile. "I believe in you, Cole, because you are a good man. Constantly working to grow and be a better person. Alec isn't worried about being a better man. He's like a child stomping his foot to get his way, only he's using violence to do that. Look at the site we just came from. Attacking you—us. Runt said that guy was going to kill you."

Tox folded her into his arms. "I wish I could see this the way you do." She did have a point. So did the professor. So why couldn't Tox let it go? Why couldn't he accept that he was different from Alec?

"You weren't meant to fight this alone. On our own, we are nothing," Haven said, her voice soft. Her eyes pleading. "God gave you this team, and me. It says in Exodus that He will fight for us, if we will just be still."

That pried a small smile from his unwilling lips. "Chiji says God chose me." He shrugged. "If I am to stay still, what did He choose me for?"

"That others may see His might through you. That you learn the humility of obedience." Haven smiled. "Don't hate me for saying that. Obedience and stillness are often the two hardest things we have to do."

Tox snorted.

Dr. Cathey appeared in the doorway, hugging a stack of papers to his chest, his face drawn.

Alarm pierced Tox. "What is it?"

The professor rushed in, dumping the documents across the mattress. "I think . . ." Frantic, wild eyes took in the papers. "I think we're in trouble."

THY STERN
AVENGER BE

Stuffing on his greaves, Thefarie stood at the door, eyeing through the sliver of an opening his brother-knights mounted and ready to return to their quest. His heart hung heavy in his chest.

Gentle hands took the second greave from him. "You will return to me, aye?"

He stared down at the dark-haired beauty and into the softest brown eyes he had ever beheld. He touched her cheek, anxious to remember, to brand into his memory the moment she looked up to him. Admired him. Loved him.

Because if he failed . . .

The Grand Master's words came sailing back from that day a fortnight ago.

"I can make no promises," he said, his words low, like his spirits.

337

"Aye, but you should. To make me feel better." She smiled, lacing the armor tight about his sides.

His hand went to her rounding belly. His progeny. He'd caved—she, Miryam, daughter of a scribe, had lured him out of his self-imposed isolation. Convinced him to taste pleasure. But his gut roiled—if he failed, he could not return home. It would be better for him to be dead. Then, at least, his wife and child would be cared for. But if he were shamed, she and the child would be mocked. Perhaps beaten or stoned.

"There is much in your eyes this day, Thefarie." Miryam ran her fingers over his beard. "Fret not, my beloved. This will not be our last meeting."

"If I fall, if anything happens to me, return to your father. Go to him—"

She pressed her finger against his lips. "Nay." Her eyes blazed. "I will not hear this. You will return to me."

He caught her shoulders. "Miryam—"

She touched her mouth to his. Then ducked out the door, calling to his brother-knights. "You should hurry before he changes his mind."

Thefarie glanced around their humble home. A one-room dwelling with a table, two chairs, and cushions. Some pottery. Little, yet plenty when he considered what he really had—her love.

Lifting his helm, he folded himself through the exit. He stepped into the bright morning to the laughter of his brother-knights. Miryam stood nearby, waiting to see him off.

"See what happens when you take a woman?" Giraude laughed. "You grow soft."

Swinging onto his destrier, Thefarie allowed himself a smile.

"Do you jest?" Ameus said. "Soft for Thefarie is a rock to us. For you—soft is water."

"You have room to talk," Giraude replied with a laugh.

They rode out of the city in silence, thoughts heavy with admonishment and the challenge of the Grand Master's warning. As Poor Fellow-Soldiers of Christ and of the Temple of Solomon, they took their oaths seriously—especially the "poor" part, owning no other clothing save their mantles and armor. The dwelling he shared with Miryam wasn't even their property, but loaned to them by friends.

As they left Israel's embrace, they paused and turned, staring back at the Holy Land. He would not fail it, his orders, or Miryam.

"Softness has no place in our lives now, brother-knights," Thefarie warned. "There will be no mercy. There will be no grace. There will only be the stern avenger of the Lord Jesus."

33

"Thanks for linking up," Cole said after the feeds came online with SAARC, DoD, and CIA. "Dr. C has something he wanted to share."

"What's that?"

"I don't know yet. He insisted on waiting until we were all here." After glancing around at the team, Cole nodded to the professor and took a seat next to Haven.

Dr. Cathey cleared his throat. "Considering the events that have happened with Mr. King and comparing them against events purported to be influenced by this crown in ancient history, I believe we are about to see a significant escalation of violence."

"Hold up," Cole said, pulling forward in his chair. "How can you possibly know that's going to happen?"

"It's a theory," Tzivia put in, arms crossed over her chest. "He's notorious for them."

"Perhaps," Dr. Cathey said with a nod, "but even you must admit my theories often prove to be true."

"Escalation?" Iliescu repeated. "Haven't we seen enough? How does one escalate—"

"He will do things that do not make sense."

341

"Killing innocents doesn't make sense," the director said.

"But these will be things that have no connection. His hunger for the crown's influence will force him to do things just for the surge of power. But to be sure, let's take a look at history. I should first mention that I agree with what Ti Tzaddik said about the three markers evident in the lives of those who wear the crown: the inability to be stopped, the notable arrogance, and last, the descent into madness. As Mr. Tzaddik also pointed out, the crown most likely originated in the Middle Assyrian era and appears to have affected the reigns of Shalmaneser I and Tukulti-Ninurta I."

"But only one of them wrote about a crown that fell from heaven—Nimrod," Haven said.

"True, but it is not outside the realm of possibility that Tukulti-Ninurta was in fact so deeply affected by the crown's properties—whether they are supernatural or borne of some emitted frequency—that he hallucinated or perhaps even honestly believed he saw it fall from heaven." Dr. Cathey smiled as he peered over the rim of his glasses at the team. "One cannot know for sure, except to say he indeed wrote of the crown and he indeed was shut away by his son and later murdered."

"We know all this," Cell moaned. "You woke me for this? Do you know what I was dreaming about?"

"Maangi in a kilt?" Thor asked with a laugh.

The Maori slapped the back of his head.

With a click of his tongue, Dr. Cathey resumed his explanation. "There is a story about Shalmaneser, that he burned a village to the ground with a fire so hot that there were no bones to be found." Dr. Cathey gave a mournful shake of his head. "There is another story that said he slaughtered cows and livestock until blood drenched the fields. For no apparent reason other than to exert his dominance, to show his power. If you look at the lives of these Assyrian kings, you will see that they all ascribed to themselves some form of deification."

"So you're saying King is going to start slaughtering cows?" Tzivia asked.

"That might have already happened," Cole said. "There's the slaughtered livestock that Haven was unlucky enough to encounter."

Grieved, Dr. Cathey shook his head. "If you follow the journey of

Mr. King's killings since coming into possession of the crown, you will see a pattern of escalation, albeit a slow one. At first, he was killing to right a personal wrong. Then, he began killing those not connected to him."

"Then the dismemberment in the village where Keogh died," Maangi said.

Dr. Cathey nodded. "And the livestock."

"So . . . what, he's going to nuke a city or something?" Cell asked.

Quiet fell over the room, and Haven couldn't help but notice Cole had covered his mouth and sat staring at the table. But then he shifted. Straightened. Looked at the feed camera.

"Do we have any information on his location?"

"Negative," Rodriguez said. "The most we have is that RFB your guy picked up. It's our only lead."

"Is there any way to jury-rig something to detect his signal?"

"To do that," Cell said, "we have to know his exact frequency. And we don't. It's why we're running three steps behind him. The last time we caught his signal was the strongest, but I had to stay on the plane"—he glowered at Cole—"in Israel, and in Ashur, there was no RFB." Cell hesitated, shook his head. "We're not anywhere near close enough."

On his feet, Cole started pacing.

"We have to assume he knows what we're trying to do," Ram said.

"So that'd mean finding the jewels—" Thor said.

"Legacies," Tzivia corrected.

"Whatever."

"Back up," Ram said. "We need to anticipate that he'll be where we're headed, Berlin and so on."

"Or that he's already been there," Cell said, "which is better, because then I can get a lock on that frequency."

"True. But he's not worried about us. He's got the crown."

"I disagree," Haven said calmly. "He is worried—not about all, but about one of us."

"The sarge," Cell said.

"Yeah," Runt cut in, "but this guy has an agenda, right? So what's the endgame? What's he trying to do with this crown thing?"

Cole rubbed his jaw. "Wake up the armchair generals and the political machine stalemating combat engagements."

Runt nodded. "He probably wants a big impact then. A big mark."

"We need to look at upcoming events. See if we can get ahead of him, ahead of this thing." Cole resumed pacing.

"Events?" Haven's stomach churned.

"Where else would he have enough people to target?"

"There are events all over the world—football, rugby—"

"No no," Cole said, rubbing a hand along the back of his neck. "Personal. Even though he hit that village, it was still connected to the military. It's still personal to him, despite going outside his immediate circle of friends and knowledge."

"So, something military," Ram suggested.

The screen went crazy with people moving, chattering, and secondary feeds sliding along the screen, showing data that Haven couldn't process fast enough. She turned her thoughts toward an event that would have enough draw for Alec, enough payout of violence.

"He'd need to feel it was justified," Haven agreed. "The target would have to directly or indirectly have wronged him. He seems to blame his superiors." She gasped, her heart racing as she thought of the fundraiser she'd been working on with Charlotte. She swallowed and caught Cole's gaze.

He'd frozen, expectation hanging in his blue eyes. "You have something?"

She wet her lips, afraid to offer this. "I . . . I don't know."

"No, you do." Confidence and assuredness met her gaze. "I see it in your eyes."

"Give it to us," Cell urged.

Should she be excited he knew her well enough to say that, or scared that he could read her so well? "I . . . I've been volunteering"—she probably shouldn't mention Charlotte—"with a charity. They're holding a gala in a couple of days. I'm not integral, and they have a large support staff, so I haven't been doing much with it—"

"Haven."

She took a breath in. Let it out . . . slowly. "The Endeavor of Patriots gala."

Several curses filtered through the room, including from the feed.

"It's in two days." She nodded. There was more certainty to her supposition than she wanted to admit. "It's in Maryland. Brass from every branch, along with award recipients that include the Purple Heart, Audie Murphy, and—" Her dry throat trapped her next words, held them hostage.

Iliescu spoke from the screen. "The president will be there, too."

Palms on the table, Cole stared at the screen. "Of course . . ."

"This is a long shot," Almstedt mumbled. "There's no way to know he's targeting *this* event, or that he's even targeting one at all."

Cole had locked onto Haven. He stared as if willing her to understand his thoughts, hear the anguish roiling through him. And she did.

"No," she said loudly. "No, it's the Endeavor event." It made entirely too much sense.

Straightening, Cole said, "This is where he'll hit."

"Why are you so sure?" Iliescu asked, looking at Haven. "Because his brother is going to be there?"

"No," Haven said, breathing harder, "because it's being held at his parents' home." Not only did Alec want to sucker-punch Tox, he probably wanted to upend Charlotte and Eric Russell's lives. Shatter them by revealing that Cole was alive. Resolution cemented her words. "*This* is personal to Alec. He's mad. At Cole."

"Whoa. Wait. Why is this a thing against Tox?" Cell asked, his young face a mask of confusion.

"Because Alec invited me to the party, and I didn't show," Cole said. "So now he's going to punish me."

* * * *

Tox shouldered into his ruck and placed his M4 inside the Jeep. He was fed up. Irritated. Ready for this to be over. Annoyed, yet again, that Chiji wasn't around. Then again, his friend's proverbs would probably only grate right now.

"Sarge?" Shoulders hunched, Cell came toward him. "Can I have a minute?" He snapped his head to the side, indicating where they could talk alone.

What was this about? Tox followed him to a spot a few yards away. "What's up?"

"I . . ." Cell scratched his scruffy jaw. He had only appeared fifteen when they met, but lately his looks seemed to have caught up with his age. "I have a theory."

"About what?"

Cell glanced at the others. Scratched his chin again. "How to stop King."

Arms folded, Tox planted his feet and leaned in. "You have my attention."

"Thing is," Cell said, suddenly bashful, "it's not the best answer."

"It's the only answer we have."

Bobbing his head a few times, Cell shrugged. "I think . . ." He rubbed his jaw. "I *think*—in theory, if I could nail down this frequency, I might—again, this is only in theory—"

"Cell."

He huffed. "I think I could turn it back on him."

"Turn it back?" Tox wasn't sure he liked the sound of that.

"Yeah, see? The crown is emitting this frequency, and I think if I can get close enough, maybe . . ." Another shrug. "I'm thinking if I send back a burst at the same frequency, maybe it'll fry the one the crown's emitting."

Surprise leapt between them. "That'll work?"

Cell quirked one side of his mouth in a grimace. "Maybe. I'm not sure."

"But sure enough to bring it to me."

"Yeah, well, see, I've been testing it on some spare equipment, and it works, but—"

"Make it work, Cell."

"Thing is, Sarge—"

"What?" Tox snapped, irritated with his indecisiveness.

"I have some friends stateside, at a certain university that should remain nameless." Cell cleared his throat. "I had them run some experiments with the RFB. They did trials . . ." He wouldn't look at Tox as his expression fell. "They failed."

"How?"

"The outbound frequency has to be high enough to create a feedback loop on the inbound frequency, scramble it. But the gray matter"—he tapped his temple—"isn't protected. I mean, I'm totally winging this. It's beyond theoretical and unproven. But that's why the crown works, I guess. Because the brain is unprotected from the RFB. If it's hitting King's gray matter—that's why it's affecting him. If I back-charge it, so to speak, then it'll back-charge his brain, too."

"So it'll hurt him?"

Cell snorted. "Yeah. If by *hurt* you mean turning his brain to scrambled eggs."

"Unacceptable." Tox glanced at the team, thinking. Knowing they had no other options. "Keep working it—find a way to turn it back without hurting Alec. If it can't be done without killing him, it's not an option."

"But isn't it?" Cell frowned. "I mean, we might have a way to stop him—he's killing people! We take out terrorists like him all the time."

"Just get it to work." Tox took a step away, then stopped. "And keep this between us."

"Roger that," Cell muttered.

"Good work, Purcell."

"Right."

Tox nodded, his gaze snagging on Tzivia talking animatedly with Dr. Cathey. She pointed to a tablet she'd placed in the professor's hands, tapping the screen in emphasis. Her mentor slowly gave a nod, angling the screen away from a sun glare, then his bushy eyebrows wagged. And he was nodding, too.

Tox felt hope surge and started toward them. "You got something?"

Tzivia quickly closed the gap. "I think so." She looked furtively at Dr. Cathey, who was working the tablet. "When Haven mentioned the gala, I remembered attending a fundraiser here last year. Dr. Cathey was there as well. The wife of the host wore a medallion, which she said was from a recent excavation. She had it on loan from a museum—that happens with big patrons sometimes. The piece was in the design of a sun, but the important thing—it had a red stone."

"Carnelian," Dr. Cathey corrected, peering over his glasses and thrusting a finger in the air. "I distinctly remember it. Lovely piece."

Catching on, Tox wondered if things might be coming together for them finally. "You think it might be the amulet of red Thefarie wrote about."

"Possibly," she said with a shrug. "I know it's a long shot, and we'd have to examine it to be sure. . . ."

"Where is it?"

Tzivia wrinkled her nose. "That's what we're not sure about."

"And what gives us the most pause," Cathey added. "It was an Egyptian exhibit, co-sponsored by the Egyptian antiquities community."

"That's why I remember it so well—the sun shape."

"What? I thought the Egyptians worshipped Ra," Tox said.

"Yes, but that medallion wasn't Ra. He's depicted as a human figure with the head of a falcon and a sun disk resting on his head, or as the infamous Eye of Ra, or a sun disk with two cobras. They've even discovered reliefs with him as a cat and a crane." Tzivia's eyes brightened as she talked about the ancient world and its legacy. "But never like a pointed sun—and that's what this medallion looked like. It was the symbol of the god Shamash, who was Babylon and Assyria's god of justice."

Dr. Cathey's hands glided over the tablet. He turned it toward Tox and showed him the image. "As you can see—very distinctive."

"You said you don't know where it is, but do you have ideas where to look?" Tox glanced at his watch. "Dr. C's plane should arrive soon."

"I sent a message to a friend with the National Museum of Iraq," Dr. Cathey said, head still down, wiry hair sticking out in a sunlit halo.

"It's there?"

"That's where it should be," Tzivia said, "and despite a great proclamation that anything found on-site belongs to the state, some pieces go missing."

"Happens everywhere, really," Dr. Cathey put in. "Thievery is not limited to Iraq."

"What's going on?" Ram asked, joining them, bringing the others.

"I think we might know what the 'amulet of red' refers to," Tzivia answered her brother. "The trick might be—"

"Ah, it's there." Dr. Cathey finally brought his gray eyes to Tox, then Ram with a large smile. "My friend confirmed it's at the museum."

Tox's heart rapid-fired. "He has eyes on it?"

"Yes," Dr. Cathey said with a big smile. "He has verified its location. Even sent me a picture." Again, he turned the tablet toward them.

"That's it." Tzivia gasped, enlivened. "We have to go now! We're ahead of him."

"Ask if anyone is inquiring about it," Tox said, not too excited about possibly running into Alec's men again.

Dr. Cathey typed in a message to his contact, then waited, stroking his beard as he stared at the screen. Anticipation suspended conversation as they waited in silence. A bleep made the professor look closer. "Brilliant." He met Tox's gaze. "No other inquiries."

Ram straightened. "If we get this, then we have two of the five legacies." He winced. "But that museum is in Baghdad—a five- to six-hour drive."

"By bird under an hour," Maangi suggested.

"Same time to Kalhu," Ram argued. "We get to Nimrud, snatch that legacy."

"But we don't know that Nimrud's artifact is still there, or even where it is on site," Tzivia said. "Or *what* it is."

"But it's reasonable," Ram suggested, "to believe it's in the area your friend just discovered. Right?"

She shrugged, reluctant to acquiesce. "I suppose."

Tox suddenly felt as if they might be finding terra firma in this insanity. "If it's there and we get the Shamash medallion from Baghdad—"

"We have both legacies by the end of the day." Ram adjusted his beanie.

"Which means we're winning," Cell said. "Good guys: three, bad guys: zip. I'm liking those stats."

"There is the chance we chase both and lose both," Thor muttered.

Cell backhanded Thor's shoulder. "Way to a kill a moment, dude."

Tox rubbed his jaw, staring at the tablet even though he couldn't see the screen. He knew the answer but didn't want to say it. Didn't want to weaken them any more than they already were simply out of exhaustion. "We need to split up."

"One team to Baghdad," Ram said, "the other heads to Nimrud?"

Tox nodded. "And Dr. C to Germany. Cell, get SAARC on the line. We need a helo out to Baghdad. I'll ask Iliescu for diplomatic back-patting so we are in and out in record time."

"I should go to the museum," Tzivia said. "I—"

"No," Ram countered. "You go with Tox to Nimrud—it's an active site. You know the team, and you've already been there. He needs someone who can get around the site without causing trouble. I'll do Baghdad and the medallion."

"Maangi with Ram," Tox said, tugging out his phone.

"Who's going with Dr. C, then?" Tzivia asked.

Tox hesitated. "Runt, you're the junior historian—you go with the professor."

"Understood," Runt said with a nod.

"Tzivia with me, and Thor, too, to help with Cell's equipment and overwatch."

"What about her?" Runt asked, indicating Haven.

Cell barked a laugh. "Dude, if you want your head still on your shoulders, you learn real quick, she's his." He thumbed toward Tox. "And he's possessive. Kind of like a rabid dog."

"Or VVolt," Thor said.

Tox shook his head.

"So it's possible," Tzivia said, brown eyes gleaming. "By the end of the day, we could have *four* of the five gems."

Tox wouldn't jinx himself by entertaining victory before they'd stepped onto the battlefield. But that sounded like a good day, if they could pull it off.

"If we're back before you, want us to come to Nimrud?" Ram lifted a shoulder in a shrug. "Could take hours out there, searching for something that hasn't been seen in centuries."

True, but who knew how things would play out. "Check in when you get back."

"'*Out of that land went forth Ashur, and builded Nineveh, and the city Rehoboth, and Calah, and Resen between Nineveh and Calah: the same is a great city.*'" Dr. Cathey hefted his briefcase and shrugged when the team stared at him. "I'm inspired by history and the Bible. Nimrud is mentioned in Genesis 10 as a great city."

"Not so great if it's a pile of rubble," Cell muttered.

"Be not deceived," Dr. Cathey argued, ruffled by the comment. "That city thrived for centuries. Though Shalmaneser I built it, it was under the leadership of Ashurnasirpal I that it became a glorious part of the Assyrian empire."

"You know why they failed?" Cell said. "Because their names were too long. They needed more Bobs and Janes. Some spy comes into the palace and says, 'Whatchacantremember sent me.' And everyone shrugs and lets him in because they don't know if it was Whatcha-cantremember or Whatcha*can*remember who sent him."

Maangi rolled his eyes. "Says the guy named Barclay Purcell."

"Hey, that's a proud name borne by generations of Purcells."

"Point made." Maangi bumped fists with Thor.

"And right there is how friends became *non*-friends." Cell glowered, but there was a smile behind his eyes.

"Nimrud is heavily guarded and monitored," Tzivia said. "When I visited a couple weeks ago, we had to be very surreptitious getting in and out."

"Antiquities authority?" Maangi asked.

"And ISIL." Tzivia lifted a bag from where it waited with the rest of the team's.

"I should think you would know about this place, Mr. Purcell," Dr. Cathey said with a large dose of amusement. "It is said Nimrud is the location of the largest party ever thrown."

"Now that"—Cell pointed around the device he held—"is something worth hearing about."

"Later." Tox jutted his jaw toward the plane gliding toward them. "Professor, Runt, there's your ride. If we can get these gems before Alec is aware, then we can make sure the Endeavor event goes off without a hitch."

And without my parents dying.

34

"Sarge, what's up with these vehicles?" Cell complained from the rear of the Jeep he shared with Tox and Haven.

"They're nondescript and unobtrusive." Tox eyed the Jeep ahead carrying Tzivia and Thor.

"Is that Arabic for uncomfortable"—Cell's head thumped against the hull as they nailed another city-sized pothole—"painful, and easily targeted?"

Tox snickered and nodded. The Iraqi heat had beat misery and aches into them, even though it had only been about fifteen minutes since they'd skirted Al Khidr and headed west toward the site.

"Listen up," Tzivia said, speaking through the comms from the lead vehicle. "Just thought we should have some history about the site we're going to descend upon. Dr. Cathey mentioned Ashurnasirpal—he might have built the capital and his palace in Kalhu, but he was one sick ruler. This is what he wrote after conquering the city of Tela:

> *"I built a pillar over the city gate and I flayed all the chiefs who had revolted and I covered the pillar with their skins. Some I impaled upon the pillar on stakes and others I bound to stakes*

round the pillar. I cut the limbs off the officers who had rebelled.
Many captives I burned with fire and many I took as living
captives. From some I cut off their noses, their ears, and their
fingers, of many I put out their eyes. I made one pillar of the
living and another of heads and I bound their heads to tree
trunks round about the city. Their young men and maidens I
consumed with fire. The rest of their warriors I consumed with
thirst in the desert of the Euphrates.

"And that is a lesson on the barbarism of the Assyrians," Tzivia
finished.

"That is sick," Cell said. "And here I thought we had a lot to worry
about with King going all vigilante. Though, truth be told"—he
shrugged—"a part of me was glad to finally see justice being served
and not withheld in the name of political correctness, if you know
what I'm saying."

"I think we were all glad to see a bad guy get his due," Tox agreed.

"Even though it wasn't right?" Haven asked, her surprised question
spearing the admission.

"When you see what we see day after day, it . . ." Cell shook his
head, looking at the window.

"It wears on you." Tox nodded. "Everything starts feeling futile.
Like you're fighting a fire-breathing dragon with a water pistol."

"And your ammo evaporates as soon as it leaves the barrel," Cell
added. "Not saying what Alec has done is right, but I understand
the futility."

"Except his frustration was fueled by the crown's power," Haven
said in a placating tone. "Whatever that is."

Tox met her gaze.

"Sarge," Thor's concerned voice cranked through the comms.

He keyed his mic. "Go ahead."

Dusty plaster homes of a village drifted into view. The humble
dwellings were tightly clustered, walls broken and crumbling like defeated giants in wartime.

"Engine's giving me trouble. Pulling over to check it out," Thor
said.

"Copy," Tox replied as the Jeep veered to the side of the road. Unease squirmed through him as he pulled up behind them. "Everyone, eyes out." This village could be a perfect place to find help. Or an ambush.

"Roger that," Cell said, his gaze skirting the road, front to rear, as he lifted his weapon and did a press check.

After doing the same, Tox hopped out and slammed the door shut. He gave the area a once-over, then another as he stalked to the lead vehicle. "How's it look?"

Thor was bent over the engine, which hissed its objection to the Iraqi heat. "Not great."

"Can we limp it there and back?"

"Maybe there," Thor said with a shrug. "Doubt we'd make it back."

"Let's pile into the other Jeep."

"Tight fit with the equipment," Cell commented, joining them.

"Nothing we haven't done before. I'll move it closer." Tox hustled back to the Jeep and climbed in.

"Everything okay?" Haven asked.

"His Jeep's dead." Tox turned the key. "We'll group up."

Clank-clank-clank.

Shock tore at Tox. He removed the key. Tried again.

Clank-clank-clank-clank.

"Unbelievable!" He exited and opened the hood. Examining the engine led him no closer to an initial diagnosis.

"What happened?" Cell asked as he joined him. "It was fine."

On his back, Tox checked the universal joint that ran to the back axle.

"Told you these things were pieces of crap," Cell groused.

Disbelief cut through Tox—just as someone had done to the joint. Top half had a clean line, but the lower half was jagged. He eased back. Dread drenched his shoulders. Sabotage. Who? When?

"Do we walk back?" Thor asked.

"No," Tox said. "We're in-country and running down a clock that's working against us. Locals know we're here"—he nodded to the wary faces peering from behind flapping sheets and torn blankets—"and so does Alec."

"That's a leap." Cell laughed nervously.

"Someone sabotaged the vehicles," Tox said, pointing under the Jeep. "Cut through half the universal joint."

"They didn't want us getting there," Cell muttered.

Tox heaved a sigh. "Which means we have to get that legacy before he does."

"If they sabotaged our vehicles, they're probably already there," Thor said.

Tox bit back his frustration and keyed his mic. "Command, this is Wraith Actual. We have total equipment failure."

"Copy that, Actual. We are aware of your situation and location. Working contingencies. Hold your position."

Like they were going anywhere. "Roger." It was hard not to look up, imagining himself peering into the long-range lens of a satellite.

Across the road, a ten- to twelve-year-old boy watched them, brown eyes wide beneath a dusty layer of shaggy hair. He had a soccer ball tucked beneath one arm. Two women sat in chairs on a lone patch of grass between some rubble and remains of a building. The wall behind them, crooked and damaged from something violent, hulked defiantly. As if it refused to collapse or give in to the ravages of war. Tox could relate.

"Time to work my magic skills with the locals," Thor muttered.

"Scaring kids isn't on the agenda," Cell taunted.

Thor ignored him, motioning for the kid to toss the ball.

The boy glanced at the women, who muttered something Tox couldn't hear, then the boy rolled the ball across the dirt. Thor toed the ball and bounced it into the air, hopping from one leg to the other as he tapped it with his insteps.

Tox hefted his weapon and slid his arm through the strap. He adjusted it and kept watch. Ready, monitoring the road, their six, and the impromptu soccer game that now also included Tzivia, who'd donned a hijab. Where she'd gotten it, he didn't know. But she worked sites here all the time, so she'd clearly anticipated the need.

"This is costing us time," Cell said. "What if King is there right now?"

"Nothing we can do."

Laughter competed with the tension Tox felt having half his team in the open and both vehicles down. But Thor knew how to ingratiate himself with the locals. It was a gift Tox admired. He'd never fully been able to lower his guard, to trust.

"Wraith, we have two vehicles en route to your location."

"Copy that."

Ten minutes later, plumes of dust marked the arrival of three late-model SUVs barreling down the road. Tires crunched and rocks popped as the vehicles came to an abrupt halt. The drivers of the first two exited and climbed into the third, which made a one-eighty and left. Without a word. Without question.

Tox whistled to Thor and Tzivia, who thanked the boy and women, and then helped Cell transfer the equipment. Tox eyed the village in the rearview mirror as they made their own dust plumes. It all seemed too easy. SAARC watching. Someone sabotaging.

An hour later, they jounced up to the fenced-in area of ancient Kalhu.

Tzivia used her credentials to get them past the site security and barbed-wire fence. Besides a few beat-up sedans, the place sat empty and in ruins.

"Dude—ISIL did some serious damage."

"You have no idea." Tzivia pointed to a dark blue car with a cracked windshield. She thumbed her phone. "Sending a text to Faeza. She's on-site."

Tox scanned the plains. "Anything look out of place? Wrong?"

"Everything looks wrong," Tzivia said with a begrudging sigh, referring to the destruction by radicals. "But no . . ." She brushed her hair from her face. "This . . . seems right, at least compared to when I was last here."

Tox nodded to the equipment cases. "Cell, get your gear up and check for Alec's signal."

"Roger that." Cell lugged the cases to high ground.

Tox eyed an Iraqi guard who seemed too interested in Cell. Would he have to intervene?

"So," Haven said, "this city is 'where queens are buried, in great relief.'"

The guard turned back and continued his rounds.

Tzivia's experienced gaze swept the site. "Many of the reliefs were destroyed." She motioned to the piles of boulders and bricks, then squinted at the remains of the ancient city. "There are only a few remaining, but hopefully we can find something in that new area Mehdi just uncovered."

"That would make it easy," Tox said. Too easy.

"Do you jinx us on purpose, or does it come naturally?" Tzivia taunted. "Most of the city lies in ruins, but if this letter written by Thefarie is correct, there's a clue here. Let's hope ISIL didn't wipe it out."

Boots crunching as he took in the area, Tox grunted. "Just get us in." He scanned the barbed-wire enclosure and the armed guards patrolling its perimeter.

"It's more protected than last time," Tzivia muttered, chewing her lower lip. "Guess they've had recent trouble." With a nod—to bolster her own courage or reassure Tox, he wasn't sure—she started down the path.

"She didn't seem confident."

Tox heard Haven but didn't know how to respond. Because she was right. And that made him nervous. "Thor, eyes out. Haven, stay close." He walked a wide route around their SUV, noting the few parked vehicles and what seemed like new tracks in the dusty road. Broken reeds and brush.

Five minutes later, Tzivia whistled and motioned them forward.

Surprise leapt through Tox as they loaded up and pulled through the gate. Once they were past the guards, Tox eyed Tzivia as she climbed back in. "What'd you say to them?"

"That we were with the CIA and searching for something that could stop a deadly artifact that looks like a crown."

Shock hit him, but then his brain caught up with her sarcasm. "Did you promise to give them the crown when we're done, too?"

"Well, I had to compensate them somehow."

He sighed, shaking his head. As they made their way through the site, Tox was disheartened at how much had been destroyed. How much history lost.

"Sarge," Cell called through the comms.

Tox keyed his mic. "Go ahead." He guided the SUV to the designated parking area.

"I'm picking up some serious RFB."

His gut clenched.

"So Alec was here." Tzivia pointed to one of the innumerable stone walls. It bore Alec's crown symbol.

"Wonder who his victim was this time," Thor muttered.

Tzivia snapped a look at Thor. Then grabbed her phone. "Faeza hasn't responded!" She was throwing herself out of the vehicle before he stopped.

"Tzi! Wait!" Tox wanted to curse but instead keyed his mic again. "We're going in, Cell. Keep me posted." After parking, he jogged after her, glancing back to make sure Haven and Thor were with him. "Tzi, wait."

Catching sight of more guards watching curiously as he chased her through the rubble, he couldn't get over the thought of someone bulldozing historical landmarks. It was one thing to think the paths of the past were wrong. It was another to try to erase them. If one didn't look at those mistakes and learn from them, they'd be repeated.

Realization washed over him. The bulldozing of this site wasn't too different from what Alec was doing, trying to right what he felt were wrongs.

Am I doing the same, trying to erase from my mind what happened with al-Homsi?

"Here," Tzivia called. He caught up with her as she slung her bag across her shoulder and stepped into a gaping hole, using a ladder to descend.

"Slow down," he said, glancing toward Haven and Thor.

Tzivia's head dipped belowground. "It's not like her to ignore my messages."

"Maybe she has bad reception." He motioned Haven in next. "Stand guard but stay out of sight."

"Out of sight out of mind," Thor said with a nod.

"Sarge?" Cell's voice in his ear.

"Go ahead," Tox said, his voice bouncing back to him in the enclosed area.

"This signal is strong. I mean *strong*."

Bending to accommodate his height in the tunnel, Tox navigated behind Tzivia and Haven, a lone lamp poking through the darkness as they trekked.

"He was here. Recently."

"Copy that."

"I mean, he was *here*, Sarge."

Tox wouldn't let defeat or the thought that Alec's guys had somehow sabotaged their vehicles slow or thwart him. "I heard you the first time." The point being that if Alec had already been here, then they were probably chasing nothing. They wouldn't find anything. No artifact.

"Tzi, hold up," Tox said, noting the passage was narrowing.

"I already lost Noel," she hollered back. "I'm not losing another friend."

"Let me get ahead of you," he insisted. "Rear's guarded by Thor. I ca—"

"I can take care of myself," Tzivia grunted, her voice distant, the light and air thinning.

Tox huffed. Bullheaded woman. But it was true—Tzivia had killer Krav Maga skills. He'd taken a few of her well-placed strikes and wouldn't soon forget. But he was tactically minded.

His shoulder bounced off the right wall. He shifted left—and hit that wall, too. Tightening his stance, he advanced. Soon his tactical shirt scraped both sides. "What the . . . ?"

"Keep going. Hold your breath—and your gut," Tzivia taunted. "The passage compresses, and then you slide through the opening. Maybe suck in that ego of yours, too."

"Yours fit. I should be fine." He turned sideways, shuffling. Protective instincts screaming, he monitored the women, itching to get in front of them.

Ahead, a sliver of light drew him on. The light winked out, blocked by a shadow, then returned. It happened again, and Tox realized both Tzivia and Haven had left the passage.

He threw himself forward and quickly got jammed in the narrow space. He muttered an oath, frustrated. Shifted sideways. Shimmied. The people who built this had to be small. Like, elf small.

Shouts went up. Another.

Tox pitched himself at the opening. Writhed to get through. It wasn't made for well-muscled soldiers, he guessed. When he stumbled into the new room, he was surprised to hear laughter.

"That was not funny!" a man was objecting, holding his bloody nose.

"Well, you shouldn't have attacked me from behind," Tzivia retorted.

"It wasn't an attack! It was a hug!"

Apparently Tzivia *had* put her Krav skills to use. Tox smirked as he handed the guy a bandana.

"'ank you," he muffled.

"You're alive. That's what counts," Tzivia muttered. Unabashed. Unashamed. That was Tzivia Khalon. She motioned to her victim. "This is Mehdi Jaro, who oversees this site." She glanced at her friend. "Where's Faeza?"

"In the rear, cataloguing one of the walls."

"She's alive?"

Jaro frowned. "Of course she's alive. Why?"

"Has anyone else visited the site recently? Westerners?"

His frown dug deep into his dark features. "Yes, actually. A team much likes yours is visiting the ziggurat."

Tox stilled. "Right now?"

"I don't know." Jaro shrugged. "They arrived an hour ago—heard about them on the handheld. No word since."

"I didn't see any new vehicles," Tzivia commented.

"Oh." Jaro touched his swollen nose. "Then I guess they're gone. Not much to see—the ziggurat is leveled." He started toward another slim gap in the wall.

"Ancients didn't believe in doors?" Tox mumbled, rubbing the back of his neck.

"Maybe you need to lose some weight," Tzivia said.

"Definitely not," Haven said, eying Tox appreciatively. "He's just right."

"I must agree," Tzivia said.

And they both laughed.

Now that was weird. "Okay, okay—move on. There's nothing to see here."

He waited until they passed, then took a deep breath and plunged through the opening. Haven grinned as he stepped into the new passage, which was a normal width, but shorter.

Tzivia was hugging a woman. She wasn't a hugger, so that probably meant this was the friend she'd been worried about. "I need them to see the chamber," she said. "If the ziggurat visitors are who we think, then he's the same man hunting the crown that might have come from there."

"Ah, of course." Backstepping, Jaro nodded. "Come."

Thankfully, there was more room in the chamber, though the sight of that iron cage siphoned off what little breath Tox had left. He stepped closer.

"Careful," Jaro said. "There are booby traps around it."

Tox glanced at the floor, then the ceiling, remembering Tzivia had said something about swords. "And you don't know for sure that the crown was here?"

"I have no indication of what this cage held, save the circular dust ring on the pedestal."

Tox eyed that, too.

"Do you feel it?" Tzivia asked.

"Karma?" he taunted.

"The thrum of the iron."

It was then he realized the lack of air might be the result of the vibrating bars. He wondered what Cell would think of this. "Maybe Cell should come down here, see if he can get an RFB off this."

"Wait! Look!" Tzivia hurried around the cage and pointed to a wall of cuneiform script. "This . . . this talks about the wife of Shalmaneser I."

His comms crackled. "Sarge."

"Yeah." Tox wiped his forehead as he replied to Cell, torn between the curiosity of the cage, Tzivia's excitement, and Cell's call.

"I . . . I've got something weird."

"This might be it, Tox," Tzivia called.

Excitement warred with wariness. "What's it say?"

"I'm not sure. Tzivia used her phone to video the relief as she translated. "Let's see. 'Eyes . . . her eyes of blue . . .'" Her face scrunched
as she mouthed something.

"What?" he asked.

"Well, this script." She shook her head. "It doesn't . . . it seems
off, wrong."

"Just read it. How do we find the gem?"

"That's just it—"

"Sarge," Cell said again.

"—there isn't anything."

"'Eyes of blue,'" Haven mused. "*Eyes*. Plural. Maybe . . ."

Tox watched, half listening to Cell rambling about the frequency
broadcast while Haven scurried around the stele and pointed to a
drawing of a person. "The queen."

"That's odd." Tzivia wrinkled her nose. "Most depictions are in
profile."

"I wonder . . ." Haven pressed two fingers to the queen's eyes.

The thought of booby traps and swords rushed through Tox. "Wait!"

Click! Puff!

"Oh!" Haven leapt back, staring at the stele. A small tray jutted
from its base. A glimpse of blue glared back.

Thud! Whoosh!

Air slapped Tox from behind. He turned to see the other woman,
Faeza, facing a man who hadn't been there two seconds ago. Because
there'd been a wall there.

The man snatched Faeza.

Tox lunged. In the space of a blink, the wall slammed down again,
and he collided with it. "No!"

"Faeza!" Tzivia shouted.

"The door is sealed," Jaro muttered, frantically searching its frame
for a way to open it again.

"Kind of figured that out," Tox growled, tracing the edges.

"No, this one."

The first opening they'd come through was now a wall of reliefs
just like the rest. Then, for no reason that Tox could see, the door
whooshed back open.

"This way," Jaro breathed as he darted out. "There's another opening to that passage he took her through."

Even as Tox started that way, he heard Haven call that the tray had closed. "But I saw the lapis lazuli!"

A half dozen paces down the hall, they banked right—straight into another wall.

Jaro skidded to a stop. "This—" He smacked the wall of reliefs and tiles. "This wasn't here! It goes on—"

Whoosh!

Tox peered around the corner. Tzivia stood at the opening to the room with the pedestal . . . which was no longer an opening. It had sealed. What the . . . ?

"Haven!" Tox flung himself at it. "Haven, are you okay?"

A scream lit the air. Then gunfire.

Heart in his throat, Tox threw himself at the wall. His shoulder shrieked at the pain, but he didn't care. "Haven! Haven, talk to me!" Desperation pulled his weapon to the front. He aimed it at the wall.

"No!" Jaro lunged, slapping aside the gun. "You'll destroy it."

"Yeah," Tox barked, aiming again. "Whatever it takes!"

Jaro shoved in front of him. "Just wait—"

"I'm not waiting—"

The wall grumbled as it again receded into the ceiling.

Tox pitched forward, his gaze immediately snagging on a woman's prostrated form. Though his heart shot into his throat, in that split second he knew it was Faeza.

"Haven?" He pivoted, scanning the chamber.

Dirt and sand crunched beneath a boot. Haven sat propped against the wall, staring at him. Tears streaked her face. She held her bleeding shoulder, trembling. "I'm not shot," she said, shaking her head. "He . . . he shot her. And took the gem."

"Faeza is dead!" Jaro wailed. "They killed her! Why?"

"Why are you bleeding?" Tox knelt, reaching for his med kit.

"The swords," Tzivia muttered. "The booby trap Mehdi warned you about."

Shaking her head, Haven shuddered. "He knew, Cole."

Pulling out the kit, he eyed her.

"He knew how to operate the room. Which button to push. He opened the tray. Tried to shoot me, but I . . . I think the doors and their timing saved me. When I dropped behind the pedestal, he didn't have time to kill me. He had to work fast to get the tray open and get back out before the doors changed again."

"Which means our enemy is smarter than us," Tzivia said around tears. Fire lit her eyes. "They knew opening the tray would trigger the walls to start changing."

"He just has a better source," Tox muttered. Which he'd take up with SAARC. He bandaged Haven's cut, relieved it wasn't deep. "We need to get topside, find out what happened."

"Faeza, Faeza," Jaro repeated over and over. "Why?"

Tox pivoted in his crouch and lowered his head. He'd known as soon as he entered the room that the woman was gone. He nodded Tzivia toward Jaro and turned his attention to the team. "Thor, we're coming up." He helped Haven to her feet. "Thor?"

He thought of the double-tapped woman.

"Thor. Report." He stopped, checked his comms piece, glancing over his shoulder toward the entrance, as if he could see his team. "Thor. Cell? Come in."

Nothing.

"Comms are down," he said, turning to Tzivia. "Can I borrow your phone?"

She tugged it out of her pocket and stilled. Pressed a button. "It's dead."

Not good. "Okay, everyone clear out."

Jaro clenched his fists. "I'm not leaving Faeza—"

"You can't help her. And right now, if you want to stay alive"—objection registered on the archaeologist's face, and Tox knew he needed to switch tactics—"to protect this site, you have to go now."

The defeated and shell-shocked Jaro stood, and they started the trek back to the surface.

35

"*Assalamu alaikum*," Ram greeted the woman behind the desk at the National Museum of Iraq. He slid his hands into the pockets of the silk suit he'd had delivered to the airstrip, where the limousine had picked them up. Two men were on hand to brief Ram about the museum, about their contact, provide the legends that would get them in and give them access to the artifact.

She inclined her hijabbed head. "*Wa alaikum assalaam*."

"My associate and I"—he motioned to Maangi—"are here on the authority of Safa Binte Mansoor as representatives of the Israel-America Foundation to identify and verify a medallion in the current possession of this museum."

Bewilderment shaded her eyes, dark as inkblots. "I have no note of your visit, sir. I am sorry."

"I'm sure if you check your records again, you'll find it. We did make the appointment last-minute, but it's there. I'm sure," Ram explained. "We learned only a few hours ago about an active threat against this medallion."

Those inkblots widened. "Oh." She ran her hands over the papers on her desk, then checked her computer. "I apologize, but—"

366

Ram slapped a hand on the counter. "I have no time for this! I would speak to Halim bin Fahd."

"The directo—oh." Her trembling hands dialed bin Fahd's extension, and Ram knew the director's reputation had carried into all areas of his life, not just the underground, where he went by another name. The girl explained the situation into the phone. Face chalky white, she returned the phone to the cradle.

Almost at the same time, a door opened. A thick-chested man stepped into the foyer, extended two fingers, and motioned Ram to come with him.

Silently, the man stalked the plain halls of the museum's office space, soft carpet padding his steps. The buzz of the daily grind filtered into the halls from the many offices and mazelike collection of cubicles. Finally, their guide approached a heavy door, slid his card into the access port, then palmed a panel in the wall. With a definitive *shink*, it opened. He shouldered the door aside and held it for them, exposing slick floors, hard steel, and half walls of inches-thick glass. He let it close behind them, sealing Ram and Maangi in the cold, sterile hallway.

"Keep walking," Ram whispered as he strode into the secure wing, confident. Especially when a man emerged from an office at the far end and buttoned his suit jacket, carefully placing four fingers along the navy silk.

Four minutes. They'd only have four minutes.

With an almost imperceptible nod, the man headed in the opposite direction. Ram hadn't stopped moving, aiming straight for the room the man had just vacated.

As Ram rounded the corner, he collided with solid mass. Struck shoulders with another man. The room should have been empty. Alarm sparked through his veins. Instinct drove him back as a stick aimed at his face.

With one hand he swung the stick aside and lifted the other to strike. And stopped short, realizing he was attacking a mop that reeked of antiseptic. Bent and startled, the janitor cringed—cowered.

Ram waved him past.

Hurrying, the janitor wheeled a mop bucket out the door, mumbling an apology.

Grunting his frustration, Ram scanned the room. "Close it," he muttered to Maangi, who secured the door.

Rows of tables straddled the long, narrow room, and the walls were the dark gray of bullet- and fire-proof vaults. Each held an artifact, preserved and protected from the elements. Only the last table was lit, a black box waiting ominously. As Ram swept toward it, he plucked cotton gloves from a box on the wall and pulled them on. Everything here was about preserving the past, protecting the artifacts.

Pointing to the box, Maangi huffed. "There's a lock." He stuffed his fingers into a pair of gloves.

Ram carefully gripped the top of the box and nudged. It opened without complication. Smiling that the contact had done his job, he leaned over the preservation box.

Black velvet stared back. He lifted the thin scrap of fabric. Only more black. His heart jolted. It wasn't here. But the contact wouldn't have acknowledged him, confirmed the package without the amulet.

"Where is it?" Maangi asked. "What—"

Mind springing backward— "The janitor." Ram threw himself toward the door, yanked it open. Nearly cursed when he saw the mop bucket abandoned in the hallway.

Through the window in the secure door, he spotted the janitor at the end of the corridor. "Hey!" Drawing his weapon, Ram lunged at the door.

Locked.

He aimed and fired twice at the lock. It crackled and popped, smoke rising from the mechanism. He drove his heel against the jamb. It surrendered. He plunged through and sprinted down the hall.

A man stepped out of his office. "Hey, what's—"

"Move!" Ram shoved him aside and kept running. Momentum flung him wide around the corner. Thirty meters ahead, the janitor headed for an exit.

Ram snapped up his weapon and fired two shots.

The janitor slammed into the door, his right shoulder hitting hard. He fell against it, clearly having taken a bullet, but kept moving.

So did Ram. He dove for the door, but it clapped shut. Blood smeared the steel barrier. Ram crashed through it, weapon sweeping right and left. The silence of the empty foyer stunned him. The receptionist looked on the verge of a heart attack.

Behind him, Maangi trotted up. "Where'd he go?"

"Where is he?" Ram demanded of the receptionist.

Hand shaking, she pointed at an exit to the right.

Ram pitched himself at it and barreled into a narrow hall. His shoulders thumped the walls as he ran. Broke out into a side alley. Shadows and stench lurked in the darkened space between the museum and the parking garage.

And there, on the side of the dumpster, spray paint still wet and bleeding red down the steel container: Alec King's symbol.

36

As they neared the tunnel opening, Tox noticed a shadow shift ahead. He slowed, raising his weapon as the shape came into view.

Shrouded in shadows, Thor stood a half dozen feet from the base of the ladder with his weapon aimed at them. "Glad you're alive," he muttered as he swung his sights back up the ladder. "Lost you on comms."

"I think they failed."

"Negative—been talking to Cell."

Tox yanked out his piece and checked it. "Mine's dead. Let me borrow yours."

Thor removed the wire and earpiece, then handed them over.

"And our phones are dead," Tzivia added.

Wiring up, Tox jutted his jaw toward the entrance. "What's happening?"

"Guards went ape. Started running east. Cell said to get down, that they were shooting." He pointed his muzzle at the ladder. "Fish in a barrel."

Tox nodded. "Smart." He eyed the opening. "Cell, you there?"

"'Bout freakin' time!"

"Is it clear?"

"Copy that. Guards are huddled, but the shooting stopped."

"We're coming up." Tox drew his Glock 22, very much wishing for his M4, but they'd come in light, wanting to appear friendly so they could gain access. "Ready?"

"Anytime, anywhere," Thor said.

Tox nodded for the others to stay, then reached for the ladder. Weapon aimed up, he began to climb. Even though Cell said it was clear, Tox wasn't taking a chance. No sense playing whack-a-mole with his own head.

Barely clearing the hole, he swiveled around, checking for threats. He spotted the distracted guards in the distance and drew himself out. He crouch-ran to a nearby boulder. "Clear," Tox called.

It took two minutes for the others to climb out. Tox had point, Thor took rear, and they trekked back in the direction they'd last seen Cell. They rounded a corner and spotted him, squatting in front of his gear.

"Cell."

Weapon in hand, he rotated toward them. Then sagged as they grouped up around him. "Dude." He shook his head and turned back to his equipment.

"What's going on?"

Cell shifted, his face chalky. "This is muffed up."

"Everything is muffed up when you're involved," Thor said lazily, his gaze scanning the site.

"No," Tzivia said, wrapping her arms around herself, "I've got a weird feeling here, too."

Irritation scraped Tox's spine. "Cell."

Static crackled through their comms. "Wraith Actual, this is Wraith Five. Come in."

Tox turned away from the others, relieved to hear Ram's voice. "This is Actual. Go ahead, Five."

"Bird's inbound. You still on-site?"

"Roger, on-site."

"Coming your way in three mikes."

"Negative."

"Come again?"

"Possible hostile situation. Rendezvous at Stryker in two hours."

"You need backup?"

"Negative. Packing up now."

"Copy that."

"Did he get the medallion?" Tzivia asked.

"Unknown." Tox jutted his jaw toward the guard hut. He looked at Cell. "What were you saying?"

"Just remember"—he wagged a finger at them—"I said it's muffed up. And I have to say, I'm freaked because . . ." He swallowed. "King has figured it out."

"Figured what out?"

"That we're tracking him, in a sense, through this."

Tox cocked his head. "The RFB?"

A scowling Thor shouldered in. "How's that possible, that he knows we're trying to find him? Nobody knows but SAARC and DoD."

"And that's about fifty too many hands in the pot," Cell groused. "Who knows how he figured it out, but he not only knows we're detecting him, he knows *how*."

What little Tox had eaten that morning began to sour in his gut. He took a step back and glanced away. They were close. They needed to be close. The danger of Alec committing some large-scale murder hovered like a sandstorm.

"So someone's feeding him information," Haven said.

"That's the only answer," Tox said. "After the puzzle box down there—"

Cell frowned. "Puzzle box?"

"Never mind." Even as a hot breeze dragged its annoying fingers across the back of his neck, dumping buckets of sweat down his shirt, Tox saw the way Cell shifted. Kept looking at the box. He hadn't told them everything. "You have something?"

Again, Cell swallowed. "Yeah. A message—from King."

"What do you mean, a message?" Tox's gut twisted. "You know what? Never mind—were you recording?"

"From the second I powered up."

"Then let's pack up and head back. Play it back at Stryker. I want out of this place."

* * * *

FOB STRYKER, IRAQ

"Play it." Tox nodded to Cell as they gathered in the conference room back at the base.

Cell's gaze flipped to Haven, then back. "I just . . . maybe it's . . . sensitive."

"Everyone here has clearance," Ram said.

"No, not sensitive like that." Cell cowered beneath whatever secret he protected. And somehow, Tox had a feeling this secret was connected to himself. His gaze hit the box. What could Alec have possibly done? "I don't get it. How'd he send a personal message? I thought ghost skips were trapped radio signals."

"They are. But this isn't. It's different from the RFB of the crown, but I don't exactly know how, just that it is."

"I thought you were the comms expert," Thor taunted.

"I'm a communications specialist, not an expert. And this is a lot of pressure, right here." Cell scratched his head. "Look, his guys shot up the place, so maybe he was nearby, transmitting. I don't know."

Maangi shifted. "King was on-site?"

Cell grunted. "All I have are guesses." He glanced at the machine. "And the recording."

"Play it. We're all adults here," Ram said.

But Tox wasn't so sure.

And neither was Cell. He eyed Tox, hesitating. Hiding would only make matters worse, whatever it was. He gave a curt nod.

With a long intake of breath, Cell dialed in and flicked a knob.

Static squawked. Squealed.

"It's on a loop. Keeps playing," Cell explained. "He sent this deliberately, knowing we'd look for the crown's frequency and find this."

" . . . *loyal will they be once they know everything? Keep a watchful eye out, brother, because this is far from over. Count their lives. Count the minutes. Because their clocks are ticking down.*"

Static crackled. Hissed.

Cell held up a hand. "There's more—that's just where I picked it up."

"Once we know what?" Maangi asked, angling closer to the box.

"Wait, is this guy threatening us?" Thor demanded.

"Of course he is," Ram bit out.

"His brain's fried, remember?" Cell added.

Tox didn't want to hear more. That first line kept repeating in his head, gnawing at him. Once they knew everything? He knew what secret Alec was about to splay open. And these men? They'd be gone.

This couldn't happen. Not right before they took down Alec.

That's his plan. Destroy the team. Destroy our chance to stop him.

Which meant Alec was probably pulling out the stops. But what did he have on Tox? There was no way he could know about al-Homsi. About Brooke. His gaze fell to the floor. Could he know? But . . . how?

Someone had put Alec onto the team, told him how they were monitoring him. And that someone had to be high enough up within SAARC, DoD, or the CIA to have access . . .

Oh no. Crap.

" . . . *No man left behind,*" blared through the speaker.

"Turn it up."

"Turn it off." Tox's command competed with Ram's. His heart beat faster as Ram's gaze struck his. And Tox saw it—the desire to know what had happened.

"*That's what they tell you,*" Alec's voice droned. "*They hammer that into us as brothers-in-arms. We go out, and no man gets left behind. It's a code cemented with blood, sweat, and tears. Trial after trial. Attack after attack. Until we trust no one but the ones wearing the same uniform. We trust each other that we won't get left behind. We won't be abandoned. But it's a code you seem to have forgotten, Tox.*"

His ears rang with the words—words that couldn't be farther from the truth.

"*One I had been so sure you were not just following but leading with. But I finally see it—you actually think you're better than me. You think you know more. That you're smarter. You put trust in men we both know are not worthy of that trust. Yet you handed it to them. For what? For what, Tox?*"

"Wait—how are we not worthy?" Thor balked.

Each beat of his heart felt like the *thwump* of rotors. His hearing grew hollow. His fears screaming. *He knows. Somehow, Alec knows.*

It took everything in Tox not to back up. Not to react. React, and he'd look guilty. Stand firm, and you defend your actions.

But should he? Could he?

"The men surrounding you now, the men whose hands you put your life in, how likely are they to keep that code once they know the truth? And that lovely blonde you've gotten a taste of—what if she knew about her sister, Tox? How loyal would she be then? And your men, when they know what you did, the blood you spilled to buy their cooperation? Or your country—when they find out about al-Homsi? How loyal will they be once they know everything? Keep a watchful eye out, brother, because this is far from over. Count their lives. Count the minutes. Because their clocks are ticking down."

There it was.

Tox straightened—but his legs swayed. He lifted his gaze to the ceiling. Ignored the silence that dropped with nuclear force.

Alec had just dumped a crapload of trouble on him, but Tox had to know—"Can you track the message?"

Complexion pale even though he'd had more time than the rest to process the words, Cell nodded. "It's the best signal we've had, but it's not the crown's signal. That was there, too, and strong. But that message was a recording." A shrug. "But yeah. King was here. And within the last twenty-four. We're catching up."

* * * *

"So that's it?" Ram demanded. His words pulsed with as much uncertainty as Haven felt in her spinning head.

She tried to look at Cole, but her gaze defied her. Never made it past his chest. What did Alec King mean about Brooke? And what was with Cole, his rigid avoidance? His quieted voice? His shaken demeanor?

Alec knew something. Something terrible supposedly committed by Cole.

And Cole *must* have done it—it couldn't be false accusation, because he wasn't arguing. He wasn't angry. He was . . . accepting, in an avoidant, noncommittal way.

"What did he mean about Brooke?" she asked.

Cole stilled, staring at the floor. His gaze slid to the side, but not to her. "Not now."

"No, I think now is the perfect time," Ram said. "What'd he mean about al-Homsi?"

"That's the hot-shot senator who got blown up," Runt said.

"We know who he was," Ram sniped, turning his attention back to Cole. "But what did you have to do with it?"

The sigh Cole hefted seemed to bear the weight of a megaton bomb. "I'm not supposed to talk about this—"

"Hey, if King's lording it over us, we need to get it out there, get answers."

"Do we?" Haven hadn't realized she'd said it out loud until the guys turned to her with uniform scowls. "Think about it—if Cole could tell us openly and without hesitation, don't you think he would have?" She felt the tremble in her words, because she wasn't even sure of that answer. "Just because we want answers doesn't mean we have a right to them." And she definitely wanted answers.

"So just because the sarge has it bad for you makes it okay to side with him?" Thor asked.

"Hey," Cole and Ram barked.

Thor wasn't deterred. "Doesn't it bother you? This involves your sister!"

"Hey!" Ram snapped again, louder, but the damage was done.

Haven hesitated, sliding a look to Cole, who had his head down, shoulders sagging.

A ringtone split the silence. Cole straightened and pulled his phone from his pocket. "It's him, Alec."

Ram strode toward him, nodding to the team. "Speaker. For everyone."

"Is that smart?" Haven wasn't sure she could take any more of Alec's revelations.

Cole nodded at Ram, and held up the phone. "Russell."

"I take it you found my message, thanks to your clever little comms specialist."

"Trying to divide my team. Clever tactic." Irritation and anger pounded Cole's words as he speared Thor with a glare, as if to make the point.

"I thought you should know there's a price for those in your path, Tox. A steep, lethal price."

Jaw set, nostrils flared, Cole said nothing. Waited.

"Speechless, are we?" Alec said with a chuckle. "Well, the truth remains—innocents will suffer. When you kick the hornet's nest, there's a price to pay. Perhaps, say, children who play soccer with American soldiers?"

It took the space of a heartbeat for the words and threat to register. "Alec—"

"Kharouf!" Thor lunged at the phone. "You piece of—" Spinning away, he hurled a flurry of curses at the non-present Alec, kicking a chair across the room. Spun toward Cole. "We have to go! He's going to kill that boy!"

37

The past was roaring back with a vengeance.

The rotors of the Black Hawk thumped hard, hammering Tox's conscience as they raced back to the village where Thor had played soccer with a preteen boy. The big guy pounded the hull of the chopper, his anxiety fever pitched.

A boy could die because of Tox. He turned his attention to the warbling heat waves riding the surface of the Iraqi plains.

"Two mikes," the pilot called on the comms.

Double-checking his weapons, Tox peered south, where the city seemed to grow as they raced to the village just outside it. Like ghosts of the past, the war-chewed buildings grew on the horizon. Rubble. Debris. And amid it all, normalcy. Cars. People. Beside him, Ram snatched up his handgun. Racked back the slide for a press check, verifying a round in the chamber. Then he lifted his M4 and expelled the mag into his hand. He glanced at it, popped it in, then drew back the charging handle. A second later, he dropped the mag again and glanced at it before slapping it back into place. He repeated the same process for Tox's rifle and declared it ready. Thor, Cell, and Maangi were prepping their weapons, too.

378

Thor slapped the pilot's shoulder and pointed to a cluster of buildings to aim for. But it was too tight. They'd have to get dropped farther out. Frustration roiled across Thor's face.

They hit the ground running, hearts in their throats. Anger in their veins.

Helmet on and weapon up, Tox ignored the heat baking his body as he scurried to the nearest structure. While Thor sprinted across the open, straight toward the building the boy had emerged from with his mother, Tox made quick work of clearing buildings and dilapidated structures as he made his way around the area.

He stepped into a house. Wide eyes in a mahogany face stared back, shocked. Whispering an apology in Arabic, Tox aimed his weapon down but didn't lower it. In his best but broken Arabic, he asked about Kharouf.

The teen boy merely stared at him.

Beside him, a young girl stirred. She pointed behind Tox.

"Sarge, King's crown. It's here," Cell subvocalized through the comms.

Tox backed out of the house, pressing his spine to the wall so he couldn't be ambushed. Turning, he let his gaze take in the scene—located Cell, who pointed to a partially hidden wall that bled with the crown of Alec King.

"It wasn't there before," Thor said, his voice broken and nervous through the earpiece. "Right, Six?"

It hadn't been there. But *they* had been there. That was the point. Maangi and Cell were standing watch, weapons tucked against shoulders, helmets baking their skulls just as Tox's was his, protecting the team. Ram and Thor were hurrying along the other side of the courtyard.

"Kharouf!" Thor shouted, slinking around the other side of the buildings. "Kharouf!"

Tox motioned at him, urging him to not call the boy. If Kharouf was still alive, better to have him out of sight than in the open and a prime target. He scurried up to the next building. They had no idea what they were facing—shooter, bomb. No idea. The kid might already be dead. But Tox had a feeling that wasn't the case. Alec drove them here. He wanted Tox to see it.

This kid could die because of him. *You're Toxic. Alec is just prov- ing it to everyone.*

Shouldering aside the condemnation, Tox gritted his teeth, know- ing they'd played right into Alec's hands. He was here. Watching. Had to be. Tox's gaze scanned the rooftops. The higher buildings in the distance.

A soccer ball burst from the narrow alley between two homes and bounced against the hard-packed earth.

Tox flinched. The impact seemed deafening.

"Kharouf," Thor shouted in relief as the kid broke into the open, his face alight. Until he saw the soldiers—saw Tox and Ram. His smile slid away as he swung his gaze to Thor. The large man waved him closer, urging him to come quickly and quietly.

"Hurry," Ram said in Arabic. "There's danger."

Kharouf stood five paces from the alley, smudged in dirt and sweat. An uncertain smile on his thin lips. Mop of black hair dusted and matted to his face. He glanced back into the alley, where the voices of other children drifted into the tension.

Tox's heart stumbled at the thought of involving more kids. "Tell him we have to go *now*."

But Ram's terse Arabic words had the opposite effect. The boy froze. Then backed up.

"No!" Thor held out his hands, placating, begging. He went to a knee, sliding his weapon around to his back. "It's okay. Come. Tell him I'll get him to safety. We'll find his family."

Ram translated, but the boy didn't answer or move.

Dust and fear hung in the air, drenching their muscles with adrena- line. The clock was ticking. "Just grab him," Tox said, not willing to be in the open any longer.

Kharouf smiled and took a step toward them.

Then he crumbled in a heap. Lay still.

The ball rolled to Tox's feet. Thumped against his boot.

"*No!*" Thor screamed, lunging at the boy. He hauled Kharouf into his arms. Hugged him to his chest.

"Shooter on the roof! Shooter on the roof!" Ram yelled.

A series of cracks responded to the murder of the innocent boy.

Maangi and Cell flew into action, sprinting across the road and chasing the shooter.

Tox clapped a hand on Thor's vest, and with Ram's assistance, dragged him into the cover of the nearest building.

Still hugging the boy tight, Thor released broken sobs that echoed the wrenching dread suffocating Tox. Numbness spread through his limbs. He'd seen the killing of innocents more than once. But this time . . . this time was different.

The game had changed. Alec had played them. He'd treated the innocent lives he'd taken like moves on a chess board. Tox slid down the wall, crouching beside Thor and the boy. Ran a hand over the boy's thick mop of black hair. *I'm sorry.*

It was stupid. Senseless. Sick. Perverted justice.

No, this wasn't justice.

It was murder.

All to punish me.

Enough was enough.

Alec had gone too far. He'd pushed too hard. Lost his bearings. Lost his compass. In fact, there might not be a compass for him anymore.

Time to call it. End this charade of vigilantism.

The thought rattled Tox. But he surrendered the battle. He surrendered the hope that he could save Alec, turn him back toward the light. It was impossible to save Alec because he didn't want to be saved. He'd go down in a blaze of glory.

They had to bring the game to Alec. Deliver that crown to the history from which it had come. Bury it.

Bury Alec.

38

"Wheels up in twenty."

Tox glanced at Ram. "We just got back. Where are we headed?"

"SAARC wants us to rendezvous with Cathey and Runt. Then we're headed stateside."

"But we don't have the legacies yet."

"I think they're worried about your revelations." Ram adjusted his beanie, eyes glinting. "They're not the only ones."

"What?" Thor's voice prowled through the hangar near where the Black Hawk had deposited them. "*What* can you be hiding that is so awful he will kill kids?" He touched his fingertips, still stained with Kharouf's blood, to his temples. "I can't even—tell us what's worse than that."

Tox tucked his hands under his armpits and scanned the area. They were alone, but anyone listening could get a clear shot or record anything he said. This talk needed to take place in a more secure location. The plane.

"Hey." Ram aimed Thor toward a door. "Go clean up."

"Nah, man. I want answers."

"We all do," Ram snapped. "Clean up."

382

Tox and Ram exchanged a glance, but there was no understanding in it. Only an awareness. It couldn't be avoided any longer. If Tox had to guess, Ram's expression insinuated that this would have been better handled a year ago when Tox had resurfaced. He was probably right. But the gag order . . .

What would happen if—no, *when*—he told the guys what happened? Would he get yanked and tanked?

Like they say, better to ask forgiveness than ask permission.

A black Suburban lurched to a stop between the plane on the tarmac and the hangar. Levi Wallace emerged, arm in a sling and neck bandaged. He wore a light blue shirt and black slacks. Before the door even closed, Haven was halfway across the hangar, concern etched into her face. Though Tox didn't want to read into it, he did. Especially in light of the new bomb sitting between them. She'd asked about Brooke, and he'd put her off.

Once the team boarded the SAARC plane, Tox planted himself in a seat and buckled up. As soon as they reached altitude, he unbuckled and started toward the conference area. It seemed each step he took unclicked another belt. Steps padded behind him. They knew. He knew. It was time.

He pushed past the leather chairs and pinned himself into the corner, the hull brushing his shoulder blades, his hands planted on a chair. There wasn't enough room here for maneuvering or excuses. Almost not even enough for breathing.

Somber faces held fast as they slipped into their seats. Except Thor. He stood by the door, Ram next to him. Haven sat next to Levi and Tzivia. Cell and Maangi behind them.

Tox locked on to Thor. "This must stay here. It can't go anywhere. I'm breaking the law by telling you, but"—he shrugged and sighed—"it's time. Alec wants to break up our team. We're close to stopping him, and he knows it. I'm going to come clean in the hopes you'll put this aside. Hate me later. Quit the team—later."

"But Alec's ahead," Cell protested. "He has two of the artifacts. We only have one. Why worry about us?"

"Because he knows I won't quit or relent. I believe the same about each of you."

"What law?" Shoulders squared, Thor lifted his chin. "What law are you breaking?"

"Four years ago, I signed a document agreeing to never discuss my mission with anyone without the express, written permission of the Secretary of Defense, Director of the CIA, or the president."

"So it's high up the food chain," Maangi noted.

Tox gave a curt nod. "After Kafr al-Ayn, we were all locked away—you know that. They wanted scapegoats for Montrose's death. They got them. You. Me."

"Yeah, I still don't get that—nobody made him go back in after you. Montrose got himself killed," Cell said. He shrugged when the others looked at him. "What? It's true."

Nobody made Montrose try to save Tox, but he had. And then the team disobeyed orders to go in after him. A snowball effect unleashed when Tox decided to save the president but couldn't get himself out once he had.

"So." Ram inserted himself. "He died. We didn't. The American public wanted someone to blame. We went down in a blaze of glory."

"Pssh," Cell said, sarcasm and frustration boiling into a pot of misery, "I missed the glory part. Unless by *glory*, you mean losing everything, including your girlfriend."

"You and me both," Maangi muttered.

"There a point?" Thor snapped.

Cell came to his feet. "Dude, back off. You weren't even involved in Kafr al-Ayn—"

"But I sure as heck was involved today when Kharouf was murdered six feet from me."

Tox shifted forward. "Cell. It's okay."

"Nah, it ain't," he said, lowering himself back to his seat. "Respect, man. This is about respect."

Tox needed to get on with it. "I was in prison when"—he probably shouldn't mention Barry Attaway, his brother's chief of staff—"an offer was made. If I took a mission, they would clear all charges against you. Records would be sealed so nobody could bring this to bear on you again. I took the offer."

"What was the mission?" Ram asked quietly.

Tox glanced at the slick, gray table. Dug deep for some courage missing from his arsenal. There was no way around this. He met Ram's gaze again. "Amir al-Homsi."

Something shifted in Ram. Shock. Surprise. It rippled through his olive complexion. "*You* killed him."

"I killed him."

"Wait." Cell held up a hand, his brow knotted. "Didn't he go down in Baltimore, a car accident?"

Tox nodded. "That was the official story."

"But we can't act on U.S. soil," Cell countered weakly.

"Which is why this can't get out," Ram said and adjusted his stance against the galley bulkhead. "So you killed him. Then what?"

The rest of that deadly night in Baltimore was a blur. And it had to stay that way, too. "Official record: I was murdered in a riot at the prison. They notified my parents I was dead. I left the country." Tox forbade his gaze from drifting to Haven. "Vanished. Made my way to Nigeria, where I . . . ended up with Chiji's family."

"And that's where you were until they lured you back in?" Cell asked.

Tox nodded again.

"So what's the big deal about all this?" Shrugging, Cell looked around the room. "Because he killed someone on U.S. soil?"

"He *murdered* an *American* citizen on *American* soil," Wallace said, his tone graver than anyone else's. "It's a capital crime."

"Except they made him a deal."

"Doesn't make it right," Wallace said, his gaze piercing.

"It wasn't right," Tox agreed, his pulse a little uneven. "Killing al-Homsi went against everything I believe in, every code I've ever lived by. Even after they showed me documented proof that he wasn't an American citizen, it still felt wrong."

"Wait," Maangi said, "he wasn't?"

"Yet you did it." Though Wallace threw that fact out there, it was hard to tell if he was enjoying this or frustrated by it.

"They used us," Ram said. "They got you to do their dirty work by buying our freedom."

Mutters flitted around the plane, nervous and humming. Let the jury deliver their verdict. Tox would neither defend himself nor incriminate himself any further. He said nothing.

"That's interesting," Maangi said, his brown eyes probing and his tone less than convincing.

Tox waited, nervous about the coming point.

"I got wind of the unofficial report on al-Homsi's death." Maangi squinted. "Explosion caused by a collision was official report. Unofficial was two sniper shots."

Heart crashing, Tox shook off the words with a wave. Surprised anyone knew that, let alone someone on his own team. He managed a half shrug. "We're not all crack shots. Can't be responsible for collateral damage."

"Collateral damage," Maangi muttered.

Tox regretted his choice of words.

"That's wrong, having you kill someone so they didn't dirty their hands," Cell finally snapped. "Ticks me off, using us grunts, then later blaming us."

"If they showed you documented proof al-Homsi wasn't an American citizen," Wallace said, his words tempered, "why do you say it went against what you believe in?"

The words were even, logical—and they pulled Haven's gaze from Wallace to Tox.

He folded his arms. "Anything could've been doctored. They wanted me to remove al-Homsi from the equation. It's possible they gave me the proof they thought it would take to get me to agree." Tox bounced his shoulders.

"You think they doctored the documents?"

He shrugged again. "Possible."

"But you did it, killed him," Wallace said, leaning forward in his seat and pressing a fingertip to the table as if to make a point, "knowing it was possible they doctored the proof, that it was possible he was legitimately an American citizen. You violated your conscience to *appease* your conscience—to free your men."

The words were cruel. Left Tox raw. But they were also true, when it came down to it.

"Hey, I saw al-Homsi at a rally once," Cell said. "Never trusted him. He made me feel like it was green-on-blue."

The words haunted Tox. They referenced attacks where those trained by Coalition forces turned on their mentors, killing them.

Tzivia shifted in her seat, seemingly bored. Wallace stared at Tox. And still, Tox refused to let his gaze meet Haven's. "Look," he said. This meeting had gone way better than he'd expected, so he half expected it to blow up in his face. "If you have questions, ask them now. Because after this, I won't answer any more."

"There's nothing else to answer. You told us what happened, what they used against you as their means to an end. As far as I'm concerned, we're done," Ram said. "King wants us divided, but this?" He adjusted his beanie. "This just cements my loyalty to you, as much as it does yours to me, to this team."

"Yeah, I'm kinda thinking King's plan here backfired."

"Unless there's something else," Maangi suggested softly.

"What?" Cell snorted. "I mean—everyone knew al-Homsi was planning to run in the next election, but he died. It's done and—"

"Tox's brother is still president," Wallace said.

Tox held his peace.

"Is that why you did it?"

"No."

"That's a quick, easy answer," Wallace pushed. "Easy to say on this side of it, right? I mean, you can shrug off the results because—"

"I didn't know the details before I agreed." Tox felt his pulse jam, constricting his throat. He swallowed. Shouldn't have mentioned that.

"Wait." Cell came forward, spreading his arms wide over the table. "You didn't know what the mission entailed? That they wanted you to kill al-Homsi?"

Tox clenched his jaw. "They came to me. Said they had a mission, that if I took it, they'd clear all of you."

"They didn't tell you what you'd be doing?" Wallace asked.

Cell's eyebrows rose. "And you took it?" Disbelief filled the question.

"No choice."

"But there *is* something else." Haven's voice was calm and quiet. Yet loud against his conscience. "Because when Maangi asked you a question earlier"—she pointed her pen at the Maori—"you gave three signs of deception."

Defying every ounce of his willpower, Tox's gaze slid to her. Locked on, the truth riveting his attention to her. His heart thudded. Stalled. Crashed into the once-potent belief that he could have something special with her.

Was it possible Haven would understand, that she'd know . . . ? Fool's hope.

"Dude." Cell gave a shaky laugh. "Seriously? What three signs? How do you even do that?"

But Haven didn't answer. "My sister."

He was done. Done keeping secrets. Withholding the truth from her.

While he and Haven stared at each other, Tox vaguely noted the guys move. The room emptying. Only when Wallace stood and started toward the door did Tox blink. "Wallace."

The special agent hesitated.

"Stay." It hurt to say it, but he did. "Please."

Haven frowned. "No." She nodded to Wallace. "Go on."

"No," Tox argued. "He should stay."

"I disagree. Go," she said to Wallace firmly. She was on her feet now, coming around the table toward Tox. "This is between us." Her words did that crazy-soft thing that always went sideways in his gut. "Right? You. Me." She had reached him now. Touched his arm. "Brooke."

He couldn't move if he'd wanted to, the storm so violent, the fallout so deadly.

✳ ✳ ✳ ✳

Not since she had sat at Arlington National Cemetery beside Charlotte Russell did Haven feel so absolutely wrecked. Yet somehow, this was worse. She was scared. Because the confident, unwavering man she'd come to love had vanished. Before her stood a *boy*. Desperate for hope. Desperate to be believed.

Her nerves thrummed. "Cole?"

He remained rigid, eyes drilling into her with a cold dread.

"Alec mentioned my sister. Brooke."

At her name, he flinched.

Haven swallowed, not wanting to make the connections, not wanting to believe any of the outlandish theories bobbing on her churning thoughts. But the connections had been made long ago. The uncanny timing. The coincidence. The fact that al-Homsi died the same night as her sister.

Even though the Democrats lost the presidential race, young Senator al-Homsi found himself catapulted to the head of his party, which had control of the Senate, and was slated to chair the Select Committee on Intelligence, which would have given him access to highly sensitive intel critical to national security. He and the president-elect's wife—both dead the same day.

"She died." There. That was easy. Well, not easy, but more easily said than anything else tumbling through her brain. "But earlier, when Maangi mentioned the shots that killed al-Homsi, you not only gave three signs of deception, you mentioned collateral damage."

He flinched again.

"By all reports, al-Homsi was alone, so how could there be collateral damage from his death? The driver wasn't killed—in fact, he was under suspicion for a while. The media covered it heavily." There was a connection in there somewhere. It hovered beneath the surface of this whole nightmare and rippled around them like a rip current.

Still, he watched her. Desperation pooled in his blue eyes.

"You're not making this easy." Nerves forced her to laugh. There was nothing funny. "Brooke was shot at home. Whoever did it used the gas stove to burn down the house."

"That's what they want you to believe." His voice was hoarse. His words strained. Raw agony roiled through his expression. The effort it took to keep himself composed was working against him.

In the back of her mind, she thought she might be shaking her head.

"You *know*, Haven," he said, searching her, willing her to say it. But why wouldn't he? "You're smarter than that, to believe she was killed by some random burglar in Arlington."

She did shake her head this time, the weight of her thoughts clanging. A wall stood between them—not his wall. Hers. She didn't want to move past it. Didn't want to find the ugly truth lurking behind it.

A scowl dug into his brow. "She wasn't at home when she died."

Her objection hung suspended between her open lips.

"She was in al-Homsi's limo."

Air sucked at the back of her throat. Made her cough. "No. She had a gala. I was waiting on her and got mad—she knew I don't like those things, not like she did—so I called her. Yelled at her for standing me up." Her eyes swam in tears. "The baby-sitter was late. Brooke was running behind—"

"When did they ever bring in a sitter for Evie?" Tox growled. "She was with my mom."

"Your—no. Your mom would've told me." Haven shook her head. "Evie was with a sitter."

"They never hired a sitter for her. Ever. You know that, if you think about it. If you stop trying to hide from the truth."

Haven drew back, startled at his animosity. "Don't do this, Cole. Don't put this on me."

"Brooke was with al-Homsi that night—in his limo."

Her mind scrambled for purchase. "But those limos are armored. Shots wouldn't have penetrated."

"They had to use a different limo. Last-minute engine trouble."

Haven swallowed, realizing what he was saying without directly saying it. Someone had *created* the trouble. Just like someone had with their vehicles in Iraq.

The answers were there. But she wouldn't believe them. They were too terrible. "No." Tears blurred her vision. She sliced a hand through the air. "No. Your mom would've told me she had Evie. What would my sister even be doing with someone like al-Homsi?"

"I don't know, but she was there!" he snapped, his face reddened. "And when I took the shot, I somehow—" His jaw clamped shut. He stopped talking. Moving. Was he even breathing? His blue eyes sparked with panic, his rugged features contorting. As if the words he'd nearly spoken were trapped within his own war. A fight between self-disgust and terror. He cocked his head. "I—"

"Stop." Haven wasn't sure why he was so angry with her. And she wasn't going to be a casualty of this scenario. "They wanted you—"

"It wasn't them, Haven. It was me."

She stilled, hands trembling. Heart trembling, hovering on the verge of words she knew were about to change *everything*.

"I killed Brooke."

AND GOD FORGET US IN THE HOUR

Steel clanged against steel. Vibrations wormed through his gloves, but Thefarie used his height and size advantage against the Saracen. He pushed him back, shouldering in as he freed his dagger and drove it into the enemy's side.

The man gaped. His eyes bulged.

Thefarie stepped back. Held his sword in both hands and delivered the man's body of its head.

There was no time to revel in the death, for two more Saracens came at him. They were relentless. And many. So very many. With Thefarie were a hundred soldiers and just as many brother-knights. St. Amand had given him one last chance to drive back Salah ad-Din and retrieve the crown.

Dealing with the next Saracen, Thefarie forbade his thoughts from drifting to his wife. To his newborn child. He knew not if he had a son or daughter. It had been more than a year, and no word had come. He refused to return home and be made a mockery of in his failure. Best to remain in the battle, reputation intact.

"Sandstorm!" someone shouted.

Thefarie glanced back and saw the great brown wall crawling toward them. Howling pervaded the battlefield. He tied a cloth around the slats in his helm to protect himself, knowing the Saracens would seize the storm, think it an advantage. It would not be the first time.

Even as he thought it, a sea of Saracens flooded over the northern rise, descending on them.

"God have mercy," Giraude railed from nearby.

Perhaps even God was angry with them—why else would there be so many attacks, so many failures? Had God turned his back on them?

Thefarie swung his sword again, hitting another enemy. Then another. He deftly avoided several strikes but felt more than one glancing blow off his armor. Were he not tall and strong, he might have succumbed to the strikes of the smaller Saracens. But he was not going down. Not today. Not until he had that accursed crown.

A shriek went up.

Thefarie jolted and saw Giraude stumble, go down, his arm dangling bloody at the side.

Rage tore through Thefarie, sighting the Saracen attacking his brother-knight unyieldingly. He was there in a flash, swinging. Arcing. Driving the man back in a rage of furious strikes.

"We must retreat," Ameus said. "We're badly outnumbered."

"And surrounded," Thefarie shouted, going to Giraude's side and helping him to his feet.

"Get me on my horse," Giraude grunted, his knees buckling as he walked. "Tie me on."

"You've lost your faculties," Thefarie said.

"No, just my arm." He pointed with his sword. "My horse!"

But even as he helped Giraude toward his mount, the storm reached for them. Sand felt like shards of glass, tinkling against their armor. Needling into their chain mail. Rubbing between steel and flesh.

Thefarie saw the swarm of Saracens closing in and did something he rarely did—he hesitated.

"God have mercy," Giraude said.

"I think He has forgotten us in this hour because I have failed again."

"Do not be so quick to give up on God," Giraude said. "He has not given up on you."

"I think you may be wrong."

"If I am not, I want your mercenary sword."

Thefarie nearly smiled, but the *tsing* of a blade drew him around. Two men surged toward them, wielding swords. Thefarie defended himself and Giraude, who had collapsed to the ground without Thefarie's support. The Saracens drove them back, unrelenting in their blows and fury.

Thefarie felt his own fury, his thoughts flinging out toward Tveria. Toward Miryam. He would die, not in shame, but in defending their Lord Jesus Christ.

But failure—if he died, was that failure? Would they—

A *clang* rang out, knocking him back a step. Only Giraude was there. Sand and Saracens before him. Thefarie shifted, and his boot caught on something. He went down hard.

The Saracens lunged.

Darkness dropped over Thefarie, pitch black. Confusion rankled him as his mind warred to sort out what had happened. He hung his head, trying to stop the sandstorm from filling his helm, and waited.

It had happened before, a storm like this. They waited it out. And even before the veil of darkness lifted with the storm passing, the Saracens were fighting again. They were used to this. The knights were not. Even Thefarie, who had been here far too many years. *I fear this may be my last.*

Only then did he realize he and Giraude had been covered by something. A tarp of some kind. Why had they been protected?

When the howling of the raging desert died down, Thefarie fought to free them. Even as he did, he found the Saracens springing out of the sand.

One flew at Thefarie.

He shoved upward, but his legs got caught in the tarp. Useless, he fell back again. His heart vaulted into his throat as he watched the sword coming down.

Shapes shrouded in black leapt from the grains, like their own mini-storms. Whirls of shadows. Moving lightning fast.

His mind struggled in confusion for a second longer. Then the battle was over. A man in head-to-toe black stood over him, legs straddling Thefarie's. Only his eyes were visible through a slit in the fabric covering his face.

The man looked around, drawing Thefarie's stunned gaze to the surrounding area. Bodies littered the field. Two dozen black shapes like the one standing over him converged. The man turned back to him and tugged off the hood.

Recognition hit him hard. "Bahir."

"I want the one they call Thefarie," a voice boomed in the distance.

Thefarie came to his feet with the aid of Bahir. To his great shock, the entire host of Saladin's army sat perched on the plain, apparently having chased the storm to gain the advantage.

Gripping his sword tight, Thefarie started forward.

"He will kill you," Bahir hissed, catching his arm. "We can protect you here. But not there."

"Get my brother-knights to safety." He slid his sword into its scabbard. "God has forgotten me. It is just as well that you should, too."

Hope abandoned, faith flagging, Thefarie started forward. One might think courage advanced him, but this was a death march. Behind him, he heard his brother-knights shouting at him.

But he would not fail his honor. He would not walk darkly back to Tveria. To Miryam. He would not give Grand Master St. Amand that satisfaction, to strip the great Thefarie of Tveria of rank and dignity.

A black horse and its rider galloped forward.

So. It was to be one-on-one.

A fleeting dart of hope shot through him. He might have a chance in hand-to-hand combat. He let that tendril of hope sprout through his chest.

Until he saw the rider.

Saladin. The great sultan himself.

Thefarie stopped. Spread his feet.

The ground rattled as the destrier barreled toward him. Saladin rode a tight circle around him, dust and rocks spitting at Thefarie.

Then he drew the horse around in front of him and let it stamp its feet.

"*Dawiyya!*" Saladin shouted, using the Arabic name for the Templars. "You are everywhere, contaminating the earth with your blood."

Holding his peace, Thefarie watched the revered general, his face partially shielded by the protective plate of his helmet. Saladin was in battle gear. Not ceremonially, though this conversation was clearly a display for his army. For Thefarie's shame.

"The crown," Thefarie said. "Clearly even you know it is too much weight for your shoulders."

In a fluid move, the sultan slid from his mount and stalked over to him. "You seek the crown." Amusement tinged his heavily accented words.

"You know I do. I sought it in your camp. I seek it now."

"And if I do not have it?"

"I will pursue you until I recover it."

"To the ends of the earth?"

"To hell, if I must."

Anger glinted in the Saracen's eyes. "You will not have it. No man will. Ever." His gaze darkened. "It is a wicked thing, this crown."

Thefarie studied him. Studied the emotion roiling through his hard features. "I will recover it. I must. I have been sent by God."

"And God has told me to bury it from all mankind." He shook a finger. "No, you will not find it. No one will. It is gone!" He waved dismissively.

"I will not cease my pursuit until I have recovered it and delivered it to the Grand Master for destruction."

"Then your journey will be long and fruitless."

"Whatever it takes. If I must raze your home and army, I will. I will not fail."

"If you do this, Thefarie of Tveria"—the sultan's tone of cold malice chilled the air—"you will see my fury. Here against your knights, and in all your homelands. *I* will not stop until you are all wiped from the face of the earth!"

"To the last one standing."

Nostrils flaring, Saladin inclined his head. "As you will it, *Dawiyya*."

39

Ripping his chest open and crushing his heart, Haven walked out of the plane's conference room. Silently. No tears. No screaming. No anger. Just stunned silence, leaving an icy trail in its wake.

He wanted to call after her but this was what he'd expected. What he deserved. She couldn't love the man he had become. The monster she'd vowed he wasn't.

It was over.

Alec had won.

He groaned and slumped against the table, palms to the cold surface. Knew it. He knew he'd lose her with the truth.

He'd lost himself that night. Brooke, bleeding out in his arms. Apologizing to her over and over. Some suit showed up fast. Too fast. Told Tox he didn't belong there. That he had to leave before authorities responded to the incident.

But he couldn't leave Brooke. Couldn't extricate himself from the asphalt collecting her blood. Watching tears slide down her face. Perfectly styled hair askew against his arm. She'd broken his heart a decade earlier by eloping with Galen while Tox had been at Basic. He'd wished the two of them dead many times. Never meant it.

His ears popped, and Tox lifted his head from the memories and grief, realizing the plane was descending. How long had he been in the conference room alone? He glanced at the wall clock. Still, he stayed in the room. Alone.

Only when the tires screeched on the runway did he consider getting up. But there was still too much pinning him to the seat, to the past. He'd thought taking that deal would even things out, buy the guys back their lives. He'd already lost everything. Then they dragged him back into the game, and he reconnected with his men. A side bonus was the reintroduction to Haven. A reintroduction to love.

Now he was hollowed out, hope gone.

Where was Chiji when he needed him? He always had a good Bible verse or Igbo saying for any situation. Tox sure needed one now. But maybe there wasn't a saying or verse for him now. Because he wasn't sure this could be fixed. Maybe he was just on his own.

As it should be. He'd accepted four years ago that he'd be alone for the rest of his life. But he'd had a taste of happiness—Haven. Now he'd lost her.

Why are you taunting me, God? Rubbing my nose in this, just to remind me I'm not good enough?

A soft click pulled his gaze from the table.

Ram stood in the doorway with his arms folded. "What happened with you and Haven?"

"She left." He stared down at the brown surface again.

"Nice try. Now—what happened?"

Keeping the secret didn't matter anymore, but the truth wasn't easy to push across his tongue either. "I killed her sister that night."

"Same sister you had a thing for, the one your brother stole?"

"She only had one sister." He could still see Brooke, hear her breathing go ragged, then shallow. As her pulse went thready. "In the same second I eased back the trigger to kill al-Homsi"—he tightened his jaw—"someone moved into the line of sight. Into the path of the bullet. Someone who shouldn't have been there."

Ram heaved a sigh. "That's why it took two bullets."

"First one hit her, then him, going wide." Numbness spread through Tox. "Second finished him."

"Why was she there?"

Tox shook his head, pursing his lips. "No idea." Swallowed against a tight throat. "Couldn't get answers. Sure made a lot of noise trying, though. Got me nowhere. They said if I didn't leave that night, I'd hang for everything."

"So you left?"

Another snort. "Told them I wasn't leaving until I had answers." He'd really thought he was in control back then.

"Let me guess. They said they'd renege."

"Not just renege but take you all down in flames. Throw everything at you, buy the verdict. Death penalties across the board."

And now, years later, it had all gone down in flames anyway. Was there any way to get Haven back?

Only if he could resurrect Brooke.

"Attaway?"

He blinked at Ram. "What?"

"Was Attaway behind this?"

"Yeah. Maybe." He shrugged. "He was involved, but to what extent, I don't know."

Ram nodded. Drew a breath. "Well, hate to break up your tortured moment, but Iliescu and Rodriguez pinged us. The professor and Runt are en route, then we're wheels up and headed home."

"Home." Tox stood up, the pain washing away as the mission surged to the forefront again. "The gala."

Ram nodded.

Tox felt sick. The gala meant his parents and his parents' home. "I can't be there."

"Iliescu has some ideas. Once the team is gathered, we'll go over that."

So Ram was taking charge again. "What about you and Tzivia?"

"Another fight for another day."

"Tends to be a lot of fights on a lot of days with you two."

"That's what happens with a bullheaded sister."

"You mean strong and admirably intelligent?" Tzivia's silky voice crooned as she sauntered into the room. Her gaze hit Tox's and he saw a question, a concern. Probably about Haven. But she knew better than to ask and instead tugged off her brother's beanie.

"Tzi!" Ram snatched it back as the rest of the team filed in, a heavy silence weighting the room. He nodded toward the screen and pressed the power button.

Faces sprang up on the monitor, stern. Voices spirited in and out across the three-way split that featured Robbie Almstedt, Dru Iliescu, and Major General Rodriguez.

Chatter carried down the plane, followed by laughter.

"We're back," Runt announced with a cocky grin as he entered the conference room. "With police escort."

Mopping his brow, Dr. Cathey shuffled in behind them. "Escort," he grunted. "More like *pursuit*. I'm sure there were more than a few bullets zinging past our ears."

Runt laughed, slapping Dr. C on the back. "This one is pretty sly. And spry for his age."

"Watch yourself, young man."

"Even I didn't see him switch the ring."

Tox shifted gears—well, most of them. A few were still jammed around Brooke's death. "You got the ring?"

Ram smiled. "That'd be about the only thing that's gone right."

"Of course," Runt said around another laugh, "the Germans weren't very happy once they discovered his switcheroo. There are warrants out for him, and Interpol is looking for us. You should be proud!"

"Already on that security problem," Iliescu said.

The ominous words made Tox a little uncomfortable, but only because they were so similar to the ones spoken when he was vanishing four years ago.

"All we have to show for our efforts," Ram said, looking at Maangi, "is this cloth left behind when the medallion was taken."

"Brilliant!" Dr. Cathey's face enlivened. "I believe that may be as old as the gems." His salt-and-pepper beard twitched into a slow smile.

"We also found a black piece of cloth with the ring." Runt nodded. "We think they may be part of the sheet Tukulti-Ninurta saw coming down from heaven."

"*We* think?" Tox tapped the newbie on the shoulder. "You an expert now?"

"As near as can be," Dr. Cathey laughed. "I'm afraid I couldn't stop talking once we left. He's heard the entire history of the ring and its possible journey. But that fabric—the fibers are very old. The dye exquisite and rare."

"Where's the ring?" Tzivia demanded.

The professor lifted a small box from his satchel and handed it over with another warning to be careful. They passed the ring around, which wasn't a glamorous piece of jewelry by today's standards. Square and large, the jasper gem easily covered a person's finger from knuckle to knuckle. The gold wasn't highly polished. Hieroglyphs were carved into the jasper.

"Thought this was Akkadian," Cell muttered. "Why are there Egyptian symbols cut into it?"

"How do you know the difference?" Thor asked.

"Because some of us have brains."

Thor swatted at him, but Cell dodged.

"It is believed that Ramesses II had it carved with a curse, should anyone remove it from the ring and use it elsewhere."

"Curse?" Cell shifted away from Haven, who now held the ring.

"Is it gold?" Haven asked.

"Most likely, but it's possibly some other metal, perhaps bronze." Dr. Cathey peered at the piece over his glasses. "It'd take a metallurgist to know for sure."

"Which we can look into later," Almstedt intoned from the wall. "So we have the onyx, now the jasper."

"Correct," Dr. Cathey said, turning his attention to the large screen and the faces there. "And two sections of the black cloth." He compared them next to each other. "They appear to be a match."

"But what we failed to secure," Almstedt went on, "are the other two gems. Correct?"

Tox rubbed the back of his neck.

"The carnelian and the lapis lazuli," Dr. Cathey answered. "But if they're going to be in DC, we can steal them back."

"And the fifth legacy," Haven put in. "Whatever it is."

"We don't have any other choice, do we?" Almstedt snapped. "And once we have them, what are we supposed to do with them? This artifact doesn't have a cradle, does it?"

"Return them to Ashur," Tzivia said, "to the cage. I don't know how, but I know it needs to be there. There were probably instructions in those reliefs I sent you photographs of, Dr. Cathey. We had to leave fast after Faeza was murdered."

Dr. Cathey muttered an apology, peering at Tzivia over his glasses. "I've been working on translating them, but I have not found a way to neutralize it."

"And what if we can't get the crown away from him?" Iliescu asked. "Can we just kill him?"

"Sure," Ram said, half annoyed, half confident. "But then if someone else gets the crown, it's murder and insanity all over again."

"What about those RFBs?" Almstedt asked, rubbing her temples. "Is there a way to do something with them?"

Tox shared a look with Cell, who shook his head. Apparently, he still hadn't figured out a way to turn the frequency against the crown without injuring Alec.

"What was that?" Thor demanded.

"Nothing," Cell said.

"That was a lot more than nothing."

"Cell is working on a theory, but it's only a theory."

"What theory is that?" Almstedt burrowed closer to her camera. "Mr. Purcell?"

Cell shifted uneasily in his chair. "I'm trying to isolate a way to turn that RFB back on the crown. It would take a massive burst."

"Excellent," Thor said.

"No," Cell snapped. "Right now, I can't figure out a way to do that without killing the subject."

"So we get it away from him one way or another," Tox said, glancing again at Cell and the team. "Neutralize it offsite."

"That would work. Maybe," Cell said, nodding.

"Mr. Purcell," Almstedt said, "if I sent some physicists your way, think together you can figure out how to neutralize this crown?"

Sitting a little straighter, Cell considered the offer. "Maybe. It's all theoretical. I mean—the iron itself shouldn't even be *emitting* a frequency. That it's otherworldly changes things. So who knows? But we can work on it."

"They'll be en route within the hour."

"I think," Dru Iliescu said, "you have to come to terms with the fact that we *do* have a way to stop Alec King."

Tox squared his shoulders. Lifted his chin.

"Even if it means his death, if that's the only way to stop him, to prevent more lives from being lost," Iliescu said, determination carved into his words, "we have to seize this chance."

40

He was back home. And though home hadn't been a warm friendly place in decades, now it felt . . . desolate. Crazy how he'd established so many plans without even realizing it—all involving Haven. Where they could live, if things got serious and they took the plunge. Close enough to SAARC headquarters and yet far enough from the insanity of DC traffic.

Now he had the home but not the girl. It was a recurring theme in his life. Toxic. Would he ever be rid of that moniker? Forget the nickname. Would he ever not be that way?

Haven had said he wasn't. Said he wasn't toxic. That he wasn't Alec. He'd tried to warn her.

"We're bringing in forensic artists to help us give you a new look."

From his seat at SAARC headquarters, Tox hesitated, eyeballing the general. "Come again?"

"We need you on-site to read the situation and Alec, but with your parents there as well, you can't look like yourself."

"Right." Tox sighed. "Not permanent, though, right?"

"I could have one of the guys make it that way," Ram offered.

406

"Stay out of this," Tox teased. "So, any new intel or sightings of Alec and his team in the area?"

"No sightings yet," Iliescu said. He pointed to a wall plastered with photos of Alec's known associates: Jason Bollinger, Maury Sagel, and Guy Jeffries.

He'd known these men once. Not like he knew his team, but Bollinger and Sagel had worked a couple ops with him in the early years. Jeffries had been a great quarterback for inside-the-wire ball games during down time.

"Positive ID!" Wallace announced. "We have positive ID on Maury Sagel driving a 2007 Toyota Avalon on the Beltway," he said from a bank of computers where a half dozen navy suits worked to locate Alec's team and the man himself.

"Can we stop him?" Tox asked.

"No," Wallace replied. "Car was flagged using the express lane without a tag. That was an hour ago, though."

He hated this. One of Alec's men heading right into the area of his parents' home. "So they're converging," he said, turning to Rodriguez and Iliescu, who sat at a table with the team and an impromptu task force composed of military and intelligence personnel.

"We've swept the estate with detectors and dogs—no explosives," Rodriguez said. "That was easy to accomplish, since your brother is on-site and those things were happening regardless. But we added a few additional steps without drawing attention."

"Milk that for all it's worth. So what's Alec going to hit them with?" Tox wondered aloud. "Poison? A gas?"

"A bomb? Drop it in. That'd be quick and easy."

"No," Tox said. "Too impersonal. He wants to make this hurt not just those he's killing, but their families."

Rodriguez nodded. "Everything is personal with this guy."

Wallace leaned against the table. "He has to know you're on to him after Mosul, so he's going to know he can't get anything big past us."

"That arrogance," Iliescu said with a shake of his head, "is how we miss things. It's quite easy to get the elements in place for a large explosive without anyone being the wiser. He could've done it weeks ago. We've been the ones chasing our butts. And he could do a little here, a little there."

"But King hasn't been the little-by-little kind," Thor muttered from the side wall he was propping up. "He's the type to spray and pray."

"True," Tox said. "If the crown's affecting him like we think it is, then he's losing his ability to reason and think clearly. That means mistakes will be made—"

"If he's been planning this for a while," Ram countered, "then he probably already has things in place. We can only count on him making mistakes with anything he does now. And while he may be wearing that crown, his guys aren't."

"Good point."

"The location is problematic, too," Rodriguez said. "Woods to the north and west. Hilly. Then the waterfront and the Potomac itself. A lot of scenarios present for quick infil and exfil. Impossible to cover them all."

"But only one road in and out," Tox said. "And you shut down flights over it, right?"

Iliescu nodded. "But only during the event, and they were screaming holy terror at me for that order."

"They'd be screaming louder if two hundred military personnel got wiped out." Tox looked at Iliescu. "What about my parents? What do they know?"

"Nothing. They were told the heightened security was due to the brass attending."

"My dad bought that?"

Rodriguez smirked. "Not even close, but he said he wouldn't ask. Yet."

That sounded more like him.

"We're keeping this low-key and limiting the number of people read in to reduce cross-contamination."

"What about Cell? He made any progress?"

Rodriguez nodded. "I've heard the team he's working with is testing a resonance burst or something." He shrugged. "Not my area of expertise, but they're getting close."

"Close," Tox repeated.

Rodriguez eyed him.

"We need better than close."

Thor shifted. "Still holding out hope that we can save him?"

He shared a glare with him. "No, I'm more concerned about my parents and the two hundred guests."

"Good. Because this is happening tonight. We can't play it again somewhere else," Rodriguez said. "We might be behind him, but we're not far."

A woman crossed the room with two large boxes, escorted by a SEAL, who carried a third. "Sir," the SEAL said to Rodriguez. "Ms. Marcey. General Rodriguez."

The general greeted the woman and asked how her trip in had been.

She glanced around, then back at the general. "Look, this was last-minute, and I have a flight to catch—"

"Understood." Rodriguez turned to Tox and grinned. "Time for your makeup, Tox."

Whistles and cat calls spirited through the facility. Ms. Marcey shot a glower around the room.

"Ignore them. That was for him," Rodriguez said, pointing to Tox as he came to his feet. "What do you need?"

"You have prosthetic artists?"

Rodriguez indicated a huddled group in a curtained area.

"Okay, then a room and lights."

"This way."

Rodriguez started across the open warehouse. Tox took the box from the SEAL and followed Rodriguez to a small room away from the main hustle and bustle. Chairs and a cabinet crowded the space, and a desk with only three legs was pushed against the table. The overhead light sprang to life with an incessant buzz.

"This do?"

Ms. Marcey stepped in, setting her gear on the table. "I guess it'll have to." She drew a chair to the middle of the room. "Where's my skull?"

Rodriguez grinned broadly. "Guess that's you, Tox."

41

Finding out the man you loved killed your sister sort of changed the way you viewed the world.

As soon as they arrived in Virginia, Haven had slipped out of the hangar and driven herself to the Metro station in downtown DC. She withdrew several hundred dollars from an ATM, then bought a day pass and just rode the commuter rail, thinking. Praying.

Prayers were the only thing keeping her sane and her anger in check.

She finally disembarked somewhere in northern Virginia and walked until she had no idea where she was—save close to the river. She paid cash for a room, thankful for her ability to read people so that she could leverage the clerk's drug habit to buy her way around showing an ID to check into a room overlooking the Potomac.

Hugging her legs, she sat on the balcony, cradling a large cup of coffee. Cole hadn't known Brooke was with the presidential candidate that night. But still . . . Haven glanced at the notebook and pen on the table beside her. Scanned her Known and Unknown lists. Eventually she pushed her gaze back to the sky, because she had no answer, save the undeniable peace that had been with her since she and Cole were reintroduced six months ago.

Reintroduced.

She sighed. Such a sanitary word to describe the way their lives had collided. The way he'd stepped into her life and yanked her perfect, ordered world into dizzying chaos of love and abandon.

Resting her chin on her knee, Haven peered out across the sparkling water. She loved him. And he loved her. She was sure of that, though he had never voiced the words. Cole, she believed, was as afraid of love as he was of facing his own demons. But she'd known that all along.

So could she leave this? Leave the fact that he killed Brooke on the ground and walk away into a future with him?

If they didn't solve the dilemma with Alec King, he might not have a future.

And you walked away.

She had needed to. It was impossible to think with his blue eyes constantly homing in on her, looking for reassurance, affirmation.

She wasn't angry with him. Which made her angry.

Wouldn't a normal person be insanely enraged over something like this? In normal circumstances, one would be angry with the individual responsible for killing a loved one. But this wasn't normal. It was convoluted and complicated. He had been put in an impossible situation. He'd been contracted to kill al-Homsi. That alone was startling. And Brooke had been the collateral damage.

He'd kept this from her. Hidden it. She knew he wasn't allowed to tell her, but he should have. Right? Yet he didn't. Because he was Cole. Honor-driven, code-bound Cole Russell.

The questions pummeling her included the biggest of all—why had Brooke been with Amir al-Homsi that night? Was she having an affair? It seemed too incredible. Brooke loved the powerful life she led as a congressman's wife and then aiming for First Lady. Why would she ruin that?

A gust of wind kicked up, blowing against her face. Nudging her hair from her shoulders. The pages of her notebook flapped, tipping its balance. It slipped over the edge of the small table and clapped shut against the ground.

Haven lifted it and fanned it back to the page she'd been writing on. As she did, the entries from the search for the crown's gems caught her attention. Something snagged in her memory as she saw the notes Thefarie had written.

Lapis Lazuli cuffed me in failure and shame.

Lapis. Blue eyes. The queens.

An image clicked in her mind of the relief—the queen in that relief wasn't in profile. Haven scrambled into her room and snatched her phone from the table. She ignored the texts and missed call notices from a dozen different people and went to her photos. Scrolled through the ones she'd taken at Nimrud and found one of the queen.

Wearing a bracelet with a blue gem.

"No!" Haven stared, stunned, at the image. "There's two . . ." She switched to her contacts but quickly realized that calling anyone from the team might give away her location. She wasn't ready for that.

She pulled up her browser and searched for Ti Tzaddik. But found nothing. One result was for a Tiberius Tzaddik, but he'd relocated, so how was she supposed to find him now? It might not even be the same person. Was Ti short for Tiberius? A few more searches indicated it was a distinct plausibility.

Only Mr. Tzaddik had information on Thefarie of Tveria, which was what she needed right now. Knowing Google and other search engines eliminated smaller words like *of* and *the*, she did the same. And hit enter. The varied results essentially contained the same basic information. She slid over her notebook and copied it into a fresh Known column.

* Thefarie = Etruscan cognate of Tiberius
* Thefarie = Latin praenomen, borrowed from the Etruscan or river of the same name
* Tiberius considered Latin
* Name Tiberius used by Latin, Oscan, and Etruscan families
* Widely used across Italy

Wait. So . . . Tiberius was Thefarie.

But why had her search for Tveria brought that up? She retyped *Tveria* alone this time. And gasped, unable to move beyond the first search, which provided a translation key:

Tiberias (Hebrew: טְבֶרְיָה, *Tveria*; Arabic: طبرية, *Tabariyyah*; Ancient Greek: Τιβεριάς, *Tiberias*)

Numb, she wrote out *Tiberias = Tveria*.

And the Etruscan cognate of Tiberius was Thefarie. Not exactly the same. Yet . . . in a way, wasn't it? "So," she whispered to herself, "Ti is Tiberius is Tiberias, which is Tveria, which is Thefarie." She wrinkled her nose. "Sort of."

Dumbstruck, she stared at her notes. How could that be a coincidence? She went to her contacts list again, drew up a phone number, and hit talk, not caring who found her.

"Hello?"

"Are you still with the team?"

"Ha—"

"Please. No names."

"Yes and no. I'm sitting here with Dr. Cathey. We're not allowed in with all the mission planning stuff." Tzivia's voice faded. "And we're all wondering about you. Your Clark Kent went all FBI on us, searching for you."

"I just needed some space."

"Right."

"Listen, I think I might know what Thefarie missed."

"What? How?"

"First I need to talk to Tiberius."

"Who?"

Haven stared at her notes again. "Sorry—my notes and brain are jumbled. I meant Mr. Tzaddik."

"Dr. C might have his number. Hang on."

Moments later, Haven was dialing Mr. Tzaddik. Nerves pushed her into the chair at the small dinette in her room.

"I wondered when you might call," he said in greeting.

How on earth did he know? "I . . . I wondered if you could help me with Thefarie's journals." It wasn't a deception, not really. "A question I need answered, to be more exact. We didn't get to read everything."

"What do you need to know?"

"Did Thefarie ever mention—" Haven went cold, staring at the poem she'd written from memory.

Lapis Lazuli cuffed me in failure and shame. "Cuffs." Her heart beat a little faster.

"My dear?"

Haven's heart tripped at his voice, but hesitation gripped her tight. Why did she think she could find something a Templar knight dedicated to a singular purpose couldn't?

"Haven, are you there?" His voice had changed. Sounded closer. Different.

"I think I know what he couldn't find." Thoughts pinging, she realized that by having written that last line, Thefarie had known what he'd been looking for. He just hadn't been able to find it. "The cuffs," she repeated, her mind racing. "There were *two* cuffs. But only one was still in Nimrud. Alec only has one."

"I knew you would figure it out."

The voice came from behind her. Haven spun, shocked.

And found in her hotel room none other than Ti Tzaddik.

42

"Mr. President, we need to talk."

Galen Russell turned from his date—an interestingly leggy foreign diplomat—and took in General Rodriguez and the two Navy officers with him, one of whom was Tox, standing stiffly in a captain's uniform and facial disguise. It was weird how Galen looked right through him. But then Galen's gaze hit someone behind them.

As the dutiful officer he was supposed to be, Tox slid his attention that way, too. Barry Attaway. The vulture had locked onto them. Tox tried not to react. He shifted back to the president, subtly shouldering into Barry's line of sight.

Galen stayed Barry with an upheld palm, then nodded to the general. "Sure. This way." He led their entourage down the hall, past Secret Service agents guarding the family rooms from revelers, and into a cozy library. One Tox had loved growing up, especially during the winters, when a fire roared and their father read letters, sipped brandy, and talked politics.

Tox eased the pocket door closed behind them as the general started talking. "Sorry for the intrusion, Mr. President, but—"

"You're on his team, right?"

415

Staying calm and neutral was tough, but Tox maintained the role. Brought himself about casually and stood at attention.

There was little doubt whose team Galen had been referring to.

"I think the correct phrasing is that he's one of mine," Rodriguez corrected. "Yes, sir."

Galen smirked. "What can I do for you?"

"We have reason to believe there is an active threat against this event tonight."

His brother tensed. "My security didn't alert me—"

"We asked them not to," Rodriguez asserted. "We need the target to show up, reveal his hand. If he thinks he's compromised, he won't come."

"So," Galen said, moving to the bar and choosing a snifter. *Just like Dad.* "You believe there's an active threat, you've informed my security but haven't increased it, and you're still letting him walk in here, where he can endanger or kill not just my parents, but me—the president of the United States."

"That won't happen, sir." Rodriguez's gaze darkened as he watched Galen pour a drink. "And I never said we hadn't increased security."

Glass halfway to his mouth, Galen paused. Set down the glass. That was a nice change, seeing his brother off guard. "Why are you telling me this now?"

"Frankly, because it's time to tell you. Tox—all of us—are concerned for your parents. Their safety and yours."

Hearing his name nearly made Tox flinch.

"If he's worried about us, why isn't he here doing something? Why didn't he come himself?"

Oh, he would rub this in Galen's face for the rest of his life when it was over. Assuming they were all alive afterward. Then again, maybe he wouldn't because it almost sounded like Galen was upset he hadn't seen Tox in a while.

"You know that's not possible, sir."

"Right." Galen tossed back the liquor. "He's dead."

"Who's dead?"

Galen jerked around, and it took everything in Tox not to do the same when his mother glided in from the side patio. "Mother, what—"

She waved him off, and that simple gesture—one so small but *so her*—nearly buckled Tox's knees. "This is my home," she sniffed. "I wanted some fresh air. Not my fault, Galen, that you chose to have your private meeting in here." She nodded toward the liquor. "You'd do well to leave that alone tonight, too." With an appraising look at the general, his mother scowled. "Where is your security team, Galen?"

"Outside the door."

"You know this man, these two officers?"

"Of course. This is General Rodriguez." Galen strode across the room and rolled his eyes at the general. "I think that's her way of ending our tête-à-tête."

"There are a lot of extra security personnel here, General," his mother noted, and Tox bit back a snort. She never missed a thing. "I hope you don't plan to interrupt the Endeavor—"

"We have no such plans, Mrs. Russell."

She nodded, glancing around before her gaze came to rest—like a two-ton anchor—on Tox. Everything in him ached for her to see him, to know. It would screw everything up, but the longing was there all the same. She broke his gaze and drew in a breath. "Well. We should be getting back to the event. Your father will hang me for sneaking away."

Galen offered his arm, and his mother tucked her hand through.

Tox let out a stiff breath as they left. He'd been about to break cover and tell Galen it was makeup and prostheses that made his nose crooked, his eyebrows thicker, and the brow line over his eyes more prominent. A plug concealed the small dimple in his chin that his mother would've recognized immediately. She'd often said he got it from being too rebellious. Too rambunctious, climbing trees, hills, houses.

"She didn't even recognize you," Ram said, turning to him with a grin.

"When she stared at you there at the end, I was sure she'd call it," Rodriguez said.

"You and me both."

"Told you Marcey was the best. We paid her an arm and a leg, too." Rodriguez considered him. "Don't worry—we won't let him hurt them."

Tox appreciated the sentiment, but it wasn't something anyone could guarantee.

"If Sagel, Bollinger, King, or any of his men show, they won't leave alive."

Tox nodded. "Sounds like a plan."

"Remember, stick to the perimeter. Extra security and all that."

They exited the library and moved into the open hall with its tall ceilings and massive paintings. He remembered being in awe as a boy that they were bigger than he was.

"You lived here?" Ram muttered.

Nodding, Tox took in his former home. It had been a long time since he'd been here. But it still felt the same—too big and too . . . much. Tables for the gala were set up on the lower level and spilled out into the garden. The gazebo hosted a live orchestra, whose notes carried over the lawn. How much had Haven helped coordinate?

"Heads up. We have eyes on Bollinger," said a voice through the tiny device tucked into Tox's ear. "Coming through the front entrance with an invitation."

So Alec had been planning this for a while. Less hope that his "descent into madness" would aid them, then. And if Bollinger was here, so was Alec, or would be soon.

Tox negotiated the crowds, making his way back to the main hall where most of the guests were enjoying libations and lively chatter. A burst of laughter shot through the room and snagged Tox's attention. His gaze swung in the direction of an older couple surrounded by a younger crowd. His gut cinched at the sight of the man at the center of the group.

Mr. Linwood. Haven's father. And beside him, her hair in an updo, Mrs. Linwood. The parents of the two women he loved.

Tox forced himself to turn away, and when he did, he met Wallace's gaze. He stalked up to the agent. "Did you find her?" he asked around gritted teeth.

"No. But she texted. Said she needed time. Excuse me." Wallace shouldered past.

"You're enjoying this."

Superman came around. "Seeing you break her heart, prove to her

418

what I've been saying all along?" He huffed. "Not hardly." He then strode toward the Linwoods, clearly rubbing it in Tox's nose that he was able to be himself and mingle with her family. That he now believed he was protecting Haven from Tox.

Mr. Linwood's face lit up. "Levi! Good to see you."

"Thank you, sir. Good to be here. You look beautiful, Mrs. Linwood."

"Kiss up," Thor muttered through the comms. "I could shoot him and nobody would know."

Irritated—whether at himself or Wallace, he didn't know—Tox rotated away from familiar things. Though that was impossible in this home.

"Do I know you?"

The voice was unmistakable. Tox glanced over his shoulder, hoping—praying—she wasn't talking to him. But knowing blue eyes met his. Eyes that had called him on a thousand lies. "Pardon, ma'am?" He put as much twang into his reply as he could muster.

"You're familiar," his mother declared. "I'm very good with faces. Never forget one. And I know you."

"Sorry, ma'am." He dipped his head as someone barked through the comms that Tox needed an interception. "I was hired to work security for this gig—"

"En route, Actual," said a voice in his ear.

"I'll remember." She had a warning gleam in her eyes, amused with herself. "Before the night ends, I'll remember. And then you'll owe me an apology, young man."

You have no idea.

* * * *

UNKNOWN LOCATION

Tickling along her arms and legs lured Haven awake. She blinked, but only darkness enveloped her. Maybe it was still night. Something tickled her forearm again. She twitched, sure a spider or bug had crawled over her, but her hand wouldn't move. She tried again. Something bit into her flesh, holding her in place. She reached toward it with the other—but that hand wouldn't move either. What on earth . . . ?

Even in her struggling confusion, she sensed it. Shifting. Tightening around her body. The tickling sensation—not ants or bugs—sand! She . . . she was sinking! In sand!

Where am I?

A light, feathery sound filtered into her awareness. Though she could see nothing, she smelled the air. Hot. Arid. Like a desert. Fear swirled through her veins.

Don't panic. Don't panic.

How did she even get here? The last thing she remembered . . . "Ti." Tiberius. Tzaddik. At her hotel room. She blew out a breath—then thought better of it. The sand would fill the gap the expelled breath would leave, and then she'd have no room to breathe.

What had Ti done to her?

But wait—they'd talked. He said he'd seen her getting off the metro. He warned her that Alec's men had been tailing her, but that he'd help throw them off her trail.

They'd talked about the bracelet. He said there were more writings. That Thefarie had, in fact, located a bracelet with a lapis lazuli gem, but he'd figured out too late that there should have been two cuffs. It was, Thefarie believed, the attempt of ancient priests to ensure the crown could never again be used to its full power.

Then Mr. Tzaddik left, certain he knew where to look for the final bracelet. He promised he'd get it to Cole. She'd taken a shower and gone to bed.

Then . . . woke up here, head throbbing.

Panic tempted her again. She had to get out of here. She yanked her arms, hard. Gravity released its hold on her, and she dropped. With a yelp, she felt the gritty sand in her mouth and eyes. Felt her legs sink further. She tensed, whimpering. Afraid she'd sink completely.

With a hissing *whoosh*, the earth gave way. She plummeted with a blood-curdling scream.

Air. Sand. Fear. Terror.

Like a bungee cord, she snapped to a stop. Her right shoulder surrendered. Pain exploded through her joint. Sand poured past her, its gritty torment almost teasing. Strange how it almost felt like a warm bath. She stared up and saw that she was hanging in a cistern of some sort, a speck of light mocking her from above.

Terror cocooned her. Strangled her.

"Help!" she screamed. "*Help!*"

* * * *

RUSSELL ESTATE, MARYLAND

"Uh, heads up." Cell's voice came through the comms an hour later as Tox lurked on the perimeter and avoided his mother. "I'm getting serious readings."

"Then Alec's here," Tox subvocalized, his gaze sliding over the attendees.

"Or the crown is," Ram said.

"Crown won't be here without him," Tox suggested, noting a cluster of young women gathering nearby, fluttering their eyelashes at him. He relocated himself.

"I have eyes on Bollinger," Runt muttered. "Yellow Two."

Tox's gaze shifted to the area by the library and spotted the red-headed grunt who'd done some dirty work for Alec.

"King's not, like, on the guest list or something, is he?" Cell asked teasingly. "'Cause I have his RFB. It's there, guys. The crown has to be."

"Mr. Purcell," snapped Almstedt's voice, "you ready with that resonance burst?"

"I . . . uh, yeah. But those physicists didn't help much. This thing will kill Alec. And likely damage the ears of anyone who's close enough."

"Just be ready," Almstedt ordered.

"Wait," Tox gritted out. "We agreed—"

"Remember, we need the other stones," Tzivia spoke through the comms, drawing Tox's attention to where she stood with some other women in gowns. She cleaned up nice.

"There's no guarantee frying Alec's head will fry the crown, too," Cell warned.

And since Alec wouldn't let it out of his sight. . . "Eyes out." Tox noticed the guests moving toward the tables, settling in for the boring part of the evening. "Speeches and dinner coming up."

"Perfect, tight target for a hit," Maangi said.

He was right. The guests would all be gathered in one area. Hit them, and it would guarantee mass casualties. But with what? Tox wandered to a window and glanced out. The orchestra members were taking a break, walking down to the water's edge. The guests on the patio adjusted their chairs to listen to the speech given by his father, who stood at a lectern perfectly placed so everyone had a nice vantage.

A gasp shot through the crowd. Heads swiveled to the side. Tox saw the entourage and drew himself into the shadows. Striding toward the crowd of tables, Alec and a woman created an enormous stir. Not because of their unannounced, uninvited presence. But because he wore a large gold crown.

How had he gotten through security? "King's on-site," Tox growled.

"As I said," Cell groused.

Shadows lengthened in the deep crevices beneath Alec's eyes. Skin a sickly yellow, he laughed. Taunted the crowd. Waved at them. Kept moving.

"Yeah, and he looks like death warmed over," Cell said.

"Not even that good," Thor muttered. "Should we put him down?"

"Not until we know where he has the other legacy stones," Tzivia said.

"She's right," Almstedt said, "Mr. Purcell, can you do a half burst?"

"Seriously?" Cell snorted. "It's not like I can only half melt his brain. It'll just give him a really bad headache—which'll probably tick him off. And then we're screwed."

"Who's the woman with him?" Ram asked.

"Working on that," Iliescu chimed in.

"Good evening," Alec proclaimed, motioning the woman with him into a chair near the front of the crowd. "This is the Endeavor of Patriots gala, right? For military personnel, the beginning of a charity for the families of military and government workers." He laughed. "Am I right?"

Stricken faces gaped at him.

"Then I'm in the right place." When a dozen Secret Service swooped into the room, Alec lifted a hand. "Ah-ah-ah," he said, holding up a device, then motioning in a circle around him. "You enter this ring of tables, you swift little agents, and this entire room goes up in flames."

Hesitation slowed their approach.

Galen motioned them away.

"Let us take the president and his family away," an agent insisted.

"Heavens, no. Don't you know?" Alec exclaimed, feigning insult. "Our president and his parents lost a very, very dear family member. He was killed"—his gaze went a little blank—"I can't recall. How did their son die?"

"Prison riot." Several guests scowled at the suit who'd provided the answer.

Alec's face brightened and he pointed at the man who'd spoken. "Ah, yes! Thank you, good sir."

"Actual," Tzivia said in a calm voice, "his date has the amulet."

Sure enough, around her neck hung a large medallion. "Copy. Cell," he subvocalized, maneuvering to a more strategic position, "Alec has an ignition switch. What's it for?"

"Working on that," Cell said.

"You got that burst ready?" Almstedt hissed through the line.

"Already told you I do," Cell groused. "But everyone knows I'm not pressing this button unless Actual says to, and I can't do two things at once, so a little quiet, please."

"You are under the command of the—"

"I trust one man tonight, and you ain't him. Just sayin'," Cell snipped.

"What is that?" a woman in the crowd asked Alec from behind her husband's shoulder. "Is that a bomb?"

Alec laughed. Hysterically. "Oh Haven, no."

Tox's heart jump-started, and the comms went nuts.

"Did he seriously say *Haven*?" Thor asked.

"Do we have eyes on her?" someone from Command asked.

"Send a team now."

"Negative."

"Haven, no," Alec repeated around a laugh, pale eyes glittering as he looked around the room and settled on someone. "This isn't a bomb."

Several women tittered nervous laughs while the team erupted in curses and frustration.

"He did it again."

"Used her name. Please. A double tap," Cell pleaded.

Heart thudding, Tox angled around the side of the room, staying to Alec's back for a stealthier approach. But then a strange noise caught his ear. He stilled. Drew out his comms piece for a second, aiming one ear toward Alec, the other homing in on the noise. It drew him back . . . back. Outside. He tucked the comms piece in again.

On the patio, he closed his eyes, listening. Listening hard. Shutting out the white noise. He turned more, angling the ear without the comms piece back toward the lawn.

"Tox, you okay?"

"The river," he subvocalized, descending the steps to the lawn. "I hear something. Can you see anything?"

"Nothing," Iliescu said. "No movem—wait. Heat signatures. There are heat signatures in the water. And—oh crap!"

Tox jogged down the sloping lawn, noting ripples stretching across the river, reaching for shore. A boat chugged into view. "What about the boat?"

"No bodies," Iliescu noted. "But it shouldn't be there. Bravo and Charlie—converge on that boat!"

Which was exactly what Alec would anticipate, right? Or did he intend to use something on the boat to—

Tox skidded to a stop. Pivoted and shot a look back at the house. Alec wouldn't do that, would he? He wouldn't take down the entire house with himself in it? "We have Aerial One and Two?" Tox asked.

Rodriguez answered. "In the air as we—no!"

Even as the general cut off, Tox noted the SEALs in the water jerking violently, then going deathly still. His mind ricocheted back to Nimrud, when their devices had died. Some type of electrical current?

Alec had electrified the water so they couldn't stop whatever was on that boat.

"Our birds are being jammed," Rodriguez announced.

The glow of the moon slid its caress along a long, straight line on the boat's deck. "A rail," Tox breathed, his gaze finally lighting on the fins at the end. "Missile!"

They had no way to take down that boat. An inbound bomb would take several minutes to strike. In a heartbeat that felt like minutes, Tox eyed the house. The ambient lighting. The ominous silence save Alec's squawking voice. Hundreds of people sitting captive. Hundreds about to die.

Decaying moral judgment.

He would. He would totally take them down with him.

Tox sprinted toward the house. "Cell, send the burst."

"Sarge?"

"Light him up! Do it now!"

WE CEASE TO THINK OF THEE

"It is personal."

Countess Eschiva faced the sea, the salty breeze rustling her hair carelessly about her face. "Is there any other way, sir knight? One war over dirt, one over a slight." She sighed. "And here . . . both sides fight for a sliver of land they both view as holy. The dome for the Muslims. Solomon's Temple for the Christians. Whether you see it as a Christian land or the Turks'—it is significant." She turned, hands clasped before her. "And that significance speaks to me. Dark calls to dark, and light to light."

Thefarie inclined his head. "Aye, my lady." He and his men had been ordered to Tveria to intercept Saladin on his war trek from Acre. To create an ambush. With the years that had passed and the crown yet unrecovered, Thefarie would have been stripped, but an expected . . . delay came with the death of the Grand Master. So the vigil for the crown's destruction endured, as did Thefarie's mission.

"'*And the Philistines came up yet again, and spread themselves in the valley of Rephaim . . .*'"

Thefarie gave a start at that last term, a knot twisting in his gut. How could she know his legacy? "My lady?"

She smiled and sighed. "Do you know it? The story of David and the giant, the mercenary?"

He tried to stop his swallow, but it pushed down his throat. "I do, my lady. But of what—"

Turning back to the sea, she sighed. "David inquired of the Lord if he could defeat the Philistines, and the Lord told him to go."

Thefarie shifted. "I am afraid we face no giants here, my lady."

"Don't we? I fear the Saracens are giants in their own right, their own might." She smiled at him over her shoulder. "King Raymonde and my sons are too far away to save us, Sir Knight."

"My brother-knights and I will not give up while breath yet remains in our lungs."

"Ah, see?" she said with a rueful smile, peering at him over her brocaded shoulder. "Again there are giants. Salah ad-Din would behead them."

"Their laws do not allow them to kill prisoners of war." He knew better than the words he spoke, but he would not wish her to fret.

"He follows his own laws, Sir Thefarie."

Indeed. Especially with that crown. *To the last one standing . . .*

But then her gaze and smile fell away. Focused on something. She blanched as a shout went up from the city. "I fear we are lost."

Thefarie glanced back to the south gate in the distance. The Saracens flowed into the streets like ants. "My lady—to safety."

She nodded, lifted her skirts, and hurried to the stone steps that led down into the Citadel. There, they were met by Giraude and Ameus.

"Miryam?" Thefarie asked, anxious to ensure her safety as well.

Slowing, Ameus paled. "But she said . . ."

Heart seizing, Thefarie recalled her concern for their neighbors, for her brothers. "No . . ." His gaze struck the barred door. "How long since she departed?"

"She left shortly after the nooning meal."

Covering his mouth, Thefarie turned a slow, painful circle. He could not leave the Citadel and the countess. He was charged with their protection.

But Miryam and Ayla . . .

A knight was bound to honor the Order and the Rules, to obey the word of the new Grand Master and the king. It was these powers that had pulled Thefarie back to Israel, back to his home. Back to those he loved.

And it was the incompetence of King Guy along with the desperation of Raymonde and his treaty with Saladin that had Tveria besieged. The countess holed up and staving off the Saracens with her small band of knights.

To abandon her would be to abandon his station. He would sin in the pursuit of selfish endeavors and thus be expelled from the Order.

For the last year or so, the world had watched as Saladin swept Israel, claiming victory after victory in his march south to Jerusalem. Though it meant another conquest for Saladin when he claimed the sea city, it also meant he could reach a certain family. A quieter one. Lesser known.

Tveria was . . . personal. The sultan sought revenge against Thefarie. Against his unrelenting quest to secure the crown.

It had been fourteen years since the fires in Syria. Since he and Rashid, the Old Man of the Mountain, had attempted to drive the sultan back to Egypt. Seven years since the sandstorm vow.

Tried and failed. Though Thefarie had escaped, he had failed. Failed to recover the crown. All these years, it had not been seen, not on Saladin's head nor in his possession. Nor in anyone's. Though the Grand Master spoke not of his failure, it hung over Thefarie. Why had they not seen it? Could it be that Saladin had truly done away with it somehow?

Thoughts of the crown were lost as Thefarie mentally fought to navigate the terrain. Was there a passage he could take to quickly reach Miryam?

And abandon his post? No. He could not. Would not. He had surrendered his flesh, his family, his home, to serve. This—this was why he had never before allowed himself to indulge in the flesh. Why he had always chosen to espouse only the Lord and the Order. Until now.

"Sir Thefarie." Cold, clammy hands covered his. "Go." Confusion held him fast as he stared down at the Crusader princess, as she had come to be called. "Go to them, your Miryam and Ayla."

"I cannot abandon my post."

"You must obey the orders of your sovereign, yes?"

Thefarie felt the gazes of his brother-knights as he nodded to the countess.

"I am the last and only representative of the king here in Tveria. And I order you to secure the innocents in the streets, especially a young woman and her daughter."

Hope lurched in his chest. "I will return immediately."

"Already you slow success of your new mission, Sir Knight."

Thefarie fought the tangle of bodies as he pressed himself through the small gate to the great gates. He turned to take a small passage.

"Thefarie!"

He slid to a stop. Backed up. Turned.

Saladin sat upon his mount. He held up his sword. "To the last one standing!"

43

Sand teased her bare calves as it trickled in from above. It had taken what felt like hours for the grains to reach her ankles, then her knees. All the while, she tried to stay atop the grains filling the cistern. For each inch she gained, she also sank a little. Though it panicked her to slip, she couldn't get buried. So she'd fought it. Tried to toe the hard walls, but her toes barely reached. They were raw now, but what was a little pain compared to death?

Exhaustion plied her arms, her legs. Her shoulder ached, and pain had become a constant and insistent friend. She struggled to stay coherent, but the numbness spreading through her was a sure sign her body wanted to shut down.

She would die here. And nobody would know.

Cole.

"Oh, God—please," she pleaded, eyes burning, but the tears had long dried. Her hope long shriveled. She didn't want to die here, not without letting him know that she forgave him. That she didn't hold Brooke's death against him.

How could she?

Well, she could, but she wouldn't. There had been enough torment in

431

their families for too long. Too many reasons to hate. Too many reasons to hold a grudge. The subtle tendrils of bitterness were watered over years as wounds were left to fester, the person believing their wrong, their hurt more important than healing. Than letting go.

Bitterness rotted the soul. And she, Tox, and his team had seen over the last four weeks what happened to someone whose soul had rotted.

She didn't want to hate Cole or be angry with him. She ached to love him. To show the man who'd never liked himself that he was one of the best men on earth. He wasn't perfect, but he was perfect for her.

Somehow, she realized she loved him more. He'd been put in impossible situations. Faced with cruel missions and outcomes. How was he still walking upright? She'd have crumbled beneath that load long ago. There had to be a way to get free, to get back to him and let him know how she felt.

"God, please." Only darkness and that lone speck of light answered. "Please." The last tear in her ducts squeezed out. Resting her cheek against her swollen, throbbing shoulder, she closed her eyes. But that would be giving up, and she couldn't give up. She would not give herself permission to die in a cistern. "God!" she shouted. "God, help me!"

A strange noise sluiced through the vacuous silence. Haven stilled, searching the shadows. The dot of light.

Whoosh.

Something dropped past her.

Thump.

Haven sucked in a hard breath, aware that something had joined her in the cistern. Frozen, she listened.

A growling moan filled the air.

＊　＊　＊　＊

RUSSELL ESTATE, MARYLAND

"Take his team!" Tox launched himself up the steps to the house and threw himself through the crowd. He jumped over a chair that skidded into his path. Aimed for the dais.

His onetime friend turned widened eyes on him. He went rigid.

432

As he shook violently, he lifted his hand—the remote! Smoke rose in angry tendrils from his head, curling around the filigree of the crown.

Tox dove through the air. He drove his shoulder into Alec's chest, and they barreled backward. Crashed against a table. Shouts and screams rang out. The table collapsed beneath their weight, sending china and crystal smashing to the marble floor.

Adrenaline jacked, Tox hoisted himself up, weapon drawn and aimed at the man beneath him.

Alec's mouth hung agape, the crown still mounted on his white-blond hair. Blood streamed from his eyes, his ears, his nose. Though Tox expected Alec to fight, there was nothing save a wheeze from his lungs.

Ram was there, kicking the remote from his hand.

"Alec," Tox said. In a grotesque display, the crown and Alec's forehead were melting into a marred mess. "Where's Haven?"

Screams shrieked around them.

"Get them back," Ram ordered. "General, security needs to gather the guests onto the lawn. Nobody leaves."

"Where is she?" Tox demanded, grabbing Alec's collar. "What did you do to her? Help me, Alec. Help me save her, and I can save you, too."

The sizzling hadn't stopped, so Tox used his forearm to bat the crown off Alec's head. It peeled away, taking a layer of flesh with it. Alec cried out, arching his back then slumping in agonized defeat, a seared red line across his forehead.

"Save me?" Alec's lips quirked upward. His eyes grew unfocused. Bloody saliva slid over his lips and trailed down his neck. "Brother. Too late . . . can't save me," he mumbled. His head lolled. "Or her."

"Come on, Alec. Tell me!" He wanted to strangle him. "Where is she? This isn't you. I know you—we don't kill those who deserve to be protected. Save her, Alec! Help me save her."

"Restore . . . restore the crown." Even in death, he was defiant.

"Forget the crown!" Tox pounded Alec's chest. "Where is Haven? What'd you do with her?"

Alec's eyes focused on Tox for the space of two heartbeats, and then he drifted away again, turning his head to the side. He didn't respond when Tox shook him. "Restore the crown. Right the wrong." His lips quavered. "It came from heaven. A gift."

"He's gone—not dead yet, but might as well be," Ram said quietly.

"Augh!" Tox banged his fists on Alec's chest. As he hovered over the dying man, rage biting him, defeat clawing at his courage, Tox noted the crown being hefted into a case by his team, securing it. They had the crown. And the amul—

"The woman." Tox was on his feet, searching the crowds. Scanning faces.

Ram whipped around. "Where's his date?" he yelled to the uniforms around them, then keyed his comms. "Find King's date. Now!"

Alec's hand lifted. "You . . ."

Tox knelt, gaze sweeping the room for the dark-haired beauty who'd come with Alec. Then suddenly the air around him sizzled. A split-second blur, familiar from when the Arrow & Flame Order had wreaked havoc on the world with phosphorus arrows.

Disbelief pummeled him as he looked down and found a glowing arrow protruding from Alec's chest, the acid already boiling through his skin. Alec convulsed twice and then fell still.

"Back!" he shouted, pushing away, heart hammering. The tremor of rage roiled through him.

"You have *got* to be kidding me," Cell yelped through the comms.

The AFO had just killed their only way to find Haven. "Augh!" He shoved a chair across the room. Balled his hands into fists and growled.

The rest of the team whipped toward the open doors that led to the lawn. But hundreds of people milled around in the dark. Tox thought about hunting down the shooter, but the point was moot. In this kind of confusion, they'd be long gone. His gaze hit Ram's and they shared a long, angry look filled with questions. Was the AFO shutting Alec up? Did they want Haven dead? Were they behind the crown?

A crash sounded at the back of the house near the library, followed by a shout that sounded a lot like Tzivia.

"The woman!" Ram guessed.

They darted down the hall, rounding the corner to the library. Behind them, a herd of security followed. There—movement in the corner.

The woman who'd been with Alec threw a wild punch at Tzivia, who—all grace and ease—deflected the blow like someone swatting away a fly rather than fighting for their life. She flipped her hand onto the woman's wrist. Stepped to the side as she yanked the arm back and under, twisting—

Crack!

A shrill scream pierced the air.

Groans of sympathy pain rose behind Tox as the onlookers watched. Ram lunged forward and dropped on the woman, pinning her to the floor.

Tzivia stood over her conquest, then lifted something toward Tox. "The amulet." And in her other hand— "Lapis lazuli."

Admiration ran through Tox as he set eyes on the cuff she'd ripped off the woman. He nodded his approval as the agents moved in and secured Alec's accomplice.

"I help you," she said, her English broken. "I know where girlfriend is. She die if you no listen to me!"

"Hold up," Tox snapped to the security detail. "Where is she?"

"I want deal."

"All you'll get is more time with her," Tox said, nodding to Tzivia. "Now tell me where she is, or these agents will walk out of here for a coffee *break*."

Holding her broken arm closer, the woman cringed. "He took her to place where crown must be returned. He know you go there. He want you to find her drowned. *Dead*," she snarled at him. "And I hope she is!"

"Rodriguez," Tox said through his comms, "did you get that?"

"Loud and clear."

"Tox."

He pivoted toward Ram. "Yeah?"

"That's Iraq."

"How'd he get her there?" Tzivia asked. "When's the last time anyone saw her?"

"When she got off the plane yesterday," Tox surmised.

"Iraq is a twelve- or fourteen-hour flight." Ram's eyes were bleak. Meaning even if they left now, they'd probably be too late.

"Six by Learjet."

Tox turned, surprised to find his father on the other side of the room. And for a second, he forgot—forgot about the prostheses. Forgot he didn't look like himself. Forgot about the years that had put distance between them. He stood before his father, feeling every ounce of rejection and disappointment he'd supplied in his thirty-two years.

"I have a Learjet," his father said. "My pilot will meet you at Dulles."

But six hours . . . Tox swallowed. "Thank you."

His dad gave a nod, lifting his phone in acknowledgment as he left the room.

Bewilderment fastened Tox to the hardwood floor. "He didn't even recognize me."

"That was the point," Ram said quietly, moving toward the hall.

It *had* been the point, but Tox hadn't expected it to hurt that much. How could a father not know his own son? Then again, his father had always seen what he'd wanted to see. Not what was really before him.

"You certainly made a mess of my home tonight, gentlemen," his mother said in a light but disapproving voice as she entered the library, Ram tailing her.

"Sorry about that, ma'am."

"I hope you got what you were after."

"Most of it, ma'am." *Nod and leave. Nod and leave.* "Thanks." Stiffly, he angled around the furniture, which brought him dangerously close to her.

"You never were one to clean up after yourself."

Tox stilled. Felt the thrum of adrenaline buzzing in his veins. Did she really know who he was? Or was she talking to someone else? Maybe Galen? Should he check the room? Frozen in indecision, he waited. Then slid his eyes to his mother. His heart pounded. Did he acknowledge it? There were so many repercussions. "I think you might have me confused—"

"You might be confused, but I'm not." Her eyes watered, but she maintained that control she'd always had. "Did you really think I wouldn't know my own son?"

Abashed, he stood there. Feeling like he had at eight years old when he'd been caught testing his father's hunting rifle. "We hoped . . ."

She half laughed, half sobbed. "It *is* you, isn't it?" she asked, pleading in her voice. Arms spread in openness and affection, she welcomed him. "It's really you, Cole Russell."

Years of heartache, disappointment, and grief melted away as his mother wrapped him in an embrace as only a mother could. Crushing yet comforting. Loving and urgent. Theirs had never been a particularly affectionate relationship, but she always knew him. Always jerked him by the collar. Straightened him out. Challenged him. Loved him.

He might drown in this moment. But— "I have to go, Mom. Haven . . ."

She gasped and drew back. "It's you—you're the one she's in love with." Her laughter, so light and beautiful, rippled through the air. She reached up and cupped his face with her cool hands. "I should've known."

He ached. Haven wasn't in love with him any longer. "She's in danger. Dad's loaning us the Lear—"

"He knows?"

"About me? No." The pain scoring his heart still shocked him, but he managed a semblance of a smile. "But he offered the Lear."

"That daft man—he didn't recognize you."

Tox removed her hands. "I'll come back. We'll talk. I promise. But I have to find her."

"You'd better come back, or I'll hunt you down."

He smiled. "No doubt." Planted a kiss on her cheek and heard her quiet sob. "I'll be back. Love you."

"Actual! Need to move."

The shout drew him around. With one last, furtive nod to her, he was out the door, hurrying toward the chaos.

44

The king cobra puffed its hood. Threw itself at Haven's leg. Fangs stabbed her flesh with piercing agony, and she screamed. Kicked her legs. Tried to lift herself, but she had no strength and her shoulder protested. Hot tears streaked down her face as the fiery venom coursed through her muscles.

The snake released her, then puffed again, arching back.

"God, *help*!"

The cobra didn't strike again, but it also wasn't leaving. But then, where would it go?

"God does not leave me nor forsake me," she cried, her muscles aching. Her heart stuttering. "Exodus says you will fight for us, Lord. Please—fight for me. Your Word says no weapon formed against us will prosper, but there's a fierce one pumping venom into my body."

As her panic subsided, she realized the snake hadn't coiled around her. Hadn't struck again. She couldn't see it anymore, but her leg burned like crazy.

Maybe the Bible verses and prayers were working. She kept quoting them. Pulling on years of church services and Bible studies.

The snake had to still be there. Why wasn't it attacking again?

438

Why hadn't it slid up her body and wrapped around her? It could have constricted the air from her lungs.

Cobras were poisonous. She had to limit her movements. Slow the spreading of the venom. How long would it take? Minutes? She'd whisper her prayers and climb the ever-rising sand, eyes on the light above, just as she kept her eyes on the Father above. She found an ounce of comfort in the fact that she was now only a foot or two from the lip of the well. She cried out—but her voice caught in her throat. Dried from dehydration, it refused to cooperate.

Defeated, exhausted, aching, Haven closed her eyes and mouthed the verses and prayers. She would do it for as long as she could. Time fell away and took the sunlight with it.

She didn't know when she'd fallen asleep or for how long, but Haven awoke to a tightness in her chest. Was it the venom? Losing lung capacity? But as she wondered, a frightening realization fell over her. Darkness. Tightness. It wasn't the venom making it hard to breathe. The cistern had filled. Sand cocooned her shoulders.

Oh no. Oh no no no.

✳ ✳ ✳ ✳

SOMEWHERE OVER THE MIDDLE EAST

Though the six-hour flight to Nimrud was half the length of a typical trip from Dulles to Iraq, it was still five hours and fifty-nine minutes too long for Tox.

Haven could be dead. *Because of me.*

It had been a game. One he'd been all too ready to play, convinced he was in control. Convinced he could control the life of another, the outcome. Convinced if he saved Alec, he could save himself.

But he couldn't. Couldn't save Alec. Or himself.

Alec had died. Would Haven die, too?

He couldn't do it alone. That was the point, wasn't it? Bringing him to the end of himself.

God, I need help. . . .

"Hey." Ram came down the gangway with Cell, who had a laptop. "They found some things I think you'll want to see."

"Who?"

"Iliescu. This was yesterday morning, right after we landed in DC. They pieced things together." He sat and angled the screen. "Haven took the rail into Arlington and got a hotel room."

Tox leaned in. The video showed Haven leaving a check-in desk at a hotel. The next image was—

"What?" Tox couldn't believe his eyes.

"Exactly," Ram said. "Ti Tzaddik visited her."

"How did he even know where she was? Did he take her?" He felt sick. "Was he working with Alec this whole time?"

Cell held up a finger. "Just watch." He played another video. "This is security footage from outside the hotel, east entrance. Less populated." He nodded at the screen. "Tzaddik emerges. Bright-white glare washes everything out, and then things are normal."

Tox shrugged. "So did he—"

Amused, Cell held up his finger again. "I slowed down the footage. Filtered out the glare as much as I could." He grinned. "Now watch."

The video played again. But this time, the bright white glare was a streak. From a phosphorus arrow.

"Snagged right out of the air by Ti Tzaddik," Cell announced.

"Pause it." Disbelief squirmed through Tox as the footage clearly showed Tzaddik's hand around the shaft of the unexpended arrow. "No way."

"Exactly. But then!" He laughed and pointed to the screen, narrating what happened next. "The old man attacks the two men who come at him."

Another flare of white swallowed Tzaddik, and the alley lay empty.

"I don't . . . I don't understand."

"The dude vanished. But he caught that arrow in like a split second."

"Vanished. How?" Never mind. All he cared about was Haven. "Did he take her?"

"No, but I think he was there to draw attention to this." Cell made a few more clicks and brought up a third video. "These two bring out a laundry bin. But there's only one parcel. And it's heavy—look how they're struggling to get it out of the cart."

Bile rose in Tox's throat. "Haven." They put her in a freakin' box.

The feed showed Tzaddik come out the side door after them. "Then they tried to kill him with those sick arrows."

Ram leaned on the back of a seat. "They're with the AFO."

"A fight for another day. Haven is our concern now." Tox looked at Cell. "Did you trace the van? Do we know—"

"It's a dead end. Van disappeared."

"Ladies and gentlemen," the pilot droned, "we'll be landing for a refuel. No more than twenty minutes, and we'll be airborne again. Flight path has been cleared for a straight shot into Mosul."

"Black Hawk will take us the rest of the way," Ram said.

Tzivia peered over her brother's shoulder. "I've already talked with Mehdi, and he said they were forcibly removed from the site about six hours ago. No idea what's going on."

"Alec's men," Tox said, more convinced than ever. "She's there. We need to be ready to hit and hit it hard."

MOTHER OF GOD! THE EVENING FADES

— 1187 AD —

TVERIA, ISRAEL

The crush of bodies held him fast. Thefarie stared over the citizens as he always had, the blood of time running through his veins. His gaze, locked on the sultan, saw but one course of action—battle. War. Bloodshed.

Yet his heart cried another—love!

Miryam. Ayla.

He pivoted, the rocks beneath his boots strangely loud in the chaotic din, and launched himself against the flow of bodies fleeing to the water to escape the siege. Though Saracens before Saladin had taken prisoners, rumor had raced across the Levant that Saladin was

443

slaughtering captured knights. And he would make no exception for Thefarie. In fact, Saladin would take pleasure in cutting the breath from him. But Thefarie would not grant him the lives of his wife and daughter.

Large and powerful, Thefarie shoved through the crowd. The people clawed at him, begging for help, for protection. "To the water," he urged them. Boats would take them across the Sea of Galilee to safety.

Thefarie pushed himself up the terraced cobbles. Two more turns. Past the baker's house . . .

A shout came from his right.

He twisted, freeing his sword before he even saw the Saracen. The crowd around him dispersed with screams. Steel struck steel, vibrations rippling down his arm, but he swung again, advancing. Forcing the Saracen back—into a crowd. The man was young, not experienced. His death would be quick. Thefarie arced up and brought his blade down at the soft spot between shoulder and head. The Saracen fell, shock frozen on his dark features.

Thefarie did not wait. He hopped away, sprinting for the archway that separated homes from the market. Even as he rounded the corner, he spotted the sultan at the far end, his army slaughtering the people. Livid eyes fastened on him before Saladin glinted with excitement and urged his horse ahead.

He goes for Miryam.

Thefarie swung around and went up a winding passage. Around the cobbler's hut and down a street lined with small homes. Thrusting aside people as he would branches on an overgrown path. They cared not either, fleeing for their lives.

One more row. Just one more row of houses, and he would be there. But the clopping thunder of hooves raced him. His heart beat faster, in cadence with the Saracens. Slapping the walls slowed his momentum enough to take the corner. Thefarie willed himself faster. Pleaded with the Lord God to grant him this one favor. Though he had earned none, despite his years of penance. One could not forgive the unforgiveable. He had no purity. He had known unconditional love, and somehow, it had not been enough.

That was long ago. A foolish, wicked, grievous mistake.

That he would relive for all time.

He crashed around the bend. Launched himself over the small pen at the edge of the city that held Baruk's milk goats and a handful of sheep. Tripping and stumbling around the bleating, smelly animals, Thefarie sighted his small home. There at the door, clutching Ayla to her chest, Miryam looked around in fright. Eyes wide, her head covered, she scanned the panicked crowd.

"Miryam!" he called. "Come, come!"

She started toward him, but horses erupted in the narrow passage, cutting Thefarie off from his wife and child.

A destrier stomped before him, the rider edging it closer and closer. Taunting. Mocking.

Thefarie locked gazes with the sultan, separated from him by three horses. "Leave her and I will let you live!"

The sultan laughed. "I think you mistake your position, *Dawiyya*!"

"I think you mistake who—*what* you deal with." Thefarie felt his old self rising. The one not satisfied with purity and perfection. If he could but unleash it by a fraction, he could end this. "She is not to be harmed, nor the child!"

The nearest Saracen extended a scimitar at him.

Thefarie seized it, mindless of its sharp edge, and hauled the rider off his mount. Straight into his fist. When the rider struggled, Thefarie landed another blow—this one lethal beneath his rage.

Silence dropped hard, save for the clops of hooves as the destriers shifted nervously. Thefarie drew closer to both his family and the sultan. A shout rose, and several Saracens fell on him. Fury and precision were his allies as he fought. A dagger to the throat of one, quick work. A sword driven up through the belly of the next. And still he advanced, closing the gap between him and his wife.

Though he felt steel pierce his thigh—a dagger—Thefarie ignored the pain. Focused on his mission. Dealt violently with the attackers. A nick stung his cheek. He swung his sword. Stabbed. Punched.

"Thefarie!"

Miryam's voice froze him. She no longer stood at their home. He scanned, fending off yet another Saracen.

"Think, *Dawiyya*," the sultan said, his sword laid across Miryam's shoulder as he pulled her against his horse, "think on the shame you will feel if I take her life and let you live."

"If you let me live," Thefarie said, aware that the other fighters were easing away as he advanced toward the sultan, "all my days will be spent hunting you. When you breathe your last, it will be me standing over you."

Where was Ayla?

He stepped over a body and stopped. He stared up at the sultan. "Release her. Act in honor."

Saladin laughed. "That is brave talk for one whose wife feels the sting of my steel."

Miryam stiffened, whimpering. A thin line of red sluiced down her neck.

Thefarie drove his gaze from his wife's teary face to the hard planes of the sultan's. "Last chance."

"Yes," Saladin said. "It is. You are a knight. You fight in the name of your god. Will you surrender?"

"You know the answer."

Nodding, Saladin smiled crookedly. "I do." And with a flourish, he drew the sword against Miryam's throat. She slid to the cobbles, limp, her blood seeping into the grooves between the stones.

Rage threw Thefarie forward, his sword coming with him. He vaulted his large frame at the sultan. Knocked him from his mount. They scrabbled on the ground, Thefarie struggling to gain control.

Steel bit into his side, a dagger searing through his armor. He growled but focused on driving his blade into the sultan. Hefted it up and aimed.

Weight plowed into Thefarie's spine. Pitched him forward. His head hit the hard stone, his hearing rang hollow. Pain exploded through his back. He cried out and dropped against the road, feeling the sting and warmth of blood beneath his mantle.

Hooves and shouts erupted in a dizzying whirl of combat. A hoof hammered his hand against the cobbles. "Augh!"

He scrambled out of the road, panic beating him into the corner of a hut, his gaze only on Miryam, crushed beneath the horses as a small band of soldiers struggled to push back the Saracens.

446

The sultan! Where had he gone? Thefarie searched through the tangle of legs and hooves. Spotted Saladin being dragged to safety by his men. Defeat pushed Thefarie back down. It was a lost cause. Failure at the most egregious level.

Tears ran down his cheeks as the edges of his vision blurred.

"Brother," Giraude called in a stiff, frantic voice.

A flicker of movement in the pen snapped Thefarie alert. Small and round, a face peered from beneath Baruk's fence. "*Ayla . . .*"

Giraude pivoted on his heels and gave a cry. Rushed to the pen and plucked Thefarie's daughter to safety.

The day—and life—quickly grew gray. "Mother of God! The evening fades . . . as do I."

*   *   *   *

As dawn spilled over the horizon, Thefarie crouched at the eastern edge of the Sea of Galilee, watching smoke spill from the citadel. Despite the few who braved to fight, Tveria had been taken by Saladin. His armies now marched to confront Guy and the Frankish army. Tveria was lost. A total loss.

Miryam. Her laughter. Her love. Her resolute belief in him, which he did not ask for nor deserve. Though he had sought to do well by her, he had failed. Just as he had failed in recovering the crown. And now he was dead by all official accounts.

"Are you yet healed enough?"

"Aye." Thefarie glanced down, leaving this piece of himself here at the water's edge, where they'd first met. "They will care for her well?"

"They are good people," Giraude said. "Ayla will be cared for. You are sure—"

He climbed up onto his horse. "It must be this way. She must not know I live." His gaze again struck the burning city. His home. "No one must know."

45

Shouldn't I be dead?

The blurry thought ached against her pounding temples. Haven pried open her eyes, gritty with sand. She groaned, aches permeating every cell of her body. Her eyelids were heavy. She couldn't feel her arms or legs anymore. Her tongue felt five sizes too large for her mouth. She swallowed—and choked on her own tongue.

A man stood before her.

No. No, not possible. She was in a sand-filled cistern. She had to be hallucinating. Probably dehydration and the venom of the cobra, which had vanished. Maybe buried in the sand? She had no idea. Didn't care, as long as it was gone. Sand blew against her mouth.

Sand?

She blinked away her confusion, realizing the grains had risen to her chin. Startled, she tried to tip her head back to free it of the sand. But there was no way to lift it. She was buried. Couldn't move.

I can't breathe! I can't breathe!

Panic clawed through her, fighting her tenuous grip on self-control. "God," she rasped. Her heart raced.

Her eyes drifted closed. They were so heavy. Life was heavy. Breathing was heavy. She just had to rest.

"Haven." A deep, resonating voice whispered against her ear. She was in a warehouse in Israel. In Cole's arms. His lips against her ear. "Haven."

She loved him. He loved her.

Grief wrapped tight fists around her heart and squeezed. She had walked out of that briefing room and right off the plane without ever saying another word to him. He'd think she hated him. She'd die, and that would be the last thing he remembered—that she left him.

"Haven!"

Her eyes fluttered, the voice cracking against her eardrums. Dizzy and vision blurring.

"Haven!"

She snapped open her eyes. The cistern was a blur of oranges and reds. Golds. Beautiful. Fiery. She grunted, confusion addling her mind. A man hovered above her. He seemed familiar. Sounded like . . . someone.

"Hold on, Haven."

Her mind tripped and fell against the familiarity of his presence. She squinted. "I know . . ." Dryness scratched her throat. She coughed— and with each intake of breath, sand sucked into her throat.

Panic tore at her anew. She would drown—in sand! Lungs would fill. She screamed. More sand. So much sand.

She wanted to thrash. Couldn't.

Sand. Sand sand sand!

A strangled sob beat against her temples. "God, please!" God heard. He heard the cries of His children. She knew that. She *knew* it.

A hot, stirring breath blew against her face. Powerful. Pushing back her hair. Drying the tears on her face. With it, a hollowing in her ears, she heard, "Peace."

She gasped.

As she fell away into an exhausted darkness, she saw him looming over her again. The man with a thousand names that all meant the same thing.

"Tiberius . . ."

* * * *

NIMRUD, IRAQ

"Five klicks out."

Adrenaline jacked, Tox watched the ancient site grow in the distance. She was there. Haven was in there. Alive?

She'd better be alive.

A tap on his shoulder drew his gaze back. Runt crouched nearby, pointing at something, tracing his hand in a swerving arc. Canals. Tox saw the impression of them now, though they hadn't been very visible on the ground.

Satellite sweeps revealed two armed tangos guarding the road to the site from a vehicle with a mounted machine gun. Four more were posted at the entrance to the tunnel they'd used to reach the crown's hidden chamber. So it was a good bet someone had already messed up or destroyed the pedestal and cage.

"Two klicks. Going silent."

It was their only chance to buy as much time as possible to get close to the hot zone before engaging. The bird would not be setting down. The team would fast-rope in. Neutralize the tangos.

Tox linked up with his carabiner and stood poised, ready to jump. The cord was hot in his gloved hand as he hopped into the air, weapon out and ready. He used his boot and hand to control descent. His feet thudded against the ground, and he went to a knee, scanning the terrain.

Shots peppered the air to his eleven. They were shooting at the bird. Tox took aim and fired at the man running wildly toward the chopper with a weapon. He stumbled. Fell face-first into the dirt.

Tox pushed up and hustled to a nearby mound of dirt and rocks for cover. A quick glance around gave him the condition of the team. Fanned out, they were hunched and ready. Their mission parameters started with finding Haven. Then taking care of the crown, which Tzivia had in her pack.

He peered back over the mound to the cluster of guards.

"Tox." Tzivia pointed to something in that direction. "The well. Remember, the woman said Haven would be drowned."

His heart skipped a beat. With hand signals, Tox sent Ram and Thor up the west side. Maangi and Cell east. They would come up and flank the cistern, while Tox and Runt would advance straight on. He whipped around and leapt into the open.

The ground spit at him, bullets impacting at his feet. He zigzagged and dove into the dirt. Scrambled up to the edge of a half-blown wall and aimed his M4. Providing suppressive fire, he waited for Runt to cross the distance.

"Tango down," Ram announced.

Runt patted Tox's shoulder, telling him he was ready. Tox burst forward. Saw a man step from behind a wall. He eased back the trigger and fired at the tango, took him down. Used the man's presence as a clue, advancing steadily, pulse speeding. Stock tucked into his shoulder, he scanned the area for more threats.

"Clear," Cell shouted as he closed up on them. "We're clear."

Wariness crowded Tox, but he hurried to the cistern marked by a stone wall maybe two feet high. When he looked over the lip, he sighed. Maybe three feet down, all he saw was sand. "It's filled." He drew back. "It's not—" His gaze snagged on something.

Runt pointed at the same thing that had silenced Tox. Iron bolts driven into the top of the well. Chains fed from them down to two small mounds.

Not mounds. Hands! Bloody knuckles. A strangled cry vaulted into his throat when he saw the glitter of blond hair. The pink forehead. He almost didn't notice her eyes and nose, covered in dust, the sand clogging her nostrils. Reaching over, he swatted the sand away. "Haven!"

Green eyes watered, blinked rapidly. Sand puffed beneath a faint breath.

He clawed at the sand, so she could breathe. Hands around her face, he did his best to protect her air as Runt worked to clear away the sand. "Stay with me, Haven!"

The others joined in the digging.

But her eyelids slid closed. "Haven."

"Whoa." Runt pinched the sand and held up a wide metal bracelet. A blue stone winked at its center.

"Lapis lazuli!" Tzivia exclaimed, looking at Haven. "How'd she get that?"

"*Dig!*"

Haven blinked several times, tears spilling from her eyes and darkening the sand. Again, he pushed the grains away, but more flooded in from the side. He grunted and flung it away from her face. Frantic, he did it again. But the sand fought him. "What the heck?"

"Stop, stop, stop!" Tzivia shouted as she went to her knees at his side.

Tox didn't.

"Sarge, I think you should listen," Cell said, bending over the cistern as well.

"They said it's a trap."

"What?" Tox slowed, hand still protecting Haven's mouth and nose. "What trap? Who said?" He looked at Runt. "Get me an oxygen mask."

"I found two of the workers from the site," Tzivia explained. "They said that since she was put in the cistern, the sand from the tunnels has been collapsing. Vanishing."

"That doesn't make sense—it's full!"

Tzivia leaned over the edge of the cistern. "The cistern is connected to the crown's cage—it's all booby-trapped, remember? One wall closes, another opens? Same here—one place empties, another fills. This well fills. To get her out, we have to put the crown back."

Beside him, Runt handed off the mask, then turned to work the small oxygen bottle.

Tox's only concern at this instant was getting Haven some O_2. He fought to secure the mask over her face, feeding air into her lungs so they could focus on extracting her. Still, the weight of the sand could crush her lungs. There were no guarantees.

"Look." Tzivia pointed to the inner lip of the cistern. A one-inch gap ran along the interior, bleeding sand. "It's pouring *into* the well. And those iron chains"—she indicated the rings that anchored Haven's hands and were pulled taut—"they go into the earth. I think I know where they come out. They're attached to the iron bars of the cage."

Tox stared at Haven, her eyes moving, the face mask slightly fogged with her breath.

"We free her hands," Thor said. "Her wrists look broken. Do that and just drag her out."

But it hit Tox. "No. She'll sink with the sand."

"I think so," Tzivia said. "The chains will release, and with it the rest of the sand. Come on, Tox. Let's go."

"Where?" He scowled, tearing his gaze from Haven. "I'm not leaving her."

Sighing, Tzivia looked morose. "We don't have much time. *She* doesn't have much time. Trust me."

Haven's eyes widened. Fear coated those green irises. But there was another message in their depths—a message to listen.

Tox stilled, anxious—desperate to do whatever she wanted. "The crown."

She blinked her answer

He turned to Tzivia. "Show me." To the team, "Stay with her. Do not let her sink."

Tzivia spun and he followed her back to the tunnel. They descended the earthen steps into the darkened passage. Dull light flickered from the torch lamps placed along the path. They turned a corner, then came into a cavernous room. Tzivia rushed to the tiny opening in the wall and squeezed into it.

This time, Tox didn't hesitate. He dove through. In the chamber beyond, he dusted off his hands and pants, then stilled. Saw the iron shackles dangling against the cage.

"The chain follows the ceiling into the wall." Tzivia drew her hands along an invisible path. "That direction runs toward the cistern."

"And you think replacing the crown will release her shackles."

"I do. Tox, I . . . I have to be honest. This scares me."

His gut cinched. "Why?"

"You can't tell me you believe Alec's men alone are responsible for this. How did he even know about the crown to retrieve it? He was a soldier, not an archaeologist," she spat. "And this chamber—with its puzzles and secrets! He worked them like a master. How? He loved that crown—why would he want it destroyed?"

Tox let her talk, but he circled the cage, trying to figure out how to free Haven. "Then who?"

Quiet draped the chamber. "I don't know. But that arrow . . ."

"AFO. It would make sense for them to know."

"But why would they enable him?"

"To kill me."

"Maybe." She brushed bangs from her face. "But—"

"Tzi! Stop." He nodded to the cage. "Haven needs our full attention. Let's put the crown back."

Shrugging free of her pack, Tzivia took a knee. She set down her bag and drew out the crown. Then she held up the lapis lazuli cuff Runt had found in the cistern. "Get the stone free. How do you think Haven ended up with this?"

"No idea. Maybe Tzaddik."

She grunted. "I'm not sure I like that guy."

"Don't have to like him for him to be useful." Tox used his KA-BAR and pried back the prongs holding the gem to the cuff. The stone tumbled to the ground. "What's going to happen when we replace it?"

"Who knows?" Tzivia grabbed it and slipped it into the center mark of the crown with the other lapis lazuli. She had spent the flight restoring the other legacies to the crown. "No more shame, Thefarie," she muttered.

The ground rattled. A hum ran through the air. Tzivia gasped and looked up.

Expectation churning, Tox shifted as an iron bar slid into the floor. "What's that?"

"It's the 'door.'" She handed him the restored artifact.

Aiming the crown at the opening, Tox realized it was just wide enough for the piece to fit through. He prayed swords wouldn't cut his hands off as he set it on the pedestal. He quickly stepped back, anticipation high, his mind swinging to Haven stuck in that cistern. "Nothing's happening." He fisted his hands. "What's wrong?"

Tzivia came to her feet, palm to her forehead. "I . . . I don't know."

"The stones," he said, thinking it through. "We put the stones back. That's all it said." But in the back of his head, he heard Haven's complaint to Tzaddik. "The fifth legacy." A great cavern opened in his gut. "We . . . what is the fifth legacy?" Standing there, his attempt failing, he suddenly understood what Thefarie must have felt.

455

Tzivia grabbed his hand. "The cloth pieces!"

"What?"

Kneeling again, Tzivia dug into the pack. "The pieces Ram and Dr. C found—they're original to the crown. They must be the fifth legacy." She handed the scraps to him.

After giving them a speculative look, Tox set the cloths on the crown. "I hope thi—"

CLANK!

Alarm and awareness shot through him at the lightning-swift blur of movement. He snatched back his hand, iron skimming his knuckles as the bar banged shut.

Clank-clank-clank-clank-clank-clank-clank!

"The door!" Tzivia threw herself at the exit, sliding under seconds before it slammed into the ground with a resounding thud that vibrated against his feet. Tox froze, stunned to find himself sealed inside the chamber. Then he watched, speechless, as the chains rattled up and out of the conduit until they pulled taut. Haven . . . what did that mean for Haven?

"Puzzle box," he muttered, turning, searching for an out. An escape. A newly opened door. But there wasn't one.

"Sarge! Sarge!" Cell shouted through the comms. "Something happened. The clamps released."

He sucked in a hard breath. "Goo—"

"She sank! She sank right into the cistern. The ground ate her. She's gone!"

456

46

Crack! Boom!

The ground shook as Tox palmed the walls, trying to find an out.

A groaning sound brought his attention back to the cage. He watched helplessly as it and the pedestal began lowering into the earth at his feet. Smoke and heat seeped through crevices in the floor as the crown slipped out of sight. Cracks and thuds resounded through the stone chamber, as if it were collapsing in on itself.

"Not cool," he said, eyeing the walls. Thin, veinlike cracks spirited through the stone. He keyed his mic. "Wraith, I have a problem."

A strange sound emanated from the back wall. Splintering cracks fingered out, reaching toward the sides. The noise pushed him back. Trembling vibrated through his boots, drawing his attention to the ground. The walls dribbled chunks of stone. A hand-sized block fell away.

It's going to collapse.

Tox dove backward just as the upper section of the wall gave way. Sand vomited into the room, peppering his face and eyes. Rushing over him. He scrambled to the other side, but then saw a large shape slide into view. A body.

457

"Haven!" He pitched himself toward her, but the sand acted like water, slowing him. Making his run a struggling trudge. Defying his efforts to reach her as more poured in from the wall.

She lay facedown, unmoving. The oxygen mask, askew on her face, had cracked.

"Haven! Haven, talk to me." He caught her shoulder. Pulled her to himself as he brushed the hair and dirt from her nose and mouth. Was she breathing? "Haven, please." He laid her down. Listened for a heartbeat. Had the sand crushed her lungs? She coughed, but didn't come to.

"Sarge." Cell's tone was panicked. "Sarge, you got a load of trouble coming your way."

How could it get worse? "I've got Haven," he said. "What's happening up there?"

"Uh . . . well, whatever happened down there, it opened some water source."

"It's the canals," Runt announced. "They're flooding from some underground source."

"Tox." It was Ram this time, his voice even. Too even. "It's coming your way. We can't stop it."

"Water?" He looked up at the opening Haven had fallen through. The sand had slowed. Beads of water cascaded over the lip, the sand turning nearly black as it became saturated. A trickle at first. Then a stream. "You have got to be kiddin—"

A roar swallowed his words as water flooded the room. Maybe the cracks in the walls would bleed the water out enough that it wouldn't rise. But even as he considered it, he noted the waters rising fast.

Crap. He had no time left. Water sloshing around his ankles, Tox grabbed a strap and threaded it through Haven's belt loop, then through a carabiner on his tactical belt, anchoring them together. He lifted her and propped her back against him so she wouldn't drown in the rising waters.

He shouldered out of his pack and freed his oxygen bottle as water cocooned his knees. Tightened the mask over Haven's face, noting with relief that she was breathing shallowly. This might give her a chance to live.

458

The water encircled his waist and lapped at her chin. Hooking her underarms, Tox came to his feet. Pulled her up. The chamber was sealed save for the opening the collapse had created to deliver the sand and the water. Staying here wasn't an option. They had to get out. He couldn't hold his breath forever, so they had only one choice.

A bad one.

A really, really bad one.

Grateful the water buoyed her, Tox slipped a harness around Haven and anchored them with yet another carabiner. He eyed the only means of escape—the tunnel she'd fallen through. Then keyed his mic. "Cell?"

"Yeah?"

"Be ready up there."

"Uh, okay. For what?"

He gritted his teeth. "To resuscitate us."

Tox treaded water, holding Haven close. He let the rising flood carry them up . . . up . . . Palming the wall, he guided them toward the opening, refusing to think about the fact that Haven hadn't moved. Hadn't come to.

With three quick breaths, he cupped her head to his chest and pushed beneath the water. Wiggled through the opening—with two of them pancaked together, it was tough to negotiate, but he used the pressure of water to help. It rushed into the tunnel, creating displacement that Tox would ride up like an air bubble. Their shoulders scraped the walls, the water violent around them as it thrust them upward.

Up . . . up . . .

Light, he saw light above. But far above. Would they make it?

He gritted his teeth and forced himself to relax. Straining would only tire him quicker. Make him want to take a breath.

Suddenly, Haven jerked awake. She flailed in his arms. Thrashed. She could drown them both! She was wild with panic, terrified, he imagined, at finding herself trapped in a well. Tox held her tight, willing her to work it out. To realize they were getting to safety. Bracing himself, he fought to hold her. Not to lose her as they rose through the darkened tunnel.

She suddenly went limp, flopping against him as the torrent of water beat against them.

No. God, no—please.

He closed his mind to the possibilities. To the likely reality that she'd drowned in his arms.

C'mon, c'mon, c'mon.

The light grew brighter. He pushed himself. Kicked higher. Higher. *Haven, stay with me. Stay with me.*

His back arched, the current dragging them up and over some incline. Temples pounding, he fought the urge to take that breath. Just a little farther . . .

Hands pawed at him. Tox surged. Clamped onto one of the hands. Let them haul him out. As they freed Haven from him, Tox slumped onto the ground. Coughed. Hauled in a breath, staring at Haven, who lay on her back with Maangi and Runt bent over her, working. Compressions. Breaths. Compressions. Breaths.

Exhaustion weighted his limbs, but he dragged himself toward her. Touched the blond hair matted against her face. He brushed it back. "Haven." He pressed his lips to her head as the compressions continued. "Come back to me, Haven. Please." He smoothed her hair. "Please."

Around them, the dizzying chaos of a team ordering a medevac, securing the scene, trying to save a life. But for Tox—one thing—Haven.

"I love you," he whispered against her ear.

Breaths. Compressions. Breaths.

She coughed.

Maangi rolled her onto her side as she coughed again and vomited.

Tox pulled himself to his knees and shifted closer. When she slumped against the dirt, breathing raggedly, trembling, her green eyes hit his. A weary smile filtered onto her face, but then came a torrent of tears.

Tox slid alongside her, nudging out Runt, and drew Haven up into his arms. Cradled her against his chest. "Thank you." He kissed her temple. "Thank you for coming back."

460

EPILOGUE

Tox stood over Haven's gurney in the med-bay, watching as a nurse took her vitals, checked the bandages on her wrist, and the one on her leg. Bite marks, Haven had said. From a cobra.

"I'd say you don't have to hover," Haven whispered around a smile, "but it's kind of nice."

He swept the back of his hand along her face, eyeing the cuts from their ordeal. "I'm surprised you want me anywhere near you after . . . everything."

She closed her eyes, still smiling. She'd slept most of the morning as the team drew up their AARs. Tox had refused to leave her side.

"The guys are saying you should break up with me."

"Good thing I'm the only one with a vote."

"What about me?"

"Not even you." Her eyes were still closed, the oxygen mask still in place until her levels evened out. "Not right now," she said. Her green eyes peeked beneath her lids.

"But . . . Brooke . . ."

She seemed to breathe her next smile. "If you had done what Alec

461

did, if you had deliberately set out to kill my sister, that would be one thing. But you didn't."

He thumbed her forehead again. "Cell says you're too reasonable. Said we should give you a nickname."

Haven arched an eyebrow, the lights of the room reflecting through her irises and making them shine like emeralds. "Yeah?"

"Cobra."

She snorted, then started coughing. "If I didn't have the bite marks to prove it, the doctor said he wouldn't believe I'd been bitten. He said there was no trace of venom in my system." Her expression turned serious. "Ti Tzaddik."

Tox stilled. "Haven, you should—"

"I saw him."

He angled to the side so he could meet her gaze straight on. "Where?"

"He was at the cistern."

His heart thudded.

"He saved me. Kept the sand from my face so I could breathe."

Disbelief tightened in his chest. It sounded so much like his experience in Syria.

"I wasn't delusional." She wrinkled up her face. "I should've died, but I didn't. Several times. And he was there."

How . . . how could that be possible?

"You don't believe me."

"We have footage of him in DC. When you went missing."

She pulled her gaze away, looking wan. "I knew you wouldn't believe me. It's crazy. *I'm* crazy."

Cole laid his hand on the rail of the gurney and leaned in. "I believe you," he whispered. "A man who looked like him saved me from a tunnel collapse four years ago." He sighed. "And Tzivia suggested he's the one who put you in the cistern. Did he give you the final legacy?"

She frowned. "The cuff . . ." Her eyes widened. "He had the other cuff. He made sure nobody could put the crown back together for its full power."

"So he put you in the cistern?"

462

She shook her head. "At least, I don't think so. I never saw who did it, but it wasn't him." Her eyelids drooped. "Just woke up there . . . alone."

Tox bent down and pressed a kiss to her forehead. "Rest. I'll be here when you wake up."

* * * *

— DAY 33 —
FOB STRYKER, IRAQ

"Dude, it was so Indiana Jones!"

Tox glared at Cell, who had been bouncing with energy and excitement since they'd returned from Nimrud. The team had been through days of debriefs, Command getting stories straight and preparing cover statements that would shield the team's efforts from the media. Now they were all gathered for a final meeting before heading stateside. The team, Haven, Tzivia, and Wallace.

Hand fisted, Tox had cemented his decision days ago, when he'd held a dead Haven in his arms. Just as he'd held her sister. Haven had been resuscitated, but Tox wasn't doing that again. He finally had a chance and an anchor to tether himself to a normal life.

"What?" Cell laughed. "One second that cistern is full of sand. The next it's empty. She's dropping into that chamber with you, the door slams shut—"

"We almost died." Tox shook his head, noting the rest of the team had gone strangely quiet. This mission—watching one of their own go crazy and try to kill people with a crown—had changed them.

Cell's eyes went wide. "But you didn't. You totally Jonesed it."

"How did that even work?" Thor asked. "I don't get how that cistern with sand . . . and the chamber . . ."

"What I figure," Cell explained, still excited, "is that whoever built that chamber for the crown—"

"Saladin, according to the history of the crown," Ram said. "Thefarie couldn't find the crown or the final piece. So it had to be Saladin."

"No," Tox argued. "Dr. Cathey said some religious sect at the time of Nimrod's son dismantled the crown, scattering the jewels. Saladin couldn't have known the weight needed to set up the cage."

"Whatever." Cell waved a hand, dismissing their theories. "So it detects the crown's weight with jewels and the fabric, and it triggers the release of a spring. But as a counterbalance—the cistern empties. The cage slides into the earth, which trips the trap that releases the cistern floor. But that also breaks the dam, unleashing a flood. Whoever built it made sure this crown wouldn't be found again."

"I should mention," Haven spoke from his left, "that I did some research. Did anyone else know that Mr. Tzaddik's name is Tiberius?"

"Ti, short for Tiberius. Guess it makes sense," Tox said.

"And Tiberius is another variation of Tveria."

Tox frowned.

"And even the name Thefarie was a cognate of Tiberius. All the names are connected."

"So . . . ?" Runt shrugged. "You think they're the same person?"

Cell snickered. "What? This guy's been living for centuries?"

"Shut up, man." Thor tossed a wad of paper at Cell. "Be nice."

As a raucous taunting session broke out among the men, Haven leaned closer to Tox. "I know this will sound crazy," she whispered, "but . . . do you think . . . ." She wet her lips. "What if he's Thefarie?"

He scowled.

"Think about it—Tzaddik has said things to us that he couldn't know. He called Alec your 'friend-soldier,' which is the same construct Templar knights used: brother-knights. Then, when we were reading the journals, he knew exactly which passages were there, and several times, when we questioned him, he looked as if he were remembering something. Once, he even said *he* wrote it a certain way, and when I asked, he blew it off. And how many times has he seemed to read your thoughts as you're arguing with him?"

"You do realize what you're saying, right?"

Haven sighed, sad or depressed, he couldn't be sure. "That maybe I lost more oxygen than I realized." She hunched her shoulders. "But I can't ignore what I see."

General Rodriguez entered with Dru Iliescu and Robbie Almstedt.

"Thanks for waiting. We've been over your AARs in great detail. We're satisfied and feel we should move on."

"Move on?" Tox lifted his head. "To what?"

"Maybe you forgot how Alec King died," Almstedt said.

"Forgot? His brain melted because of a resonance burst," Tox growled. "Not easy to forget."

"He also boiled out."

Tox slumped. Closed his eyes and sighed. Defeat choked him. "You're sending us after the AFO."

"It has to happen," Almstedt said.

"No," Tox countered. "It doesn't." He stood. "Not for me. I'm done."

"I'm not sure you can do that," Almstedt said, looking to the general. "Can he?"

"Tox, I have a better idea," Rodriguez said.

"I'm not going out there again. I won't put Haven's life in jeopardy, and I'm not going to put myself at risk when something is finally right in my life."

"We want you to take Command."

Tox jerked. "Sir?"

"Coordinate efforts from here in DC. The team continues, with Metcalfe staying on. He's agreed." Rodriguez nodded to Runt. "And we have some dossiers for you to consider in backfilling the team."

"Backfilling." Vacancies left by Keogh. Palchinski.

"Not to sound callous, but you're a gifted soldier. We need you to take down the AFO. We'll give you whatever you need, but I also think you're not the type of soldier to walk away from an unfinished mission."

Tox shuttered his eyes.

"Help us put an end to them. After that, we can readdress your request."

He sighed. What else would he do with his life? He wasn't good at anything but being a soldier. And with the AFO out there, nobody would have a quiet, normal life.

But then, there would always be an enemy to fight, a dragon to slay.

"Sorry. Did my time."

* * * *

DAY 62
CATOCTIN MOUNTAIN, VIRGINIA

There were times for conversation. Times for silence. Tox had experienced both in the month since Alec's death and nearly losing the one person who had seen something in him that he couldn't see.

"Charlotte said you two had dinner again," Haven said.

They sat on a rocky ledge, peering out over Catoctin Mountain Park and the sparkling Potomac. His heart thudded a little harder. The purpose of that dinner had been intentional on his mom's part—agenda-driven. Her agenda, 14K gold and more than a hundred years old, sat in his pocket.

If he could just muster the chutzpah to follow through with *his* agenda in inviting Haven on this hike.

Had the meeting with SAARC, the DoD, and the CIA not gone as he'd intended, no way would he be sitting here, staring down the biggest challenge of his life—owning up to his feelings for Haven.

No. Not owning up.

Embracing. Accepting that he did not want to do life without her.

But a piece of him—a shredded, frayed, torn piece—couldn't fathom life outside Wraith. Without the action. Adrenaline. And the danger, a two-headed serpent that pushed him to walk out of that briefing.

"Your dad seems to be coming around."

"That's one way of putting it." More like his old man knew he couldn't stop Tox from returning from the dead, so he just looked the other way. "I'll never be good enough for him."

"Or for yourself?"

He slid a gaze to Haven, who gave a knowing smile. "Give a guy some credit."

"Okay, you've definitely come a long way after the ordeal with Alec, but you still think of yourself as Tox."

"It's who I am."

"You're Cole Russell, the best man I've ever known."

He studied the ridge again for breathing space, since there was little between him and Haven. "If we abandon the past, we lose the ability to prevent repeating it."

"But we can't let it control or dictate our future."

He nodded. "Agreed." Which was why he needed to take this agenda out of his pocket and put it on her hand. What was wrong with him? Why hadn't he done it already?

He thought of Alec boiling out. "You know, as long as the Arrow and Flame is out there . . ."

"Even if they weren't, there would always be someone, some evil to combat. You don't have to wear a uniform to be in a battle."

Storms had always assailed his life. But Haven . . . she was his QRF, his quick reaction force, in the ambush of life. "I'm still amazed you're sitting here after what I—"

"No." Haven touched a finger to his lips. "You're not allowed to bring that up again."

Confusion forced him to look at her. The sun's light lazily traced her oval face, softening her cheeks and complexion. Those rose-pink lips.

"It's forgiven. Done." She swiped her hands across an invisible counter, as if clearing it off. "It doesn't have room in our relationship or life. Clear?"

"You're sexy when you take charge."

"Am I clear?" she growled.

Tox grinned. "Yes, ma'am."

Thick dense fur pushed against Tox's shoulder as VVolt inserted his eighty-two pounds of intensity between them. Haven laughed, wrapping an arm around the Belgian Malinois.

"Stand down, airman," Tox teased the now-retired MWD. "I was here first."

VVolt's pink tongue dangled contentedly as he panted and squinted out at the sunset.

"I'm not sure I'd try to make him move," Haven said around a giggle.

"Back up," Tox ordered.

VVolt's tongue vanished as he snapped his snout closed. His ears went straight, head snapping to their six. The change in behavior brought Tox to his feet, and he turned, scanning the tree line just beyond the path, mentally reaching for the weapon holstered at his back. His heart crashed against his spine when a man emerged from the shadows.

But not the shadows of the trees.

Shadows of . . . something that wasn't there.

Taking point, VVolt growled. His hackles rose.

You and me both, buddy.

VVolt took a step forward, snout partially open and teeth bared. His tail flicked rapidly, ready for a command to attack.

"Mr. Tzaddik," Haven said, her greeting breathy and surprised.

Tzaddik swiped his hand through the air and across—the hand signal for "down." Unfortunately, VVolt complied, though he did so with a disgruntled huff and kept every muscle contracted, ears high. As if he obeyed despite his instinct. Despite his training.

Tox could definitely relate. "What're you doing here? What do you want?" Like VVolt, he felt like he'd been commanded to heel or stand down. Everything in him ordered Tox to confront this man. To send him packing. But all he did was spout off lame questions. "How'd you find us?"

Tzaddik gave a wry smile. "You have many questions."

"Which is why I asked them."

"Yes," Haven said, "including an explanation of your name."

"No, start with the truth—did you put Haven in that cistern?"

Intelligence glinted behind Tzaddik's brown irises as his smile deepened and he fixed his gaze on Tox. "You have chosen her well. I knew I liked this one from the first moment we met."

Tox didn't appreciate the way he looked at Haven. Didn't like that he was here. That he treated Haven like some pet. Skin crawling, awareness blazing, Tox felt his instinct go primal. He stepped in front of Haven, palming his Glock 22 as he did. "You need to leave."

"I will leave when my purpose here is done."

"What is that?"

"You need to return to SAARC."

"Not happening." Tox felt Haven's touch on his back. "I quit."

"I'm afraid that must change," Tzaddik said, walking to the edge of the cliff Tox and Haven had been sitting on moments ago. "Just as

you sit on this precipice, there is a much larger one confronting you."
A shadow crossed his face, though the sky was clear. "Confronting
all of humanity. You must return to the fight, guardian."

Something hot and weird tumbled through Tox. He wanted to pitch
Tzaddik over the edge. Get rid of him. But something anchored his
feet to the rocks. Anchored his thoughts to the strange notion that
centuries of shadows slid across Tzaddik's life. "Like I said, I'm not
with Wraith anymore."

Tzaddik smiled. "No, no, you're not *with* them. You *are* them.
And you must return."

Tox reached for Haven, enfolding her hand in his. "Sorry. I'm done.
We're done."

"You're not," Tzaddik said. "And if you were to walk away, you
would undo with your rebellion centuries of work done in prepara-
tion for a great battle."

Tox scoffed.

Tzaddik's gaze struck Haven. "You spoke of my name."

It felt like a warm stream wrapped around them. Buffeting them.
Embracing them. Restricting them. Strange. Frightening. And strangely
euphoric.

"Tell me." There was an urgency in Tzaddik's demand. "Tell me
what you've reasoned."

"It's—" Haven licked her lips. "All your names mean the same
thing or point to the same thing."

Tzaddik seemed amused. "What is that?"

Haven hesitated. "Tiberius."

"What does it mean?" His questions were quick, urgent. Strident.
Separating the discussion, changing it from a talk to a revelation.

"I . . ." Haven shot a look at Tox. "You're Thefarie."

"Impossible." Tox spat the word out before he could stop himself.

"Yes." Tzaddik lunged forward a step—but he hadn't. He still stood
in the same spot, yet he seemed to breathe in their faces. "Isn't it?"

"That's how you knew so much about the artifacts," Tox heard
himself saying, yet chiding himself. Telling himself to shut up. This
made no sense. "It's how you knew the location of the mace's cradle.
And the codex. Now, the crown."

"Yet this is impossible, as you yourself have said. Thefarie of Tveria lived centuries ago." Tzaddik pointed at Tox with a wry smile. "You yourself saw the documents written in his hand."

"The same hand the journals are copied in," Haven added. "When you said you wrote them, it wasn't a mistake. You really did."

"Why are you telling us this? Why argue this? Why hide for the last year and now insinuate you're thousands of years old?"

"Do *I* insinuate that?" Tzaddik smirked. "Why, you ask? Because centuries ago, there were many guardians. Our number, our kind have dwindled and reduced until there are but a handful."

Tox gritted his teeth. "Our kind?"

"You are a guardian, and the darkness that is the Arrow & Flame will only fall at the hand of one."

"This is insane."

"I agree with you, Roussel."

"Russell."

Tveria smirked again. "The days are numbered, guardian. In a great battle, two foes will converge—light and darkness. Warriors of light and the fathomless creatures. Rephaim and demons of Resheph. To know your path, you must search out your ancestor. He held the secret, and it died with him."

"Ancestor?"

"Giraude Roussel."

ACKNOWLEDGMENTS

Dr. Joseph Cathey: Once again, my friend, thank you for your incredible help in brainstorming and getting things right.

Dr. Brian Reid: You taught my daughters chemistry and give so tirelessly to your science students, and now I thank you for brainstorming the crown within this story to make it plausible and, well, cool.

Ordnance Experts: Anthony Amato and James Dobbs, thank you both for your service and for your help making my explosive content (ha!) accurate and plausible.

Carrie Stuart Parks: Thank you for once again helping me craft Haven's character and develop her ultra-cool deception skills. You are amazing, friend!

The Rapid-Fire Fiction Task Force: Thank you, team, for always going above and beyond the call of "duty," for promoting my titles and encouraging me so many times. Thank you, Narelle Mollet, Emilie Hendryx, Linda Attaway, Lydia Mazzei, Jamie Lapeyrolerie, Brittany McEuen, Elizabeth Olmedo, Heather Lammers, Mikal Hermanns, and Steffani Webb.

Emilie Hendryx: Thank you so much for the Tox Files logo and gear you designed for Rapid-Fire readers.

Ronie Kendig is an award-winning, bestselling author who grew up an Army brat. She's penned over a dozen novels, including the bestselling *Conspiracy of Silence*. She and her hunky hero hubby have a fun, crazy life with their children and a retired military working dog in Northern Virginia.

Sign Up for Ronie's Newsletter!

Keep up to date with Ronie's news on book releases and events by signing up for her email list at roniekendig.com.

More from Ronie Kendig

When an archaeological dig unleashes an ancient virus, paramilitary operative "Tox" Russell is forced back into action. With the help of archaeologist Tzivia Khalon and FBI agent Kasey Cortes, Tox races to stop a pandemic, even as a secret society counters his every move.

Conspiracy of Silence
THE TOX FILES #1

You May Also Like . . .

When a terrorist investigation leads FBI agent Declan Grey to a closed immigrant community, he turns to crisis counselor Tanner Shaw for help. Despite the tension between them, he needs the best of the best on this case. Under imminent threat, they'll have to race against the clock to stop a plot that could cost thousands of lives—including theirs.

Blind Spot by Dani Pettrey
CHESAPEAKE VALOR #3
danipettrey.com

In the biggest case of her career, attorney Kate Sullivan has been appointed lead counsel to take on Mason Pharmaceutical in a claim involving an allegedly dangerous new drug. She hires a handsome private investigator to do some digging, but when a whistleblower is found dead, it's clear the stakes are higher than ever. Will this case prove deadly for Kate?

Deadly Proof by Rachel Dylan
ATLANTA JUSTICE
racheldylan.com

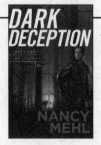

Four years ago, Kate O'Brien and her twin were attacked by a serial killer—and only Kate survived. She's been in witness protection ever since her testimony led to a conviction. When new evidence is found suggesting they got the wrong man, Kate is terrified. With a target on her back, can U.S. Marshal Tony DeLuca keep her safe until the new trial begins?

Dark Deception by Nancy Mehl
DEFENDERS OF JUSTICE #2
nancymehl.com